Day Reaper

Also by Melody Johnson

Eternal Reign

Sweet Last Drop

The City Beneath

Day Reaper

A Night Blood Novel

Melody Johnson

LYRICAL PRESS
Kensington Publishing Corp.
www.kensingtonbooks.com

To the extent that the image or images on the cover of this book depict a person or persons, such person or persons are merely models, and are not intended to portray any character or characters featured in the book.

LYRICAL PRESS BOOKS are published by

Kensington Publishing Corp.
119 West 40th Street
New York, NY 10018

All Kensington titles, imprints, and distributed lines are available at special quantity discounts for bulk purchases for sales promotion, premiums, fund-raising, educational, or institutional use.

Special book excerpts or customized printings can also be created to fit specific needs. For details, write or phone the office of the Kensington Sales Manager: Kensington Publishing Corp., 119 West 40th Street, New York, NY 10018. Attn. Sales Department. Phone: 1-800-221-2647.

First Electronic Edition: April 2018
eISBN-13: 978-1-60183-427-0
eISBN-10: 1-60183-427-6

First Print Edition: April 2018
ISBN-13: 978-1-60183-428-7
ISBN-10: 1-60183-428-4

Printed in the United States of America

Acknowledgments

I've been writing Cassidy DiRocco and Dominic Lysander's story for over five years. They've become an integral part of my life, and it's with a bittersweet excitement that I've reached the fourth and final installment in the Night Blood series. Day Reaper is especially dear to me as it's my first series finale, and as I write Cassidy and Dominic's last pages, I'm reminded that every journey's end is really just a new beginning.

Acknowledging everyone who impacted my life and my writing during this five year journey would be impossible, but I'd like to give a special thank you to the people who put their time, effort, and talent into my work and whose generous contributions helped shape my story, the one I was writing as well as the one I was living:

My fellow members of First Coast Romance Writers, for sharing your experience, encouragement, advice, and enthusiasm. Our guest speakers are invaluable, but they are nothing compared to the bond of our community, which I appreciate more deeply than words can describe.

Nicole Klungle and Margaret Johnston, for reading it rough and giving it to me straight. Your feedback was, as always, on point and priceless.

Carl Drake, for your creativity and continued friendship. Your fabulous bookmark and postcard designs are only rivaled in my affections by your Netflix account.

Nancy and Leonard Johnson, for your unwavering support, constant love, and the uncountable hours you've listened to me blab on the phone about everything and nothing.

Derek Bradley, for filling my heart with laughter and love.

Prologue

Transform me into a vampire.

The words had just left my lips, more shape than sound since I still couldn't speak without vocal cords, and Dominic Lysander, Master vampire of New York City—who had supposedly seen all, knew all, and wasn't impressed by any of it in his four hundred and seventy-seven-year-long-life—stared at me like I was an alien, like I was an otherworldly creature he'd always known probably existed, but was wholly unprepared to confront. I knew that horror-filled, struck-dumb look all too well; I'd been wearing it pretty consistently over the past several weeks, ever since Dominic had shoved me against the brick exterior of my apartment building and commanded me to look into his eyes, and my body had unwillingly obeyed. I knew that sometimes events were so devastating, both physically and mentally, that all you could do was stare blankly at the destruction and hope to God you didn't lose your shit.

But in all his four hundred and seventy-seven years, this was not the time nor the place to lose his shit.

Use my necklace, I mouthed, both encouraging him and reminding him not to use the blood in his veins, weakened by the Leveling. I would have ripped the pendant from my necklace and raised the precious drops of his formerly powerful blood to my lips myself, but I'd lost the use of my arms. My body was numb, my awareness drifting, my vision a starburst blanket of blackness covering my face, and still, Dominic just stared.

What are you waiting for? I snapped, as much as I could snap under the circumstances.

"Another solution to present itself," he finally admitted, looking over my injuries, the movement of his eyes darting and frantic.

I raised my eyebrows, or at least, I tried to. *Cold feet?*

Dominic let loose a long-suffering sigh. Some of the horror left his expression, but not all of it, and what little did leave was replaced by weary resignation. I didn't understand his reaction—I didn't understand *him* and maybe never really would, not as a human anyway. After weeks of attempting to seduce me, not only into his bed but into his coven, this should be his golden, shining moment, the pot of gold at the end of this violent, blood-soaked rainbow, but by the sick, nearly choked expression on his face, instead of bathing in his good fortune, he was drowning in it.

"The temperature of my feet has little to do with this decision," he said blandly.

I opened my mouth to correct his misunderstanding, to explain that "cold feet" was just an expression, not a literal physical discomfort, when I noticed the tilt to the scarred half of his lips. He was teasing. I was exsanguinating in an alley between East Fifty-Seventh Street and 432 Park Avenue, my vocal cords in shreds, breathing more blood than air into my lungs, and fading fast. And he was teasing.

I laughed and blood sprayed like a geyser from my esophagus.

Dominic choked, coughing up physical blood from his metaphysical injuries. My injuries.

The blanket over my vision thickened, filling the gaps between starbursts. I didn't have time to doubt my decision and consider why Dominic would hesitate—which wasn't so much a decision as it was a last resort, and perhaps therein lay Dominic's hesitation. I didn't have time to convince him that my decision was more choice than he'd been given for his transformation, and if my decision was more about living than it was about a life with him, he'd have to suck up his pride and be grateful I was making this choice at all: the right choice, according to him, under different circumstances. I didn't even have time to catch my breath.

One moment, blood was spraying from my torn throat, soaking Dominic's shirt front and mixing with his own blood spray, and the next, I was opening my eyes without even having realized I'd ever closed them.

I wasn't in the gore-spattered alley anymore. I wasn't sure where I was, but I wasn't on the corner of Fifty-Seventh and Park Avenue—I wasn't even outside—and my body wasn't numb.

My body was on fire.

I bucked up off the bed and screamed. Or at least, I opened my mouth. Blood expelled from my mouth instead of screams, from my mouth instead of my ravaged esophagus.

I lifted my hand and touched my throat. My smooth, untorn esophagus.

With the rush and thunder of the flames engulfing my body, combined with the shock and disorientation of waking in an unfamiliar room on an unfamiliar bed, my brain was slow to absorb anything else. I tore at my clothes, screamed up more blood, and thrashed against the burning, but a crushing weight was holding me down, bracing me on the bed and preventing me from extinguishing the flames.

It may have only been seconds, but being burned alive had a way of elongating time into excruciating increments. In what felt like hours later—years, maybe—I became aware of a voice in my ear—something besides the thunder and fire and blood of my screams—and a hand in my hand, anchoring me to the present.

"You must accept it. Embrace the transformation, Cassidy."

Dominic. His lips were moving against my ear, and his hand was the hand in mine. His body was the weight over me, bracing my body back against the bed.

"I'm on fire," I croaked. My voice, though hoarse, still spoke through a gurgle of blood. My vocal cords were miraculously intact, although considering the blood my throat was choking on, perhaps not as miraculously as I'd first thought, unless you considered the healing qualities in Dominic's blood a miracle.

At the moment, it felt more like an execution.

His hand tightened. "No, you're not. You're just rejecting my blood, as usual."

I'm not on fire, I thought, but my next thought was as devastating as if I were. *The fire is inside me and can't be put out.*

Not for three days, at least, according to Walker.

"We've been here before," Dominic said, his voice calm and soothing, and I wanted to tear his eyes out. I was on fire, damn it; there was nothing that could soothe that.

I shook my head. I'd never burned like this before, not from Dominic's blood.

I must have said as much, because Dominic answered, although I didn't recall anything intelligible passing through my lips, only blood-garbled screams.

"You have more of my blood within you than you've ever had before. Last time, I was only healing you. Now, you've lost enough of your blood that I'm transforming you. But you must embrace the transformation, Cassidy."

"It's killing me," I gritted between clenched teeth.

Dominic's grip on my hand tightened painfully. "It's saving you. My blood is life. Feel the gift of its strength coursing through you, healing you, empowering you. Feel beyond the burn to the power that stokes its flames, the power that lives inside you now."

I tried to listen to Dominic, I really did, but the memory of Walker's voice inside my head was louder.

They say night bloods feel intense, focused burning over their entire body, Walker had explained, back when we'd first met, when he'd been more than willing to share his knowledge and weapons with me against the vampires, before the possibility of something more than friendship wasn't a canyon between us. *And they feel that sensation during the entire three-day transformation.*

I would be on fire for three whole days.

My fear turned to resistance, and the burning inside me raged.

"Cassidy, no! Don't you dare do this to me, not after everything we've survived, not after the lengths we've traveled to come this far and this close."

His grip on my hand was painful now, crushing the small, fragile bones in my fingers. He was desperate; I could hear it in the tone of his voice and in his last-ditch effort to force my will to his command.

"Cassidy DiRocco, you will accept the blood I've given you as your own," Dominic intoned, but the Leveling had depleted all his strength and abilities and given them to the very woman who had betrayed him. I didn't feel the answering spark, like a tuning fork inside my mind at his command. I didn't feel anything except the unrelenting, consuming sensation of my body being incinerated.

"Not. Working," I panted between screams.

"Not trying!" Dominic accused.

He talked about the infusion of strength and healing and new life from his blood, but Walker's scientific explanation for the transformation resonated with me more. The regenerative properties in vampire blood had healed my throat and wouldn't necessarily transform me, except for the fact that I had suffered such catastrophic blood loss. With more vampire blood than human blood in my body, the rapidly regenerating vampire cells would spread through my circulatory system, into my organs and muscles to regenerate those cells, and eventually, into my brain until vampire blood regenerated every cell in my body and became my blood.

I didn't want to change. I liked exactly who I was—bum hip, fragile body, dulled senses and all—and I wanted to stay that way. I didn't want to be more entrenched in Dominic's world, in a world of darkness and shadows, blood and hierarchy and power. I didn't want more from life than my career, Nathan—and hell, even Dominic—but he could leave all his damn baggage at the door before he entered.

More than anything else I wanted, however, I wanted to live, and no matter how unfathomable the cost, that meant letting go of all the rest.

In the end, it wasn't Dominic's words of encouragement, his hand holding mine, nor the promise of enhanced strength, abilities, and senses that saved me. The choice was never whether or not I wanted to remain a night blood with my human ailments and Dominic's eternal frustration or allow all my supposed potential to come to fruition and transform into a vampire. No matter the pros and cons of such a decision—of which there were many, and they were as catastrophic as the injuries that had brought me here—the choice was a matter of life or death, and that was no choice at all.

I'm going to live, I thought, and unlike anything else that Dominic could say, the knowledge that I would live anchored me in purpose and determination. I couldn't necessarily find comfort in the knowledge that I'd survived worse, because the hell of being burned from the inside out was the worst sensation I'd ever experienced, but I'd be damned if I wouldn't survive it.

Life as I'd always known it extinguished, leaving me in darkness.

"The face she sees in the mirror might be new to her, but I saw the potential in her human form long before her physical transformation. To me, nothing about her has changed besides the overdue assurance that I can hold her in my embrace with my full strength, and she will not shatter."

—Dominic Lysander

Chapter 1

Seven days later

A bird was squawking, and after several minutes of attempting to ignore its repetitive, shrill bleating, I came to grips with the fact that it didn't seem inclined to stop on its own. I snapped open my eyes, prepared to reach out the window and stop it myself, with my bare hands if necessary—I'd never heard such an obnoxious bird in my life, not in the city, not on the West Coast, not even on my one excursion to visit Walker upstate—and froze. There was no window. And if the vents Bex used to filter fresh air into her underground coven were any indication, there was no bird. Although the vents here resembled the ones in Bex's coven, I didn't recognize the room as the inviting, well-decorated step back in time that Bex had created either: no extra furniture for lounging, no scented candles, no gerbera daisies, and no kerosene lamps pulsing in a hypnotic, romantic beat.

This room contained only sparse necessities: vents for underground-air filtration, a bare bulb for light, a door for privacy, and, of course, a bed. I was in a strange room in a stranger's bed, its dimensions and décor familiar only by its unfamiliarity, and suddenly, the last moments of my memory smashed into my brain like a semi.

Jillian tearing out my throat. Dominic healing me. The blood and burning. The transformation.

Someone was speaking in the room outside this bedroom's door, and even through the scarred door and the cement wall, I could hear every word being said and recognize the voice speaking: Ronnie Carmichael.

"Lysander said he would. There's no reason to think he won't, so I don't think—"

And following Ronnie's voice was the squawking of that damn bird.

"Exactly. You don't think," Jeremy snapped.

"Lysander said that he would *try*," Keagan said patiently, his voice nearly drowned out by the bleat of that insufferable bird. "His priority is Cassidy and our safety. He won't take unnecessary risks, like remaining aboveground, away from Cassidy longer than absolutely necessary."

"Yes, he said he would try," Ronnie insisted, but her voice was faint now. "Lysander doesn't say anything lightly."

The bird squawked even louder, in time with Jeremy's audible groan, triggering a memory of Ronnie's little-girl voice and something she had confided in me: *I never even knew he thought of my voice as grating. I never knew someone's annoyance had a sound, let alone that it sounded like a squawking bird.*

I was right about the bird not being underground, but unlike anything I'd ever heard, the sound wasn't a bird at all. The squawking was the sound of Keagan's annoyance at the grate of Ronnie's whining voice. Unlike Jeremy, Keagan was too well-mannered to audibly express his frustration with Ronnie, but among other vampires, he could no longer hide his true feelings. His unspoken annoyance had a sound—as loud, obnoxious, and obvious as Jeremy's audible hostility—and Ronnie could no doubt hear it, too, over the calm, reasonable tone of his words.

I could hear it.

I could hear the sound of Keagan's annoyance.

The weight of the sheets covering my body was suddenly suffocating. I raised my hand to tear them from my body, but someone else's hand whipped into the air. I gasped at the skeleton-skinny joints of each finger, the knobby protrusion of its wrist and the elongated talons sprouting from each fingertip instead of nails. I ducked under the hand, trying to avoid its attack and swallow the scream that tore up my throat, but the hand moved with me, moving with my intentions, attached to my body. I froze again, for the second time in as many seconds, and raised the hand in front of my face. It looked lethal. With one wrong move, it could eviscerate me. As I ticked each finger, the long talons swept the air as I counted—one, two, three, four, five—and each moved on my command. Like the inevitability of a rising sun, I realized that the hand was mine. Fear of that hand turned to horror and then to a kind of giddy resignation. Hysteria, more likely.

I had ducked against the attack of my own hand.

A swift peal of laughter burst from my mouth.

I stopped laughing just as abruptly. Even my voice was different: guttural and sharp, like shards of glass scraping against asphalt.

The voices outside my door and the squawking bird had abruptly stopped, too, and in the sudden silence following my outburst, an uncomfortable, aching vise circled my chest. The pain wasn't physical, but its presence triggered a dull burn in the back of my throat. I had the immediate urge to destroy everything, to pound the cement walls into crumbs with my fists and tear the sheets into ribbons with my nails—my talons—and fight my way free from this prison. I held myself motionless, resisting the urge, and I realized with a belated sort of curiosity that the aching vise was panic. Without a beating heart to pound and without a circulatory system to hyperventilate, I hadn't recognized the emotion without its physical symptoms, but even so, it felt the same in one way. It felt horrible.

I took a deep breath to dispel the panic, purely from habit, but the action wasn't calming. My heart that wasn't pounding didn't slow, and I couldn't catch a breath that I hadn't lost. The vise around my chest tightened. I squeezed my hands into fists, trembling from the force of my will to remain still and silent. Something sharp pierced my hands, and I gasped, the raging panic stuttering until I looked down at my bleeding fists. My talons were imbedded in my own palms.

A door slammed somewhere outside this room, farther away than the voices directly behind the door, but I didn't hear it slam with my ears. I felt it slam from its flat slap against my skin. Never mind that the door wasn't near enough for me to see, nor in this room; never mind, the impossibility that I could feel its sound waves; my entire body felt its sting as if I'd been smacked from all sides.

"Why are you just staring?" His words were impatient and aggravated, but no matter the tone, hearing his voice made the aching around my chest both loosen and worsen.

The clip of his tread across the cement floor stung like the warning barbs of a wasp. I knew the physical pain on my skin was only the tactile manifestation of sounds—first, the door slam, and now, his walking—but that didn't change the fact that the sounds really did hurt my skin. I tried to rub away the lingering sting and realized my hands were still fisted, my talons still imbedded in my palms, so I just sat on the bed, motionless and bleeding, like someone trapped without an EpiPen, waiting for the inevitable swelling, choking, death: trapped within a body that had betrayed me.

"Did you have time to—" Ronnie began, but her voice was too small and too fragile not to crumble under the weight of his will.

"You heard her waken," he accused. "Don't you smell the blood?"

I could actually taste the pungent, freshly sliced, onion musk of their silence.

The door swung open, and suddenly, inevitably, Dominic entered the room. He didn't need permission to cross my threshold, not anymore, and he didn't bother with the perfunctory acts of knocking or requesting my consent to enter. He simply strode inside and slammed the door behind him with a final, fatal bee sting.

He'd recently fed. I could tell, as I'd always been able to tell, by the bloom of health on his cheeks, his strong, sculpted figure, and the careful calm of his countenance, but my heightened senses could now also smell the lingering spice of blood on his breath and hear the crackle of it nourishing his muscles. From the top of his carefully tousled black hair to the soles of his wing-tip dress shoes, Dominic was insatiably sexy, but his physique was an illusion of his last meal. I knew his true form. Upon waking, before feeding, he appeared more monster than man. Although not many people look their best in the morning, Dominic by far looked his worst.

The way I looked now.

That thought made my fists tighten, embedding my talons deeper into my own flesh.

Despite his grievance with Ronnie, Keagan, and Jeremy for their inaction, he, too, just stared, immobile after entering the room, but his gaze absorbed everything. I felt the slash of his eyes slice across my face, down my body, and eventually settle with dark finality on my fisted palms.

He didn't move or make a sound, but I heard the unmistakable rush of wind. There were no windows underground and in the stagnant stillness of the room—the tension between our bodies like an electric current stretching to complete its circuit—no relief from the heat of his presence. The sound wasn't wind, it only sounded like wind, but whatever it was the sound of, it was emanating from the only other person in the room.

I blinked and Dominic was suddenly, but no longer impossibly, beside the bed. His movements were just as inhumanly fast as ever, but with my enhanced vision, I could track his movement, see his grace and fluidity. I heard the slide of air molecules parting for him, felt the electric snap of his muscles flexing, and smelled an emotion he wouldn't allow me to interpret on his carefully neutral expression. Whatever he was feeling was spiced, sweet, strong, and dangerous with overuse, like ginger.

He reached out and carefully wrapped his palms around mine to cup my fists. His voice was steady when he spoke, but I knew better. The rush of wind emanating from him heightened, the smell of ginger became chokingly pungent, and his heart, which didn't need to beat to keep him alive, contracted just once. I could both hear the *swoosh* of his blood being pumped through each chamber and taste the silky spice of that sound.

My hands were injured, yet his trembled.

"Relax," Dominic murmured. "I'm here. I should have been here when you first awakened, but I'm here now."

I blinked at him. With him here, everything was somehow simultaneously better and horribly worse.

"Mirror," I growled. I tried to form a complete sentence, to demand, *Get me a mirror, so I can see the horror of a face that matches these hands!* but my throat was too dry. Even that one word rattled from my vocal cords like flint scraping across steel, and the resulting sparks flamed the back of my throat. I sounded dangerous and angry and monstrous. If I had stumbled upon me in an alley, I would have run.

Then again, I'd stumbled upon Dominic in an alley, and look how that had played out.

Whether Dominic saw my anger or thought me a dangerous monster now wasn't revealed by his carefully masked countenance. He stroked the back of my hand with the soft pad of his human-feeling thumb. "You need to calm down."

Calm down? I thought. I jerked my hands free from his gentle hold and shook my fists between us, in front of his face. *All things considered, this is calm!*

Dominic sighed. "I can't see your claws from inside your palms, but did you happen to notice their color before stabbing yourself with them?"

I frowned. I had claws, for Christ's sake. *Claws.* No, I didn't take note of their color.

"I'll take that as a *no*," he said, still gentle, still careful, and so fucking infuriating.

A comforting flood of hot anger blast-dried my shock and sorrow. I spread my fingers, tearing said claws from my palms and ripping wide my self-inflicted wounds, but I didn't take the time to note their color. I swiped at Dominic.

My movements were lightning. Dominic's movements were just as fast; he leaped back, dodging my claws. I lunged off the bed after him. A familiar sound rattled from deep inside my chest, a sound I'd heard emanate from Ronnie, Jillian, Kaden, and Dominic, a sound that coming from them had raised the fine hairs on the back of my neck. Now that sound came from my throat. I was growling.

Dominic somersaulted out of reach. I watched his movements, fascinated by the strength of his muscles as he leaped into the air, his coordination as his legs tucked and his arms caught his knees, and his athleticism as he stuck the landing and raised his hands to block my advance. He was the epitome of power and grace under pressure, and with the enhanced ability of my heightened senses, I could actually see it. He wasn't just a blur of movement, but a perfectly choreographed symphony of muscle, control, and honed skill. I watched, and unlike the jaw-dropping awe of impossibility that Dominic's physical feats would normally inspire in me, I was just inspired.

I attempted to mimic Dominic's movements with a matching forward somersault of my own, but instead of landing on my feet like I'd intended, like Dominic had stuck so effortlessly, I landed in an awkward, bone-jarring heap, flat on my back.

Dominic leaned over me, his mouth opened with concern, surely about to ask me if I was all right. My pride was more injured than my body, and the hot embarrassment fueled my anger, as every strong emotion could fuel my easily provoked temper. Taking advantage of his concern and close proximity, I raked my claws down the front of his shirt.

Buttons severed from their threads, but before the pops of their little plastic heads hit the floor, Dominic was airborne again, back-flipping away from me before my claws could do any real damage. I lunged after his leaps and twists and rolls, milliseconds behind his acrobatics, but even without the advantage of his fancy gymnastics, my body's newfound abilities were astonishing. Each muscle contraction burned beneath my skin, but not like human muscles burning with fatigue. Mine sparked to life, twitching with power and reveling in unleashed speed and strength.

I'd never been particularly athletic; my entire life, even before being shot in the hip, my skills were better served in an intellectual capacity—interviewing witnesses and writing articles. After being shot, my physical abilities had shriveled to the point where I could barely walk. Now, I could not only walk, I had the potential to fly. I was a force in both body and mind, and the limitlessness of those abilities after being physically limited for so long was intoxicating.

Time suspended. Our battle raged in the timespan of a blink, but within that blink, we fought and danced and completely trashed the little utilitarian room in what felt like years—a lifetime of limitations revealed and obliterated with every movement and newly discovered capability. Our movements were lighting, the evidence of our devastation scattered across the room—Dominic's torn clothing, upended and smashed furniture, pillows gutted and their insides fluffed over the rumpled comforter and upended mattress—the cause unseen.

I made a move of my own instead of following Dominic, cutting him mid-leap and smashing him facedown into the box spring. He was vulnerable for a split millisecond, me at his back, my razor claws splayed across his shoulder blades, his neck bared as he craned to look over his shoulder at me, and I had him. If I chose to, with a swipe of my hand, I could sever his head from his body. My claws were sharp, his skin was soft, and unlike in any other physical battle I'd waged in my life, I had the advantage.

My body's speed and strength were new to me, but the feelings of rage and intoxicating addiction were not. Memories of being addicted to Percocet and the bone-deep reasons I'd fought to overcome that habit kept me grounded when I would have taken advantage of Dominic's weakness. I nearly let strength and power overwhelm reason, but I knew when to stop. I knew when the need and heat felt too good to be good. The rage reminded me that despite the claws sprouting from each fingertip, despite the fact that I might look like the devil and have the strength of God, I was the same flawed person I'd always been.

I was still me, and despite his flaws, I loved Dominic.

I jerked my hand from his back, ripping fabric with my movement but not skin, and fell to my knees.

Dominic somersaulted over me. He landed at my back, but I didn't turn to face him. He knew I'd resisted the opportunity to kill him. Our battle was over, but mine had just begun.

He fell to his knees behind me, wrapped his arms around me, holding my hands, cradling my body, and it was only then, with the steady press of his cheek against mine, that I realized by the solid stillness of his arms holding me that I was shaking.

I burst out weeping. The sobs wracked my body and tears bathed my cheeks.

Dominic's arms tightened. He stroked my hands and murmured promises into my ear that I knew better than to believe, promises that no one could keep, but having him hold me, his lips moving against my ear and the familiar tone of his voice resonating like a blanket cocooned around my body, was comforting anyway. I sobbed harder at first, relieved that he was here, that I wasn't alone, that he'd experienced this, too, and had survived and eventually thrived. Buoyed by the knowledge that I, too, could survive and eventually thrive, I calmed. My weeping slowed, the sobs wracking my body lessened, and my tears eventually dried.

I relaxed into Dominic's embrace—my back flush against his chest, his arms cradling my arms, our fingers entwined. His breath fluttering my hair wasn't winded, and I noted with a detached sort of astonishment, that neither was mine. I was suddenly struck by a wary sort of certainty that my new, debatably improved physical form would continue to astonish for a very long time. I stared at our entwined fingers—his perfectly formed human hands still larger than my emaciated fingers, but not nearly longer than my elongated claws—and I pulled into myself, embarrassed that he was touching them.

"Don't," he murmured, tightening his hold. "Some aspects of the transformation might take some getting used to. You're already becoming accustomed to your heightened senses and increased strength, which is impressive. In a few days, you'll land that somersault, I assure you. And eventually, you'll look into a mirror and recognize yourself, but for tonight, let me be your mirror." He raised his hand and urged my face to the side to meet his gaze. "Let me show you how beautiful you are."

My physical appearance wasn't the only aspect of the transformation that shook me, but when he cupped my cheek in his palm and ducked his head, pressing his lips to mine, I kissed him back. My lips felt foreign against the long protrusions of my fangs, but his lips were soft and the texture of his scar familiar. His Christmas-pine scent enveloped us, and with my enhanced senses, I felt its chilled effervescence simultaneously heat and create goose bumps over my body. I turned in his arms, angling for more access, and a rush of blood filled my mouth.

Dominic stiffened.

I jerked back, startled by the blood coating my tongue, a taste that wasn't entirely unpleasant—was, in fact, not unpleasant at all. The blood was absolutely delicious, which was also startling, not to mention disturbing. Dominic had a gash across his lower lip, and I realized that I'd cut him.

I swallowed the blood in my haste to apologize and choked.

Dominic covered my lips with a finger and shook his head. His thumb swiped back and forth over my cheekbone as we stared at each other, and before my very acute eyes, I watched the intricacy of Dominic's body heal. The split sides of his lip filled with blood, and that blood pooled in the crevice of his cut, coagulated, scabbed, and flaked to reveal new, shiny pink skin. That skin darkened to a faint thread, and if he'd still been human, the healing might have stopped there, but his body healed the scar, too, until his lips bore not one sliver of evidence of my clumsy lust. What had once seemed to occur instantaneously and magically was now a simple bodily function, but I suppose that in itself was a kind of magic.

I touched his lips, grazing my fingertips carefully over the perfection of his newly healed skin to the divots and pucker of the permanent scar gouging through the other side of his lower lip and chin, a reminder of his human lifetime and for me, a reminder of the few things we had in common. Although looking at the skeletal, talon-tipped hand touching him—the hand that I controlled but didn't resemble anything I recognized as mine—we had much more in common now than I'd ever anticipated having.

He touched my lips with his fingertips, mimicking my movements with the human-looking version of his hand, and I couldn't help it. Regardless of the impossibility of this situation and the state of my hands and what I could only imagine was the state of my face, I smiled.

"Sorry," I murmured. Dominic's blood had moistened the scratch in my throat, so it didn't feel like my vocal cords were raking my esophagus with razor blades anymore. "I'm not myself this morning."

Dominic grinned—full and genuine and lopsided from the pull of his scar—and the warmth and affection in his expression widened my own smile. I let that warmth soak into me, filling my unfamiliar body with hope, reminding me that I could survive. That I *wanted* to survive.

"No one looks or acts their best upon waking, not even you when you were human," Dominic reminded me. "Not even me."

I sighed. "I will miss working on my tan, though," I said, only half-jokingly. The feel of the sun's warmth on my skin had become a safe haven after discovering the existence of vampires. Having become one, I supposed the necessity was moot, but that didn't mean I wouldn't miss it.

Dominic grunted. "Many things about you will never change despite the transformation, including your ability to enjoy the sun—and your stubbornness, it seems."

I raised my eyebrows. "My stubbornness won't cure a fatal sun allergy."

"Look at the color of your claws," Dominic said drily.

Ignoring the urge to resist looking at my claws just to defy him, I looked. The skeletal appendages coming from my body were long and knobby and honestly grotesque, a monster's hands with four-inch, lethal talons sprouting from their tips.

And those talons were silver.

Dominic was right, as usual, and unfortunately, so was our dear friend, High Lord Henry. I was a vampire, but I wasn't allergic to the sun.

I was a Day Reaper.

Chapter 2

The blood that Dominic raised in my direction wasn't any more appetizing for having been poured into a wineglass. I couldn't pretend it was anything but blood; besides its general crimson color, it didn't resemble any red wine I'd ever enjoyed. I envisioned its sticky thickness clinging to the walls of my throat the way it clung to the sides of the glass and gagged at the thought of having to swallow it.

I leaned away from the glass and shook my head. "Unappetizing," I said, but the few drops of Dominic's blood that had wet my throat had already dried; my voice was nothing but a rattling growl again.

By the frustrated lines between Dominic's eyes as he glared patronizingly down on me, he could understand my words just fine through the growl. "You need to drink now, here in privacy, before you come into contact with anyone. You don't know it yet, but you're ravenous, and once you realize it, it'll be too late."

I considered the blood-rimmed glass in Dominic's hand thoughtfully, but I didn't reach out to take it from him. "Shouldn't I crave it?"

"If it was fresh blood pumping through a human's veins, yes. And the first time the hunger hits, you will be overwhelmed by the inescapable urge to drink. I don't want that urge to strike in public while others are watching, while you may be near someone like Greta, who won't forget, or someone like Meredith, whose death you'd never forgive."

"Don't need the full cow to eat a hamburger," I grumbled, throwing the logic he'd used on me multiple times in the past back in his face.

"No, you don't, but the first time the hunger hits, it's all-consuming. You won't know restraint. You might not need the whole cow, but the cow will die anyway," Dominic explained.

He lifted the glass minutely closer. I wrinkled my nose.

Dominic rolled his eyes, grabbed my arm, and forced the blood into my hands. My claws clinked against the glass as I cradled the bowl carefully. I didn't trust myself to hold the stem and not snap it in half.

When it became obvious that holding the wineglass didn't necessarily portend drinking its contents, Dominic tried a different tactic. "I'll give you a mirror if you drink."

I narrowed my eyes. Two could play that game. "I'll drink if you give me a mirror."

Dominic sighed heavily, my stubbornness one of the only forces of nature strong enough to test his iron patience.

"I have been a vampire for nearly five hundred years, and within that time, I've transformed dozens of night bloods, perfecting my technique with each vampire."

"I don't see how—"

Dominic held up a hand. "In all that time, after all those transformations, I know a thing or two about raising a healthy, contributing member of my coven. Drinking blood upon waking is essential. You must drink before coming into contact with your first human and before gazing upon your reflection."

"I don't think that—"

"This is important, Cassidy. I've learned from past transformations. I've learned from past *mistakes*. This is one pool you cannot simply dive headfirst into. You must acclimate your body to the temperature of this habitat in order to thrive in it." His expression was imploring when he met my eyes. "Please, Cassidy."

I considered his words, I really did, but I didn't consider what he was describing as acclimation. It was a delusion. I could see my hands and imagine the face that matched those hands. Waiting until after I'd fed to look at myself was more than acclimation; it was a lie.

I lifted the wineglass carefully to my lips and swallowed one sip. The blood was still warm and fresh; I shuddered to think where he'd procured it.

"Happy? I drank," I said. "Now let me see myself."

He stared at me, his expression unreadable.

"You didn't specify how much I was required to drink," I defended.

Dominic's expression didn't change. Without taking his eyes from me, he strode to the bedside table, opened its drawer, and pulled out a hand mirror. He strode back to me, flashed the mirror with an imperceptible flick of his wrist, and just as quickly, hid the mirror behind his back.

I held out my hand.

Dominic shook his head. "I just showed you your reflection."

I glared at him.

"You never specified how long you wished to gaze upon yourself."

I snorted. "I couldn't see anything. You moved so fast, I was nothing but a blur."

"You drank so little, I can barely perceive an improvement in your complexion."

"If you gave me the mirror, I could determine the improvement for myself."

Dominic didn't move, he didn't even breathe. The only indication of his fraying patience was a low, nearly imperceptible rattle deep within his chest that I might not have even perceived without such acute hearing.

"I've never been physically strong before, but I've always been a strong person, Dominic, and that strength is based on a foundation of truth. Waiting until after I've fed to see myself is a lie, and someone once told me that I'm in the business of revealing the truth. And that applies to myself too. I need to face reality, Dominic, literally. I need to see my face."

Dominic shook his head. "Seeing yourself now will not reveal the truth to you. After having transformed over a period of seven days without nourishment, you don't look well. You will never look as poorly as you do in this moment ever again. Tomorrow morning will be a more accurate representation of your day form, and at that time, I will gladly give you a mirror before you feed."

I stared at him, shocked into silence. "How many days without nourishment?" I asked.

He pursed his lips as if having bit into something sour.

But my perfect hearing didn't need him to repeat anything. "*Seven days?* You don't think you could have led with that instead of the blood? Seven days," I repeated, shaking my head. "What's happening out there? Did you defeat Jillian? Did you regain control of the coven? What about your strength and abilities? What about the Damned? What about the Day Reapers? I missed *seven days?*"

Dominic closed his eyes and rubbed his temple methodically."You had the potential to transform into a Day Reaper. What did you expect?"

"I—well, I—" I stuttered, baffled. "I don't know what I expected! I was dying, not thinking," I snapped.

"Granted, seven days is exceptional," he said, ignoring my outburst. He looked me up and down, from the top of my greasy, unwashed head to my clawed feet and grinned. "I expected nothing less."

"Exceptional?" My voice couldn't possibly squeal any higher. "How is losing seven days *exceptional?*"

"The longer the transformation, the more powerful the vampire. An average transformation occurs over three days. Day Reapers, considering their increased speed, strength, mental acuity, and natural resistance to silver and sunlight—all necessary skills to enforce Council law and execute those who break it—typically transform in five days. I transformed in four. But you..." he shook his head at me, and with my heightened senses, I could literally feel the prick of his thoughts graze the fine hairs of my skin. I'd always known he'd had grand plans for me, plans I'd worked doggedly to ignore, but now those plans were coming to fruition, and by the calculation in his eyes as he looked me over, they were unfolding better than he'd ever imagined. "Seven days. You could rival the Lord High Chancellor himself."

I opened my mouth to wipe the awe-filled anticipation from his expression, but he pointed at my wineglass before I found an appropriately cutting response and said, "But no matter how powerful you will become, you are not that powerful now. You need to drink."

I took another measured sip, more than the first time, but not nearly as much as I knew he wanted.

Dominic held up his hand in surrender. "Compromise. Drink half your glass and I'll give you the mirror, assuming you promise to finish every drop afterward."

I didn't like it—half a lie was still a lie—but that was the best deal I'd probably get from him without physically fighting him for the mirror.

That thought actually gave me pause. I could physically fight him for the mirror and potentially win. The option to fight was no longer a paltry option, but one open for serious consideration. With my newfound strength and enhanced senses, I didn't have to just roll over and compromise. I could take what I really wanted by force.

I stared at Dominic's scarred, nearly deformed lip. The physical wound I'd inflicted by accident only a few minutes ago was completely healed, but I could still recall the shock and choking need to apologize. That wound had been an accident. Was I willing to battle him, to slice him open on purpose? Over a mirror?

I relented and drank half the blood, holding my breath against its tepid, clinging texture. It wasn't unpalatable, but like stale bread compared to a fresh loaf, lukewarm blood from the glass was unpleasant at best.

No sooner had the wineglass left my lips than Dominic held the mirror between us. I nearly spat the blood out of my mouth in shock—the image in the mirror was the most frightening, horrific creature I'd ever seen. The creature swallowed something, something unpleasant by the expression of disgust wrinkling its grotesque face—as I choked down the remaining swallow of blood in my mouth. I watched it swallow as I swallowed. It shook its head in disgust as I shook my head, and I realized belatedly, even knowing I was looking in a mirror, that the creature was, in fact, my own reflection.

I gasped as the creature gasped, its shark-like, solid blue eyes widening. Its fang-filled mouth gaped, and its long ears elongated to sharp points. I stared at myself and the stranger that was my reflection stared back with equal revulsion.

I'd anticipated the eyes and fangs. I'd even expected the ears and the emaciated sallowness of having a day form—I'd seen enough of Dominic in every form to know exactly what to expect from my new body—but I hadn't considered the fact that newly transformed vampires didn't drink while they transformed. I hadn't received nourishment in an entire week; if I were human, I'd be dead, but I wasn't human anymore. I was a vampire, so I only looked like death.

My skin was gray and shriveled like spandex around my skull, highlighting the sunken corners of my eye sockets, the divots of my temples, and the sharp cut of my jaw. My cheekbones were painfully prominent, my skin so tight around them they might actually split from the tension, made only more painful-looking by the scooped hollows of my cheeks beneath them. How could Dominic even look at me, let alone touch me, hold me, and comfort me? He'd stroked the prominence of that emaciated cheek and looked at me with warmth and affection as if I was more than an animate, skin-wrapped skeleton. He'd kissed me, and looking at the thin, shriveled skin around my fangs, it wasn't any wonder my fangs had sliced into Dominic's lips. I didn't have lips to kiss. I didn't have a complexion. I didn't have anything that would resemble a living creature, except the fact that I walked and talked and growled. I barely had any hair, but one wrong move—a sneeze, a breeze, a blink—and I wouldn't have that either.

Even as I stared at a stranger, I could see the blood's effect on my appearance. My complexion did pinken slightly from just the half-glass I'd already swallowed. My skin smoothed the edges and divots of my scalp, my lips darkened and plumped, my hair thickened, and my ears and talons retracted slightly. The blood didn't make much of a difference to my overall reflection, but considering I hadn't swallowed much, the immediate and visible improvements to my appearance was riveting. I still looked like death but more newly dead instead of years of being six feet under.

"Your eyes will change in sunlight," Dominic said softly. "Like the other Day Reapers, you will have irises and sclera even in your day form. You are not considered fully transformed until your first bath in sunlight."

"You kissed this," I said, touching the thin, cracked skin of my barely-there lips.

"I tried," Dominic murmured coldly.

I snapped upright, not realizing I'd hunched in on myself, but when my gaze met his, I narrowed my eyes. His eyes were anything but cold. His eyes were blazing and barely restrained.

"You promised. Every last drop," he reminded me.

The anticipation in his eyes crackled like a wood-burning hearth. Watching me drink blood obviously pleased him. The last time I'd seen that focused anticipation in his expression I hadn't been drinking blood, and seeing that expression now stoked an answering blaze in me.

Even if I hadn't promised, even if he wasn't looking at me like I was something he intended to devour, I would have drunk the blood anyway. This wasn't a day form, the true face of a vampire before its evening meal. This was Ronnie starving herself for fear of killing someone. This was Jillian serving a life sentence in a silver prison in the Underneath. This was the face of death, not my face, not even as a vampire.

I didn't tell Dominic he was right. He knew it, and if I acknowledged every time he was right, his head wouldn't physically fit through a threshold, permission or not. Besides, my willing consumption of the rest of the blood, every last drop, was acknowledgment enough.

Dominic took the glass from me when I'd finished, set it on the bedside table, and slanted his mouth over mine. My fangs didn't slice into his lip this time—I had lips again!—but I only had that one moment of clarity to revel in my improved appearance before the insistence and distraction of Dominic's tongue stole my lucid mind. I became the taste of cinnamon, the scrape of his calluses down my stomach, and the smell of pine and spice of Christmas and chai. The bite of his insistent desire against my thigh as his lips left my lips and kissed down the side of my neck blazed a trail of goose bumps lower and lower, until my thigh felt a different bite followed by the accompanying heat of his breath, the pressure of his tongue, and I—

Someone took a jackhammer to my temple.

I flinched away from Dominic's lips. Pain split through my skull, but when I touched my fingers to my head, the skin was smooth and dry. My brain wasn't bleeding from a hemorrhaging head wound, no matter the insistent pounding that claimed otherwise.

Dominic glared at the door over my shoulder, and I realized that the sudden, vicious physical pain inside my head wasn't a physical injury but an auditory stimulant manifesting as one. Someone was knocking on the door, and the rap of knuckles on wood interrupting our kiss felt like someone driving rusted nails into my skull with a power tool.

Jesus Christ.

"Lysander? Cassidy? Are you okay in there?" Ronnie asked, her hesitant, little-girl voice like a cheese grater scraping my eyeballs.

The bird in the adjacent room squawked again, one shrill, impatient bleat.

I pressed my palms forcefully over my eyes. Every sound had a feeling and every feeling had a smell and every smell had a taste, and the strange combinations of everything I could sense was suddenly unbearable. She knocked again, and even knowing the jackhammer against my temple was just the feeling of a knock, I winced anyway.

I couldn't breathe.

I reminded myself that I didn't need to breathe to live, but that didn't loosen the vise suddenly constricting my chest again.

I felt Dominic lift his head from my thigh. Otherwise, his hands and body didn't move. They nearly vibrated in their complete stillness, and I squirmed uncomfortably under him.

My movement seemed to penetrate his awareness, but when he spoke, his words were clearly for Ronnie.

"Now you interrupt? Not when she was alone and hurting and frightened, newly transformed and needing you, but now, when I am with her? When I am nearly one with her?"

My face flamed, and I squirmed more insistently. Dominic's arms still did not budge, but my squirming was stronger than his stillness. I wiggled free, and Dominic transferred his glare from the door to me.

Ronnie cleared her throat. I could feel the vibration of her embarrassment like a muscle spasm, visibly uncontrollable and painful to watch. "It got so quiet, I wanted to make sure you were both okay," she said, her voice very small.

Dominic growled. "We were not being quiet."

I pulled down my bra and twisted my shirt back into place, mortified. When had I become half dressed? When had I forgotten we weren't alone in…well, wherever the hell we were?

"You were, compared to how loud you were before," Ronnie insisted, but even her insistence sounded like a question. The bird's squawking bleats returned in full force.

"I think what Ronnie is trying to ask—" Keagan began, and the confidence in voice was solid and sure. Despite the bleating bird, I could imagine him placing his arm around Ronnie's shoulders to share in his strength and sureness. "—is if Cassidy is all right. We're all worried, we've been worried for seven days, and we're all on the edge of our seats, waiting on an update."

Keagan didn't say it, but I could hear the implication all the same. They were worried, on the edge of their seats for an update, and here we were on the floor like animals, not even having made it to the bed.

I looked over at Dominic. He met my gaze, and the heat in that one look incinerated my embarrassment. He brought out every base instinct inside me. We were on the floor like animals because together we *were* animals; I'd never felt anything more primal and passionate and confusing in my life.

"Cassidy?" Keagan asked, pounding on the door again.

I winced from the jackhammer. "I'm here," I said, my voice clear. The glassful of blood had done the trick, and my voice, if not completely back to normal, wasn't just a rattling growl. My voice was deeper than I remembered, but not in tone; it was deeper in depth, as if I had more vocal cords and although they were striking the same pitch they'd always played, the many tones that vibrated to create that pitch were richer and more alluring a sound any human throat could produce.

"And are you okay?" Ronnie insisted, obviously not convinced.

I stared at Dominic on the floor next to me. I was here, wherever "here" was, after having my throat ripped out, and after seven days, I'd survived. Seven days.

"Patience, Ronnie," Dominic answered for me. "We'll be out in a moment."

Chapter 3

The living room and kitchen outside the bedroom were as bare, neat, and utilitarian as the bedroom had been before being destroyed by my vampire-sized temper tantrum, but the many people and their suffocating emotions made the room feel infinitely more cramped. Logan and Theresa glared at me from the far corner of the room, their anger like rubber band snaps against my skin. Rafe and Neil stood beside me, their hovering proximity like flies swarming overripe fruit.

Jeremy's wary gaze looked back and forth between me, the bedroom, and Dominic as if he were trying to determine who had won, who he needed to guard against, and how much damage we were still capable of. The old me might have reassured him that my emotions were under control, that I'd obviously freaked, but I wouldn't freak again, and the old me might not even be lying. The new me let Jeremy squirm, because the smell of his fear tasted like chai, just like Dominic had always described, and I liked the taste of chai more than I liked Jeremy.

Ronnie, on the other hand, wasn't looking at the wrecked bedroom at all. She didn't waste one second looking at anything other than my face. Her fear was even more poignant than Jeremy's—sweeter, spicier, and substantially more savory—but the taste of her fear wasn't the least appealing because I almost liked Ronnie, and I still felt responsible for her. The old me definitely would have reassured her that I was fine, that we would both be fine, but even as a vampire, my guilt over her current circumstances was overwhelming. I was struggling now, but I'd adapt and eventually I'd survive. I honestly wasn't sure about Ronnie.

Her face was like looking into the mirror at myself that first time—her sallow cheeks, prominent features, and gray complexion like the reflection of living death—but she'd been a vampire for weeks now, almost three weeks to be exact. After only a fraction of that time and a glassful of tepid blood, I looked more alive now than she did.

Keagan was the only person in the room I genuinely liked—my complicated addiction for Dominic excluded—especially now that the squawking bird of his annoyance had joined Ronnie in silence. I suspected that when I asked them to catch me up on the last seven days, the squawking would return and in full force, but I couldn't help my reaction toward Keagan any more than he could help his reaction toward the whining, helpless grate of Ronnie's voice.

My relief at seeing him and the simple comfort of knowing I had a friend in the room vibrated from my pores like a gong.

Ronnie cringed and covered her ears. Rafe and Neil tried to hide their laughter, but I could see the shake of their shoulders. Logan narrowed his eyes, knowing his son was the cause of that sound and not liking the strength of such a reaction, not one bit.

Keagan smiled, and a twitter of chirps, pleasant and light, lit the air. I opened my mouth to ask him about his affinity toward bird sounds and hesitated. I didn't have an affinity toward gongs; the sound had escaped from me before I'd barely even felt the emotion.

I glanced at Dominic, wondering what he was feeling and why I couldn't hear it on him like I could hear the minutiae of everyone else's emotions.

He shook his head. "We'll work on that," he said, which I suppose was answer enough.

"Where are we? What are we doing here?" I asked, glancing at the group of vampires around me. Having all of them here in one room made the absence of one obvious. "Where's Sevris?"

No one moved or spoke or so much as blinked. In a roomful of people who didn't even need to breathe, the silence could stretch further, deeper, and more damning than I'd ever imagined possible.

Neil broke under the pressure. He cringed and stared determinedly at the nearest wall, as if the chipped paint might produce divine intervention from my questions.

I narrowed my eyes on him. "Did something happen?"

Rafe shook his head. "That's just it. Nothing's happened. Sevris disappeared the night he left to fetch you from your apartment, and we haven't seen or heard from him since. None of us have."

I bit my lip. "Maybe he's just gone to ground to wait out the Leveling like the rest of you. He'll show up, I'm sure."

Suddenly, everyone found the walls just as fascinating as Neil had.

Dominic squeezed my shoulder. "Perhaps we should start with the easier of your three questions." He moved his hand in a flourish to indicate the room around us. "On such short notice, I constructed an underground safe house for vampires warded against the Damned. I knew we'd need it for the Leveling. Luckily, we had it for your transformation."

"Protection against the Damned sounds great, but what about the Day Reapers?" I asked. "In seven days' time, how did they not find us? God knows everyone is gunning for us, and leading the charge is High Lord Henry."

Dominic's glacier eyes cut me. "Don't call him that," he chided.

I grinned cheekily. "It's his name."

"He prefers being addressed by his full name and title, and you know it."

"He's not here to care how I address him, now, is he?"

Dominic glared at me, but even his stern expression couldn't hide the rush of Christmas pine that suddenly filled the room.

I shook my head, taken aback. "You're scared."

"No, I'm terrified. And if you fully understood our predicament, you would be too. The Day Reapers are the Chancellor's coven, and I stole his right as Master of that coven to transform you. Do you think he'll allow such a slight to go unpunished?"

"That's more than just a 'slight,'" Rafe said on a snort. "You broke Council law, and a crime of that magnitude—" he finished his sentence on a high whistle.

"What?" Neil asked, wringing his hands. "A crime of that magnitude what?"

Dominic met Neil's worried eyes with a steady, uncompromising gaze. "A crime of that magnitude is punishable by death."

"So it's true," Ronnie breathed, her words more air than voice. "Cassidy is a Day Reaper?"

Keagan's bird let loose a loud bleat.

"Of course it's true," Jeremy snapped. "Can't you see the color of her talons?"

"We'll have to paint them. I have polish," Ronnie said, sounding excited to help. She gasped suddenly, and I could hear the cogs of her mind fit some unfathomable piece into the puzzle. Literally, I heard it. "Is that why Bex paints hers?"

Keagan's bird let loose a loud string of bleats.

"What did I say?" Ronnie asked, her voice a high whine.

The bird bleated louder.

I ignored Ronnie and the telltale bleat of Keagan's bird in favor of facing Dominic. "Maybe if I avoid sunlight and paint my nails, the Chancellor won't discover the truth," I suggested.

"You will hide your existence as a Day Reaper from one of the greatest, most powerful entities of this world with nail polish?" Dominic leveled me with a look. "Like how Bex hid her true self? Are you willing to build an underground fortress and avoid sunlight for millennia?"

"It worked very well for Bex," Keagan murmured. "Until Cassidy came along."

Dominic snorted. "It worked so well she lost her Second, her night blood, and her coven."

"She didn't lose her coven. She left it," Ronnie said, her voice very small. "She left us."

For once, Keagan's bird remained silent.

"Can we focus? I'm seven days behind here and not getting any younger," I said, attempting to lighten the mood.

"Technically, neither are you getting any older," Keagan said, grinning. He'd always understood my dark humor—hence our friendship despite the age difference.

"Jokes," Logan whispered to Theresa, as if with our heightened senses we couldn't hear him. "Two of his brothers are dead, one is being raised by the man hunting us, we are vampires, the life I built for him is being trod underfoot like fucking crumbs, and he's making jokes."

Some kind of sound expelled from Keagan, but it wasn't a bird this time. Maybe the sound of a bird being strangled.

"You don't need nail polish," Jeremy said, interrupting my eavesdropping. "Locked away as they are, the Day Reapers aren't our biggest problem at the moment."

I blinked. "Locked away? What are you talking about?"

"Maybe we should all sit for this conversation," Dominic suggested. His hand was suddenly at my waist, leading me to the nearest couch before I'd even conceded to sitting. I pulled away from Dominic just to be obstinate and sat of my own volition next to Keagan and across a coffee table from Jeremy and Ronnie. Rafe and Neil shifted to flank Dominic.

"Happy? I'm sitting." I said, primly. "Now, start talking."

Dominic nodded. "We needed a safe haven, somewhere that Jillian, the Damned, and daylight couldn't touch you. I briefly considered your apartment, but I needed to remain at your side for the transformation, and your apartment was designed beautifully to keep vampires out, not safeguard them once inside. So I brought you and everyone here," he said, waving a hand to encompass our little dysfunctional family, "to wait out the remaining hours of the Leveling. Jillian had amassed too much of my power and strength for me to fight her and win, and combined with her army of Damned, the threat of Day Reapers, and your vulnerability as you transformed, I had no choice. My one advantage was that Jillian thought that killing you had killed me. Once the Leveling passed, I anticipated regaining my abilities and power as Master vampire of New York City, and Jillian would realize too late that I still lived."

"But you didn't regain your abilities and power?" I asked.

"No, I did. I regained all my strength, power, and abilities just like I thought I would."

"But?" I pressed.

Dominic's expression hardened. "But I didn't regain my coven."

I frowned. "You regained your abilities and power, but you're no longer Master?"

"I regained the abilities and power of a Master, but not of New York City," he specified.

"I don't understand. You lived. She lost, so just march over there and take back what's yours. She doesn't have the abilities and powers of a Master anymore. You do, so what's stopping you?"

"An army of the Damned and a coven of vampires who no longer want me as their Master."

I shook my head. "You don't know that. They could be missing you. They could feel held hostage by Jillian and the Damned. They—"

"They opened their hearts to her," Dominic said, and the words scraped from his throat, each syllable taking its own slice. "It's why I can't feel their presence like the ebb and crash of an ocean tide around me, pulling me in multiple and often conflicting directions, sometimes buoying me up and just as often dragging me under, but always moving, ever changing, and constant. I am not linked to them anymore, not like I once was as their Master. And the few of us," he said, gesturing at everyone in the room, "are no match against them."

I bit my lip, the synapses in my brain firing, dismissing, and generating new thoughts faster than I'd ever imagined possible. "We're no match against them," I agreed after a moment, "but we're not alone. We have Greta and her police force, Meredith, Dr. Chunn, and Rowens. We have more allies than just 'the few of us.'"

"They're human and nothing but a liability."

"In a fight, sure, they're a liability. So was I, yet you kept me around. Just because you're the brawn doesn't mean we can't use their brains. We also have my brother, who is both brawn and brains, and Bex, who—"

"We don't have Bex," Jeremy said. "Not anymore."

"Not that we ever really did," Ronnie muttered.

"Yes, we did. We *do,*" I corrected myself. "She's our ally, and when push comes to shove, she'll have our backs."

Ronnie looked away, a petulant skeleton. Jeremy, for all his snide bravado, didn't reply, and even Keagan wouldn't meet my gaze. Theresa and Logan hadn't resumed their conversation, but they hadn't joined ours either. They just watched, Theresa's eyes darting between Dominic and me, cautious and wary, and Logan's filled with something mutilated, like the remains of a Damned's victim. Two Damned's victims in particular, I supposed.

"Dominic?" I asked, gently at first, but when he wouldn't meet my eyes either, I snapped "Why don't we have Bex? What the hell happened?"

"Jillian happened," Dominic finally said, running a frustrated palm down his face. "While we waited out the Leveling and your transformation here, Greta and her SWAT team raided 432 Park Tower."

"Oh God, is she—"

"Greta is fine," Dominic interrupted. He closed the distance between us and squeezed my shoulder, rubbing his thumb in comforting circles over my skin. Damn my body's reaction to him. I didn't know what I took more reassurance in: his words or his touch. "And so is Rowens and most of their team, but Greta and Rowens are the only ones who remember there was even a raid. When her team infiltrated the tower and confronted the Damned, the Day Reapers entranced everyone, protecting their goddamn secrets better than they protected anything else, even themselves."

I narrowed my eyes. "What are you saying? I've seen them in action myself; the Damned are no match for the Day Reapers."

"They shouldn't have been, but when the Damned attacked, the Day Reapers couldn't simultaneously fight the Damned and entrance the humans. With their efforts and focus divided, the Damned won."

I covered my mouth. "Is Bex d—"

"I don't know," Dominic said. His hand tightened on my shoulder, but I didn't draw any comfort from his touch this time. "More than likely, she's imprisoned with all the other Day Reapers in the Underneath, the silver-lined crypt beneath the coven where I imprisoned Jillian during her punishment."

"Okay," I said, trying to let everything that had happened in the last seven days soak into my brain. It felt like a nightmare, unbelievable and unreal, but just because I hadn't lived it didn't mean it hadn't happened. Didn't mean I couldn't fix it. "Okay. I need to talk to Greta."

"Greta?" Ronnie asked, her voice more an expulsion of air than actual sound.

"After hearing everything that's happened, you want to talk to *Greta*?" Jeremy asked, his tone scathing, but just as full of disbelief as Ronnie's.

I looked between the two of them and raised my eyebrows. "I'm sensing you have a problem with me talking to Greta. I've worked with Greta for years, and she—"

"She's the reason the Day Reapers failed!" Logan exploded. He knocked Theresa's fluttering hands aside and charged toward me. In another life I might have stepped back, but in this life, I calmly watched him approach. He was a large man, barrel-chested, muscular, and over six feet tall, but he strode across the room with human-slow steps. In this life, I was stronger and faster, and as I'd just proved to myself with Dominic, I no longer had to avoid a physical altercation. Strangely enough, the fact that I didn't want to avoid it was what held me in check.

Logan loomed over me on the couch, using the full intimidation of his height to his advantage as he shouted, "If it wasn't for Greta, the Day Reapers wouldn't have been distracted. They would have won against the Damned and stopped Jillian's ascent to power."

I nodded and then tipped my head sideways. "And what would have happened to all of us?"

Logan froze in his hovering. "What do you mean?"

I spread my hands to indicate the barren walls around us. "Dominic couldn't fortify this bunker against the Day Reapers because I'm a Day Reaper. So if Greta hadn't interfered and the Day Reapers had won against the Damned, what do you think would have happened to us, considering that Dominic, not High Lord Henry—"

Dominic groaned.

"—transformed me?" I finished.

Logan pursed his lips.

Keagan raised his hand next to me.

I nodded at him. "Yes, Keagan?"

Jeremy rolled his eyes. "We're not in high school anymore, idiot. Still, you manage to become teacher's pet."

"Still, you manage to be an asshole," Keagan shot back. To me, he said, "The Day Reapers would have attacked us and punished Dominic for transforming you. *We* might have been the ones imprisoned in the Underneath."

"Precisely."

Logan let loose a low growl, and Dominic, who had previously been watching this all play out without interrupting, growled back.

"Greta didn't know what she was doing when she did it," Logan said roughly, refusing to back down despite my logic and Dominic's growl. "She planned a raid under the mistaken confidence that she could win against the Damned and protect the city. And look where that got her! She lost, the city is in ruins, and our only chance to overthrow the Damned is locked away, as good as dead!"

I shook my head. "Listen to what you just said. 'Greta didn't know what she was doing when she did it.' She did the best she knew how under the circumstances. She did what she thought was in the best interests of the city. The Day Reapers, on the other hand, knew exactly what they were doing. They prioritized the secrecy of their existence over protecting the city from the Damned, and look where that got them!"

I took a deep breath. Knowing it wouldn't loosen the pressure around my heart or calm my temper, I took it anyway. "Greta and I are a team. Together with our medical examiner, our environmental-science expert"—I tipped my head at Dominic—"and a whole team of police officers and lab techs, we uncover the truth, solve crimes, and bring the guilty to justice. But it only works as a team; Greta didn't know what the hell she was doing when she did it, and since I wasn't there to help her, this mess is just as much my fault as it is hers. We failed this city, and I need to talk to her so we don't fail it again."

"There's something else you don't know." Dominic reached for my knee again, his thumb stroking gently, and I knew that whatever he was about to say would cut deeper than anything else he'd told me so far.

"What more could there possibly be?" I asked, warily.

"Jillian is in power, Cassidy. What has she always wanted? What was her ultimate goal?"

I blinked. "To take control of the coven and rise to Master vampire of New York City."

Dominic shook his head. "No, that was just the means necessary to get what she really wanted. Had I given her what she wanted when I was Master, she never would have betrayed me."

I gaped as realization dawned. "She was sick of living in secrecy. She wanted humans to know about the existence of vampires."

Dominic nodded deeply. "It's why the Day Reapers attacked, but Jillian was victorious. The Day Reapers are no longer in power to enforce our most sacred law, and Jillian has revealed our existence, and that of the Damned, to the world."

"And I'm sure she didn't hold a press conference for her big reveal," I said testily.

Dominic snorted. "Press conference or no, there were cameras and the footage went viral. The hunt, the blood, the destruction and massacre—all of it just a click, a like, and a share away."

"What do you know about social media?"

"I know that the undeniable evidence you sought to prove that vampires existed beyond a shadow of a doubt wasn't found in a laboratory. The public saw the Damned and their slaughter online, and that was all they needed in order to believe."

"Jesus," I whispered. "What the hell is Jillian's endgame in all this?" I raised my hand against Dominic's opening mouth. "I know, I know; she wanted freedom from your secret existence, but what about afterward? What's the point of freedom if we're living in the middle of World War III?"

Dominic shook his head sadly. "I am no longer in a position to know her mind. Even when I thought I did, I obviously didn't know her well enough."

I grunted my agreement. "Fine. It doesn't signify anyway; we need to focus on *our* endgame. Does the government realize this is homegrown or are they pointing the finger at terrorists?"

"I don't know."

"Well, what's the press coverage? Are they planning a counterattack? Will they be sending in troops or just bomb the problem away?"

"I don't know."

"What do Greta and Rowens have to say?" I asked. "Surely *they* know."

Dominic just stared at me.

"You haven't talked to Greta and Rowens," I said, deadpan.

"I couldn't leave you."

I flung my arm out at our ragtag little coven. "What about them?" I turned to face Ronnie, Keagan, Jeremy, Logan, and Theresa, eyeing them each in turn, but no one could meet my eyes, not even Keagan. "Not one of you could leave me? We have friends on the inside, people who might know what we're up against, and you didn't ask? The United States' military might be minutes away from nuking this entire island, and all you can say is *I don't know?*"

Silence.

Pain sliced through my palms, and I realized that I'd fisted my hands. I was impaling myself on my talons again. Shit.

Dominic's hand was suddenly heavy on my shoulder, but the movement of his thumb against my neck was a feather's flutter. "Greta and Rowens are your friends, not theirs, and barely mine. They only tolerated me and my expertise because of you. Considering who you are now, you must consider the possibility that they may not be your friends anymore either."

I frowned. "What are you talking about? Why wouldn't they—"

Dominic's hand left my shoulder to cup my cheek. "You are a vampire, and vampires are not their friends."

I shook my head, dislodging his touch. "A vampire is *what* I am. *Who* I am is Cassidy DiRocco, and not even you can change that."

Dominic let his hand drop, but his lips curled in a lopsided grin. "Nor would I want to."

"What about Nathan?" I asked. "In the last seven days, you must have at the very least talked to Nathan."

Silence. Damning silence.

"Damn it, you didn't even tell him I was okay? That I survived?"

"Your brother is still with Greta," Dominic said, a miserable mockery of his previous smile from a moment before twisting his scarred lips. "I couldn't talk to him without risking a confrontation with her."

"You could have called him," I said, and then I froze. "Could you have called him? Are cell phone towers still working?"

Dominic stared at me strangely for a moment. "The Damned have been hunting in Brooklyn for seven days, not seven years. Cell phones work. Wi-Fi works. Electricity works… well, it works in neighborhoods where the power lines are underground. The Damned did knock down a few power poles and a transformer."

I blinked, regrouping. "Great. Then you could have called Nathan."

Dominic hesitated for a moment, and I could tell he was hedging the truth when he said, "He didn't answer the phone."

"Whatever," I grumbled. "I'll tell him I'm alive myself when I talk to Greta."

"I don't know if leaving the confines of this bunker is a good idea," Theresa interjected, her voice quiet and steady and as raspy in death as it ever was in life. She wrung her hands. "The city isn't the same as you remember it. Nothing is."

I nodded. "All the more reason to leave. I've got to see for myself what we're facing."

Jeremy snorted. "So you can look upon the wreckage and see how far we've fallen. So you can see with your own eyes how badly we failed?"

I unclenched my hands, carefully unsheathing my claws from my palms. "This isn't about failure or blame. I need to see the city and what's left of it for myself, so I can see how fiercely we need to fight to get it back."

Chapter 4

Travelling from Dominic's underground safe house near the far side of Prospect Park in Brooklyn to Kings County Hospital Center should have been a fifteen-minute taxi ride, sans traffic—but even then, twenty tops, assuming, of course, there were taxis to hail and traffic to contend with. There weren't. Cars sat gridlocked in the streets, but they didn't move when the lights turned green. Drivers didn't honk their horn, scream obscenities, or flip the bird when the cars in front of them remained motionless. There weren't any drivers. The sidewalks were deserted, too, except for the scattering of purses, pumps, and briefcases that people had left behind in their haste to run. Their lives had been more important to them than their belongings, but they hadn't escaped with either.

Bodies littered the streets and sidewalk. Some still had their hearts intact. Some had a crater in their chest cavity where their heart had been, and some didn't even have anything resembling a chest, just blood and the spill of internal organs. As reluctant as I'd been to choke down the additional three glasses of blood that Dominic had forced down my throat before I showered and travelled to meet with Greta, I was unaccountably grateful for his foresight and insistence. I grieved for my city and her lost lives, but that didn't prevent me from salivating over the smell.

I remembered having a similar reaction when Jillian had leached onto my mind; I'd felt her physical reaction to the sight and smell of blood as my own. Her cravings had been horrifying and undeniable, and now they were my cravings. Thanks to Dominic, however, as delicious as that blood would have smelled, I wasn't hungry. These were dead humans; their blood smelled stale and unappetizing, and I could move through the streets without diving headfirst into the gore.

As inconvenient as not having public transportation might have been, walking through the unmoving traffic and around bodies and debris wasn't really what made an hour walk stretch into three. Had I left by day, I could have traveled much faster under the protection of the sun where not even Jillian and her army of the Damned could touch me, but that would have meant not only facing my final transformation into a Day Reaper, which I wasn't wholly ready to confront—I was just barely holding it together as a regular vampire—but also traveling alone, which was equally unacceptable. If I barely recognized my new self, how could I expect anyone else to see the creature I'd become and accept it? I wasn't ready to confront Greta and Meredith and Rowens and Nathan as a vampire on my best day; although this was decidedly not that day, I suspected that that day wouldn't dawn anytime soon, and if the state of the city was any indication, we didn't have the luxury to wait.

With that logic in mind, we'd only waited until the sun had set before leaving the safe house, and even then, we'd slunk shadow to shadow, human-slow to avoid detection. Jillian hadn't attacked Dominic's safe house, perhaps because the rooms were well hidden, but maybe, just maybe, she hadn't found us because she wasn't looking. After slitting my throat and gaining the coven's favor, she might think us well and truly dead, and far be it for us to correct her. So instead of tapping into my new abilities and strength, the only vampire super-skills I employed throughout our three-hour, ten-block nocturnal journey downtown were patience and stealth, which in and of themselves really were super-skills. What I'd thought was Dominic's ability to materialize from the shadows was simply the ability to move really fast from shadow to shadow and remain stone-still within their concealing darkness. Such an ability didn't seem particularly impressive, not compared to magically materializing from thin air, until a group of Damned converged on a café a half block ahead of us.

There were five of them. Three rained from the sky like missiles, breaking through the roof of the café headfirst. The other two landed on either side of the building and waited. Dominic and I waited, too, unmoving, unblinking, and unseen in the shadows of the alley across the street. A scream pierced the silence, punctuated by a round of gunfire, both of which abruptly stopped before their echoes had even really begun. Another minute passed in silence.

The whining scrape of plastic on plastic shifted the air. If not for my enhanced hearing, the night would have remained silent, but I wasn't the only one with superhuman hearing who could detect the second-floor window of the café open. A young girl slipped through the crack. I wasn't the only one who could hear the accelerated beats of her heart. I wasn't the only one who could taste the brown sugar, vanilla scent of her shampoo, or smell the cloying, burned-hair scent of her grief and fear.

I stepped forward, unsure exactly what I was about to do but needing to do something. Dominic wrapped his hands around my waist and yanked me back into shadow. I opened my mouth to argue—we could help this girl and still make our meeting with Greta. Someone needed to do *something*—and in those two seconds, one to open my mouth and the second to inhale in preparation to speak, one of the Damned waiting on the street jumped up onto the window ledge, punched its clawed fist into that little girl's chest, and ripped out her heart. She didn't even scream.

The creature tipped its head back, upending the heart whole into its mouth, and the little girl tumbled from the roof like a limp doll, landing with a hard crunch on the pavement. I wasn't the only one who heard her skull crack against the sidewalk on impact. I wasn't the only one who choked on the release of her bowels or felt the shudder of her last breath after she'd already been butchered and fallen, but I was the only one who cared.

I glared back over my shoulder at Dominic, sickened and needing a target.

Dominic wouldn't meet my gaze. Instead, he pulled my body flush against his with one hand around my waist and cupped his other hand around my ear. I felt the movement of his lips against my cheek as he whispered, "They haven't noticed us yet because they're distracted by the hunt, but once they finish, they'll hear your outrage like the police siren it is. We must remain under the radar. Calm yourself. Anchor your emotions."

I don't know how, I thought, but then, Dominic knew that and continued without me having to admit my ignorance.

"Focus on the brush of my breath against your ear, and when you start to feel desire, focus on the thought of me not speaking to your brother, and when you start to feel anger, focus on being reunited with Greta and Meredith, and when you start to feel nervous—"

I squeezed his arm where my hand was resting on his bicep, understanding the gist of it. Learning how to hone my vampire senses would be more enlightening than I'd imagined with Dominic as my teacher. All the times that I couldn't quite discern Dominic's kaleidoscope emotions, all the times I'd thought him conflicted or cold—maybe he'd just been hiding one, strong, very *un*conflicted emotion.

I rotated my emotional kaleidoscope as Dominic instructed while the Damned dismembered the girl and thrashed her body to shreds right there on the sidewalk. Presumably, the three Damned butchered whoever remained inside the café, too, but there were no more screams, there was no more gunfire, and no one else attempted an escape. Five years passed in the span of five minutes while I held my silence and felt everything it was possible to feel about life except for the outrageous tragedy in front of me. Eventually, there were no more beating hearts for the Damned to eat, no more flesh on which to beat out their rage, and Dominic's emotional kaleidoscope worked. They didn't sense our presence and moved on.

I again opened my mouth and inhaled to speak, but this time, Dominic spoke before I could voice my complaint. "If you had interfered with their hunt, we would have lost all advantage of Jillian believing us dead," he said, his voice infuriatingly calm, like a parent lecturing a small child on why they couldn't have dessert before dinner.

"How could you stand by and watch that thing eat her heart and do nothing? She was just a little girl!" I kept my voice to a whisper, not wanting to attract the attention of the Damned, because Dominic was right. If the Damned discovered us it would blow our advantage, but just because Dominic was right didn't mean it felt right.

"What I want to do and what I must do are two separate things. Of course I wanted to prevent the Damned from killing a child, but I must protect our anonymity. If Jillian were to discover us now, we may very well lead her directly to Greta, Rowens, Meredith, Dr. Chunn, and Nathan, whose anonymity is their only protection."

I shook my head. "We are their protection. Who was there to protect her?" I said, gesturing at what remained of the girl's tiny, broken body.

"There are dozens, if not hundreds of little girls in this city needing protection. Are you willing to protect that one only to forsake all the rest?" Dominic said, his voice so calm and reasonable, I could have happily strangled him. "One life is not worth losing the entire city."

"Really? Not one life?" I asked, spreading my arms out like a target. We were in this mess because he'd willingly risked losing the entire city, his entire coven, his own life to save one life: mine.

His expression darkened. "That's different, and you know it."

"I fail to see how—"

"One *stranger* is not worth losing the entire city. One loved one is worth everything." Dominic sandwiched my face in his palms, his voice no longer quite so calm and collected. "You are worth everything."

I wanted to continue arguing my point—that little girl, although a stranger, was worth just as much as any other life—but I couldn't, not after he'd just qualified me as a "loved one," not while his hands cupped my face and his eyes bore into mine with the intensity, heat, and destructive power of an incinerator. My words turned to ash before ever leaving my mouth because I felt the same way about him—he was worth everything—and I couldn't in truth say otherwise.

I pulled away from Dominic and continued walking shadow to shadow down the block, avoiding the hard truth in his eyes and displayed in broken, bloody detail on the sidewalk across the street.

Chapter 5

Kings County Hospital Center's visiting and office hours were long over, but gaining entrance wouldn't be an issue. The entire hospital was deserted; not just closed for the night, but completely forsaken. It wasn't just the vacant halls and empty rooms that gave the building that hollow feeling, although they certainly contributed to it. Like the stranded cars lining New York Avenue and the forgotten shoes, briefcases, and purses scattered across the sidewalk, the hallways, rooms, and office areas had been dropped mid-use and abandoned.

Clipboards and paperwork remained on the front desk and welcome stations, discarded and unfiled. Gurneys filled the hallways, some with rumpled sheets, some still soiled, and a few spattered with blood. Food hadn't been packed away in the cafeteria. Gravy and marinara sauce had congealed in their silver tubs, uncooked chicken and beef patties had attracted the attention of flies at the grill station, and trays, plastic ware, and half-eaten meals littered the tables. Chairs were pushed back or overturned; people had obviously fled the cafeteria mid-meal, and I could only imagine the kind of panic that would cause people to leave their personal belongings behind—evidence of the same panic we'd seen in the street.

Unlike the street, however, the hallways of the hospital were not littered with mutilated bodies. The people who had been here either were hiding, had survived the attack, or more likely, had fled like the young girl futilely attempting to escape from the Damned. I replayed the horror of that memory over in my mind one last time before letting it go. As much as it pained me to admit it, as much as it always pained me, the evidence here and on the street proved that Dominic was right. That girl's death was a tragedy, but it was only one of a thousand tragedies. We couldn't save the one if we wanted to save the next thousand.

Wherever that thousand were, however, they weren't here.

No one was.

"They aren't here," I whispered. I don't know why I whispered it, but in the silence of the empty hospital halls, I felt conspicuous and out of place. "We should have come during the day. Greta and Meredith won't be here now that the sun has set."

"They're here," Dominic assured me.

"No one's here," I argued. "It's after dark. They're probably bunkered down at home, not working."

"This isn't work anymore; it's survival. They're here."

I rolled my eyes. "You can't know that for certain."

"I do."

"How?" I challenged. "How are you so sure that Dr. Chunn and Greta would be here of all places, when no one else is? Why not at the precinct or at home or dead?" I forced myself to say. Looking around at the evidence of everyone's obvious absence and the gore outside, I couldn't ignore the cold, hard fact that New York City and her citizens had suffered a great loss in the last seven days, and it was more than possible—likely even—that so had I.

Dominic pursed his lips, obviously struggling with whatever he was about to say. I prepared myself, but after a long moment, the words he whispered were not the words I'd expected to hear.

"I know they're here, because it's where they're keeping Nathan."

I blinked, startled at first by his admission and then suspicious of his wording. I narrowed my eyes. "What do you mean, *keeping*?"

"Come. See for yourself." Dominic stepped to take the lead and turned the corner down the last hallway toward the morgue.

I followed, feeling that vise around my chest tighten painfully again. My heart couldn't beat and my breaths couldn't quicken, but fear for my brother's well-being sliced just as deep as it always had. When Dominic paused at the doors to the morgue, his hand hovering at the handle instead of pushing it open, my fear got the best of me; I elbowed past him and attempted to cross the threshold. But I didn't think of it as a threshold. To me it was just a door, and I'd opened and stepped through doorways my entire life without asking permission or being injured or encumbered.

But that life was seven days past.

I rebounded off the threshold like I'd hit a live wire and landed hard on my back. I blinked, stunned more by my sudden view of the ceiling than by the ache blanketing the front of my body, but it did ache. I'd walked into nothing but air, and the air had smacked me back with the force of a Mack truck.

Dominic's face swam into focus, blocking my view of the ceiling. "Are you all right?"

"Who taught Dr. Chunn to fortify her morgue into a fallout shelter?" I asked, my voice more a groan than actual words. "Keagan?"

Dominic lifted an eyebrow. "Keagan hasn't left our fallout shelter in seven days, let alone constructed one for a group of humans."

"Cassidy? Is that you?"

Nathan. At the sound of his voice—clear and strong and sharp—the aching urgency around my chest loosened minutely. I needed to see him with my own eyes, to touch him and hug him and know that my seven-day absence hadn't hurt him as much as it had obviously devastated everyone else in this city, but hearing his voice, even disembodied, was better than nothing.

"Nathan, it's me." I winced at the guttural sound of my voice and tentatively explored the elongated fangs suddenly crowding my mouth. "Kind of," I amended.

I took a deep breath, purely out of habit. I didn't need air and taking in such a large quantity didn't produce the calming effect it used to—if anything, it produced the very opposite, slamming home the many ways I was no longer still me. I needed to get control over my emotions, or at the very least, practice hiding them like Dominic had taught me. It was bad enough that I looked like microwaved leftovers. I didn't need extra fangs to improve my appearance. Two were damning enough.

"Why are you loitering in the hall? What do you need, an embossed invitation? Get in here, quick, before the Damned sniff you out."

Just like that, from one moment to the next, something in the air released, like the vacuum seal of an opened jar. The morgue hadn't existed at the end of the hallway, not for me—a void I'd have noticed if I hadn't been so overwrought with worry and urgency over Nathan—but with three thoughtless little words, "Get in here," the seal unlocked, the void was filled, and I could walk wherever I willed.

And just as suddenly as the morgue had opened to admit me, a barrier of my own contriving prevented me from entering: unadulterated fear.

"I can't do this," I whispered. "Nathan can't see me like this."

Dominic pulled me to my feet with a steadying hand. We stood, forehead to forehead, and he brushed his knuckles across my cheek. "Yes, you can. He will see you, and he will accept you."

I shook my head.

"I know exactly what you're going through, Cassidy. You're stronger than this fear. You will survive it. Moreover, you and Nathan will survive it together."

"How do you know what will and won't survive?" I snapped, unaccountably and irrationally angry with him.

"I know because I lived it. Nearly five hundred years ago, I was a newly turned vampire with human loved ones too."

His words startled me into silence. For as long as I'd known Dominic, we were two very different creatures, with different morals and priorities and tolerances, but since the very first grudging compromise between us, we'd come together to defeat a common enemy: the rebel vampires. Over time, I'd realized that we had more in common than just enemies, and little by little, those commonalities, combined with Dominic's irrefutable actions of bravery and sacrifice and loyalty made the truth, no matter how unlikely, undeniable: appearances aside, we were very similar people. Now that we were actually the same creature, you'd think that moments like this, when we shared a common moment, wouldn't rock me like it used to, but it did.

"You revealed your transformed self to human loved ones too?" I asked, but if the grief and sorrow etching his features was anything to go by, I already knew the answer to that question.

He nodded deeply.

"Your father?" I guessed.

He nodded again. "When he gazed upon me, I was naught but a demon, returned from hell to torment him. I'd known better than to seek him out as the creature I'd become—I'd thought myself a demon at first, too, and wasn't wholly convinced even at that time that I wasn't—but in those first few years following my transformation, I couldn't accept what I'd become, let alone accept everything I'd lost."

I reached out to hold his hand and stroked my thumb across his knuckles. I knew that feeling all too well, long before I'd ever been transformed.

"Revealing myself was a grave error in judgment. I did it to assuage my own feelings of grief for the life I'd lost, not thinking of my father's grief, nor how seeing me in such a state would affect him. My Master entranced the memory from his mind, and I never again revealed my existence to another human." He gave me a weary grin. "Until recently."

"I'm so sorry," I said. "I really am, but if your story was meant to convince me that my relationship with Nathan will survive this"—I indicated myself with a sweep of my hand—"it fell short."

"Your brother is a very different man than my father, separated by five hundred years and awareness of the reality of these circumstances. Nathan will not think you a demon."

I snorted. "Not in the traditional sense, but I'm not human anymore either."

"Neither is he."

That thought gave me pause. Nathan was half-Damned now, but I'd seen him fully-Damned—an eleven-foot-tall, fanged, ferocious monster. At least I was still my general size and shape. I'd retained my memory, and I wasn't hunting the beating heart in his chest. I'd never thought the memory of discovering Nathan as one of the Damned would bring me comfort, but I could look in the mirror and know that Nathan had survived worse. I looked terrible, but seeing me like this was nothing compared to seeing him Damned.

"Despite the creature that Nathan has become, you accepted him," Dominic insisted.

I nodded.

"Give him the chance to accept you."

I nodded again and stilled the quiver of my non-beating heart. Just because it no longer kept me alive didn't mean that breaking it wouldn't kill me.

I stepped past Dominic, crossed the threshold into the morgue to face Nathan squarely, and gaped, fears for myself forgotten.

Nathan looked as whole and hearty as his voice indicated, but Dominic's word choice, describing him as being "kept" here, was a gross understatement.

Nathan was inside a cage.

And not just any cage, if his pinkened complexion and the noxious steam wafting from his skin was any indication: he was locked inside a silver cage.

I growled, low and deep and menacing in the barrel of my chest, and any attempt to come into this room with my emotions and vampiric features in check was blown to hell on the explosion of my rage.

"Cassidy?" Nathan's low, suddenly guarded voice brought me back to myself, but only slightly.

"Who did this?" I asked. I suspected that I knew the answer to that question, but the answer was so unacceptable, I needed to hear it out loud.

"Calm down." His eyes darted to the right. "I'm fine."

"Like hell," I spat. "You're caged, like an animal."

"I *am* an animal," he said, and the matter-of-fact way he said the words was just as infuriating as the words themselves.

"Bullshit," I snapped. "Who did this?"

"I really am fine. See?" He grabbed the bars with both hands, and after a darting glance to the right again, bent the bars like they were Play-Doh. He stepped through the hole and outside the cage, lifted his arms in the air at me like he was performing a magic trick—ta-da!—jumped back into the cage, and bent the bars back into position with a final, darting glance to the right. He met my gaze and grinned. "I'm fine."

I stopped growling, shocked. "You're allowing yourself to be caged?"

His eyes darted to the right again. "Shhh," he hissed. "Keep your voice down, or they'll hear you."

I narrowed my eyes. "Who is 'they'?"

"If it gives them peace of mind while they run their tests, it's worth it. If I were them, I'd fear me too."

Run their tests, he said, and that was admission enough for me. "If I were them, I'd fear me more."

The high squeal and slap of a swinging door opened, and the subject of our conversation strode into the room. Dr. Susanna Chunn was a petite woman, fine-boned and delicate, but strong enough to balance the five binders, countless manila files, laptop, cell phone, and variety of pens and markers piled in her arms. Her thick, yellow hipster glasses rode low on the tip on her nose as she stared over them at Nathan, eyeing him critically and without fear. Her heartbeat increased slightly and the lilac of her body lotion blended with a natural, nutty scent, but the scent and increased heart rhythm stemmed from excitement. She was enjoying the mystery that Nathan presented. She wasn't frightened of it.

She wasn't frightened of him.

I checked myself before my thoughts became too hopeful. She didn't know he could bend the bars, because if she did, she would run screaming from him, from this hospital, and smack into another Damned, just like the young girl in the café. She didn't know that he was allowing her to run the tests. She couldn't see past what he was to the truth of who he was; otherwise, she would see that she didn't need a cage around Nathan to keep herself safe. She would see that he was on her side, that we were all on the same side.

Until everyone figured that out, we were all just screaming blind.

Greta stepped into the room behind Dr. Chunn, but unlike the good doctor, whose attention was focused solely on science and Nathan, Greta noticed the uncaged threat in the room.

Greta's eyes locked on me, and she pulled her gun.

I didn't bother raising my hands. The four-inch talons that had erupted through my fingertips upon seeing Nathan in a cage hadn't retracted; raising my hands would only look threatening. I smiled instead.

Greta paled, and the high, sharp, whistle of her fear pierced the air.

Fangs, I realized belatedly. They probably weren't any more reassuring than my talons.

Dominic growled softly and moved to step in front of me. I shook my head, not daring to take my eyes from the barrel of Greta's gun. If I didn't do this myself, she would never see me in the vampire I'd become.

Even though I was mostly still me, I couldn't deny that Greta's instinct to defend herself was dead-on accurate. The urge to tear her throat out and guzzle her blood was there—I couldn't deny that as a passing thought. It had merit, especially when the savory flavor of her fear, like wafting grill smoke, made me salivate—but like with any addiction, I could simultaneously crave it and know I'd regret it. Choosing to resist that craving was just that, a choice, and one I'd probably have had more difficulty making had I never previously experienced and overcome addiction. I knew what the bottom of the gutter looked and smelled and felt like. I knew the hell of being completely abandoned by my last loved one and knowing it was all my own fault. No matter how irresistible a craving seemed, I knew it for the illusion it was, and no matter what form it took—pills or blood—I would never make the wrong choice again.

Although, looking at Nathan trapped in that cage, I had to strongly remind myself that he could escape of his own free will if he really wanted to. We were all on the same side: I was just the only one who knew it.

"Hey G," I said, overlooking the sight of her gun, the smell of her fear, my brother in a cage, and Dr. Chunn's horror-movie shriek as she whipped around at the sound of my voice and dropped everything in her arms. The binders and laptop crashed to the floor. The loose paper inside her manila files burst into the air and slid across the room in random sweeps, and the half dozen pens in her hand clattered over the mess like sprinkles on a sundae.

Greta didn't flinch. Her hands were rock-solid. If the silver cage surrounding Nathan was any indication, Greta probably had silver bullets too.

Meredith poked her head through the swinging door. More than anything, even Greta's gun aimed at my head, the sight of Meredith made me freeze with dread. I wasn't ready for this. If I hadn't been ready to face my half-Damned brother, I certainly wasn't ready to face my full-human, best friend.

"I heard a scream. Is everything al—" She blinked at Greta's gun. "What are you—" And then she invariably followed Greta's aim to me and didn't blink at all. "Oh, God."

"No, just us," Dominic rumbled behind me, attempting and failing to bring some levity to the conversation. "But I understand the confusion. Happens all the time."

I didn't have the ability to contribute with a witty rejoinder and prove to everyone that everything was fine and under control. It wasn't—I wasn't—because Meredith wasn't. Her confusion and fear and relief and grief bowled me over like a gale force wind. My ears were deafened by the howl of her denial. My skin was shredded from the grate of her terror, and my mouth was flooded by something thick and cloying. It had the consistency of honey but the flavor of acetone: tar, maybe, or wet cement. Whatever it was, it constricted my throat, and when I breathed, all I could smell was cinnamon.

My talons, which I still hadn't successfully retracted, unwillingly extended another inch.

"Meredith," Greta said, her voice so calm and careful, I wanted to scream. "Please return to the lab."

No one moved.

"It's me," I said, finally breaking the horrible, flesh-eating silence. "I know it doesn't look like it, but I'm telling you, it's me. I survived, and I'm here to help."

I might have been more convicting if my last few words hadn't ended on a growl. It came rumbling up my throat of its own accord, like a growling stomach, never minding that friends don't growl at each other.

I tried to mask the noise by clearing my throat.

"What should I tell Rowens?" Meredith asked, and it took me a confused moment to realize that she was speaking to Greta.

"Tell him," Greta eyed me up and down. Whatever she saw made her sigh. "Tell him Susanna needed her notes."

"My notes are on the floor," Dr. Chunn whispered.

"Her other notes," Greta snapped. "And Susanna will stay here for now. Until I need *my* notes."

"Right," Meredith said. She ducked out of the room without a second glance, and the dead muscle in my chest throbbed. All of Meredith's aching emotions remained in the room, flaying me even worse in her absence.

It killed me not to go after her, but no one would see that as anything but an attack. I turned away from the swinging door to face Greta and her gun instead. "Sorry I missed all your meetings this past week. Want to catch me up?" I asked, striving for normal and failing miserably.

Greta narrowed her eyes. "Have you seen the streets? Take a look around; it's pretty evident what happened."

I crossed my arms. "I know what happened. I want to know what you're going to do about it. What's the plan? What's our next move?"

"'Our' move?" Greta shook her head. "You bailed on me, DiRocco. Whatever plan I have is my own."

"That's bull, and you know it. You *wanted* me to bail. 'Get out of the city,' you said. 'Get Meredith, Rowens, and Dr. Chunn as far away from ground zero as you can.'" I shook my head. "As if."

"You disobeyed a direct order."

"I'm not one of your officers, G. I don't take orders."

"And look what happened to you." Greta's voice cracked. She didn't put up her gun, and her hands never wavered, but the stone-cold shield of her expression faltered. "Jesus, Cassidy, look at you."

I caught myself before I could wince from the disgust in her expression. Regret was there too; I could taste its bitterness and swallowed the knee-jerk urge to apologize for the creature I'd become, as if I'd willingly chosen to switch teams. As if I was even playing for a different team.

Never apologize for surviving, I reminded myself, and lifted my chin up a notch.

"I think you look great, sis," Nathan interrupted from behind his bars. "Better than you'd look if Lysander hadn't saved you."

Behind me, Dominic snorted.

"Thanks, bro. It's always a comfort to know I look better than death."

"Anytime." Nathan smiled, and his grin was all fangs.

Dr. Chunn gasped. As if Nathan had pressed a reset button, she unfroze from her fright, pounced on the nearest pen and paper scattered on the floor, and jotted a note.

I eyed Dr. Chunn pointedly before settling my gaze warily on Greta. "I don't need to look in a mirror to know who I am, but seeing how you're treating Nathan, I'm not sure I know who *I'm* looking at."

"He's dangerous. Until we know what we're dealing with—"

"He went with you willingly," I reminded her.

Greta winced.

"He agreed to help you find an advantage over the Damned, to discover his weaknesses and find the chink in his strengths. He came here to lay bare his darkest secret for your scrutiny, to give you the ultimate power over him, and this is how you repay him, caging him like an animal?" By the end of my sentence, my words were all growls, but I didn't care. Now that I'd started, I couldn't seem to stop. "Where did you even get a silver cage on such short notice? I doubt you had one in storage next to the spare test tubes and eyedroppers."

Greta sighed. "The cage is just a precaution."

"An unnecessary precaution. An insulting precaution, considering he came here of his own volition. I let him go with you because I trusted you." I pointed at the cage. "This is a betrayal, Greta, and you know it."

"What I know is that I *don't* know. I don't know shit about the creatures we're up against, and that ignorance got hundreds of people killed." Greta swallowed, and for the first time since she had entered the room, her rock-solid aim slipped slightly. "My raid failed, just like you said it would, because we didn't have adequate weapons to use against them."

I glanced at the cage. "Well, it looks like you're well on your way."

Greta pursed her lips and with one last, long hard look, she put up her gun. "Look, Nathan is safe here. The cage aside, we're caring for him, feeding him, and guarding him."

Dominic made a strange noise behind me. "Even lambs are cared for, guarded, and fed before the slaughter."

Greta blushed. "It's just a precaution."

"Just a precaution," I muttered. "Hitler's Jewish ghettos were just a precaution, and look how that ended. Next, you'll have me in there, but unlike with Nathan, you won't have the excuse of science to back you."

"Don't be ridiculous," Greta scoffed.

"We could probably learn a great deal from you too," Dr. Chunn chimed in, only listening enough to know when a scientific opportunity might be presenting itself.

Dominic growled.

"Sounds like an excellent idea to me," a male voice drawled, deep and lazy. Ian Walker stepped out from behind the swinging door. He was tall and lanky, his height all in his legs, and his head was topped by commas of golden curls. His brown, velvet eyes—a gaze that had once looked at me with the heat and devastation of molten lava—now spread chills down my spine. Everything had spiraled so out of control so quickly the last time we'd been together. We'd gone from friends—near-lovers—to enemies in less than thirty-six hours. Meredith thought he was the man who had attacked and nearly killed her last week in her apartment, and considering how we'd left off, I honestly wouldn't put it past him to maim or kill anyone in his path if it meant subsequently hurting me.

We'd parted on horrendous terms, at the end of his crossbow, and I didn't know what slayed me more: the things we'd said to each other or the things I'd allowed to go unsaid. And all of that would remain unsaid, since it seemed we were picking up almost exactly where we'd left off, with a gun aimed between my eyes.

"How many more people do you think Greta has stowed away back there?" Dominic muttered.

"Hello, Walker," I said, ignoring Dominic. My voice sounded as flat and dead as Walker's gaze. He smelled like mint, as always, but beneath the mint, I could smell the heat and spice and everything Dominic and every vampire I'd ever met had said smelled so damn nice. The smell of his night blood was intoxicating. I swallowed, and the walls of my throat scraped like sandpaper. "Nice to see that, even after all this time, we can pick up right where we left off."

Greta's gaze never left mine, but she wasn't talking to me when she said, "We're just talking here. Stand down."

"We don't talk to vampires," Walker said. "We kill them."

"That's not just any vampire. That's DiRocco."

Walker shook his head. "That *was* DiRocco."

"I can attest that I'm still me," I said, warily. "Not that anything I could do or say would convince you otherwise."

"He turned you against me long before he turned you into a vampire. I should have killed you then."

"As if leaving me for dead wasn't the same damn thing," I snapped.

"And yet, here you are, mission unaccomplished." Walker's expression twisted painfully. "We were friends once. More than friends. We were—" His voice broke, and whatever he'd been about to say, he dismissed it with a quick shake of his head. "I was wrong about you. And I was wrong to let you live."

I heard the strain of his trigger finger contracting, and I realized that dodging a single bullet as a vampire would be as easy as avoiding oncoming traffic while crossing the street as a human—I simply needed to keep my eyes open for danger and side-step accordingly. I felt a sudden sorrow for Walker. He'd been fighting this battle his entire adult life since losing his fiancé and blaming Bex for her death. He'd sacrificed a great deal in his personal war against Bex: a normal life and our friendship. He'd even killed other humans in the effort to kill vampires, all because he thought no sacrifice was too great in the effort to win his personal war against Bex. But what Walker didn't realize, what his passion and vengeance would never allow him to truly grasp, was that his efforts were futile and self-destructive, tantamount to a fly waging war against the hand swatting at it.

Walker's finger muscles were still contracting on his trigger and I was still debating my next move in our conversation after I dodged his bullet when someone slammed into me, knocking me back a step into Dominic and shielding the two of us from Walker, as if we needed shielding.

Walker's finger muscles froze and every other muscle in his body began to tremble.

"Ian," Ronnie whispered, her voice a soft plea. "Please, don't shoot."

Chapter 6

A few strands of what was left of Ronnie's tinsel-thin hair fell from her emaciated scalp in her haste to shield my body with her own. I winced at both the sick straggles of her hair and at her misguided attempt to protect me. I could dodge Walker's bullet, and if I was wrong about the power and capabilities of my new body or overconfident against Walker's weaponry, I could probably survive being shot. Dominic most definitely could survive a bullet. I'd witnessed dozens of bullets turn his body to Swiss cheese, and the injuries, which would have killed a man on impact, had only pissed him off. But somehow, we'd ended up in the opposite order—me in front of Dominic and Ronnie in front of me—so the weakest person was the front-row target of Walker's shot.

But he didn't shoot.

Walker's jaw clenched, his hands physically shook, and I'd never smelled a more aromatic scent than the cinnamon-mint effervescence wafting from his pores—unadulterated horror, I realized. A little part of me hated that I salivated at the scent of his suffering.

Considering he was still aiming a gun at me, a very little part.

A rattling growl swelled the room. I opened my mouth to admonish Dominic; the growl became louder, and I realized the noise was coming from me. I cleared my throat and tried again. "Ronnie, stand down."

Ronnie didn't move. Walker's trembling worsened as he studied her, from the dead strands of her tinsel hair to the bony knobs of her ankles and every emaciated feature in-between. Walker shook his head in denial.

Ronnie nodded back and took a step toward him.

Dominic and I simultaneously lunged forward to drag her back.

Our movement snapped Walker out of his shock, and he re-aimed his drooping gun wildly, targeting me and Dominic and even Ronnie before settling back on me.

Ronnie sidestepped into his crosshairs.

"Stop it, Ronnie," I said. "You can't—"

Ronnie held up her hand, but when she spoke, it wasn't to me. "I know this is hard."

Walker wasn't looking at her. He was still aiming at me, but he was also still shaking his head.

"I never wanted this. I never could have imagined in my wildest nightmares that we would come to this, that you could ever point a gun at me, and that I—" Ronnie's voice broke. She cleared her throat and started again. "I've loved you my entire life, and I always thought that despite the vampires, despite everything, we would marry and live happily ever after."

Walker shook his head, more insistent now than in denial, and I tried to stave off the inevitable.

"Ronnie," I pleaded, "maybe we should—"

"Even when you were engaged to Julia-Marie," Ronnie forged ahead, ignoring me, "I was thrilled for you, but a part of me still dreamed. Even after everything with Bex, and you turned so cold and distant, even after you brought home Cassidy, I still remained hopeful that maybe one day it would all work out for us. We were good people, and good people deserve to be happy. And the years just flew by, and I just kept hoping, maybe one day."

Walker's head stopped moving. In fact, even with my enhanced senses, the only movement coming from him was the involuntary contraction of his heart. He'd even stopped breathing.

Ronnie took a step toward him, and this time, Dominic and I let her go.

"It wasn't until I woke after Bex's attack and realized that I wasn't dead, that I was a vampire, that I knew one day would never come. Maybe we never would have been happy even if I'd grown old and died human, but suddenly, even the hope of happiness was gone. Completely, utterly gone. I looked at my claws that were once hands, cut my tongue on the fangs that were once my eyeteeth, and felt bloodlust burn the back of my throat, and greater than the fear of the creature I'd become was the dawning horror over the fact that there was no hope for you and me. Your love for me was just a foolish girl's dream, but there was nothing questionable about your love of killing vampires."

Ronnie took another step forward, an arm's-length away from Walker now, close enough that, depending on the size of the bullet he had loaded, the exit wound might blow apart the back of her skull.

Walker didn't move a muscle, not even to blink, but tears filled his eyes and spilled over his cheeks.

"Nothing about this is easy, Ian. Realizing that we were over was the hardest moment of my life. I still can't come to terms with it. Looking at you now, finally seeing you again, your face...God, your face—" Ronnie reached out a shaking hand. Walker finally moved, just one twitch of his eyes to Ronnie's raised claws, and she froze. She sighed and let her hand drop down to her side. He met her eyes. "I missed you," she said. "More than my whole human life, the one thing I miss most is you."

"I'm sorry," Walker said, and his voice was nothing but gravel. I didn't know what he was sorry for. Was he offering an apology for ignoring Ronnie's feelings for most of her life? For not being there for her when she was attacked and transformed? Or preemptively for killing her? Really, I didn't think it mattered anymore.

"I know," Ronnie said, "because this is the hardest moment of *your* life. The day you face not one vampire, but three, and you don't kill any of them."

Walker was back to shaking his head, but when he spoke this time, he wasn't looking at Ronnie. "What's wrong with her?"

I blinked. "There isn't a clinical term, but I believe they refer to what Ronnie is suffering from as heartbreak."

"Are you depriving her of blood? Are you punishing her to get to me?" Walker asked, and the tears kept flowing.

I gaped, taken aback. "Of course not. We're vampires, not monsters, Walker. Oh, that's right, you could never tell the difference."

"Cassidy," Dominic growled. "Not that long ago, neither could you."

I sighed and tried again. "Ronnie's transformation only took a few hours. She's been struggling with basic vampire skills, like feeding and entrancing, and although we've tried to teach her those skills, it's not going well for her."

Walker looked back at Ronnie, waiting for her response.

Her smile was small and so, so sad. "What does it matter if you're just going to kill me anyway?"

Walker froze again, nothing but heartbeat.

Ronnie took one last step forward, close enough that the handgun's barrel pressed against her chest. I glanced at Dominic to gauge his reaction, but the expression on his face was resigned. *We should do something*, I thought, but we'd already warned her. We'd already tried to stop this from happening, but no effort would be enough to get this derailed train back on its tracks, with or without casualties. And there were sure to be casualties.

Ronnie raised her hands and wrapped her bone-thin fingers around Walker's fist. Her claw-tipped thumb threaded through the trigger guard and over his index finger. "What does it matter, since I'm already dead?"

Ronnie tensed to pull the trigger.

Walker flicked the safety on with his thumb.

They stared at each other for a long moment, the gun and the safety between them like a life preserver neither could find the heart to let go of.

"I thought Bex had killed you," Walker whispered.

"Didn't she?" Ronnie murmured back. "Isn't that what you always said, that being transformed into a vampire was as good as being dead?"

Walker's expression hardened. "I searched for you. As much as I could while caring for Colin, I searched for all of you." He blinked, nearly startled by his own thoughts. "What of the others? Are Logan, Keagan, Jeremy, and—"

"We were all attacked and transformed."

Walker nodded, his expression still unyielding. "What are you doing here?"

Ronnie blinked. "Seriously?"

Walker frowned, as much as he could frown while already wearing such a somber expression.

"Why is anyone here in New York City right now? Sightseeing?" Ronnie snorted derisively, and I had to bite back a smile. I'd never heard her speak like that to Walker—I couldn't remember hearing her be anything but meek and tender toward him—and if his gaping jaw was any indication, he couldn't either. "I'm here to help take down Jillian and stop the Damned from taking over the world," she said.

"Taking over the world might be a bit of an exaggeration," Walker said drily.

"They took over New York City easily enough," Ronnie reasoned. "Who's here to stop them from taking over the next city and the next and the next one after that?" She looked around at our little group, Dr. Chunn and Greta on one side of the room, with Nathan caged behind them and Dominic and I on the other side of the room, tensed for action. "If we're the only hope the world has against these creatures, the world is doomed."

"Only because we're divided," I interjected.

Walker's eyes flicked to me, and Dominic flinched beside me. Walker's gaze was filled with so much anger and revulsion, I was reminded just how close his thumb still was to the safety.

"Cassidy's correct," Dr. Chunn said.

Silence stretched, and I could feel the heavy weight of doubt settle on Dr. Chunn from everyone's collective, unresponsive stare.

"She is," she insisted. "Detective Wahl and her raid might not have failed if the Day Reapers hadn't shown up and tried to save the day on their own."

"They'd won against the Damned once," Nathan said. "I'm sure they thought they could do it again."

"They probably could have, but not with dozens of entranced humans in their way." Dr. Chunn shook her head. "We were an ill-equipped, divided front, and Jillian used that to her advantage and won."

Walker snorted, and I realized where Ronnie had learned to sound so derisive. "And having an army of nearly a hundred ten-foot-tall creatures with talons like sabers and scales like armor didn't have anything to do with it."

"It did, of course," Dr. Chunn said, frowning at his tone. "But we didn't help ourselves either. We didn't stand against them with our best, united front. We didn't punch back with planning and precision. We were desperate, and the Day Reapers were overconfident, and that, in combination with our lack of solidarity, was a disaster. The Damned are stronger and taller and more lethal, but we have intelligence where they only have instinct and orders. We could have won against them—but we didn't—and Cassidy is right when she says that one of the main reasons we didn't is because we were divided."

"One of the reasons?" Walker raised his eyebrows. "As in, there's more than one?"

"Yes, and I'd like to show all of you." Her eyes shifted to the gun in Walker's hands and pressed flush against Ronnie's chest.

Walker looked down at his gun as if just realizing he was still holding it, and then he lifted his gaze back to Ronnie. "I'm not okay with this," he said, his voice a low rumble.

"And I am?" Ronnie shook her head, and her expression said very plainly that she thought he was an idiot. "You think that I'm okay with being the very creature I've feared my entire life? You think I'm okay with attacking people to drink their blood and entrancing them to survive and being the weakest, most pathetic vampire because I can't do either of those things? You think I'm okay with losing my hair and looking like death?" she shrieked.

Walker's mouth opened and closed without uttering a word.

Ronnie let go of the gun. "I'm not any more okay with this than you are, but I can't just wiggle my nose and fix it. I can't do anything except live with it, assuming I get to keep living," she said, eyeing Walker's trigger finger.

Walker didn't move; not even his thumb hovering over the safety so much as twitched. And then he put up his gun.

I sighed in relief, releasing the breath I hadn't realized I'd been holding. "All right, doc, let's see what you've got."

Chapter 7

I stared at the charts and figures that Dr. Chunn had created, obviously painstakingly and thoroughly, and I tried not to let the disappointment show in my expression. Seven days wasn't a lot of time to produce scientific results under normal conditions, and there was nothing normal about conducting experiments inside a morgue on a caged, unclassified creature while New York City was being slaughtered into the Stone Age. She didn't have a mail system to send samples to specialized labs or a team of scientists at her back to delegate work to anymore. Everyone else either had evacuated, was missing, or was dead. All Dr. Chunn had at her disposal was her equipment here at the morgue—which was substantial, considering the size of her facility—a dead Damned and my live brother as lab rats; and an unofficial, unqualified team of two: my partner from the *Sun Accord*, Meredith Drake, and Supervisory Special Agent Harold Rowens.

At least Meredith could help run and monitor the software, providing valuable technical skill in support of Dr. Chunn's efforts, but I couldn't say the same of Rowens. He was sharp and skilled in his own right, but he belonged in the field, not the lab. Despite my assumptions, however, he stood next to Dr. Chunn, his shoulder holster strapped over an apron and wearing protective eyeglasses, looking surprisingly in his element.

I resisted teasing Rowens, for which I was proud, and hugging Meredith, which made me depressed as hell. Her furtive, frightened glances grated against my heart, but my self-control could only withstand so much. I indicated the rows, columns, and charts of printed results between us with a wave of my hand and gave up on tact. "This isn't anything we didn't already know, and we're out of time. We need real answers," I said.

Meredith frowned, but when she would have normally defended her work, she remained silent, cutting me with the hesitation in her eyes.

Dr. Chunn crossed her arms. "We might have known that the Damned's scales were impenetrable except by the Day Reapers and their maker, but now we know why." She jabbed a finger at one of many stacks of statistics and findings I didn't need to decipher to know we were screwed. "It's more than just the Day Reapers' silver talons, although silver is enough to penetrate Nathan's scales, because he was created before the Leveling. The Damned that Jillian created while in full possession of Dominic's Master powers are resistant to silver, yet they are still susceptible to injury by a Day Reaper. An enzyme in Day Reaper blood prevents the Damned's injuries from healing after the silver penetrates their scales. That's why the silver trackers penetrated their scales but were expelled from their bodies. And it's why the silver tracker coated in your blood penetrated their scales and didn't get expelled; an enzyme in your blood prevented the wound from healing. If we can replicate the enzyme, we can build weapons that not only penetrate their scales but do some real damage—without having to bleed you dry."

I shook my head. "Your findings are nothing but theories unless we can test them."

Dr. Chunn stared at me and smiled.

I sighed. "Fine, let's say you draw my blood and create a synthetic enzyme that you apply to weapons to kill the Damned. Which Damned do you plan to prove your theory on?" I asked. "You can't just shoot Nathan."

"I don't see why not," Walker grumbled.

"At that stage, lab experimentation would no longer be applicable," Dr. Chunn smoothly interrupted. "We would field test, of course."

"Of course," I said, shaking my head. "I'd be more willing to open a vein for your experiments if I hadn't witnessed your hospitality firsthand." I glanced at Nathan standing docilely in his cage and shook my head. "Excuse me if I refuse to willingly walk into captivity for the cause."

Nathan grabbed the bars suddenly and shook the cage violently. "I am not an animal!" he screamed in his best Charlton Heston impersonation.

Which was, admittedly, spot-on.

The *Planet of the Apes* reference was lost on most everyone. Walker, Greta, and Rowens all pulled their guns. Ronnie flinched back violently, equally terrified of both Nathan and the firepower. Dominic blinked noncommittally. I stared at my little brother—not so little anymore, but just as exasperating—and shook my head.

But Meredith, bless her, Meredith knew better. She burst out laughing.

Dr. Chunn eyed all of us as if she'd prefer to cage everyone, not just for scientific purposes.

Nathan lifted his hands innocently, and we watched as the boils and open sores on his palms healed. No matter the science, and no matter my enhanced senses, which could actually see the healing process—Nathan's newfound abilities still shook me to my very core.

A thought escaped from the deep, dark box inside myself where I stuffed, locked, and hid the memories and emotions I was too chicken to examine. Typically, I was a seasoned pro at self-preservation, and that box stayed airtight, but witnessing Nathan's antics and abilities, seeing him caged like the animal he claimed he wasn't, had weakened its seal, and I thought, *Thank God Mom and Dad aren't alive to witness this.*

For the first time in over five years, I felt something other than horror, denial, and rage at the thought of my parents' passing, but this feeling, something akin to morbid gratefulness, wasn't much of an improvement.

Rowens glanced at Meredith speculatively. "Did we miss the punchline?"

Meredith nodded, wiping her eyes. "Yes, you did."

Dr. Chunn settled her gaze, once again, on me. "I'm not caging you. I didn't even want to cage Nathan. I just need a sample of your blood."

"And yet there he is, caged," I reminded her.

"It made Walker feel better," she said, sighing. "It's perfunctory anyway. He can escape at any time."

Everyone's gaze, which had once been focused on Nathan, shifted instantly and simultaneous to Dr. Chunn.

"He can what?" Walker asked, his voice a low rumble.

Nathan rolled his eyes.

"Oh, fuck it." I conceded, feeling more pressure from the unstable hostility in the room than anything else. "Yes, you can have a sample of my blood. Happy?"

"Ecstatic," Dr. Chunn said, unsmiling.

"In all your findings," Ronnie began, her voice fluttering nervously, "have you come across anything pertaining to the Damned's eating habits? Why do they specifically crave aortic blood as opposed to blood in general?"

"Yes, actually, I have a theory about that as well," Dr. Chunn said, but I had a sinking suspicion she had a theory about everything—which did not necessarily indicate she had answers about anything.

"Why do their eating habits matter to you?" Walker asked sharply.

Ronnie shrank back. "If Dr. Chunn can determine why the Damned crave aortic blood, maybe she can figure out why I crave blood, but can't stomach it. Maybe—" Ronnie glanced at the crowd around her and curled in on herself. "I know we have a lot to worry about, and the Damned come first. But I was just hoping…I mean, it's just that I'm—"

"You're starving," Dominic interjected plainly. "I'm sure that Dr. Chunn can apply her findings to you as well. You are not alone anymore, Ronnie," Dominic said kindly. He placed his arm gently around her shoulders, and somehow, she seemed bolstered by the weight. "We will figure this out together, and you will heal." He glanced at me. "We will all heal, and we will all survive."

Walker glared at Dominic, the expression on his face somehow both possessive and disgusted. "She was never alone."

Dominic raised an eyebrow. "Does she have the look of someone who has been well cared for?"

"She looked a sight better when I was the one caring for her!"

Ronnie deflated under the sharp prick of Walker's words.

I turned away from the strange and convoluted emotions between Walker and Ronnie to focus on the facts, which were confusing enough without distraction. "Please, continue Doc. You were about to explain why you think the Damned crave aortic blood."

Dr. Chunn pointed to a stack of papers on the far side of the lab bench. Rowens alternately eyed the stack of papers and Nathan, compliant behind bars. With only one hand, he had to choose: put up his gun and pass Dr. Chunn the papers or ignore her and continue aiming his gun at a calm, caged man. After a moment of hesitation, he put up the gun with a heavy sigh and passed the indicated stack of files to Dr. Chunn. Their fingers brushed as the file changed hands, and Dr. Chunn blushed a bright, tomato red from the chaste touch. Rowens's expression was lecherous, but he didn't say or do anything beyond that little finger caress. I tried to ignore the fact that I could smell the mingling scent of their arousal and the realization that, because of my heightened senses, I would be fastidiously ignoring personal insight into people's desires and emotions for the rest of my life.

"Doc?" I prompted.

"Oxygen deficiency!" Dr. Chunn blurted. She cleared her throat and tried again. "It seems that Nathan has an oxygen deficiency."

I narrowed my eyes. "Nathan has an oxygen deficiency, so he craves human blood," I said doubtfully.

Dr. Chunn shook her head. "He drinks human blood because he's a vampire. He craves aortic, oxygen-rich blood because he has an oxygen deficiency. People who suffer from an oxygen deficiency typically experience irritability, irrational behavior, memory loss, depression, dizziness, muscle aches and pains, circulation problems, and fatigue.

Give a twelve-foot-tall, three-hundred-pound, muscle-bound, bloodthirsty creature those symptoms, and you have the Damned."

I held up my hand. "If a human—say, Meredith—had an oxygen deficiency, she would get dizzy and depressed and feel achy." I gave Dr. Chunn a look. "The Damned are slaughtering people."

"Meredith isn't predatorial. She doesn't drink blood as a main food source, nor does she have the ability to smell, hear, or taste the oxygen in aortic blood. Meredith with an oxygen deficiency isn't dangerous. Give a vampire an oxygen deficiency—"

"—and you get humans with missing hearts," Greta finished morosely.

Dr. Chunn nodded. "Exactly."

"So if we treat their oxygen deficiency, the Damned will stop craving human hearts?" I asked, but I couldn't keep my eyes from settling on Nathan.

"There's no fixing this," Nathan said. "This is who I am now. You saved me the best you could, the best that was possible, but there's no going back to the way I was before being transformed."

"You don't know that," I said. "You heard Dr. Chunn: you crave aortic blood because of an oxygen deficiency. It's something that can be treated."

"She didn't say that. *You* said that."

"He craves human blood because Jillian escaped," Dominic said flatly. "If we kill Jillian, his maker, we seal the transformation like we should have weeks ago."

Dr. Chunn shook her head. "Killing his 'maker' to 'seal the transformation' isn't a real thing."

I raised my eyebrows. "What is it?"

She shrugged. "Folklore?"

Dominic narrowed his eyes. "I've done it before. I transformed Jillian from being Damned to a vampire. She no longer craved human hearts because I sealed the transformation by killing her maker."

Dr. Chunn was still shaking her head. "Correlation does not imply causation."

"English, Susanna," Rowens reminded her.

She sighed. "Just because Dominic killed Jillian's maker and then Jillian was suddenly no longer Damned does not mean that killing her maker necessarily caused that to happen."

Dominic crossed his arms. "The simplest explanation is usually the right one."

"I eat a carrot, and an hour later, I become violently ill: did the carrot cause my illness?" Dr. Chunn asked.

Dominic rolled his eyes. "That isn't at all akin to—"

"Maybe I ate improperly cooked chicken a few hours earlier," Dr. Chunn continued, speaking up over Dominic's exasperation. "Or maybe I contracted an illness from a germ. Or maybe I'm pregnant. Assuming the carrot caused my illness is not only presumptive, but dangerous, because I might stop eating carrots instead of cooking my chicken more thoroughly."

"I concede your point," Dominic said. "But it's still *possible* that it was the carrot."

"Not likely," Dr. Chunn said stubbornly.

I shook my head. "When we transformed Nathan, we mimicked everything based on Dominic's experience with Jillian. His master drained him and fed him non-Damned blood. Everything was the same, except that we didn't kill his maker to seal the transformation."

Dr. Chunn laughed. "There are so many differences between Jillian's transformation and Nathan's that they don't even compare: the locations were different; the masters were different; the blood you used to transform him back was different. You made a valiant attempt to fully transform him back into a night blood, but there's simply too many differing factors to determine exactly which one, if it was even only one, that caused him to retain his oxygen deficiency, not to mention his heightened senses and the ability to shift between forms at will. Given enough time and resources, I might be able to isolate the necessary factors, but—"

"Time isn't exactly something we have in spades," Greta grumbled.

"Neither are resources," Rowens added.

I raised my eyebrows. "Are we on a timeline?"

"We're on a ticking time bomb," Rowens said grimly. "The military already attempted and failed a covert mission to take out the Damned without realizing what they were really up against. Afterward, they bombed the bridges and collapsed the tunnels to isolate the city from the mainland."

I blinked. "They what?"

"They've completely cut off any means of escaping New York City except by air. I was able to get word to my superiors that innocent people are still here, but..." Rowens shrugged, the muscles of his residual limb twitching slightly. "Really, it's just a matter of time."

"Which is why my time will be more efficiently spent determining how to create a synthetic version of the Day Reaper enzyme," Dr. Chunn said.

Greta raised her eyebrows. "Can you do that?"

Dr. Chunn pursed her lips, warily looking over the stacks of statistics and results. "Can I afford not to try?"

"What do you need to get it done?" I asked, and then smiled just as warily. "Besides my blood."

"May I point out that until your body bathes in direct sunlight, you are not technically a fully transformed Day Reaper?" Dominic interjected.

"My blood had the enzyme even when I was a night blood," I reminded him.

Dr. Chunn waved away my point. "Fully transformed or not, samples from two different Day Reapers to confirm my results would be ideal," Dr. Chunn confirmed, as if we could just run an errand to the nearest supermarket to pick one up.

Ronnie frowned at Dominic. "The Day Reapers aren't exactly our friends right now," she reminded him. "When they find out that you transformed Cassidy, they'll want your head on a pike."

"In general, you are correct; the Day Reapers will not approve of my actions," Dominic said. "But one specific Day Reaper will understand. Bex is our ally, and I think she will help us if I ask nicely."

Ronnie made a noise between a snort and a low whine.

Dominic eyed her askance. "Please, speak."

"Sorry. I just don't share your confidence where Bex is concerned," she admitted. "She's never been *my* ally. She abandoned me."

Dominic eyed Ronnie thoughtfully before returning his attention to Dr. Chunn. "You will take Ronnie's blood as well, and test it for deficiencies."

Ronnie's expression brightened.

Dr. Chunn blinked. "Bulimia isn't a blood deficiency. It's a mental-health disorder."

"No, I—" Ronnie began.

"Admitting you have a problem is the first step," Walker said softly.

"No, you don't understand. I was *anorexic*. I didn't throw up my food; I hardly ate." Ronnie swallowed, and even that small movement sounded painful. "I had a problem, I know that, but this is different. This is a new problem, and it's killing me."

Dominic leveled his eyes on Dr. Chunn. "You will take and test her blood and determine what is wrong with her."

Dr. Chunn rolled her eyes. "Sure, I'll just squeeze that in between creating a synthetic vampire enzyme and discovering the cure for vampire oxygen deficiency."

"We all have our problems to solve," I murmured, "and yours isn't any more impossible than us finding you a spare Day Reaper to conduct your experiments on."

"Or finding the families of the Damned and breaking it to them that their loved ones are ravenous, heart-eating creatures slaughtering the city—assuming their loved ones are still alive." Greta said. She waved a hand dismissively. "But no worries, I can tell them it's just an oxygen deficiency we can't treat yet."

"Or having said oxygen deficiency," Nathan interjected.

"All right, okay, enough with the pity party; we all have our impossible problems to solve," Walker said. "And anyway, hunting Day Reapers takes the cake."

I raised my eyebrows. "No one is *hunting* Day Reapers. We're saving them."

"We're saving one." Dominic clamped a hand on my shoulder and moved me gently aside, so he could confront Walker. "And you are not the face Bex will want to see upon her rescue."

I'd never seen a grimmer smile than the one on Walker's face in that moment. "It's not a matter of want, but a matter of need. I'm your best bet to infiltrate the underground of your coven undetected."

I shook my head. "This isn't a good idea."

Dominic crossed his arms. "I'm more than capable of infiltrating my own coven."

"Not undetected. Jillian was your Second—she knows every secret passage and unmapped tunnel in the coven that you know of," Walker reasoned. "I have forged passages to infiltrate your coven without your knowledge, and therefore without her knowledge. With me, you'll have the element of surprise."

"Bullshit," Dominic snapped. "I know all passages in and out of that coven; it holds many secrets, but none from me."

"Let me prove you wrong. If I show you a passage that you already know of, by all means, leave me behind," Walker said, his expression somehow cruel despite the helpfulness of his offer. "But if it's a passage I've kept secret, even from you, then I get to come along."

I squeezed Dominic's shoulder, digging my talons into his flesh. "I don't care what he knows; this is a bad idea," I insisted.

"This is a rescue mission, not a staking," Dominic reminded him. "Why do you even want to attend? When has saving a vampire ever interested you?"

"Bex saved my life once. Maybe I want to return the favor." Walker shrugged noncommittally.

I squeezed my talons in deeper. "And maybe he wants to lead us deep into a secret passage where no one will ever find the ash of our bodies."

"I would kill him before he could even twitch a finger," Dominic said drily.

Walker snorted. "You would try."

Dominic's ears elongated. "Should I try now?"

Walker aimed his handgun.

"Stop! Please, stop." Ronnie lunged between the two of them. "We all agreed that being divided allowed Jillian and the Damned to win last time. If we have any hope of winning a fight against them this time, we have to find a way to work together." She eyed the two of them speculatively. "Which means not killing each other."

Dominic sighed, but he took a step back.

"Even if some of us are vampires," Ronnie finished.

Walker looked away, unable to hold her gaze, but he did finally holster his gun.

Dominic must have seen something more in Walker's gaze than grief and guilt—or perhaps, that was enough to convince him—because the next words out of his mouth made me nauseated with dread. "I accept your offer. You may show me the secret passageway to infiltrate my own coven, and if it is indeed secret to me, you may join us in our endeavor to free Bex from her confinement in the Underneath." Dominic's eyes narrowed slightly. "But I will have your word that you will not use this opportunity to kill or otherwise incapacitate, inflict pain on, maim, or in any way physically harm Cassidy, Bex, myself, or any vampire, with the exception of Jillian and the Damned, or in self-defense."

"Agreed, assuming I have your word as well," Walker said.

"If we must sign verbal contracts not to kill each other, we shouldn't be working together," I grumbled.

Dominic nodded to Walker, ignoring me. "You have my word. I will not harm you in any capacity unless in self-defense or in defense of Cassidy, Bex, or one of my coven."

Walker nodded curtly, and then fixed his velvet-brown gaze on me.

I blinked. "What?"

"Your word," Walker answered tightly.

"You're kidding, right?"

Walker stared at me, deadly serious.

"I would never harm you except in self-defense," I said, bitterly. "And until recently, I never thought I'd need that exception."

"You never would have, until recently," Walker said coldly. "But I was wrong about everything concerning you."

I smiled sadly. "It's hard to be right about someone you never really knew."

Chapter 8

Dominic, Walker, and I working together was a bad idea. I'd recognized it as a bad idea from the moment the words "hunting Day Reapers" had uttered from Walker's mouth, and I continued to believe it as Walker led us through the familiar sewer drains beneath New York City to an underground passageway that had indeed been secret from Dominic, and as Dominic upheld his end of their bargain and allowed Walker to join us in our mission to release Bex from the Underneath.

After hours of navigating the damp labyrinth of old sewer drains, we came to a passage that expanded into tunnels carved into the hard, porous rock that composed Dominic's coven. Dominic took the lead, and eventually, after what felt like an eternity of navigating winding passages and crumbling fissures, we stared down into the silver-lined Underneath.

The Underneath was an unfurnished, mildew-ridden series of chambers at the bottom of a four-foot-wide, twenty-foot deep chasm. The crevice would have been unremarkable in the porous cavern, where spider web cracks commonly snaked to wide fissures, but with my enhanced senses and sensitivity to silver, I could feel the heat billowing from this particular fissure with the energy of a furnace. Emanating from the Underneath along with the sweltering heat was the noxious scent of steaming flesh.

Bex's flesh.

Even though I was standing ten feet away from the Underneath's opening, the beating burn of its heat made my eyes water. I wiped the tears from my cheeks distractedly, imagining Jillian in that hell for the three weeks before we'd released her in the desperate attempt to save Nathan. Her body had been nothing but bone and charred sinew and tendons; feeling the blistering intensity of the Underneath's entrance from several feet away, I couldn't imagine how Jillian had been anything but ash. I pulled my hand away from my cheek and stared, somewhat unsurprised, to find blood, not tears, smeared on my fingertips.

Of the three of us, Walker was the only one capable of infiltrating the Underneath without being physically affected, and that realization only pounded home the fact that working together was not just a bad idea, but the worst idea I'd ever agreed to. Considering all the times I'd agreed to play bait for Dominic in his endeavors to save his coven and my brother, I'd agreed to some terrible ideas.

"We're sending Walker down there to rescue Bex alone," I said. It wasn't a question but a matter of common sense. Our eyes were *bleeding*, for heaven's sake.

"Since he's here, we may as well take advantage of his indifference to silver," Dominic said reasonably.

"What would we have done without him here?" I shook my head in wonder. "How do you imprison people down there without enduring the effects of silver exposure yourself?"

Dominic laughed. "I suck it up."

I wiped my eyes again and held up my bloodstained fingertip for his inspection. "If these are the effects of silver exposure from *outside* the Underneath, I can't imagine going inside. I can't imagine surviving."

"Bex is stronger than even Jillian," Dominic said, "and she's only been imprisoned for seven days. She will be starved and wasted nearly to bone, but she will recover with a simple feeding. She'll have survived."

Dominic's voice sounded certain, but I wasn't completely convinced. I glanced at Walker as he edged toward the crevice, unaffected by silver and therefore exempt from its burns—but not from the smell of other people's burns. He pulled the ropes, anchors, and harnesses of his rappelling equipment from his pack, his nose tucked into the front of his shirt.

I turned back to Dominic, my eyebrows raised. "Simple feeding?"

Dominic glanced at Walker, his brows furrowed, but as my implication dawned, his expression showed something akin to astonished incredulity. "My intention is not to feed Walker to Bex. I daresay he would consider that an attack, a break of our promise, and permission to—how did you so eloquently state—" Dominic tapped his forefinger to his lips twice in thought before holding it aloft in exclamation. "—hide the ash of our bodies where no one will ever find it."

I nodded. "Exactly."

"After seven days in the Underneath, Bex's flesh may or may not still be intact, but she will most certainly be unconscious. Walker will lift her out of the crevice, carry her to safety, and be gone from this place before anyone is wise to our presence or her absence. Only then will I procure a meal for her." Dominic grazed the hollow of my cheek with the knuckles. "And for you."

I swallowed the cinnamon burn of Walker's scent, a heady reminder of my own unsavory appetite. One day, I would have to procure my own meal, as Dominic so delicately phrased it, but lucky me, today was not that day. I had other, more pressing dilemmas at the moment. "This was too easy."

Dominic shrugged, but I wasn't fooled by his nonchalance. He felt as uneasy at our uncontested entrance into the coven as I did. "Ian Walker's passage was secret even to me, so Jillian would not have prepared a defense against that entrance."

"But she should have felt our presence when we officially entered the coven. At the very least, she would have felt *someone's* presence. As Master, you would have—or so you have claimed," I pointed out.

Dominic nodded. "It's true; to me, the coven is a living being, as animate and susceptible to invasion as my own body, but even microscopic parasites and germs may enter my body undetected."

I grinned. "In this analogy, are we germs or parasites?"

Dominic returned my grin. "Our visit tonight may go undetected."

"Or she is waiting for Walker to rappel into the Underneath before attacking, so we are torn between fleeing and fighting? In our hesitation, her Damned will tear us to shreds and devour the hearts from our chests."

"That, too, is a possibility, but the less likely scenario, I think."

I snorted softly. "How less likely?"

Dominic gave that serious thought. "Seventy/thirty, give or take a percentage."

I turned toward Walker and raised my voice slightly. "You need any help with that gear?"

Walker didn't look up from where he had secured his rigging into the rock. "I'm about ready here. I've prepared a fifty-foot line."

"That should be plenty," Dominic said. "Once you reach the bottom, you'll face a series of chambers, each containing several cells. Each cell is silver-lined and unwelcome to vampires, but being a night blood, you shouldn't feel any resistance crossing the threshold."

Walker's grin wasn't humorous in the least. "Lucky me."

"The doors are thick oak reinforced with silver," Dominic continued, unhampered by Walker's sarcasm. "They close flush against the surrounding rock, so you won't be able to determine if a cell is occupied, let alone who may be occupying it."

I frowned. "There's no window? Not even a peephole?"

"No, of course not."

"Of course not?" I asked, shocked. "I'd think a window would be necessary. Even solitary confinement cells in maximum-security prisons have peepholes. It would have been helpful specifically for this purpose, to see who's inside the room and how they're doing."

Dominic bristled. "The Underneath is reserved as a final resting place for vampires sentenced to death. You do not put windows or peepholes in human coffins to check who's inside and how they're doing, do you? Do you find it necessary to check the state of decay of your loved ones?"

I recoiled. "Of course not. Such a thing would be obscene."

Dominic nodded. "Precisely. The Underneath may resemble jail cells, but for all intents and purposes, they are graves."

I frowned. "Well, we have the forethought to mark our graves, so we know who occupies each one. We keep records of such things, so if a body does need to be exhumed, it's not a guessing game."

"As do we. But I can only account for my records and the actions of the coven while under my rule. I have no idea if Jillian has continued such record keeping." Dominic turned to address Walker once more. "Best-case scenario, Bex will be in the first sealed cell you open, and she will be the only vampire in that cell. She will be burned nearly to bone and unconscious—so you must take care not to lose any parts—but she won't be a danger to you."

I raised my eyebrows. "You think Jillian would dump all the Day Reapers in one cell, like a mass grave?"

"I cannot presume to know what Jillian has and has not done. I can only guess at the likely scenarios that Walker may encounter."

"You're not responsible for Jillian. I get the drift," Walker interrupted. "What's the worst-case scenario?"

"Worst-case scenario, the Day Reapers were imprisoned together in one cell and have somehow devised a means to use each other's power to delay the effects of silver exposure, so when you open the cell, they attack and drain you to regain their strength."

Walker blinked in silence and then burst out laughing. "Oh, is that all?" He shook his head with continued mirth.

"Most-likely scenario is that the Day Reapers are in separate cells and unconscious. You should be able to open each cell, determine its inhabitants, and either extract Bex from her cell or move on to the next. Be sure to close and lock each cell securely behind you if you open one that does not contain Bex, even if the cell appears empty." Dominic looked deep into Walker's eyes, his voice grim. "None are empty. They all contain the ashes of at least one vampire, and at the time of their existence, they were the worst of our kind. There's good reason for each of vampires I've sentenced to the Underneath to be there."

I frowned. "If they're nothing but ash, what does it matter if the door remains open? How could they possibly escape now?"

Dominic shuddered. "Never ask that question. I would prefer not to tempt fate when fate is already so far from our side."

Walker shook his rigging impatiently. "If Bex's body is nothing but bone, how will I recognize her?"

Dominic frowned, thinking.

"She only has one eye." I said softly. "Her skull, if that's all that remains, will be wearing an eye patch."

Walker pursed his lips. "Anything else?"

"Good luck," Dominic said.

"Here." Walker ruffled through his pack and dug out two walkie-talkies, one of which he strapped to a harness on his hip. He handed the second to Dominic. "I'll keep you updated on my progress. Turn it on and dial to frequency four."

"Got it," Dominic said, handing the walkie-talkie to me.

I rolled my eyes. "Got it," I said, turning the switch and setting the dial. "And like he said, good luck."

Walker didn't look up at me, or acknowledge my words. He settled his grip on his rigging, leaned back in his harness, and dropped ass-first through the crevice to the Underneath. Dominic and I waited, staring at the taut line of Walker's rigging in silence, the only sound between us the zip of Walker's descent and the scrape of his boots on rock.

Until there was only silence.

The walkie-talkie crackled to life. "Walker to DiRocco, do you copy? Over."

Dominic smirked at the walkie-talkie. "No greeting or salutation? Does Ian Walker not know the fine points of phone etiquette?"

"He does, but this is walkie-talkie etiquette," I explained. I pressed the *talk* button. "Copy that," I said into the walkie-talkie, and then remembered. "Over."

Dominic cocked his head questioningly. "Why does this device need different etiquette?"

"This technology is different than phones in that only one person can speak at a time, so you tell the person on the other end when you're done speaking by saying 'over.'"

He eyed said technology uncertainly. "We have phones. Why not simply use the technology we already have?"

"We are deep beneath the city, under God only knows how many feet of solid rock, not to mention the steel of sewer drains and the cement of the subway. We don't have service down here."

"How do the walkie-talkies have service if our cell phones do not?"

"Walkie-talkies don't use cellular service. They—"

"I've hit rock bottom. Literally," Walker said. Even through the crackle and mechanical monotone of his voice coming from the walkie-talkie, I could detect his sarcasm. "I'm unhooking my rigging now and about to explore the Underneath. Over."

"Roger that. Over," I answered.

"Who's Roger?" Dominic asked.

I shook my head. "Roger is an expression. It means that I heard and understood what he said," I explained. I gazed at the confused doubt in the beautiful, icy depths of his eyes and smiled. The rare moments in which he needed the finer points of cell phones, texting, the internet, and walkie-talkies explained to him were so adorably grounding.

"What?" Dominic asked, and I realized I was staring.

"Nothing." I pressed *talk*. "DiRocco to Walker, do you copy? What's going on down there?"

We waited, but after nearly thirty seconds of radio silence, Dominic murmured, "I don't know if this matters, but you did not say 'over.'"

I rolled my eyes. "Oh, for the love of—" I pressed *talk*. "Over."

The walkie-talkie instantly crackled to life. "All of the doors in the first chamber have markers indicating the cell's occupants. None of them say Bex. I'm moving on to the second chamber. Over."

Dominic snatched the walkie-talkie out of my hand. "Do not leave the first chamber. What do the markers say?"

"You have to press *talk*," I said, pointing to the button. "And then speak. After you say 'over,' then release the button so Walker can talk."

Dominic blinked at me. "We cannot communicate simultaneously?"

"It's not a phone. That's why we say 'over,'" I reminded him. "It's a—"

"A walkie-talkie. Yes, I understand. I prefer my cell phone." He pressed *talk*. "What do the markers in the first chamber say?" He released the talk button.

I reached over and pressed *talk* for him. "Over."

Dominic shook his head. "This technology is outdated."

I raised my eyebrows. "The problem isn't with the technology."

"If it doesn't utilize service towers, how does it—"

"The cells are labeled with names and numbers; dates, I'm assuming," Walker said, his crackling voice interrupting Dominic's complaints. "Over."

Dominic pressed *talk*. "Read the names." He glanced at me. "Over."

"What does it matter? They're not Bex. Over."

"It matters because I never utilized the cells in the first several chambers. If they are occupied, and if they are not Bex or one of the Day Reapers…" Dominic's voice trailed off, his expression pained.

I stole back the walkie-talkie. "Just read the names, Walker. Over."

"I'm already at chamber four. I'm not walking all the way back. We don't have time for a recitation. Over."

Dominic jerked violently.

"How many cells is that?" I asked.

"More than just the Day Reapers," he said tightly.

The radio crackled between us. "I'm approaching the first door on my right of the seventh chamber. It's the first that is not marked. Over."

Dominic stared into my eyes, and I raised my eyebrow, ready for his call. He pressed *talk*. "Open the cell. Over."

Seconds ticked by in years.

The walkie-talkie finally crackled. "The cell is empty. Over."

I blew out a breath in pent anticipation.

"The cells only appear empty. Remember to shut and seal the door behind you," he said. He released the *talk* button and waited.

I snatched the walkie-talkie out of his hands and pressed *talk*. "Over."

Dominic rolled his eyes. "Jesus wept."

The walkie-talkie crackled. "I have shut and sealed the door, and I'm moving into the next unmarked cell. Over."

"Copy that," I said.

Silence.

"This cell is empty too," Walker said. "Over."

I glanced at Dominic, but his expression was as hard and unmovable as granite.

Walker continued cell by cell, but after exploring all of chamber seven, eight, and half of nine, Dominic shook his head at me. "He skipped a cell. He must have. The alternative is unthinkable."

I raised my eyebrows. "What's the alternative?"

"That Jillian imprisoned the Day Reapers in random cells within random chambers. To check each cell in every chamber one by one in the Underneath would be impossible."

"How many chambers are there?"

Dominic gave me an arched look. "Enough to accommodate centuries worth of past and future imprisoned vampires. Tens of thousands of chambers."

"Oh," I said, feeling overwhelmed by the scope and magnitude of such a search. "Crap."

"Yes. Crap, indeed," Dominic growled.

"Maybe she's not imprisoned in the Underneath. Maybe—"

"She's here," Dominic insisted.

"Fine," I snapped. "If she's not in chambers seven, eight, or nine, and forgetting that she might be in chamber ten thousand and one, where else in the Underneath might she be? Bex's name wasn't on any of the occupied doors. We have nowhere to search except behind the next door."

The walkie-talkie crackled. "Unless you have a better plan, I'm moving onto chamber eleven. Over."

Dominic ignored him. "Say that again," he said to me.

"Which part? That Bex might be in chamber ten thousand and one or that her name wasn't—"

"Her name," he said, suddenly fierce. "It's not Bex."

I frowned. "What do you mean, Bex's name isn't Bex?"

He gave me a look. "You think Madonna's or Cher's mothers named them with only a first name? 'Bex' is a nickname."

I arched a brow. "You know who Madonna and Cher are, but you can't work a walkie-talkie?" I shook my head. "Okay then, what's Bex's real, full name?"

The fire in Dominic's eyes banked, and his expression returned to granite.

I blinked. "What's wrong?"

"She would not want Ian Walker to know her real, full name," he said.

"It's not as if he has the ability to use her name to entrance her, like I could as a night blood," I pointed out. "I think between the two, she'd prefer we not leave her to rot inside the Underneath."

Dominic's frown deepened. "No matter Walker's inability to entrance, informing him of her full name is still giving him knowledge over her that she would not want him to have, and if I know anything about Walker, I know he'd create some crazy plan to use that knowledge against her."

"At least she'd be alive to face him and his crazy plan."

Dominic clenched his hand into a fist as he thought over the limited options before him. Finally, he came to a decision and held out his empty hand to me.

I slapped the walkie-talkie into his palm, and he pressed *talk*. "Change of plan. Jillian may have used an alternate name to mark Bex's cell. Over."

"An alternate name?" Walker asked. "Why would she do that? Over."

Dominic's expression was unyielding as he said, "The Day Reapers have internal nicknames they use for correspondence that only Masters are privy to. Jillian may have used these alternate names to mark the Day Reapers' cells, hoping that, should someone in the coven attempt a rescue, as we are attempting to do now, we would not find them. Over."

"Tell me the name, and I'll double back through the chambers. Over."

Dominic shook his head—a slow, nearly unconscious motion. When he spoke it wasn't into the walkie-talkie. "He knows I'm lying."

"You don't know that. Maybe—"

"Yes, I do. I can hear his excitement and anticipation like the chime of Christmas handbells." Dominic cocked his head. "Can't you?"

I listened to the silence of the cave and gaped, astonished. I could hear the chiming crescendo of Walker's anticipation, the tolling of the bells. "Oh," I said for the second time in as many minutes. "Double crap."

Dominic's unyielding, granite expression broke into a reluctant smile. "Double crap, indeed." He shook his head, sobered, and pressed *talk*. "Yes, turn back and look for the name Beatrix Beautreau. Over."

The radio crackled. "You got it. Over."

Something shifted in the air, something minute, and if I hadn't been listening so intensely to the texture of emotion on the air from Walker's bells, I wouldn't have even noticed it.

I grabbed Dominic's forearm and squeezed.

"What are you—" Dominic saw my expression and froze.

I pointed to my ear and cocked my head. Dominic's gaze turned inward as he listened. I saw the exact moment he heard what I heard, whatever the hell we were hearing. His otherworldly eyes widened, and something I dreaded more than any other danger we could face crossed Dominic's expression: fear.

"What is that?" I asked.

"We need to leave. Now," Dominic said. He barked as much into the walkie-talkie, his snapped "over" like a well-aimed bullet.

"I don't understand. What—"

"It's Jillian. She knows we're here, and she's not surprised." Dominic ran a hand through his hair.

"You don't know that," I said, but even as the words came out a second time, I could hear the rising desperation in my tone. Of course Dominic knew; he knew fucking everything, damn it. "You could be wrong."

"I've heard that emotion from her before, when she ambushed me and left me for dead in that alley," Dominic insisted. "It's the sound of relief and triumph and deep, roiling regret."

"You don't *know* that!" I whisper-screamed at him. "She betrayed and attacked you months ago, and you didn't even know it was her at the time. You're projecting. You—"

"I know what I heard. That sound is coming from Jillian. She's coming for us and not coming alone," Dominic said. He pressed *talk*. "Walker, do you copy? Abort mission. Pull out now. Over."

The radio crackled. "I found a cell marked with the name Beatrix Beautreau. Over."

Dominic closed his eyes, looking pained. "If we don't leave now, Jillian and whoever she has sent to kill us will surround us. We will be ambushed."

"If we leave now, we won't have the opportunity to save Bex again," I argued.

"The bones in that cell might not even be hers. This could all be a fucking trap," he spat.

"We knew going in there would be risks. Jillian coming for us doesn't change that; it just means we need to do whatever we'd planned to do now. Right now," I said. "Because there's no going back."

Dominic touched my face, his thumb sliding slowly across my cheek. He pressed *talk*. "Open the cell. Over."

I bit my lip and tasted blood.

The radio crackled. "It's Bex. Over."

I grasped Dominic's wrist and pulled his arm and the walkie-talkie to my mouth. "Are you sure? Did you find her eye patch? Over."

"Yes, she's wearing an eye patch, but besides that, she's not as deteriorated as she should be. She's badly burned, but her burns are not to the bone. I can easily recognize her face. Over."

Dominic dislodged his wrist from my grip. "Have you crossed the threshold? Over."

"Negative. Over."

The shifting emotion on the air grew louder, like the electric gust of a summer storm.

"What weapons do you have on you? Over," Dominic asked.

"Every weapon," Walker said. "What's the plan? Over."

"Bex might look unconscious, but when you cross the threshold, the scent of your night blood may revive her. Incapacitate her before she gains consciousness. Cassidy and I will fend off Jillian up here—"

"We will?" I asked.

"—so be quick about it. Do not inflict unnecessary or permanent harm," Dominic clarified. "But ensure that she will not impede our escape. You have two minutes to get her and get out. Over."

"Copy that. Over and out."

Dominic handed me the walkie-talkie. "You stay here and guard the corridor," he ordered. "I'll stand guard at your back." He jerked his thumb at the other side of the crevice.

"We are facing whatever is coming for us alone?" I asked. "Without weapons and backup? That's the plan?"

Dominic squeezed my hand and stroked a finger down one of my extended talons. "You are our weapon," he said.

I waited for him to laugh and hand me a silver-loaded shotgun from Walker's pack, but when he just continued stroking my talon, I realized that wasn't a punch line. "You're serious," I said, stunned.

He blinked, staring at me as if *I* was the one mentally deranged. "Of course."

I felt the slide of blood down my chin and realized I was biting my lip again. Hard.

Dominic released my hands and wiped the blood off my chin with a smooth swipe of his thumb. "They're coming, ready or not." He licked my blood off his thumb.

"I'm not," I said. "If I'm all that stands between us and Jillian, we're dead meat. Literally, dead fucking meat. How can you even think that I—"

Dominic cupped my face in his hands, surrounding me with his sheer size and confidence, and effectively cut off my rant by pressing his mouth against mine. Despite the urgency of the moment, with Jillian and her coven bearing down on us from above and Walker facing Bex from below, Dominic's lips were soft and coaxing. I pressed closer, demanding more of him, needing to feel something real and solid and unmovable in my hands, something that could give me the courage and strength to face the impossible.

He responded to my duress, wrapping his arms around my back and urging our bodies hip to hip, chest to chest. He tightened his grip on my face and slipped his tongue between both our fangs. I met him stroke for stroke, fisting my hand into his shirt, clawing my nails down his back, and writhing in his arms. His muscles, like silk-wrapped steel, surrounded me, his strength held me, and his well-versed, thorough tongue scorched mine, but instead of taking all that muscle and strength and experience into me, his kiss only illuminated the insurmountable distance Dominic and I had crossed to find each other and this moment, and in surviving that journey, how much we had to lose.

Emotions that I'd never dreamed of experiencing again, and especially not with this man, bloomed from our collide: passion and trust and intimacy and understanding like I'd never believed could exist thrived in the microscopic space between his body and mine—as much one person as two people could be. The groove of his scar—what was once an intimidating addition to his frightening appearance—now reminded me of his humanity and compassion. The hard bulk of his fangs behind his lips, once undeniable proof of his monstrousness and our incompatibility, was a comforting reminder that he'd thrived in this life with dignity and pride, and that I could, too, no matter the frightening savagery of my new appearance.

Dominic tore his lips from mine, his breath harsh and uneven, and terror like I'd never felt before—minutely comparable to the horror I'd felt when coming face-to-face with Nathan as the Damned—doused the flames of our kiss.

I shook my head, frantic. "I can't lose you."

His hands tightened around me. "You won't."

"You can't *know* that." I punctuated my outburst by pounding my fists into his chest. "When we started all this—when we first met and I discovered the existence of vampires—I was alone. I didn't think I had much to lose except my life, but that was worth the risk if it meant gaining a good scoop, furthering my career, and exposing the truth. Now…" I grazed my fingertips over the jagged dip and pull of his scarred lip and shook my head. "It's not just my life on the line anymore."

"After being transformed, I thought I was stronger for surviving the loss of my humanity and family, like steel cast in fire." Dominic loosened his grip on my back and ran his finger gently over my cheek. I could hear the reverberating howl of the Damned, but Dominic didn't pull away, and neither did I. "Meeting you was like being cast into fire all over again. I am all too aware of the distances we've crossed together, of the delicate, precious bond we formed when neither of us was looking, but I'm not scared of everything we have to lose. We are stronger together than we are alone. Together, we can survive anything," he said, his voice rough with emotion. "We will survive this."

I shook my head. From the vibrating impact tremor foretelling their approach, we wouldn't be facing Jillian. Or maybe we would, but in addition to Jillian, we would be facing the Damned.

He stopped my protests with both hands on my cheeks.

"We survived our best friends betraying us. We survived your brother being Damned. We survived the loss of my coven and your humanity. Together, damn it, we *will* survive this."

His conviction was absolute, which I suppose was good, considering I had enough fear and doubts for the both of us as one of the Damned turned a corner in the tunnel and charged.

Chapter 9

Time is a puzzling thing; we mark it in years and dissect it into months, days, hours, minutes, and seconds, so we're keenly aware of exactly how long it takes for time to pass. One minute takes sixty seconds whether you're bungee jumping or waiting in line at the post office, yet one minute for the first can pass in what seems the blink of an eye and the latter can seem like an eternity. We lament the time we've lost, stress over how time flies, bemoan how time drags, and fear how little time we have, yet no matter how we perceive the speed of time, it ticks on, second upon second, a steady, man-made mechanism to measure our finite lives. Knowing all of this, time must have continued ticking after I caught sight of the Damned bearing down on us at the end of the tunnel—in fact, I know that it did, because I could hear the mechanical spring of Walker's skeleton watch fastidiously keeping time—but for me, it seemed to instantly and utterly stop.

Beyond the banal ticking of Walker's wristwatch, I could sense the relentless, consuming rage from the approaching Damned. I heard the static roar of their driving hunger, smelled the salivating anticipation of that first bite—the juicy tear and warm flood of blood from my punctured heart—and tasted the spicy pepper of its contracting muscles. The Damned were suffering, craving peace from a thirst they couldn't slake, comfort from a place that was home, and love from a woman who wasn't family.

The creature was nearly at the crevice, only a few yards from reaching us. I watched it approach, not necessarily in slow motion—I knew how fast and powerful and unavoidable a force was barreling toward us—but with an unconcerned confidence I'd never experienced before, especially not when facing such a physically intimidating creature. In my former life, I'd have been frightened to the point of being physically ill when coming face-to-face with the Damned. In my former life, my body hadn't matched the fierce strength of my spirit—had, in fact, been deteriorating without my permission for years.

Now, I was not only physically stronger than my former self, I knew by the minutiae of sights, sounds, tastes, and smells surrounding me that I was stronger than the Damned charging us, as confident as I might be in my former life if pitted against an ant. The Damned was large and fierce, and I was frightened of it because of previous experiences, but with my newly enhanced eyes, I could plainly see that as the Damned charged me, it was tensed to raise its right claw and slash at my front, swipe my body forward with its left, and tear out my throat with its teeth.

I smiled grudgingly, realizing what Dominic had already realized: as a night blood, I'd been woefully inept to bump back against the creatures of the night; as a Day Reaper, I didn't just have the strength and ability to bump back—I was the creature who bumped.

I stepped in front of Dominic and dodged under the Damned's claw as it swiped at us, like I'd known it would, and I countered its attack with a swipe of my own, letting the Damned impale itself on my talons with power and speed of its own momentum. I plunged my claws deep into its neck and pulled down with a smooth slice of my arm, gutting the creature from chest to groin. A pile of its intestines and internal organs gushed from the wound, spattering me as it stumbled, its legs still running as if they were a separate entity and not privy to the fact that it was already dead.

I blocked its sluggish counter-swipe easily, and it collapsed face-first at Dominic's feet.

Dominic glanced at the creature, gurgling in its death throes, and then raised his eyebrows at me.

I crossed my arms, annoyed. "What?" And then realized I'd smeared gore across the side of my shirt. "Oh, ugh," I groaned.

Dominic's grin channeled the devil himself. "I want to hear you say the words."

I looked away from my ruined shirt to glare at him. "I want lots of things, but it doesn't mean that I get them."

He made a circular gesture with his hand.

I rolled my eyes. "How was I supposed to know I could compete with that?" I asked, gesturing to the behemoth on the floor at our feet. "We're lucky that more haven't come for us."

The walkie-talkie crackled to life. "I've secured Bex, and I'm about to climb from the Underneath. Am I clear? Over."

I opened my mouth to give Walker the go-ahead, but Dominic touched my forearm. "Do you hear that?"

I strained my senses, listening to the depths of the Underneath with more than just my ears, with my entire being, and there it was again where it hadn't been before, a subtle shift in the air: the sound of Jillian's relief and regret. More Damned were coming.

"What the hell?" I snapped. "How does she know this one didn't finish the job?" I asked, pointing my thumb at the Damned behind us.

Dominic wasn't looking at me or the Damned anymore. He was looking at the walkie-talkie. His expression hardened. "Because she heard otherwise. How does this damn thing function without cellular service?"

I shook my head, staring dumbly at the walkie-talkie in my hands. "I don't know the particulars. It uses sound waves and air frequencies to relay what we're saying."

Dominic's eyes blazed. "Are you telling me that the words we are saying are traveling through the air at a specific frequency?"

"Yeah, frequency four, to be exact," I said, pointing to the frequency knob, "but I don't know about our exact words. Cell phones use electrical signals. I don't know exactly how walkie-talkies work. I didn't invent them," I snapped.

Dominic swore under his breath. "Do not answer Walker on this thing. And stay here; I'll be right back."

"Where are you—"

Dominic turned, giving me his back as he walked to the crevice of the Underneath, effectively cutting me off mid-question. He peered over the crevice and made a come-hither curl of his hand at Walker.

The walkie-talkie crackled. "Walker to DiRocco, do you copy? What's going on up there? Over."

The subtle shift on the air paused.

Dominic gave Walker a thumbs-up before returning to my side.

I frowned. "Is he coming up?"

"Yes, but now Jillian thinks we're dead, or at the very least incapacitated, since we didn't respond with the walkie-talkie."

"Walker did." I frowned. "Tell me this isn't your backhanded way of getting rid of him."

"If I thought getting rid of Walker was the best course of action, he'd already be dead," Dominic said, incinerating me with the heat of his glare. "When have you known me to backhandedly do anything?"

I snorted. "I noticed you didn't say that you didn't want to get rid of him."

Dominic raised an eyebrow. "I noticed you didn't produce any examples of me being backhanded."

"Then what is your intention?"

"My intention is for Jillian to think the Damned killed us, and after Walker rises from the Underneath, we will make her think the Damned killed him as well." Dominic crossed his arms. "And then we leave, all of us, very much alive. Does that work for you?"

"Anything that involves walking away alive damn well works for me," I answered, as if his question hadn't been soaked in sarcasm.

Dominic shook his head and opened his mouth to retort, but before the words could leave his mouth, Walker popped his head out from the Underneath.

"A little help here?" Walker asked, his voice strained.

He was holding Bex in his arms, but I'd never seen her look like this, even at her worst. Bex typically wielded beauty like I did anger and Dominic did stoic intelligence, to hide weakness and pain, but she didn't have her beauty to hide behind now. Her body was cringingly emaciated, her charred, blistered skin shrink-wrapped to her bones. Her hair, formerly thick, long, and luxurious, rivaled the brittle thinness of Ronnie's straggles. Her one remaining eye, however, was still intact and glaring at us from over the silver muzzle that Walker had locked around her head.

He'd also bound her arms and legs in silver cuffs; her skin was steaming where the silver touched the skin at her ankles, wrists, and mouth, and her struggles against those bonds, coupled with the acrobatics of balancing them midair over the crevice, was proving difficult, even for Walker. In another moment, Walker would lose his balance and strength, and I could tell by the set of his jaw that he wasn't letting both of them fall—and he wouldn't be the one falling.

I darted forward, took Bex's meager weight from Walker, and pulled her over the lip of the crevice.

She flinched as I laid her on the ground, but really, I couldn't avoid hurting her when what little was left of her skin was oozing blisters. I patted her shoulder, hoping she could feel some comfort through the pain.

"I'm sorry," I whispered. "We'll remove the bindings as soon as we're out of the coven."

Her glare sharpened on my elongated, silver talons on her shoulder, and her struggles stilled. She met my gaze, staring deep into my reflective, otherworldly eyes, and the knowing in her one, green, human-like eye was terrifying.

I curled my talons into a fist and pulled back my hand.

"Holy shit. Is it dead?"

I jerked around at the panic in Walker's voice, bracing for another attack, but when I followed his gaze to the object of his fear, I relaxed. He was just now noticing the Damned lying eviscerated on the tunnel floor.

"Even creatures as indestructible as the Damned find it difficult to continuing living without their internal organs." Dominic offered this hand to help Walker over the lip of the crevice.

"Nice work," Walker said, ignoring Dominic's proffered hand. He finished the climb on his own.

"Thanks," I murmured.

Walker's head whipped up in my direction, then glanced at Dominic as if in confirmation, but Dominic wasn't interested in explaining who had done what. He was more concerned, as was I, on what needed to be done next.

"Question our absence into the walkie-talkie and then scream like your heart is being ripped from your chest," Dominic instructed, pointing at Walker's radio, "so Jillian thinks she has successfully killed you and stops sending Damned to kill us."

Walker frowned. "Why would she think that?"

"She can hear us over the walkie-talkies," I explained.

"Impossible," Walker scoffed. "All the times I infiltrated this coven, and you never—"

Dominic's expression yawned wide with realization. "That's why your voice would sound different. I knew when you entered my coven by your scent, but I never knew why your voice always sounded so strangely mechanical. I thought maybe it was the vibrations and echo of your voice in the tunnels. All this time it was the walkie-talkie," Dominic said, studying said device. "Interesting."

Walker wasn't looking at the walkie-talkie. He was staring at Dominic, gaping at first and then grinding his teeth with the hard flex of his jaw when he finally closed his mouth.

Dominic, ignoring Walker's expression, pointed at the walkie-talkie. "You must pretend to die before we leave."

Bex grumbled, but gagged as she was by the muzzle, I couldn't understand her words. If her eyes were anything to go by, however, the sentiment was cutting.

Walker narrowed his eyes at all of us. "Jillian is a Master now, imbued with all the omniscient powers you once had," he said. I'm surprised he didn't choke on the sarcasm in his tone. "If she knows we're here, playing pretend won't fool her into thinking we're dead. Again."

"That's not entirely true. Had Jillian adopted the full Master's power, I wouldn't even suggest it, but she didn't. I retained the majority of my strength and heightened senses. I think we may very well be able to play pretend, and she might just be confident enough in what she thinks are her full powers to believe us. It's—how would you put it, Cassidy?—it's a long shot, but worth the risk."

Walker didn't say anything for a long moment. In fact, he didn't move at all except for the rhythmic tightening and release of his jaw muscles.

Finally, without breaking eye contact, Walker squeezed the *talk* button. "I'm nearly to the top, over." He waited a second. "Do you copy? Over." Another few seconds, and he drew a handgun from his side holster. "Where the hell are—holy fu—" Walker pointed his gun down the opposite end of the tunnel and squeezed off several rounds. He released the *talk* button and raised an eyebrow. "Good enough?"

"You didn't scream like your heart was being ripped out," I commented.

"I wouldn't scream; I would shoot," Walker said. "My version was more realistic."

Dominic's smile was all fangs. "I dare say, Ian Walker, that you missed your calling."

Bex grumbled under her muzzle, something along the lines of "always an excellent actor."

I sensed another shift in the air—not like before, when Jillian was ordering her flock of Damned to massacre us—but not like she was content, either.

"Excellent actor or not, we need to move. Now," I said, reaching for Bex.

Dominic brushed me aside. "I will carry her. If they come for us, you will need your hands free."

I stepped aside, allowing Dominic to squeeze past me to reach Bex, and my gaze wandered back to the Damned I had killed. Never mind that it had been in self-defense, the thought that I was physically capable of ending the life of a massive, twelve-foot-tall, three-hundred-pound rabid creature with little more than a swipe of my wrist was mind-boggling. I lifted my hand and stared at the length of silver talons that probably wouldn't contract back to fingernails until I'd fed. The Damned's blood was crusted under my nail beds. If we met with any further resistance on our way out, it wouldn't be the only one whose blood would stain my hands.

My claws, I amended. I could regret the creature I'd become. I certainly wasn't comfortable with it; but I was the only one capable of defending us against them. I could rage at my cravings and hind-hinged legs and deadly claws, but human hands wouldn't have saved us from the creatures trying to kill us.

"Lead the way," Dominic said. His hands were full, carrying Bex, so he jerked his head sideways in the relative direction of the passageway. Walker had already packed away his rappelling equipment. He stared at me with the same expression I remembered from that fate-filled night in the middle of the woods in upstate New York. He'd just killed Rene and shot Dominic with his crossbow, and Jillian had fled the scene, leaving me on the ground, dying from my metaphysical bond to Dominic's wound. Walker had watched me struggle to breathe with the same look he had on his face now—an unyielding, uncompromising, terrible expression I'd only ever seen him direct at vampires—right before he'd turned his back on me and left me for dead.

And I had a thought. It was an ugly thought, and the fact that it came from me—not from Cassidy the Day Reaper or Cassidy the Master vampire's lover, just from Cassidy DiRocco—somehow made it even uglier: We'd needed Walker to find the hidden entry into the Underneath, but we didn't need him to find our way out.

Bex grumbled something indecipherable under her breath. The stink coming from the silver bonds melting her flesh snapped me back to reality. I turned my back on Walker's expression and did the only thing I could do. I led the way.

"Ever since we were children, she was determined to outshine me. I got my nose pierced while she got a scholarship to Berkeley. I became a high-school track star, and she became a Pulitzer contender. I earned my EMT certification while she took a bullet, earning the respect of NYPD's finest. It was only just a matter of time that she transformed into a Day Reaper after I transformed into the Damned. Stealing the show is as programmed into her DNA as being a vampire."

—Nathan DiRocco

Chapter 10

Two hours later, we had nearly completely escaped from the labyrinth of the coven's Underneath, but dawn was only a short fifteen minutes away. Dominic said that he could feel the heat of its rise on his skin, and he wasn't even in direct sunlight. Of the four of us, he was the only one who would burst into flames should we not make it back to his underground bunker in time, but his danger was my danger; I could feel my fear for him like the shock and shrivel of ice against my skin. I'd witnessed him burst into flames once—the inferno of his body blasting my face and frying my eyebrows and lashes, his skin peeling to charcoal, my own hesitant, frantic helplessness, and the piercing pitch of his screams—and that had been quite enough. I'd never before heard Dominic scream, and I'd planned to never hear those screams again.

"If we don't make it out of here in the next fifteen minutes…" I began.

"We will," Dominic assured me, his tone and conviction unflappable.

I didn't share his confidence. "But if we don't—"

"We have to," Bex interrupted. Dominic had removed her muzzle after only a few minutes into our escape, reasoning that if she was incapacitated by the silver around her wrists and ankles, the muzzle was cruel and redundant. I agreed, but in such close proximity to Walker, I'd admittedly felt more assured with her muzzled. Neither had said a word to the other, either in sarcasm nor hostility. And since Dominic had taken the burden of carrying her, they hadn't looked at or touched one another, either.

The tension between them was somehow thicker for having remained unspoken.

"But if we don't," I insisted, "can we reach your bunker without leaving the tunnels?"

"No," Dominic said curtly.

"But maybe we could—"

"I deliberately chose the location of my bunker precisely for its complete separation from the coven's tunnels to prevent Jillian from finding me during the Leveling," Dominic explained. "If we do not escape the tunnels before the sun crests the horizon, I will be physically unable to leave the tunnels until sunset tonight."

I turned back to Walker. "How far are we from the entrance?"

"Another hundred yards or so," Walker said, sounding vaguely disappointed at the prospect of us escaping in time. "Really, the grate is just around the next bend. You'll probably make it back to the bunker with a whole minute to spare." And as he finished speaking, the disgust in his voice wasn't vague at all.

"Try to contain your relief," I said drily.

"I'm expending all my energy trying to restrain my trigger finger," he snapped.

"Why start now?" asked Bex—the first words she'd spoken directly to Walker.

Walker grinned. "Go ahead, give me a reason to stake you."

"As if you needed a reason to stake anyone before," Bex said, laughing darkly.

"Removing the muzzle was a mistake," I muttered. I could see frustration tightening Dominic's expression as he nodded in agreement.

"You attacked Ronnie," Walker said. "I staked Rene. We're even."

"You watched Nathan rip out my heart," Bex accused. "We're nowhere near even."

"You invaded my home and slaughtered my friends!"

"They're still alive, you idiot," said Bex. "You choose to shun them. You *killed* Rene!"

"You let Julia-Marie die!"

"I didn't want her to die!" Bex shrieked, struggling in Dominic's arms.

"You did," Walker insisted. "She was the only thing standing between you and me."

I closed my eyes to keep Walker from seeing them roll.

"She was dying! I tried to transform her—for you!" Bex said. "I wish I could have seen then what I see now: the man I loved—the person I saved from the fire that killed his parents—died with Julia-Marie."

"Such pretty words of regret and love lost," Walker spat, "but you were the one who set that fire."

Bex shook her head sadly. "Your parents died in a fire set by the Lord High Chancellor and his Day Reapers, not me. They set that fire to kill you because I wouldn't join them, not while there was still a chance of you becoming my night blood."

I tried not to look. I tried keeping my gaze locked on that final bend fifty yards ahead to give them a modicum of privacy in the confines of the tunnel, but my eyes seemed to move independently of my will, and I stared at Bex and her resigned, granite-like expression.

Walker shrugged. "Looks like High Lord Henry and his Day Reapers got what they wanted after all."

"Yes, they did," Bex said. "They always do. I didn't start that fire, but I never should have saved you from it. I won't make a similar mistake ever again."

We walked in silence. Walker had won the argument, but judging by his pinched, sour expression, even he—as hardheaded and stubborn as he was—knew that the conversation hadn't ended in his favor. Those last forty yards were some of the longest few minutes of my entire life, the silence yawning wider than the distance we walked.

We turned the corner, and suddenly the silence was the least of our concerns. A Damned was standing at the entrance of the tunnel and staring right at us.

I halted mid-step, stunned dumb. Walker stumbled into my back, and Dominic cursed under his breath.

The Damned opened its mouth and inhaled. It was going to alert Jillian and the others. We were so close, only yards away, and it was going to ruin everything.

I rushed forward, not thinking about its five-inch talons or jutting, razor-tipped fangs or its overwhelming height and strength and dozens of monstrous attributes that should have made me hesitate. Before the creature could let loose the roar that would give away our position—give away our lives—I slashed my claws across its throat.

The creature crumpled dead at my feet, silent.

"Nice work," Bex complimented, the first positive words from her mouth since we'd saved her from the Underneath. "Effective. But not much flair."

I flicked a glob of bloody fat from under my fingernail. "I'll work on that."

Bex glanced at Dominic from under her lashes. "Even at my most powerful, I didn't possess the speed or strength to rival the Damned until after bathing in sunlight to complete my transformation into a Day Reaper. My claws couldn't even penetrate their scales," she said, her voice softening with wonder. "Her abilities without having fully transformed are already incredible."

"Her abilities have always been incredible," Dominic agreed, "even as a night blood."

Bex nodded, and a wistful smile blossomed across her grotesque, blistered face.

I grimaced, uncomfortable with their strange, almost parental praise.

"We need to move," Walker said. "Now. Where there's one, you can damn well guarantee there'll be—"

A line of Damned flooded through our exit, slavering and ravenous despite having freshly returned from a hunt. Blood gloved their hands from the tips of their talons to their elbows and smeared across their muzzles like macabre barbeque sauce. I'd witnessed their kind kill. When my own brother had been fully Damned, I'd watched as he'd pounded his arm elbow-deep into his victim's chest, ripped out his heart, and eaten it. He'd subsequently slashed and torn and dismembered his victim to pieces—literally pieces—reducing a person to scraps of flesh and organs. The inferno of their rage-filled thirst was all-consuming. One heart was never enough. Ten was never enough. Nothing would ever be enough to ease their suffering.

I paused in awe-filled horror for just a moment, and in that moment they laid eyes on me, the only living thing in front of them in that narrow tunnel, the only thing between them and home with the dead body of their brethren lying at my feet. They roared—a deep, chest-vibrating roar—and they charged.

"This was your personal, secret entrance into the coven, was it not?" I snapped.

"Secret from Dominic, yes," Walker snapped back.

"A secret *only* from Dominic, apparently," Dominic said between gritted teeth.

"Referring to yourself in the third person doesn't become you," Bex quipped.

Dominic gestured to the riot of Damned barreling toward us. "Ignorance doesn't become me, either, yet here we are."

Their movements, which had appeared only a blur to my eyes when I was human, were an unsynchronized disaster. Unlike bees, which choreograph their individual movements perfectly in a swarm, the Damned didn't care about anyone or anything besides themselves and their relentless drive for blood. The faster, more powerful Damned trampled over the others, slicing them aside with their claws and crushing them underfoot in their mad rush to reach me. I watched the minutiae of their movements—their muscles contracting, the stringy spray of saliva as they growled, the focused rage in their eyes—braced my weight on the balls of my feet, and allowed my claws to fully extend into talons. All five-foot-two, one-hundred-and-thirty-pounds of me was all that stood between Dominic, Bex, and Walker and a stampede of Damned, dozens upon dozens of them, returning from their nightly hunt. Yesterday, I would have screamed for Dominic, even knowing that he was no match for the Damned. No one was, except for the Day Reapers.

And me.

I charged forward, meeting the Damned halfway and keeping them a healthy distance from the others. One of the Damned swiped at me with its claws. I jumped over its shoulder, wrapped my arm around its head, and with a quick twist, broke its neck. Another Damned came at me with its talons. I juked to the side, and gutted him from groin to gullet with my claws. He fell and another Damned charged. Damned after Damned, they attacked, and Damned after Damned, they fell at my feet, their dead or dying bodies crushed by the next in line, which were in turn felled and trampled themselves. And I defended our position in the cramped confines of the tunnel, a one-sided fight I couldn't lose, but because of their sheer numbers, I couldn't end.

"Er, DiRocco?" Walker's voice behind me sounded hesitant; nearly embarrassed, even, as he drew his gun from its holster. "We have company at six o'clock."

I incapacitated the Damned nearest me with a quick slice to its jugular and glanced over my shoulder. A second stampede of Damned was charging toward us from the back of the tunnel.

I cursed under my breath. "Duck down! Give me room to maneuver!" I shouted.

Dominic instantly complied, flattening himself and Bex to the ground. He tugged Walker unwillingly with him by yanking the collar of his shirt down with his fist.

I hurdled over their crouched bodies and met the second stampede head-on. We collided in a spray of arterial blood and thicker things as my talons pounded through muscle and organs and scraped against bone, but I couldn't hold them off for more than a second before the first crowd of Damned closed in. I was inhumanly strong, imperceptibly fast, and could sense the twitch of their muscles before they even truly moved, making me most possibly the biggest badass this city had ever seen, night or day—

never mind my petite stature—but I was only one person. Everyone, even the biggest of badasses, needed backup.

I strained to move faster and strike harder, but they just kept coming. A Damned behind me raised its claws against Dominic. I could feel its excitement charge the air like a feather tickling my spine. I impaled a Damned in front of me and turned to block the strike against Dominic. A second Damned swiped at Walker. Dominic curled around Bex, protecting her with his body, but Walker didn't have anything but air between his soft skin and the razor edge of the Damned's lethal talons.

Lunging forward, I covered Dominic with my body and ripped my claws through the Damned threatening Walker. The Damned collapsed over Walker, dead before even hitting the ground, but the creature attacking Dominic skewered its five-inch talons deep into my stomach.

"Cassidy!" Dominic roared, abandoning Bex for me and reaching to stanch the hemorrhage. His hands pressed firmly against my wound, and the pressure felt like being stabbed a second time.

The Damned raised its claw again. I didn't have time to scream, not in frustration or fear, and certainly not in pain. I pushed Dominic and his hovering hands aside and swiped at the Damned with my talons, ripping its throat out to expose the neat stacks of its vertebrae. Blood showered over us in a hot splash. The creature dropped to the ground, limp and dead, but there was a Damned behind that one, and another, and another.

My hand trembled as I pulled it away from my bleeding stomach to check the wound.

I blinked in shock. The wound was starting to heal. Before I could even scream from the injury or at our fate, my stomach knitted closed and began to scab. Within another few seconds, the scab might scar and the scar might smooth over as if I'd never been injured.

But there was no time to gape in awe of my own healing power—an ability to rival even Dominic's. The next two Damned in line attacked.

I shoved Dominic behind me and lunged to block the next strike against Walker. The Damned were relentless. I took hits one after another—a jab to the ribs, a claw to the neck, a bite on my arm—but trusting the wounds would heal, I used my body as a shield, gritted my teeth against the pain, and struck back between blows with jabs and claws and bites of my own. No matter how fast I could heal, however, the wounds were excruciating; after enduring and healing wound upon wound, I quickly reached the limits of my abilities and energy.

Walker tried to help, but even the weapons he'd perfected over the years to defend against vampires were nothing but sticks and stones against the

Damned. He'd already gone through several rounds of ammunition with nothing more to show for his efforts than a sore trigger finger and wasted bullets. His silver-nitrate spray burned their scales—the steam that sizzled from their hide stank—but the pain didn't slow their attack. His skeleton-watch spears couldn't penetrate their hide, and they were coming too fast for him to properly aim for their eyes. The most effective of his weapons was a new addition to his arsenal: a flashlight that beamed artificial sunlight, but even that weapon backfired. The Damned shielded their eyes against the light and roared, cowed for about the second it took for them to become completely enraged—as if they weren't already whipped into a homicidal frenzy—and then they attacked with renewed, brutal force.

"We need a plan," I screamed, taking a bone-deep blow to the shoulder. The creature's talon caught and tugged on my joint. When it ripped clean, my arm split wide open, exposing the bone and joint in a spray of blood and searing pain. I choked back a cry, reminding myself that it would heal—it was fine, I was fine. I struck down the Damned, but another sliced its talons down my back. "I can't keep up!"

Walker whipped his sunbeam flashlight at a Damned over Dominic's shoulder. "We're fucked."

"We're not!" I snapped. "I just need help."

"I'm trying to help!" Walker snapped back, taking his eyes off his aim to glare at me.

"Careful there." Dominic muttered, ducking down away from the wild sweeps of Walker's sunbeam. "You're all we've got, Cassidy."

"Not true," Bex said curtly, just loud enough to be heard above the sounds of combat.

Dominic shook his head. "Not happening."

Bex held her wrists up to me, her emaciated fingers elongated to three-inch silver talons. "Please!"

The cuffs around her wrists had melted her skin down to nearly bone. I turned away to disembowel the next Damned bearing down on us.

"You're not strong enough." Dominic grunted as he ducked under the Damned's claws.

"Then let me feed," Bex growled.

Walker laughed. "Nice try."

"We need a plan, people!" I yelled.

"I can help you," Bex pleaded.

I blocked a Damned from eviscerating Walker, and while I had my arm raised, another Damned punched its talons into my side. Pain, sudden and debilitating, raked across my back before the wound at my side could heal.

I fell to my knees, my legs going out from under me without permission, but I used the momentum of my weight to roll and avoid the jackhammer jab of claws trying to impale my chest. My side and back healed, but the distraction had been enough. In rolling to avoid the Damned's claws, I'd separated myself from Dominic.

A Damned cocked its fist in preparation for puncturing his sternum. I wouldn't make it in time to block the strike, but Bex was within arm's reach of both of us.

She thought she could help? I thought, desperately. *Fine—let's see her prove it.*

I stretched back with one hand and severed the cuffs around Bex's wrists and ankles with my talons.

Bex lunged between Dominic and the Damned and blocked the strike for me. I bounded in front of Walker, ignoring his sputtering, cursing protests, and Bex and I fought the Damned, back-to-back, protecting my lover and the man who had killed hers. She didn't attack Walker, not even for a quick nip to regain some of her strength; she didn't have time.

"On your right!" I shouted.

She dodged the Damned and impaled his chest with her claws.

Pain raked up my torso, from thigh to rib. I tore my eyes from Bex to face the Damned who'd struck me, but my knees buckled before I could land a solid blow. Bex back-flipped and roundhouse-kicked the creature in the face, midair. By the time I'd healed and stood, she'd already landed, decapitated it with a swipe of her claw, and moved on to the next Damned.

"Eyes front!" Bex chided. "I got this." And to prove her point, as if she hadn't already, she launched into the air, her claws outstretched as she spun, and decapitated the front line of Damned surrounding us. She landed on her feet, bounced into a little flip, and roundhouse-kicked the nearest Damned. It flew back from the force and took eight Damned behind it down, like bowling pins.

I grinned. "Effective. But too much flair."

"Efficient." She jumped into the air, swooped down on their heads in a flying, graceful flip of fangs and talons, and before she'd even landed, five Damned hit the ground. "You try."

I swiped out with my claw and neatly decapitated the Damned in front of me while dodging the two others that swiped for my heart. "Not… the…time!"

"Don't dodge! Strike!" Bex shouted. Another flip-twirl move and more heads rolled.

"I can't!"

"Try!" Bex said, killing four Damned.

I dodged a claw as it raked toward my face. "But—"

"Envision what you want to do. And just do it!"

From the corner of my eye, I watched as she fought with grace and flair and steel in every move, and I wanted it. I could feel the want inside me, begging me to try. Just try.

I glanced at Dominic, and the excitement and pride in his eyes filled me with something I might not have found within myself: the confidence to tap my potential.

One of the Damned who'd dropped from Bex's last roundhouse kick regained his feet and charged. I watched its clunky movements, smelled the electric twitch of muscles as his legs ran and his arms pumped and his jaw opened on another raging roar that shook the tunnel's foundation. I could easily duck under the arm that would slash at my head, lunge forward and take him out, but there was another Damned behind him, and another behind that, and Bex had her own unending line of Damned to face.

And a large part of me—a selfish, shallow, competitive part—resented that Bex was better.

I took Bex's advice. I waited for the creature to come to me instead of lunging to meet it, and with that extra moment to my advantage, I envisioned my movements: my knees bending, my thighs flexing, springing into the air, tucking my body into a ball, slashing out with propeller-like talons. Their necks giving way under my claws, and my foot connecting with satisfying accuracy into its chest.

Suddenly, the Damned was upon me. I sprang into the air, flipping with grace and power, just like I'd envisioned. The Damned's head rolled and its body catapulted back, knocking down the five Damned behind it before its head even hit the stone floor.

And I landed with a bone-jarring thud on my back.

"Good!" Bex said, but she'd already turned away to face more oncoming Damned.

I flipped back to my feet and killed another Damned, catching a barely suppressed smirk at my mishap from Dominic. I just had enough time to narrow my eyes at him before the fight was upon me again.

The end of the tunnels was only a few hundred feet away, but the space between us and freedom may as well have been miles. Even with the two of us fighting back, we were losing ground by inches, not gaining it. And time was not on our side: dawn broke over New York City.

A drainage grate over our heads scattered slivers of light into the tunnel, but even without the visual reminder, I could smell the sensitive, allergic surface of Dominic's skin beginning a slow bake. Cold, hard dread throbbed through my chest.

Bex glanced at me over her shoulder consideringly.

"What?" I yelled, not liking the knowing look in her shrewd gaze.

"Dominic, find a shadow," Bex replied. And without further warning, she reached up with her talons, tore the grate above us from its hinges, and doused the entire tunnel in sunlight.

Chapter 11

I couldn't see. Even more debilitating and terrifying than Dominic's spontaneous combustion, than Walker's shrieks as he jerked away from the flames, than the inferno raging beneath my own skin—not physical flames like those engulfing Dominic but burning all the same—was my sudden and complete blindness. I could smell the roasting char of Dominic's flesh. It mingled with the taste of rotting excrement from the Damned's breath as they panted in slavering, lusting anticipation, and I gagged. I could hear the fluttering wings of Dominic's panic, feel the smooth lick of Bex's self-satisfaction, and taste the biting bile of Walker's dread; the riptide of their emotions was drowning.

And I couldn't see any of it, not even a hint of shadow or movement, nothing beyond a blinding, bright light.

My throat clamped in panic at everything I could smell and taste and hear—everything I couldn't save us from—until I realized everything I could feel. Calm settled over me, a stillness that went beyond my body and took root deep inside my being. I could feel everyone and everything connected to me as if by the tuned strings of a violin: Dominic low on my left, collapsed and writhing; Bex standing at my side, slightly behind me; Walker to my right, and dozens upon dozens of strangers surrounding us on all sides. If I focused on each individual being, I could taste the spice of their desires, the savory heat of their hunger, the sour chill of their fear; all the varying nuances of their emotions were taut beneath my fingertips, laid bare to stroke, pluck, or sever at my will. If I released the minds surrounding me and expanded my awareness, I could feel my ties to the former members of Dominic's coven, their fear and confusion and reluctant acquiescence to the shifting tide of power. Hundreds upon hundreds of people, both the

Damned and the coven surrounded us, and at its center, connecting them all like the spokes of an ever-turning wheel, was Jillian.

The boiling, flaming tar of her rage was suffocating.

Despite my heightened awareness, I couldn't determine if the string between us connected my mind to hers or hers to mine. Should I attempt to play that string, the resulting melody might not be mine to create.

I might save us and all of New York City with just the right command. And she could as easily deflect my command and destroy us all.

Dominic was dying. Walker was defenseless, and Bex couldn't save them on her own any more than I could on my own. I pulled away from Jillian and refocused on the world directly surrounding me. To entrance a vampire as a night blood, I'd required two simple ingredients: the vampire's full name and the taste of my blood on their lips. Now, the strings between our minds were connected without these prerequisites; I could command them with a simple flex of my will.

"Stop," I said, but the words were superfluous. My will was their will, and I wanted them to halt their attack. The absolute, sudden silence was nearly as disorienting as being blind.

I enforced my will over Dominic, and the flames consuming him instantly extinguished. The ravages of his burns cooled, healed, and smoothed. He went limp, exhausted by his injuries even if no longer physically wounded; his relief felt like a brisk breeze against my fevered cheeks.

Minutely, the light blinding my eyes dimmed. My vision returned in flashes, clouded by a kaleidoscope of blue, green, purple, and red polka dots. Eventually even the polka dots dissipated, and I could finally see: Dominic unconscious at my feet; Walker desperately aiming his ineffective wristwatch at the Damned; Bex watching me, a knowing curl to her lips. And surrounding us on all sides, dozens upon dozens of Damned, their eyes blank, their expressions slack, completely still even as their scales steamed from sun exposure, waiting on my next command.

Walker lowered his arm slowly, glanced down at Dominic, and then settled his eyes on me, just as warily as he'd been facing the Damned.

"Not even you could entrance the Damned," he whispered. "Their minds don't understand language, and they can't obey commands they don't understand."

"No one can entrance the Damned," Bex agreed. "One can create them and wield them, but never truly control them."

Walker snorted and waved his hand at the slack-jawed Damned surrounding us. "Then what the hell do you call this?"

Bex's smile widened. "Our greatest weapon," she said, but she wasn't looking at the Damned.

She was looking at me.

I considered diving back into the tunnels, finding Jillian, and ending this once and for all, but we were still outnumbered, and as powerful as I felt with everyone's mind connected to mine, I didn't know if I was powerful enough to defeat Jillian and her army. The reward of overthrowing her, however, would have been worth the risk. With Dominic at my side to bolster my confidence and fuel my courage, I probably would have at least tried, because some things—fighting for freedom and against injustice, tyranny, slavery, and mass murder—were worth dying for. But more moving than causes worth dying for were the people who made the risk worth that sacrifice. Specifically, the one person lying unconscious at my feet.

The difference between what I was willing to die for and what I was willing to live without was minute, but it was everything.

I bent down, gathered Dominic's limp body tight against my chest, glanced up through the grate Bex had ripped wide open, and eyed the daylight outside the tunnels. Self-doubt swamped me. Had our positions been reversed, Dominic would have flown me back to the bunker, back to safety, but I wasn't Dominic. I couldn't even land a simple somersault on my feet.

"Just envision it, Cassidy."

I glanced down and blinked at Dominic, breathless.

He nodded encouragingly. "Feel the movements and make it happen. You can—"

Whatever Dominic had been about to say was interrupted by wracking, wet coughs and a full-body shiver.

Self-doubt or no, I'd never learn to land if I didn't leap.

"DiRocco?" Walker asked.

"Don't you dare even *think* about leaving me here with him," Bex growled.

Ignoring Bex's outrage and Walker's dumbstruck stare, I tensed. I'd watched Dominic fly through the night like a shooting star from the vantage of being wrapped in his arms more times now than I could count. Sometimes I'd been injured, sometimes we'd been running from the creatures trying to injure us, and more often than not, we'd ended our flight in a crash landing. But every time started the same, and I could envision that just fine.

The ground buckled beneath the weight of my power as I braced my legs for the coming leap—the longest, highest leap of my brief life—and I launched out of the tunnels, soaring high across the bright morning sky. I might not land on my feet, but wherever we fell, Dominic was secure in the safety of my arms.

Chapter 12

I laid Dominic on our bed in his underground bunker, safe from the sun and Jillian and her army of the Damned, but that hard-earned, newfound safety didn't stop my heart from clenching in unadulterated fear as I watched Dominic writhe in agony.

I'd saved us from the Damned. I'd entered their minds and entranced, en masse, dozens upon dozens of ravenous, raging, psychotic creatures that hitherto couldn't comprehend the English language or human emotion enough to understand or obey commands. I'm not sure that boded well for me, the fact that my commands were suddenly being given on a level they could comprehend. I'd survived being doused in sunlight, had, in fact, basked in its rays and perhaps blossomed into my full power as a Day Reaper. I'd accomplished more than I'd ever thought myself capable of, more than I'd thought anyone capable of, in the last eighteen hours, but even I couldn't do anything to save Dominic.

"You need to return for Ian Walker and B-B-Beatrix," Dominic said roughly, his teeth chattering in shock.

His body was smoldering. I'd healed him from being a Dominic-shaped blowtorch, but now that we were ensconced underground, meters of earth and thick concrete between us and the rays of the sun, his skin was still blackened, blistering, and flaking apart. Noxious steam sizzled from his body, as if embers of sunlight were still aglow in his clothing, still burning his skin.

I tore his clothes from his body, ripping his cotton T-shirt clean down the middle from neck to hem.

"Cassidy, love," Dominic murmured, a teasing glint lighting his gaze even through the pain, "as much as I hunger for you, this isn't the t-t-time for—"

"Shut. Up." I enunciated each word through gritted teeth as I stared.

My hands hovered over his chest, wanting to help but hesitating, knowing that to touch him would only cause him more pain. He was still smoldering. Somehow, even hidden from direct sunlight, without flames or even the tiniest spark of an ember, he was still physically and excruciatingly burning alive.

"You must return for Walker and Bex," he repeated, more insistently this time.

"They're fine," I snapped. "Be quiet and let me think!"

"The Damned—"

"Weren't attacking when we left," I bit off.

"Left to their own devices, they may j-j-just kill each other," Dominic pointed out.

"If they can't pull their shit together enough to get out while the going is good, then they deserve whatever happens."

Dominic leveled a knowing look on me. "Cassidy—" he began.

"I don't care," I said, shocked to realize the truth in that statement as it left my lips. We may have just risked our lives to save Bex only to lose her again, but in this moment, the only person who mattered was incinerating in the bed in front of me. "I'm not leaving you like this."

I ran to the refrigerator, swiped his emergency store of bagged blood from the door, and tore a bag open with my fangs.

Dominic narrowed his eyes. "That's your blood."

"There's no time to find a willing donor, and I won't hunt and attack an unsuspecting person for you when we have bagged blood readily available."

"Never asked you to," he panted.

Gripping the back of his neck in my hand, I tipped his mouth back, and placed the opened bag of blood to his lips."Shut up and drink."

He caught my wrist. "No. You drink," he growled. Had I still been human, his grip on my wrist might have fractured bone. But I wasn't human, and he was gravely injured. His entire body trembled violently.

"You're going into shock," I argued. "Stop fighting me and just—"

"You drink and heal m-me," he interrupted, chattering even more violently than mere minutes ago. "Your f-f-fault I'm burning. You must learn c-c-control."

"Excuse me?" I asked, incredulous. "It's *my* fault you're burning? Was I the one who tore open the cavern? Was I the one who flooded us in sunlight with less than a second of warning?"

"We are c-c-connected metaphysically. Your wounds are my w-w-wounds. Your strength is my strength and vice v-v-versa, but when I was the stronger vampire, the one who created our bond, I controlled them. I could hide from you when I was injured and take the worst of our combined injuries into my b-b-body to heal them." He gave me a pointed look. "But I am unable to heal this injury."

I narrowed my eyes. "What are you saying?"

"It would seem that since you came into your full p-p-powers, of the two of us, I am no longer the stronger vampire." Dominic's face pinched sourly. "You're in control of our b-b-bond."

"That's ridiculous." I scoffed. "You're hundreds of years older than me. How can I be stronger than—"

"I am out of sunlight, yet still b-b-burning from the inside out," Dominic thundered. "D-d-drink the blood to fuel your strength, determine why I'm not healing, and f-f-fix it."

"I don't know how," I admitted. "I've never healed a metaphysical wound before. Maybe I *should* go back and get Bex. Maybe she can—"

"You didn't know how to entrance me," Dominic interrupted. "When you were a n-n-night blood and no night blood had ever in the history of my knowledge before entranced a vampire, you entranced m-m-me, the Master vampire of New York City."

I closed my mouth, realizing that I was gaping. I felt as if I was teetering on the ledge of a very high cavern, peeking over the edge and down into the dark, unscaled depths below.

"You d-d-didn't know how to transform your brother back from being Damned, but you did. You didn't know how to transform into a vampire, or a Day Reaper, for that matter, but you did." Dominic hesitated, as if he wasn't sure of himself or whatever else he'd been about to say. Then his jaw stiffened, and he said it anyway. "You d-d-didn't know how to trust a man with your body and heart again, but you did."

I froze, from the hair follicles on the very top of my head to the soles of my feet rooted to the floor, and in the very next moment, heat flooded my entire body in a near, full-body blush.

"You, my dear Cassidy DiRocco, can do absolutely anything you want to, whether or not you've done it before or think you don't know how." The look in Dominic's eyes was inscrutable as he regarded me. Even with my newfound, enhanced senses, I could only dream what the intensity in his gaze could possibly mean. "Anything."

It felt fundamentally wrong to drink the last reserves of our bagged blood when Dominic was so injured, but looking into the depth of his eyes was very much like gazing down into the depths of that dark cavern, foreign and unknown, and by its very mystery, irresistible.

Before I could talk myself out of it, I raised the blood to my lips and drank.

The blood was cool and thick, not as viscous as Dominic's blood, but thicker than liquids like water, juice, and Coke—liquids I was accustomed to drinking for a lifetime. The blood chilled my esophagus all the way down to my stomach, but unlike human food and drink, the sensation didn't stop there. It spread in an uncomfortable, electric snap sensation through my chest, arms, and legs, but where the sensation spread, my flagging strength restored. My aches disappeared, and my body, which had grown thin and cold from the overuse of my abilities, warmed. We were underground, but the blood's chilling heat—like menthol—spread through my body, radiating health, wholeness, and well-being, not unlike the sensation of basking with my head upturned to the shining sun on a crisp, clear winter morning.

Except now, the sun came from within.

I'd always had a strong connection with Dominic, even before he'd forged our metaphysical bonds. I remembered entrancing him that first time in the bullpen at the *Sun Accord* directly following our first kiss. Although I hadn't been able to hear his exact thoughts, I had felt the very foreign nuance of his strange, kaleidoscope emotions.

Our metaphysical bonds weren't much different now than they'd been then, but instead of just a mental connection forced by my will, our very life forces were connected now, a connection that not even death could sever.

I followed the dozens of threads connecting us—all the promises we'd made to each other on the certainty and permanence of death between his life and mine. I stepped lightly over the tightrope of our connection until I found his body, weakened from the newfound strength in mine. With my mind's eye, I could see the warmth and glow of the sun's rays inside of me, protecting me from daylight and stoking my Day Reaper strength and abilities, but Dominic's body on the opposite end of our metaphysical thread was roasting, being charred slowly but meticulously into ash by my inner sun.

The light that made me strong was incinerating Dominic from the inside out.

I inhaled sharply, understanding like dawning horror shining light on his wounds. "It *is* my fault you're burning."

"How so?" he asked. Although his body was physically inches from mine, his voice echoed as if from a great distance.

"You're allergic to sunlight. Your skin is highly flammable to the sun's rays."

"We know this," he said.

"I absorbed the sun's rays into my body to awaken my dormant Day Reaper abilities. It's a light inside me, protecting my body from daylight and burning yours."

"I could hide in shadow all d-d-day and still not escape the burning of the sun now," Dominic said, not sounding near as horrified as I felt. "What can you do about it?"

"What can I do about what?" I snapped. "I'm burning you. The light inside my own body is killing you!"

He shrugged. "So give me sunscreen," he said, as if slathering some SPF 50 onto his skin was a viable solution.

I opened my mouth to say as much when a similar thought, but one with merit, struck and stuck in my mind: sunscreen wouldn't help, obviously, but maybe I could erect a metaphysical screen between us.

I envisioned a mirror, similar to the one Dominic had given me to protect my mind from being entranced, but instead of reflecting his commands, I reflected my inner sun back onto myself. Without my light blazing his body like an industrial blowtorch, I could see the destructive effects my power had on his body: charred organs, boiled blood, his wise, ferocious, four-hundred-and-seventy-seven-year-old soul nearly incinerated to ash.

I'd suffered the physical effects of Dominic's injuries through our metaphysical connection before—burned wrists when he'd been cuffed by silver restraints and a pierced heart when he'd been staked by Walker's crossbow—but for the first time, I wasn't victim to his injuries. I could actually envision them, and with that same enhanced inner eye that allowed me to see each burn and blister, like a half finished puzzle, I could finally see the missing pieces in my own hands: I couldn't heal his wounds any more than I could anyone else's without my blood or saliva as a catalyst, but through our metaphysical connection, I could take the wounds as my own.

I embraced the burns. My skin bubbled and oozed, my insides cramped, and the agony of his injuries engulfed my body until every incinerated cell was mine and mine alone, and with the nourishment of the blood I'd just consumed and the healing light of my Day Reaper abilities giving me strength, I healed myself.

I opened my eyes slowly. Doubt and fear made my heart throb as much as hope.

Dominic wasn't smoldering anymore. He still lay on his back in our bed just as I'd placed him, his shirt split down the middle just as I'd torn it moments ago, but unlike moments ago, his skin was smooth and unblemished by burns and weeping blisters. His body was more than just something to fix; the firm planes of his chest, the symmetrical ridges of his abdomen, the cords of oblique muscles—I drank in the sculpted, healthy perfection of his body.

I'd fallen for Dominic despite his physical form, which more often than not was either a cold and malnourished creature in need of blood or a malformed monster with back-hinged legs, elongated talons, pointed fangs, and primordial facial features. In their own strange and mysterious ways, those forms were beautiful, too, like the way an anaconda is beautiful in its element and environment: a wild predator to be accorded respect and admiration from a distance. I'd lain beside all three—the creature, the monster, and the man—and was living proof that a person couldn't embrace a predator without being bitten. Lying before me as he was now, even as a man, with every sense focused solely on me, I should have felt trapped in his crosshairs, but I wasn't prey anymore. I wasn't even his equal anymore. I was a wild predator, too, and as much respect and admiration I had for this man, I didn't want any distance between us.

More dangerous than even his body, his eyes—dear God, the unscalable depths of his otherworldly eyes—blazed with a fire more devastating than the one I'd just saved him from, a fire from which I'd never willingly escape.

I cleared my throat. "How do you feel?" I asked.

Dominic wrapped his arms around my waist and pulled me down on top of him on the bed.

"Ravenous," he whispered and slanted his lips over mine.

Dominic's kiss was a blade's edge: sharp, honed by time and craftsmanship, and deadly when wielded with skill. He had many skills he'd perfected throughout the centuries of his existence, and kissing was certainly one of them.

He rolled me beneath him and caged me with his elbows on either side of my head. His legs surrounded my hips, and his chest pressed against my chest, crushing me into the bed. We didn't have time for this; as Dominic had already inconveniently pointed out, Bex and Walker were likely killing each other if the Damned hadn't already. Saving Dominic was a legitimate excuse for leaving them behind, but this was—

Dominic rolled my nipple between his strong, capable fingers, and my thoughts shorted out. His hand on my breast stole my reason. His mouth stole my breath. His tongue stole my protests until all that was left in the whole world was him on top of me, his lips against my lips, his body hard on my body and nothing, not even air, between us.

His hand drifted up my arm to my wrist. He pulled first my right and then my left hand from where I'd been gouging my nails down his back and held them immobile over my head in one of his large hands.

"Let me touch you," I protested.

He'd explored every inch of my body with his hands and tongue the first time we'd made love, and although I'd reveled in his touch, I hadn't had the strength at the time to fight back, to demand control over the things I'd wanted to do to him. I'd taken everything he'd had to give and seen heaven, but it was past time he saw heaven, too.

"Make me," he growled, the challenge in both his eyes and his smirk unmistakable. Irresistible. Undeniable.

I bucked my hips against his, rubbing the long length of his delicious body against mine. His erection was proud and unyielding between us. The skin at the curve of his neck was salty and soft as I nibbled under his ear.

I licked his lobe and whispered everything I wanted to do to his cock and everything I wanted to do it with.

Despite his power, despite his strength and hands binding my wrists, his eyes rolled into the back of his head, and he shuddered.

Taking advantage of his distraction, I alligator-rolled us and straddled him. His eyes widened, but there was something more than just surprise in his gaze as he regarded me. His speed and strength had always been inhuman and miraculous. And now, to both our astonishments and what looked to me like his pride, so was mine.

He broke his hold on my wrists in the attempt to regain control of my body, but I reversed our hold and grabbed his wrists. I needed both hands; my fingers could just barely circle his wrists.

I ground my hips to his, slanted my lips over his mouth, and swallowed his groan. He sat up, attempting to wrestle me back beneath him, but I pushed him down with the sheer force of my strength. His back hit the bed, the mattress rocked, and suddenly we were airborne. Dominic flipped upright and slammed me back on the bed, exactly where he'd wanted me, but that's not where I wanted him. I used our momentum to keep flipping. We bounded completely off the bed, and I slammed him into the wall. My moves had less flair than I would have preferred, but as Bex would have pointed out, they were effective.

Before Dominic could recover, I ripped his pants from his body—literally, they split at the seams into four, dangling rags—and fell to my knees in front of him.

"You've always been hell on my shirts, but even for you, this—"

I took the entire length of his erection into my mouth and sucked. Hard.

His fists pounded twin holes into the drywall on either side of my head, and he growled. The sound was more animal than man, but it didn't matter anymore. I couldn't deny his animal any more than I could deny mine, and that feral, animal instinct inside me urged me to claim him. To mark him as mine in a way that not only let him know, but everyone who dared look at him know, that he was undeniably mine.

"Mind your fangs," he gasped between pants.

My heart thrilled. I made the man who didn't need to breathe breathless. I rocked his eternally cool, collected composure. The feeling might have gone to my head except for the fact that I'd long ago lost my mind when it came to this man.

"These fangs?" Glancing up, I deliberately elongated them and ran my tongue along their length.

Dominic bent forward in a move so fast he might have only appeared a blur with my human eyes. Now, I could see every minutia of movement—his contracting muscles, his tensed stance, the wicked intent blazing from his eyes. Yet having seen behind Oz's curtain hadn't disenchanted me. If anything, discovering the reality of Dominic's existence heightened it. I could move like him, see like him, hear, smell, and hunger like him. My brain synapses fired with lightning-strike velocity, like him, and with the playing ground finally leveled, I could appreciate his restraint and patience. Months of pursuing me, attempting to convince me to trust him, first as allies and then as lovers. Months of smelling my cinnamon-spice scent and resisting my blood. Numerous kisses and embraces and physical interaction where one wrong twitch of his talons, one too enthusiastic squeeze of his powerful arms, one misplaced lethal fang could slice, snap, and break my too-easily broken body.

Now, my body was nearly unbreakable, just like his, and if I wasn't mistaken by the gleam in his eyes, he intended to push it to its limits.

He wrapped his arms around my waist and swung me into the air, upside down. Minding my fangs like he'd reminded me, no matter my teasing, I released him, but he didn't release me. He kissed me between my legs.

I gasped and then smiled with this acceptable compromise; my mouth was still at the perfect height to give him as much pleasure as I was getting. I wrapped my legs around his neck, braced my arms on his hips, and licked him from base to tip before enveloping the entire length of his cock in my mouth.

His tongue swiped against my clit, and a coiled spring of heat exploded inside me. I wriggled against his mouth, the sensations so intense they robbed me of all my many heightened senses until the world honed to nothing but this moment and this man. Not wanting to be outdone, I lavished attention on him. I sucked harder, twirled my tongue over his tip faster, pounded the length of him into the back of my throat and pulled back from him in long strokes, followed by a burst of short, hard yanks, over and over again, until he was sucking and licking and worshiping me with the same frantic frenzy he'd stoked in me.

I pulled away first, desperate and gasping. "Now," I panted. "I want you inside me now!"

"Thank God," he growled, and with my mouth dislodged from his cock and my fangs a safe distance away, he threw me away from him and onto the bed.

He lunged to join me, but I rolled aside and pinned him to the bed when he hit the sheets. His muscles tensed, about to pull the same alligator roll I'd played on him, but I angled my hips and ground him home.

We both stilled.

We'd only just had sex for the first time eight days ago, but so much had happened in the interim, it may as well have been eight years. I was impossibly tight, he was impossibly large, and everything about this man and my feelings for him had been so far outside the realm of possibility when we'd first met that coming together in longing and love now, even having just been here a week ago, was still a dream. My enhanced vampire senses didn't help anchor me in reality either. I could smell sound and taste a touch. They were as confusing as they were enlightening, but in this moment with Dominic, they were transcendent.

The warmth and comfort of a hearth blazed between us and combined with the aching pleasure-pain of my body accommodating the intrusion of his. Heat pulsed through me from our center, incinerating my stomach and chest and arms until even my face and fingers tingled and my toes curled with the licking flames of our joining. I could smell the wood burning, taste the roast of pine nut and evergreen, and hear the crackling of split logs. Our union was more than just a physical and emotional expression; it felt like a presence all its own.

"Can you feel that?" I whispered. "The flames and pulse and—"

He nodded. "Like fireworks."

I shook my head. "Like a hearth. Something vital and comforting. Something to welcome you home."

Dominic's knowing gaze bore into mine, and if I hadn't thought my body could possibly become hotter with him hard inside me, I blushed from the edge of my hairline down to my pinky toes. "Like coming home," he said, considering. "I like that."

"But that's not how you feel. You just said—"

Dominic pressed a finger against my lips. "What I feel and how I feel are two very different things. Our senses, although enhanced, are deceptive.

Keagan doesn't have a bird inside his chest that changes its call depending on his mood any more than you have a hearth inside you or I have fireworks inside me. Our senses are useful and telling, but they aren't reality. You here with me in this moment, in my arms, that is real."

I bit my lip. "But—"

Dominic hushed me again, then stroked my cheek. "Concentrate on me. Feel what I am feeling."

I closed my eyes and concentrated, albeit doubtfully. I traversed the tightrope between us, and when I reached his mind, or what should have been his mind, my breath hitched. Dominic's thoughts and feelings were usually a modeled, kaleidoscope impression of feelings, not the feelings themselves, but this time, the intent in his heart blazed brighter and warmer and more constant than the sun.

I knew better than most that homes were fleeting. They could burn to the ground and take everything dear and precious along with them. I hadn't let anyone come near my scarred heart in years—how many wounds could a heart endure and still continue beating?—but Dominic's heart was as scarred as mine. He'd lived nearly five-hundred years longer than me, had survived five lifetimes worth of pain, heartache, and loss, but somehow, he'd found the courage to offer me the one organ he knew from experience could so easily break.

I opened my eyes. Dominic was still stroking my cheek, but he was smearing something wet across my face with his thumb now. I blinked and realized that he was wiping away tears.

"How do you do it?" I whispered. My voice was nothing but a rasp. I cleared my throat and tried again. "How do you live with the pain of love lost and still find the courage to love again?"

"It has absolutely nothing to do with courage. The loss of my father still pains me; it lives and breathes within me every day. Some days I can remember him fondly without being overwhelmed by grief, but most days, his loss still feels fresh and biting, even after all these years and new losses to mourn. The new losses don't replace the old ones; they just widen old wounds." Dominic cupped my face in both his hands. "But the thought of living without you, even knowing all the pain I'd endure with your loss, is a pain all its own."

I raised an eyebrow. "'Better to have loved and lost than never to have loved at all'?"

Dominic barked out a harsh laugh. "No, my dear Cassidy DiRocco. Better to have loved and lost than let it slip away from fear of loss. Either way, my heart will bleed, but I will have you in this moment and in as many future moments we can hope to create. And if a time should come that love is lost, we will have the memory of these moments to bandage our wounds, to keep us warm in the lonely cold, and to help us survive." His grip on me tightened nearly painfully, even for me. "Love me, Cassidy. Let's burn our pain to the ground and scatter it to the wind along with the ashes of our lost loved ones. Let's create a new home."

The words spilling from his lips vibrated through my body like a tuning fork, ringing loud and true. The pain was still present, but no longer paralyzing; I moved my hips, slowly at first, savoring the friction of him inside me, letting the dual feelings of my hearth and his fireworks envelope me in sensation and need and heat. The ridges of his cock rubbed in all the right places as I withdrew from him, and when the very tip of him caressed the very edge of me, I eased him back inside, his hard length deliciously consuming. We rocked, gently in and out, in and out, and then more urgently in and lingeringly out, in and out, and then slamming home again and again, until his tip touched the very deepest part of me, and I trembled from want, needing him somehow deeper.

He bruised my backside from the inside, demanding more, being driven wild by the same inexplicable need as me, being somehow glued together even knowing all the ways life could tear us apart. I gripped his hands in mine above his head, arched back in abandon, lost in sensation, and laughed, the tears still wet on my cheeks. I willingly, eagerly, pushed him deeper and harder and more permanently inside myself than I'd thought any man, and especially this man, would ever be capable of penetrating.

My vampire senses were overwhelming, my newfound strength and speed and longevity was life-changing but new, and as with everything new, even things that change life for the good, being with Dominic was as frightening as it was exciting, if not more so. There would be drawbacks to becoming Dominic's equal, but in that moment, with his fingers curled in mine, our bodies coming together thrust for thrust until we both shattered and he roared and I shuddered with a pleasure bordering on pain, I felt the deep grave of my past fill with joy.

Chapter 13

A frigid hand against my cheek woke me. I opened my eyes and stared into Dominic's luminous, otherworldly gaze only inches from mine. I could happily drown in his gaze, a sensation that had terrified me only a few short weeks ago. Now, if his lazy grin and the tuning fork vibration of his desire was anything to go by, he could happily drown in mine—but neither of us looked away.

I grinned back, albeit a little embarrassed. "I practically passed out."

Dominic's grin widened. "I'm not surprised. After fighting the Damned, barely escaping the coven with our lives, and healing me, it's a miracle you didn't pass out earlier."

Memories of last night, in particular everyone who hadn't escaped the coven, wiped the grin from my face. I bolted upright. "We never returned for Bex and Walker. We need to—"

"They're fine," Dominic said, placing a firm, staying hand on my shoulder.

"You don't know that. They—"

"They're here," Dominic said. "Calm yourself, and expand your senses. You can hear them in the living room."

I froze, but it wasn't their sound that struck me first. I could smell the physical waft of banana nut pancakes and the sriracha bite of someone's anger in reaction to them: Walker. Then I heard Bex's breathy drawl, and whatever she said, the heat of Walker's anger skyrocketed.

I slumped back into bed beside Dominic in relief.

"Bex and Walker managed to pull their shit together enough to escape the Underneath," I said, mildly stunned.

"And without us to keep them from killing each other," he pointed out. "Baby birds will either fly or fall when kicked from the nest."

"In that metaphor, Bex and Walker are our children."

Dominic's smile widened enough to expose his fangs.

I pretended to gag.

He swiped a thumb across my cheekbone and stared at me in silence.

I waited, but when it became apparent that he wasn't in any hurry to continue the conversation, I broke under the pressure of his gaze. "What?"

"I remember those eyes," he whispered.

I raised my eyebrows. "I would hope so."

He shook his head and smiled. "I haven't seen them in over a week, not since your transformation."

I frowned.

"You bathed in sunlight, Cassidy. You're fully transformed into a Day Reaper, human-eyed, sun-resistant, and all." He cocked his own eyebrow. "How does it feel?"

I rolled said human eyes. "I'm the one who should be asking how *you* feel." I sighed. "Except if I concentrate, and not even that hard, I can feel exactly how you feel. Should I ask anyway?"

Dominic grinned a mouthful of fangs. "Better yet, let me show you."

He kissed my lips and shifted over me, so the long line of his body enveloped mine. His flexed biceps surrounded me. His weight bore me back into the mattress, his strong legs straddled my waist, and between us pressed the hard, undeniable proof of exactly how he felt.

He left my lips and nipped a line of kisses down my jaw to the curve of my neck. My eyes fluttered closed, and I shuddered.

I leveled a cup of flour and upended it into the bowl, feeling myself settle into the comfort of doing something I did well, something I hadn't enjoyed in weeks.

My eyes slammed open, and I was suddenly back in bed with Dominic, enjoying his seduction, not making pancakes.

Ronnie, I thought, my mind racing. *That had been Ronnie.*

"Cassidy?" Dominic asked warily, leaning back when he realized I was no longer writhing in abandon from his touch.

"Sorry, I just…I was distracted." I licked my lips. "Where were we?"

Dominic cocked an eyebrow. "The fact that you must ask is quite telling. I must be losing my touch in my old age."

I grinned. "Old man" jokes were typically my punch line. "Quite the opposite actually," I said, attempting to mimic the aristocratic formalness of his usual tone. "I find that hundreds of years of practice has nearly perfected your touch."

I closed my eyes and slanted my lips over his.

The scent of batter hitting the griddle made my stomach rumble even as my heart ached. My stomach obviously didn't care who was making banana-nut pancakes, but having that creature serve me like Ronnie used to was obscene.

I tore my lips from his, gasping, and not from pleasure.

Dominic eyed me carefully. "What's wrong?"

The double sensation of dipping into Walker's mind was gone. I was in my own body again, cozy under the comforter with Dominic like a sexy icicle under the sheets, but if I closed my eyes, who would I slip into next?

Dominic's hands on my shoulders startled my attention back to him. "Cassidy," he said, sternly this time.

"I don't know what's wrong. I wasn't this distracted last night." I shook my head in denial even as a heavy weight constricted my chest. "Is this how it's like for you all the time?"

"What are you talking about?" Dominic asked sharply.

I could see his frustration, like I always could, by the pinched set of his lips, but now, like never before, I could actually *feel* his frustration. The dual sensation of my own fear and his frustration, quadrupled by Ronnie's contentment, Walker's resentment, and everyone else outside that door—their emotions just a thought away—was like insects squirming under my skin. Their thoughts and emotions, although foreign and unsettling, were inside me, and I couldn't escape from them any more than I could escape from my own.

The confines of my own body were a cage, and I could feel the walls of my captivity closing in.

"Cassidy!" he snapped.

"Sensing their emotions is challenging enough; I can't deal with thinking their thoughts, too! I have enough conflicting thoughts and feelings all on my own without having to deal with everyone else's!" I blurted.

Dominic's hands on my shoulders tightened. Had I been human it might have hurt. "Explain."

I sighed. "You once said that you felt crippled without your heightened senses, that you were essentially blind and deaf compared to the visual and auditory acuity you've become accustomed to."

Dominic nodded.

"I can't imagine becoming accustomed to this." I glanced at the bedroom door of his underground bunker, at the scratched oak and brass that should have created a barrier between us and the living room, but I didn't need to open the door and peek into the room to know who was there, what they were doing, and how they were feeling about it. "I nearly lost you last night and—"

Dominic snorted. "You have come infinitely closer to losing me on other nights. I assure you, last night was not one of them."

I held up my hand. "—and there is nowhere I want to be more than right here, reminding myself, again, that we are both still very much alive." I wrinkled my nose at him. "In existence."

Dominic narrowed his eyes on me.

"My point is, I want to be here in this moment with you, only you, making another memory just like we talked about, but there's Ronnie out there, gleefully making stack upon stack of banana-nut pancakes that only Walker can actually eat. Walker's out there, hungry and resenting Ronnie for feeding him. And if I close my eyes again, I have no doubt that I'll slip away into someone else—into Keagan or Bex or Theresa or Logan—getting lost in everyone else's mind instead of staying grounded here with you." My hands were suddenly gripping Dominic's shoulders. I didn't remember moving them there, but I held onto the solid strength of him, knowing he could take it. "I'm not just hearing the squawking bird of their annoyance or feeling the bee sting of their anger. I'm actually hearing their *thoughts in my mind.*"

Dominic blinked in surprise, and I realized that no matter his apparent powers of omniscience, he could not actually read minds. I heard the scraping chill of my own dread, like chewing ice, before I could mask the sound.

"Cassidy, I'm not—"

"You don't hear them," I said flatly.

"You're a Day Reaper now. Your abilities far out—"

"How do I block them out?" I snapped.

A weary smile tugged on Dominic's lips. "You can't."

The resignation in his tone spiked my panic and denial. I shook my head adamantly. "Can't you just, I don't know..." I flapped my hand between us, "sever my connection to them like you did with Jillian?"

He raised his hand and smoothed a very cold finger across my cheek. "There is no connection to sever. Jillian was parasitic, her connection to you was forced and unnatural. This time, *you* are the one invading *their* privacy with your highly sensitive senses. It's you, Cassidy, not them, and even if I could, I wouldn't change anything about the person you are becoming."

"The *creature* I'm becoming," I corrected morosely.

His hold on me tightened. "You are a force to be reckoned with, and the only force, I suspect, which will be capable of standing against Jillian and her army. I don't see a creature when I look at you."

I snorted. "That's because you're a creature, too."

"I see the only hope we may have left to restore the balance of power and save New York City," he persisted.

I sighed. No one person could be all he anticipated me being. "What do I do?"

He raised his eyebrows. "About restoring the balance of power and saving New York City? Can we have breakfast first? I'm famished."

"About blocking my heightened senses," I said, punching his shoulder lightly.

He grinned. "I just told you: you can't block them, no more than your former self could open your eyes and not see a crime scene. Just because it was a sight you didn't want to see didn't mean you could somehow will it out of existence. The scene, no matter how unpleasant, was present, and you as a crime reporter, needed to look. Now, you are a Day Reaper—"

"I'm still a crime reporter," I grumbled.

"—and you must endure the world around you with heightened senses." He cocked his head at me. "Were you as calm, capable, and grounded during your first crime scene as you are now, as a seasoned professional?"

I let out a surprised bark of laughter. "If you call finding a secluded alley to vomit in between interviews calm and capable, then yes." I shook my head. "I was eager and willing to learn, but no—of course I wasn't as capable then as I am now. It took years to become accustomed to my job and grow into a seasoned professional."

Dominic cocked an eyebrow.

My jaw dropped. "Years, Dominic? *Years?*" I shook my head, dawning horror breaking over me. "I can't live like this for *years*!"

He brushed a wayward lock of hair behind my ear, but it stubbornly slipped back out of place. "What is a meager few years when you have eternity?"

I poked my finger at his face. "Don't be condescending and flippant. I'm being serious."

"So am I. You saved us last night, Cassidy," he said, his voice suddenly grave.

I opened my mouth, not necessarily to refute that statement—I had certainly surprised even myself with all I was capable of—but I fell a little shy of such a pedestal. "It wasn't just me. Bex—"

Dominic placed a finger over my lips. "—could not have done what you did last night," he said, finishing my sentence. "If not for you, Bex would still be imprisoned within the Underneath. Walker and I would both be dead, and Jillian would have a clear runway to rule the city uncontested. As I've always known, you are the keystone."

I wrinkled my nose. "Keystone? Really?"

"You keep all of us unlikely players—humans, vampires, Day Reapers, whatever the hell your brother is—locked together as one team, greater than the sum of our individual efforts and, with a little luck, more successful."

"More than a little," I grumbled. I shook my head at his praise. "It doesn't take a genius to figure out that we need to work together to defeat Jillian."

"No, but without you, this team doesn't work. You bridge the gap between our insurmountable differences." Dominic's eyes blazed with a ferocity I'd never seen from him before. "You need to say it, Cassidy. You saved us last night. You need to say it and believe it. Believe in yourself."

I frowned.

"I believe in you."

I rolled my eyes. "What does it matter who saved who as long as we're all alive and still fighting?"

"Because you need to realize that although your new senses are distracting and uncomfortable and it may take years for you to truly hone them and become accustomed to them, they enabled you to save us last night. And when we confront Jillian to reclaim my coven, they will enable you to save us all."

Dominic pressed his lips against mine with an urgency that stole my comeback, thoughts, and will. I melted into his embrace, against the unyielding steel of his arms holding me, against the steady strength of his chest surrounding me, against everything that had stripped me bare and I couldn't bear to lose. Everything I'd die to save.

My eyes fluttered closed against his assault, and this time, my mind slipped into his. I could feel his unwavering confidence in me along with his own determination and fortitude, but more frightening than my own lack of self-preservation when it came to this man and everything I'd willingly sacrifice for him was the equality in his feelings for me. Dominic was entrusting me to help him reclaim the one thing that shared space in his heart with me: his coven. But I didn't share his confidence; My heightened vision, like a fortune-teller, could see the inevitable alternative should I fail. I would lose him. Just when we'd finally built a new home over the ashes of the last one I'd lost, I'd lose him. And the most frightening realization of all was knowing that if I lost him, our lives were so interwoven now that I'd undoubtedly lose myself, too, if I hadn't already.

I tore my lips from his, trembling.

"What is it now?" Dominic asked warily.

"It's nothing. I…well…" I cleared my throat, attempting to think about the happiest moments of my life: the thrill of publishing an article and seeing my words in print, of winning a verbal volley against Carter, my surly editor, the satisfaction of being part of a team who made New York City just a little bit safer, and being the one person everyone came to when they wanted the world to know the truth—anything so Dominic wouldn't sense the tsunami of dread drowning me. "If I'm a keystone, our mortar is crumbling out there," I said, jerking my head toward the kitchen outside his bedroom door. "We need to separate the children before they either kill each other or pancakes smash against the walls. Either way, it'll be a hell of a mess to clean up."

Dominic narrowed his eyes. He knew me too well, easily detecting the kaleidoscope of emotions I'd used to mask what I was really feeling—the very trick he'd taught me used against him—but he didn't say anything. He didn't contradict or fight me. In fact, he did the opposite: his arms loosened and fell at his sides in defeat. He let me go.

Maybe turning my back on Dominic after I'd felt the intensity of his feelings for me made me a coward. Maybe leaving his arms, his bed, and rejecting the confidence he had in me actually hurt me more than it hurt him—and hurt our cause worst of all—but what I'd said was true. Walker really was about to start flinging pancakes, and if he did that, there was no telling how Ronnie would react. However misplaced, her very life's purpose and happiness was mixed into that pancake batter.

However misplaced, Dominic's life purpose and happiness had somehow gotten mixed into mine.

I couldn't bear the weight of either his gaze or his regard, so I embraced the coward, turned my back on Dominic, and faced the fire I knew I could put out before I could even think of dousing the inferno blazing behind me. For both our sakes, I needed to find the courage to face the flames before they consumed us both, but for now, I let them burn.

Chapter 14

The mortar of our fragile alliance was more than just crumbling; when Dominic and I exited our bedroom and stepped into the living room, the tension and hostility between everyone was about to bulldoze our little family into dust and my senses along with it.

Bex and Walker had somehow managed to pull their shit together enough to escape the Underneath and the Damned, but now that the immediate, life-threatening danger was past, they looked more than willing to resume their personal war: They stood on opposite sides of the living room, scowling darkly. Their anger and resentment was sharp and excruciating, like my fingernails were being ripped from their beds.

Bex had changed since I'd first met her. Gone were her jeans and cowboy boots, flimsy, barely-there tops, and flirtatious, charming Southern twang. She'd obviously fed since last night and recovered most of her former figure and beauty because she wore another bombshell dress similar to the purple-and-black number she'd worn last week when she and the other Day Reapers had come calling on Dominic's coven. This one was green with black lace, and a matching green eye patch covered her missing eye. The eye patch was more of a fashion accessory than a covering; it, too, was trimmed in black lace. It made me wonder if she had a different patch to match every outfit, and if so, if she'd had them custom-made. I couldn't imagine her at a sewing machine, decorating dozens of eye patches in various fabrics and designs to match her wardrobe, but here she was in front of me, scowling at Walker with her remaining eye, a designer-esque patch over the other.

Despite the dress and eye patch, however, Bex wasn't quite at her best self, not even after having fed. Granted, her best self was nothing short of stunning. She wore the human mask of her night form well—rounded ears, yellow-green human iris, and a smooth brow—but after a week of starved, silver-exposed imprisonment, her thick, wavy bronze hair was still thin and although no longer skeletal, her figure hadn't regained its former strength and sensuality.

Walker, on the other hand, had somehow never looked better. He wore one of his many plain black T-shirts that were a half-size too small over the swell of his biceps and across his broad chest. He'd tucked the ends of his faded jeans into cowboy boots, and his riot of springy, golden curls was a little longer than I remembered. A lock fell across his forehead, and the memory of a time when I might have considered brushing that lock back into place still left a bitter aftertaste on my tongue. He crossed his arms over his chest, stretching the shirt to nearly a full size too small, and transferred his scowl from Bex to Ronnie.

Ronnie, bless her heart, had just dropped another five pancakes on the griddle after flipping seven others to golden-brown perfection. She seemed oblivious to the intensity of Walker's rage-filled regard. Her cooking filled the apartment with a warm, nutty scent, and although the smell was comforting and pleasant, it didn't make my stomach rumble like it used to. The smell of pancakes was akin to the smell of something floral—I could appreciate the scent without wanting to eat it.

I glanced back at Walker and winced. He did not look particularly hungry at the moment, and with Bex, Dominic, Rafe, Neil, Keagan, Logan, Jeremy, Theresa, and I the only other occupants in the room, who the hell would be eating a dozen of Ronnie's famous banana-nut pancakes for breakfast when she couldn't eat them herself anymore?

I stole a swift glance at the rest of the room and instantly wished I hadn't. Keagan and Jeremy were watching the drama unfold between Ronnie, Walker, and Bex from opposite corners of the couch, and Logan and Theresa were whispering their displeasure and uncertainty from the far corner of the room, as if I couldn't hear their every word. When I entered the living room, Logan and Theresa fell silent and all four pairs of eyes honed on me. I realized, uncomfortably, that they'd been waiting on me. Walker had been the glue that had bound them together as night bloods, but somehow along the way—probably thanks to Ronnie recruiting me to give entrancing lessons—I'd become the glue binding them together as vampires. And they were looking at me, the vampire Walker resented only slightly less than Bex, to talk sense into him and Ronnie, the vampire who thought she was still human.

I took a fortifying breath, less fortifying now that I didn't need air to live, and settled my eyes on Bex.

"What time did you get in yesterday?" I asked.

Bex opened her mouth to reply.

"What time did we get in?" Walker repeated, transferring his glare from Ronnie to me. "As if we were out on the town and not trapped in the Underneath and surrounded by the Damned."

Rafe and Neil shifted slightly, angling their bodies so the couch wasn't between them and Walker.

"We escaped shortly after you left," Bex answered as if Walker hadn't spoken, "but by the time I fed and tracked Walker back here, you were already abed. I hope you don't mind the intrusion. I didn't want to wake you to ask permission to enter, so I"—Bex smiled, but not pleasantly—"let myself in."

Walker flushed a bright shade of scarlet. "You need better protection around your fallout shelter," he muttered.

Dominic raised an eyebrow. "This shelter was meant to protect vampires from the Damned, not night bloods from vampires."

"It wouldn't have mattered how well-protected the walls were between us," Bex murmured to Walker silkily. "When I ask you to let me in, you always will. Nothing can prevent me from peeling your skull open like an orange rind and taking a big, juicy bite whenever and however often I want."

"Not helping, Bex," I muttered.

Walker whirled on me, his face beet red, either from embarrassment or rage—probably both. "With your super-enhanced ears, are you hearing this?" Walker asked, pointing at Bex accusingly. "We had a deal. We promised not to harm each other in any capacity unless in self-defense or in defense of each other."

Bex grinned. "I made no such deal."

"You may as well have broken your word outright and killed me yourself, leaving me with that monster," Walker said to me, ignoring Bex.

"And yet, here you stand, alive and well enough to complain us to death!" Bex rolled her eye.

Rafe and Neil stepped minutely closer, a low growl swelling in the small room.

"I apologize," I said, also ignoring Bex. "I wouldn't have abandoned you in the Underneath with Bex if I'd had a choice."

Walker shook his head, disgusted. "I should have known better than to take the word of a—"

"Dominic was dying," I interrupted before Walker could utter an insult he'd regret. "I left you in *possible* mortal danger to defend Dominic who was in *actual* mortal danger, which was well within the parameters of our agreement."

Walker laughed and the sound vibrated like a cheese grater against my skull. "I might have actually believed that except for the fact that you didn't come back for us. Want to enlighten me on that one, darlin'? When the *actual* mortal danger had passed, what prevented you from coming back to save the person you'd left in possible mortal danger?"

I struggled to hold his gaze and not glance at Dominic, my face blazing.

Walker nodded knowingly. "That's what I thought."

"Then why are you here, Walker?" I asked, exasperated. "Are we allies? Are we enemies? What do you want from me?"

Walker glanced at the kitchen where Ronnie was flipping pancakes and pursed his lips.

Ronnie, of course. A frustrated, scoffing noise scraped from the back of my throat. Even when Walker and I had been on good terms, our arguments had always somehow circled back to Ronnie.

"As riveting as this conversation is, we have more important business to discuss," Bex interrupted, and by the sharpness in her tone, like the precision of a well-aimed bullet, I could tell she was done being ignored. "You've certainly put me in quite the pickle, Lysander."

"And what pickle might that be?" Dominic asked drily. He knew exactly the pickle she was in—the same pickle we were all in—and that he'd personally placed the cucumber in the vinegar and sealed the bottle tight with his own two hands. But I could tell by the rhythmic flex of his jaw, despite his flippant words, that he was dreading this conversation as much as the rest of us.

"You and Cassidy have worked very diligently to regain my favor and rebuild our alliance. In my role as Master vampire of Erin, New York, I consider myself your ally. But in my role as Second Day Reaper to the Lord High Chancellor"—Bex tutted—"you've placed me in an impossible position."

Dominic stiffened behind me. I could actually hear his complete cessation of movement. "We have been allies for decades while you have avoided the Lord High Chancellor for just as long. The position I've placed you in is difficult, I'll grant you that, but I'd hoped not impossible. In fact, I'd think your position on the matter should be quite obvious."

"Are you deliberately sugar-coating what you've done because I know for a fact you're not that idealistic," Bex chided. Her expression was serene, almost teasing, but I wasn't fooled. Bex was a snake, waiting and eager to strike if provoked. I held my breath as she continued. "We may have been allies for decades, but he is the *Lord High Chancellor*."

"I'm not sugar-coating anything, *Beatrix*," Dominic purred, his voice in perfect decorum but his words and the use of her full name were a warning. "I know exactly what I've done, but I also know exactly where I stand. Being lifelong allies does not mean only backing one another in times of peace. It also means strapping on the armor for one another in times of war. This is that time."

"You knowingly transformed a potential Day Reaper, Lysander. The Lord High Chancellor will consider your actions an act of treason, and should I not carry out punishment, I could be charged with insubordination, at the least, if not outright treason!" Bex shook her head, all pretense of teasing forgotten. "What the fuck were you thinking?"

"I was thinking that Cassidy was dying, and between her certain death and potential charges of treason, I chose treason. Not that there was much of a choice at the time," he added drily. "As there isn't much of one now."

Bex sniffed. "You wanted Cassidy for yourself. Admit it."

"If you could go back to your own transformation, would you willingly submit to the Lord High Chancellor as your maker?"

Bex opened her mouth.

"Don't even try to deny it," Dominic scoffed. "Your centuries of living apart from him and avoiding your final transformation into a Day Reaper belie anything you might say now. You resent his rule. Admit it."

Bex snapped her mouth shut with an audible *click*.

"Cassidy, Ian Walker, and I saved you from painful, permanent imprisonment within the Underneath. Is that how you would repay my part in your rescue? A charge of treason?"

"You leave me no choice!" Bex hissed. "I could stay the Lord High Chancellor's hand when you at least put up a front of subservient obedience, but this"—Bex waved her hand in my direction—"this takes the fucking cake. Not even I can save you from his wrath now."

"When he finds out," Dominic murmured.

Bex narrowed her eye. "Excuse me?"

"When the Lord High Chancellor finds out about my insubordination, not even you will be able to save me from his wrath. But for now, he has not found out. And when he does, perhaps you did not find out until shortly before him. Or perhaps, circumstance being dire, you rescued him as soon as you were able after utilizing me and Cassidy and all other useful resources at your disposal to overthrow Jillian and free him. But until then…" Dominic shrugged. "Circumstances are dire, and another grave act of insubordination—Jillian's raging army of the Damned—must be addressed first. I think even the Lord High Chancellor would agree that stripping Jillian of her power, eradicating the Damned, and crowning the rightful Master vampire of New York City is our highest priority."

"I don't think the Lord High Chancellor would agree with anything you have to say, simply because you're the one saying it." Bex cocked her head and studied Dominic as if he were a specimen in a petri dish. It was a disconcerting look. "You saved me from the Underneath because we're allies, and you're calling on that bond now to secure my loyalty to you over my loyalty to the Chancellor?"

Dominic inclined his head deeply.

"I'm calling bullshit," Bex said.

Dominic blinked. "Excuse me?"

Bex pointed at Walker. "He is not my ally. Why did you really release me from the Underneath?"

I cursed under my breath. "I *knew* working with Walker was a bad idea."

Bex's eyes honed on me. "Something to add, my dear?"

"Yes," I said. "We all have our own motivations for what we do, but Walker's motivations don't detract from Dominic's. Dominic saved you out of loyalty. You can hear the truth of that ringing from his words, can't you?"

Bex cocked her head again, and suddenly I was the one in the petri dish. "And what are your motivations, Cassidy DiRocco? Have they changed since we last met, or are you still trying the keep the *Titanic* afloat?"

"The plan isn't about saving the ship. It's about saving the passengers," I said.

"And I suppose I play some vital role in that plan." Bex sighed dramatically.

I stared at her, gnashing my teeth.

Bex gestured with her hands for me to continue. "Come, come. Tell me the plan."

I opened my mouth and inhaled, using the extra seconds to find the words I needed to convince her. "You won't like what I'm about to ask of you, but it's nothing I'm not willing to do myself."

Bex laughed at that. "Considering everything you've willingly done yourself for the sake of others, I cringe to think of the possibilities." She waved a hand at my protest. "You've never been one to mince words. Just tell me the plan, and I'll tell you if I'm willing to participate."

I nodded reluctantly. "Dr. Susanna Chunn is developing weapons against the Damned and needs samples of our blood to further her research."

"Nothing you wouldn't do yourself," Bex murmured, "and nothing you haven't done before, if I remember correctly."

"At least she's requesting your permission," Dominic added, "and not distributing samples of your blood without your knowledge."

I flushed deeper.

"Dr. Chunn is developing weapons against the Damned using our blood," Bex repeated my words as if the shape and sound of them was a texture in her mouth. Considering our skewed senses, maybe they were. "Genius, that, considering we're the only species whose claws are capable of penetrating their hide."

"My thoughts exactly," I said. "There's merit to her theories, and I'd like to give her a chance to prove them."

"And you think these weapons that she develops will be only used against the Damned?" Bex's eyes sliced to Walker. "You don't think giving her our blood will give her everything she needs to develop weapons against Day Reapers?"

"She's our ally, and we—"

"And we are surrounded by enemies," Bex murmured.

"Dr. Chunn will continue her research whether we help her or not. She will create weapons, and when she does, I'd like to use them against the Damned. If we don't help her, we may not get to use them. In fact, we can almost guarantee they'll be used against us."

Bex narrowed her eye. "So either way, we're screwed."

"What I'm saying," I said firmly, "is that despite the fact that Dr. Chunn could use our blood against us, we need to trust that she won't. If we play on the same team now when she needs us, she will return the favor when we need her, because that's what allies do. They help each other and become a stronger force together than they were separately."

Bex raised her eyebrows, but for once she didn't have a ready comeback.

"*We* are allies," I continued, gesturing between the two of us, "and despite the fact that you could use Dominic's crimes of treason against us, I freed you from the Underneath anyway, trusting that you won't. We're on the same team here, Bex. Hell, I've held your heart in my hand and healed you with Dominic's blood. Some people might even call that friendship," I said. "And friends, real friends, don't betray each other, even if it's in their best interest to do so."

Bex considered me and my words for a long moment in silence. Eventually, she turned to Dominic.

"You play a dangerous game, Lysander."

"It's the only game anyone here is willing to play," Dominic said softly.

A sly smile curved her lips, baring a hint of fang. "Good thing it's a game we both play well."

Dominic inclined his head.

"So that's what a deal with the devil looks like." Walker shook his head. "Two devils. God help us all."

"Your pancakes are ready, Ian," Ronnie piped from the kitchen.

Walker glanced at Ronnie like he might regard smeared excrement on the bottom of his shoe. "I'm not hungry."

Ronnie blinked several times, first at Walker and then at the dozen pancakes on the plate she'd placed on the counter, as if the possibility of his lost appetite had never occurred to her. "Yes you are. You haven't eaten since arriving yesterday."

"I'm fine," he said stiffly.

"I can hear your stomach growling."

Silence, like a grenade, detonated the room with hostility.

"Fuck you and your vampire senses. I don't want your fucking pancakes."

Ronnie's blinking increased. She might be short-circuiting. "I don't have vampire senses. I can hear your stomach with my very human-hearing ears."

Walker made a rude, scoffing noise in the back of his throat, nearly identical to the noise I'd made at him only minutes before. "Whatever."

"You'll let all these pancakes go to waste out of stubbornness," Ronnie said, her voice disgusted.

"Someone else can eat them."

"No one else here eats solid food!"

My cell phone rang, thank God for small miracles.

"Sorry, I've got to take this," I said, digging it out of my pocket.

Dominic glanced askance at me and scowled. "Who is it?"

"Does it really matter?" I muttered.

"You can't just—"

But I'd already escaped back into the peace and solitude of the bedroom and shut the door, cutting off his words mid-sentence.

I answered the phone. "DiRocco here."

"It's Greta. How fast can you get to the morgue?"

"Why? What's happened?" My heart clenched on a bad thought. "Is Nathan all right?"

"Your brother's fine. He's helping Dr. Chunn in the lab."

"He's out of the cage?" I asked, surprised.

Greta let loose a very unladylike snort. "I'm not one for exercises in futility. Keeping him caged knowing he could have escaped and killed us if he'd been so inclined all along kind of defeats the purpose of caging him, wouldn't you say?"

"And he's helping Dr. Chunn?" I asked. I wasn't sure which revelation was more shocking.

"Much to Rowens's consternation, yes. And doing a damn fine job of it."

"Glad to hear it. So if not Nathan, what else hit the fan?"

"Nothing. We were just given a golden egg."

I raised my eyebrows. "Who the hell hands out golden eggs these days?"

"Seeing is believing, DiRocco," she said, throwing my favorite words back at me, "and you're going to shit your own golden fucking egg when you see this."

I laughed. "Okay. I'm on my way, G. Before you hang up, let me say hi to Nathan."

"Your sister says hi," Greta said, her voice suddenly muffled.

"Hi!" I heard from afar.

"There you go," Greta said, her voice solid again. "Anything else you have to say, say it in person. Get here pronto, *D*."

"But I—"

But I was talking to myself.

Chapter 15

Had Bex and I visited the morgue by ourselves like I'd intended, we could have traveled there from Dominic's underground bunker in minutes—the Damned be damned—but I'd failed to consider the fact that I wasn't a lone agent anymore. Where I went, Dominic would follow, and where he went, Rafe and Neil wanted to shadow, and where Bex went, Walker would stalk. Ronnie had a pile of dishes to clean and dozens of pancakes to dispose of, but I could tell by her longing looks that without domestic obligations, she would have tagged along in Walker's wake, no matter his rude, callous disregard. Sunset had come and gone by the time we'd agreed on who would join me at the morgue to further our investigation, who would help Rafe restock our blood supply, and who would play house with Ronnie.

But when Dominic, Bex, Walker, and I entered the morgue, I discovered that the tension between Walker and Ronnie and our little vampire family was apparently not the only bomb I'd have the pleasure of defusing. Greta took one look at Bex, in her svelte green-and-lace dress, waiting patiently for permission to cross the threshold, whipped her electric gaze on me, and snapped, "Who the hell are you dragging into this investigation now?"

"Detective Greta Wahl," I said, forcing my voice to remain professional despite the beating my skin was taking from the rubber band snaps of her frustration. Greta raised an eyebrow at my formal introduction. "I'd like to introduce you to Bex, Master vampire of Erin, New York, and Second Day Reaper to Lord High Chancellor Henry Lynell Horrace DeWhitt, Master vampire of London and Lord of all vampires." I turned to Bex, determined to keep the sarcasm from my voice. "Bex, I'm pleased to introduce you to my very good friend and the lead detective on this investigation, Detective Greta Wahl."

Bex grinned mischievously. "A pleasure to officially make your acquaintance, Detective."

"*This* is Bex?" Greta's lips thinned grimly. "Wonderful."

Both Dominic and Bex had fed from living, breathing humans on our way to this meeting, so they were once again glowing with health, strength, and model-perfect beauty. I'd refused their insistent offerings to share; my own driving, addiction-like thirst had been quenched by the bagged blood I'd swallowed to heal Dominic, so the pulse of a freshly sliced artery wasn't tempting enough for me to bridge that final chasm between my human life and my vampire existence. Besides, since basking in sunlight and completing my transformation into a Day Reaper, I was looking pretty glowing, too, if I did say so myself. My eyes had reverted back to their human appearance, and my skin had plumped and blushed into smooth perfection. Not one blackhead or wrinkle marred my pores. My hair, typically pin-straight from root to tip, now had some body to it, curling silkily at the tips as if I'd styled it that way.

But best of all, better than my enhanced looks and perhaps even better than my restored hip, was the ability to sheath my talons into nails. My ears were rounded at their tips. My fangs were no longer elongated, and although still razor-tipped, they fit neatly tucked behind my lips. My flattened nose, prominent brow, and back-hinged knees had all reverted to their human-like form. It was an illusion, the same illusion I'd been accusing Dominic of wielding against me for weeks, but one I was grateful for because Greta hadn't pulled her gun on me this time when I'd entered the room. Maybe the shock of seeing me as a vampire for the first time had waned, but I'd be a fool not to acknowledge that my human mask likely had something to do with her civility as well.

"May I have permission to enter, Detective Wahl?" Bex asked, her voice the epitome of gentle breeding. She wielded that soft, Southern twang as effectively as she did her beauty, a weapon as much as a shield.

Greta didn't acknowledge Bex's request. Her attention stayed riveted on me. "I don't care if she's God's right hand; I'm not inviting her into this investigation."

I blinked, taken aback. "This was our plan. Dr. Chunn needs a sample of Bex's blood to compare with mine while developing her weapons against the Damned." I raised my eyebrows. "Did that plan change?"

"Yep, it changed three seconds ago. You can tell your Master vampire and Second to the Lord of all Monsters to leave before I *make* her leave."

Bex leaned against the outside of the doorframe. "Such threats even after I saved your life," she tutted.

I glanced at Dominic. "I'm sensing some history here."

"Undoubtedly, a keen observation," Dominic murmured.

"Where's the trust, Detective Greta Wahl?" Bex's voice might have sounded like a caress, but I knew better. It was a vise around Greta throat, and she was threatening to squeeze.

"You haven't earned it," Greta said tightly.

"But I have," I interjected. "When I vouched for Meredith, you were reluctant to welcome her into this investigation, but since then, Meredith's photography and technical skills have furthered our case, haven't they?"

"Meredith has become an invaluable member of our investigative team," Greta conceded hesitantly.

The blast of an organ hitting a high C echoed from the lab—undoubtedly the sound of Meredith's glow from Greta's praise.

"I'm asking you to do the same for Bex," I said, determinedly ignoring the organ and the resulting jackhammer inside my brain.

Greta stared at me like I'd asked her to sacrifice her firstborn. "I was reluctant to allow Meredith on this investigation because she didn't have any experience working with the bureau in an investigative capacity, but at least she wasn't one of the creatures responsible for these crimes."

"Neither is Bex," I pointed out.

"She's a vampire!" Greta accused.

"So am I."

Greta shook her head. "That's different. I've known you for years, and we've worked dozens upon dozens of cases together. Human or vampire, I trust you with my life." She pointed at Bex with the whole of her hand, and the sharp sting of Greta's disapproval whipped my skin raw. "She was there the night of the raid. She entranced my team and sabotaged everything. I don't trust *her*."

"But you trust me, and I vouch for her," I insisted. Never mind the fact that the raid had been a terrible idea and doomed from the start, with or without Bex and the other Day Reapers' interference. Highlighting that point would only rub salt in the wound.

Greta eyed me and then Bex, stripping us with her human regard better and more thoroughly than some vampires. I recognized the look in her eyes; I'd seen it right before she butterfly-filleted a person in half during interrogation. "What can you offer this investigation that we don't already have?" she asked Bex directly.

Bex snorted. "What do you and this investigation really have without me? You cannot defend against the Chancellor, and I, as his Second and a Day Reaper, can," Bex said, the slash of her grin somehow weary. "You need me."

"If it hadn't been for you and all the rest of your Day Reaper posse interrupting my raid, we would have stopped the Damned and Jillian, once and for all," Greta insisted.

"You and your team were ill-equipped, unprepared, and outnumbered," Bex said, straightening from the doorframe and ticking the poor qualities of Greta's team on her fingers. "Me and *my posse* saved you that night at the risk of our lives and at the expense of our freedom. If that's not proof enough of my loyalty and intentions, I don't know what is."

Greta regarded Bex for a long moment.

"Cassidy thinks very highly of you and this investigation," Bex continued, "and since I think very highly of her, I'm willing to set aside my usual means of solving such problems in favor of hers. I will help this investigation and together, we will stop Jillian and her army of the Damned," Bex said vehemently. As if realizing the slip in her cucumber-cool demeanor, she cleared her throat and eased her shoulder casually back against the doorframe. "Or you can deny me entrance to this room and your investigation, and I'll revert to my preferred means of solving such problems."

"As I recall, your preferred means failed last week," Greta reminded her civilly.

"As I recall, your raid impeded my efforts," Bex quipped, just as civilly.

"Which is why I propose that we combine our efforts and work together rather than against each other," I interjected. "We have a common enemy and a common goal. Is it too much to ask that we set aside the rest in favor of the big picture? Who cares who's a vampire or a Day Reaper or a human or a night blood? Jillian and her Damned are terrorizing New York City, and it doesn't matter who we are—if we don't stop her, we'll all die."

"And you?" Greta asked, locking eyes with Walker in an obvious last ditch effort to align herself with someone sane. "Where do you stand on all of this?"

"Using Bex's blood to help Dr. Chunn develop weapons against the Damned was a good plan," he said. "I'm all for sticking to the plan."

Greta's lips puckered as if she'd taken a bite into something unpalatably sour, but when she looked back at me, her gaze was resigned. "I hold you responsible for her."

I nodded. "Of course."

Bex snorted delicately.

"If she betrays us or this investigation, it's your betrayal. This could break our friendship. Her actions are your actions. Her words are your words. Her—"

I held up my hand. "I get the point. If Bex burns us, I'm toast."

Greta nodded, her lips twitching upward into a reluctant smile. "I'd never put it quite like that, but yes."

"I vouch for her, G. I'm not going back on my word now. We might look like monsters, but we're your friends, and on this case, it doesn't matter who's a vampire, night blood, or human; we need as many friends as we can get."

"We'll see," Greta said noncommittally. She faced Bex. "Bex, you may enter this room."

"A dream come true." Bex swept into the room.

"And everyone can follow me," Greta said, ignoring Bex and her sarcasm. "We found something interesting and, frankly, unheard of for this case."

I raised my eyebrows. "A golden egg?"

"Yes." Greta's lips curved into a rare, hundred-watt smile. "We found a witness."

Chapter 16

Since discovering the existence of vampires, the only people I could share my fears, questions, and experiences with were other night bloods, and for the first several weeks of that time when I'd had the most fears and questions, Walker had been the only night blood I'd known. Everyone else—my boss, my neighbors, even Meredith, my best friend—were susceptible to being entranced, essentially having their memories wiped, and if they had a sticky memory, like Greta, they were susceptible to much worse. Until recently, Dominic and his vampires would resort to just about anything, even murder, to keep their existence a secret and protect the coven. Before the Damned had attacked New York City, I would have said that no one except other night bloods knew about the existence of vampires. I'd have bet my life on it.

And as usual, I'd have been dead wrong.

I'd searched far and wide and failed to find a witness to corroborate my story, *Vampires Bite in the Big Apple*, but here in front of me was a young woman, only a few years younger than myself, who claimed to know about the existence of vampires long before the Damned had attacked.

And she wasn't a night blood.

Inside the makeshift interrogation room Greta and her team had created at the back of the morgue, Supervisory Special Agent Harold Rowens was sitting beside our witness. Their chairs were close enough that he could lean against the chrome slab being used as a table and still squeeze her soft shoulder with his big, beefy hand. I'd been interrogated by Rowens in the past, and although he'd employed bad cop on me, his good cop was probably just as effective.

"Let me talk to her," I said.

Greta raised her eyebrows, amused. "You think you can grill her better than Rowens? Don't let him hear you say that."

"I said no such thing," I replied. "One of Rowens's specialties is interrogation, but of the two of us, I'm intimately more familiar with the inner workings of vampires in Dominic's coven. Leaving a witness," I said, pointing to the woman, "is simply not done."

Dominic shook his head. He hadn't stopped staring at the woman with his narrowed, creepy, otherworldly eyes since walking into the viewing section of the makeshift interrogation rooms. "Unbelievable."

Bex sniffed. "Finding a leak always is."

"I *need* to talk to her," I insisted.

Greta eyed me critically. "It's a good thing, then, that she specifically asked for you."

I blinked. "She what?"

"She asked to speak to you and has refused to divulge more information, names, or details until she sees you," Greta said, watching my reaction.

I shook my head, stunned. "She asked for me by name?"

Greta nodded.

"I don't even know her. I've never seen the woman in my life, before today."

My words or reaction must have passed some gut-check test because Greta released me from scrutiny and sighed, shifting her gaze back to the woman. Our witness.

Unbelievable, indeed.

"Whoever she is, she certainly knows you."

"Where did you find her?" Dominic asked.

"We didn't," Greta said grimly. She knocked on the window with two quick raps. "She found us."

Rowens stood, squeezing the woman's shoulder one last time in farewell before exiting the room. He waited until the door was firmly shut behind him before speaking. "She's padlocked, that one. Maybe DiRocco will have better luck," he said, nodding at me. "Glad you could make it."

I returned his nod. "Wouldn't miss it. What did you get from her so far?"

Rowens swiped a hand down his face, pulling down the taut lines of his craggy cheeks. "Not much, and yet, more than we've ever had before from a witness on this case. She's the wife of a vampire in your coven—"

"*Wife*?" Dominic blurted, his eyes finally shifting from the woman to blast Rowens.

Rowens continued, unperturbed by Dominic's interruption. "—and she is following her husband's instructions should he ever go missing for an excess of seven days: speaking to the police regarding the attacks and asking to give her statement to the reporter, Cassidy DiRocco." Rowens's eyes landed heavily on me with the same look Greta had given me just moments ago.

I lifted my palms to show my innocence. "I've never heard of or seen this woman before today." I had the feeling I'd be saying that a lot in my near future. "What's her name?"

"Mackenzie Clark," Rowens said, glancing back through the one-way window at the woman. "Tough as nails, that girl. Good luck."

She'd have to be tough, being a human wife to a vampire, I thought, but I kept my opinions to myself. Dominic looked on the verge of a meltdown without my snarky comments pushing him over the edge.

I entered the interrogation room unimpeded by its threshold because the woman had already invited me in by name, but obviously, I wasn't the person she'd been expecting. Her already large, brown, doe-eyes widened as they swept me head to toe, and her plump, shapely mouth dropped open before she could hide her reaction. Even if she had, though, she couldn't hide the electric snap of her shock. The sound was even more telling than her facial expression, but between the two, I knew without a doubt that something was wrong.

I sat across from her at the table and smiled, taking care to hide my fangs. "Mackenzie Clark, you have me at a disadvantage. You seem well acquainted with me, but I'm not at all acquainted with you."

Her mouth snapped closed. Her eyes narrowed defiantly, and I wouldn't have known she felt anything except shock and anger from her outward appearance. But I could smell the cinnamon spice of her fear permeate the room and feel the microscopic tremor in her dark, shoulder-length curls.

"Obviously, I'm not as acquainted with you as I'd thought," she said warily. "I didn't know Lysander had transformed you yet."

I tried not to gape, unsure which was more disturbing: that she could discern a human from vampire so easily when I clearly looked human—or at least, more human than I'd looked lately—or that she knew our big, bad secret. "You know Lysander?" I asked, striving for nonchalance.

"Former Master vampire of New York City?" Mackenzie crossed her arms. "I know *of* him, but before you sic him on me and mind-fuck my brain numb, I need your help. Sevris said you're the one person I can trust."

I started, failing to hide my own shock. "You know Sevris, too?"

"Of course I know Sevris," Mackenzie said, looking greatly aggrieved by my ignorance. "He's my husband."

I cleared my throat. "Right. Why don't we start from the beginning? How—"

"We don't have time to rehash my life story. I haven't seen Sevris in seven days, and I need your help to find him. Now, before it's too late." Mackenzie swallowed, tamping down a break in her otherwise calm composure. "We might already be too late for the rest of them."

"Too late for the rest of who?" I asked cautiously.

"All the other missing vampires and night bloods," Mackenzie said.

She took a deep breath, and I could actually hear the elevated beat of her pulse gradually decrease and become steady. It took a moment and more effort than I'd comfortably admit, but eventually, I refocused my attention back to what she was saying.

"The others didn't want me to come here, but really, what other choice did we have but to sit around and wait, and for what? Wait to die? Wait to become Damned? Fuck that and fuck them. Sevris said I could trust you, and there's no one in the world I trust more than Sevris." She seemed to shore up under the reminder of her trust in him; she looked me square in the eyes when she said, "Sevris isn't the only vampire who's gone missing, and I'm not the only loved one who needs help finding them. Even if that means taking down Jillian once and for all."

"You know Jillian?" I asked. Really, I shouldn't even be shocked by the vampires she knew at this point—she obviously knew everyone—but my jaw dropped in spite of myself.

"Of course," Mackenzie said, but wary sorrow had replaced the earlier frustration in her tone. "She was supposed to lead the uprising against Lysander and free us all from the confines of his rule. She was supposed to release Sevris and all the others from living in secrecy and in fear of their loved ones, husbands, and wives—like me—being discovered and wiped from existence. She was supposed to save us." Mackenzie cleared her throat, but her voice was still ragged when she said, "Sevris thought an uprising might be possible, that we might not have to live and love in secret anymore, but then everything went so wrong so quickly. I don't think even Sevris would condone what she's done—not that I can ask him. Because he's *missing*."

The interrogation room door exploded inward, and Dominic stood outside its threshold, on the verge of a full transformation. His ears were high and pointed, his nose flat and flared at its tips, his fangs and talons elongated to lethal lengths, and his forehead thickened to a menacing, protruding frown.

He stood outside the doorway, growling.

Mackenzie's eyes darted to mine, and the scorching accusation in her gaze warred with the high trill of her fear. I resisted the urge to plug my ears. "Sevris said I could trust you!"

"You can," I said, and to prove my point, I stood and stepped in front of Mackenzie to block Dominic's direct line of sight. "Dominic, stand down."

"Invite me in," he growled.

I shook my head. "Not until you calm down."

"Calm down?" Dominic's voice was grating, like gravel scraping over glass. "I thought Sevris was one of my most loyal vampires. I entrusted him with the knowledge of my weakness during the Leveling. I depended on his strength and power." Dominic cursed vehemently. "I allowed him to heal you!"

"And he did! He didn't betray you, he just"—I bit my lip, glancing at Mackenzie's rage-filled face—"didn't want to live in secret and darkness anymore. Can you blame him?"

"Can I blame Jillian for all she's done?" Dominic asked bitterly. "After all, that's all she ever wanted, as well."

I shook my head. "Jillian took the coven from you and killed dozens of people to do it. Sevris was never interested in power. To be honest, he didn't seem to care who took control of the coven as long as he survived the transition."

"And that's why I'm here," Mackenzie interjected from behind me. "I'm not sure that he survived."

I glanced at her over my shoulder. "You mentioned that there were other people concerned for their loved ones, too. Other humans?"

Mackenzie crossed her arms. "Sevris said I could trust you, no one else." She glanced pointedly at Dominic.

Dominic's expression softened. His forehead smoothed, his ears rounded, and when he spoke, he made a concerted effort not to growl. "I am Sevris's Master and as concerned about his disappearance as you are. You can trust me as well."

"Sevris's instructions were very clear, as clear as your stance on human memories. He said you wouldn't allow me to keep my memory of him, that if you discovered he'd allowed me to keep my memories of the existence of vampires, you'd not only destroy my memories and our love, you'd kill him, too." Mackenzie tilted her head. "Does that sound like a man I can trust to you?"

I winced, unexpectedly feeling the physical cut of her doubt, and waited on Dominic's reply. Everything Mackenzie said was true, and I felt for her. I'd fought for the same thing on Meredith's behalf every time she came too close to discovering the truth. I'd fought for my memories, too, when I'd been vulnerable to being entranced.

Dominic took a moment to answer, his jaw clicking and flexing as he ground his teeth in silence, but when he did speak, his voice was still carefully moderate, his anger tightly leashed. "No, that doesn't sound like someone you could trust. Had we met last week, I would have done exactly as you have described."

I glanced at him sharply. "You wouldn't have killed Sevris," I denied.

Dominic shrugged. "Perhaps not, but we were at war. Either he was with me or against me, and allowing a human to keep her memory of him, me, you, Jillian, and the existence of our coven was certainly not *with* me." Dominic met Mackenzie's gaze. "By keeping you as his wife, Sevris took an unnecessary risk and went against everything I stand for and everything I'd promised the Council under oath as Master. I'd assured them secrecy and silence, and most of all, after Jillian's rebellion, I'd assured them of my coven's obedience." He waved a hand to encompass Mackenzie. "And yet here you are, the very proof of my coven's defiance."

Mackenzie frowned. "How is this convincing me to trust you?"

"As I said, last week, I would have wiped your memory and punished Sevris accordingly for his disloyalty, but in that time, I, too, have taken an unnecessary risk that defied the Council." Dominic met my eyes and his fully softened, the anger not just hidden but completely extinguished. "I transformed my dear Cassidy DiRocco into a vampire, knowing that she would become a Day Reaper, knowing that her transformation was, by right, the Lord High Chancellor's to perform."

I snorted. "I'd hardly call saving us from certain death unnecessary."

"After a lifetime of service and obedience to the Council, enforcing their laws on pain of death and willing to die myself to protect their rule, I defied them, the Day Reapers, and my own reign by transforming you," he said, his eyes flashing sharply.

"I wasn't trying to diminish what you did." I waffled my hands between the two of them. "Carry on."

Dominic smirked slightly, but his face was once again composed when he turned to Mackenzie. "Last week, I was not a person you could trust, but the man who stands before you now is no longer interested in blindly enforcing the Council's laws or dying for their cause. Thanks to Cassidy, I can see the big picture now, and we have a cause far greater and more immediate than exacting punishment on you for simply loving one of my vampires. I love Sevris, too, and I vow that if you help us, we will find him." Dominic's eyes took on a near maniacal glow. "We will find them all."

Mackenzie didn't look convinced. In fact, for the first time since we started talking to her, she hesitated. "H-how can *I* help?" she asked on a half laugh and glanced at me. "I came here for *your* help."

I smiled, feeling back on solid ground. "And I will help, but to do so, I need to know about the other people you mentioned. You know other humans with vampire loved ones?"

She pursed her lips, but after a moment of pregnant silence, she finally, reluctantly nodded. "Some are like Sevris, with human families who haven't heard from or seen them since the Leveling."

Jesus, she even knew about the Leveling, I thought grimly.

"Others are friends and family of night bloods," she continued, "who haven't seen their brother or mother or cousin since the Leveling. It's as if they've all just vanished into thin air."

Dominic's lips compressed into a thin, unyielding line. "They certainly haven't vanished."

"What do you mean?" she asked.

Maybe she doesn't know everything. I winced. Of everything she did know, it figured the one thing we'd have to break to her was the worst news of all.

"We're going to find Sevris," I said, "but I need you to tell everyone who's missing a loved one to come here and file a missing-persons report."

Dominic raised his eyebrows incredulously.

Mackenzie scowled. "You want them to fill out paperwork? People are dying out there!"

The door opened behind me, and Greta strode in, paperwork and pen in hand, beaming. I hadn't seen her this delighted in ages, maybe ever, and it occurred to me how the years of solving crime and catching murderers had hardened her soft features. "Brilliant, DiRocco. Really, fucking brilliant," she murmured.

Mackenzie glanced at Greta and then her gaze hardened back on me. "Seriously?" Her frustration was abrasive, like sandpaper against my eyeballs. "Sevris was wrong about you. I thought you'd *do* something." She pushed back from the table and stood. "Paperwork," she scoffed.

I fought to not rub my eyelids or scream—or both—and react like a normal person to her frustration. She had a right to her emotions, I reminded myself, and my eyes were not being rubbed raw. They only felt like they were.

"This isn't about the paperwork," I said carefully. "There's something you don't understand, something you don't want to hear, but I'm about to tell you anyway because it's the truth. And if there's one thing I think you came here for besides help for Sevris, it's the truth."

She crossed her arms. "I'm listening."

"You might want to sit down."

She narrowed her eyes. "I'm three seconds away from ditching you, so I'll stand if I please, thank you."

I could physically stop her from leaving, but I knew I wouldn't have to. "The missing night bloods didn't just vanish into thin air. Jillian transformed them, but because she wasn't a Master vampire, the transformation didn't work; they became Damned." I waited a moment for that to sink in. "The Damned vampires are our missing night bloods."

She sat back down, hard.

"Oh my God," she said, covering her mouth with her hand. "Are you sure?"

I nodded. "Positive. My brother was one of them."

She blinked. "Was?"

"I transformed him back."

Greta snorted under her breath. "Kind of."

I frowned. "He's not a rampaging, mindless, murdering zombie-vampire anymore. I count that as a win."

"He still eats raw meat for breakfast," Greta pointed out.

"But he doesn't murder people to obtain said meat," I argued. "Again, win."

"Stop. Just stop!" Mackenzie said, breathlessly. "Your brother was a night blood that Jillian turned into one of her Damned? And you transformed him back into a night blood?"

"Yes," I said. I glanced at Greta and added reluctantly, "kind of."

"How?" she asked. Suddenly, and for the first time since arriving, Mackenzie looked hopeful.

"It's complicated," I hedged.

"But if you transformed your brother back from being Damned, then there's a chance you can transform back all the rest?"

Dominic's lips thinned into an unyielding, grim line, and I feared I knew exactly what he was thinking—the same thing I was thinking. I could remember the horror of saving Nathan last month like it was yesterday. I could still smell the putrid stink of his breath as he'd dismembered Jeremy's uncle limb from limb. I could still see Dominic's cheek, split to the bone, the skin loose and dangling by threads as he and Bex and Rene had fought to within an inch of their lives to subdue my brother. Myself and Jillian included, we'd been five against one, and we'd nearly died attempting to retransform Nathan. Saving one Damned had been nearly impossible; now that we were outnumbered, how could we possibly confront dozens upon dozens of them and ensure that everyone survived?

But the alternative was just as unthinkable: if we couldn't find a way to save them, we'd need to form a plan to eradicate them.

"Maybe," I said, finally answering Mackenzie's question, "but that's where the missing-persons reports come in. I was only able to transform my brother back into a night blood using my own blood. If we hope to have any chance of saving the Damned, we're going to need every loved one out there willing to bleed to get them back."

Greta nodded, adding, "If people come in person to file missing-persons reports, I can interview and organize their cases, and hopefully, determine who are missing vampires, who are Damned night bloods, and who are just"—Greta hesitated with a quick glance at Mackenzie—"missing."

I glanced up at Dominic, and I could read his wary, hopeless expression well enough that I didn't need mind-reading abilities to know his thoughts: if Sevris was part of the rebellion against him, maybe he'd deliberately gone missing. Maybe he was right where he wanted to be.

"I'll encourage everyone to come here and file missing-persons reports," Mackenzie said softly, "but I can't guarantee that they'll listen. Not everyone knows you, and the few who know of you think that you're Lysander's right hand. I came here alone today and not by choice: Everyone else is terrified that he will entrance them and erase the memories of their loved ones from their minds."

Dominic cursed under his breath.

"What if you had proof of Dominic's intentions and of our plan to transform the Damned back into night bloods?" I asked. "Would that help convince them?"

"Well, yeah, that would obviously help," Mackenzie said, "but your reputation precedes you. I don't know how you could possibly change that."

"How many Damned vampires do you think read the newspaper?" I asked.

"None. They can't read," Dominic said drily. "But Jillian might be tuned into the media."

Greta shook her head. "A paper hasn't been released in Brooklyn for eight days, not since the Damned attacked and the entire city went on lockdown. If she's plugged into the news, I doubt she's worried about local coverage."

"And what's the national conversation?" I asked. From what Rowens had already confided, however, I had my suspicions.

"Doom and gloom," Greta confirmed. "If the next wave of military are slaughtered like the last, I can't imagine what the government might do to prevent the Damned from expanding their hunting grounds."

I could imagine exactly what the government would do: the only thing they'd have left to do if ground troops failed again: with the bridges and tunnels already blocked, an air attack would be the next weapon they pulled from their arsenal. Little did they know that bombing New York City was the one, surefire way to kill everyone except the Damned. Like *Night of the Living Dead,* the Damned would rise from the rubble—and without us, unstoppable—and spread their hunting ground, like locusts, outward from New York City in search of a new food source.

Unless we could give the government a reason to reconsider their options and the people of New York City a reason to hold onto hope.

"I think it's time we tell our side of the story," I said. I couldn't help but grin even while facing the grim inevitability of our reality. It was time. It was finally time.

"Cassidy—" Dominic began, shaking his head.

"Who will stop us now, Dominic, the Damned? Who do we have left to fear, the Day Reapers and Lord High Henry's retribution?"

Dominic winced.

"The public knows about the monsters who rule the night, slaughter indiscriminately, and hunt human hearts," I argued, "but they don't know anything about the creatures fighting against them. We might live in darkness, but it's time we shed light on the truth of our existence and where we stand. Past time."

"And where is that?" Dominic asked, raising an eyebrow. "Where do we stand?"

I crossed my arms. "I know exactly where I stand, where I've always stood: protecting New York City and her people. Where the hell do *you* stand?"

Dominic's loyalties had never been a mystery: his life, his entire existence, was dedicated to his coven and the Council. But the Day Reapers were no longer in a position to enforce Council law, and Dominic was no longer in power. We needed to make a stand, now, while we still had the chance to save the scraps of New York City and piece her back together, before the Damned could completely tear her apart or the government, in a last-ditch effort to save us, destroyed us.

"Where do you stand, Dominic?" I whispered again when it was clear he didn't have a ready answer.

Mackenzie and Greta's eyes had settled on Dominic after watching the volley of our exchange, and I could feel the burn of many gazes, literally. I couldn't see Walker, Rowens, Bex, Meredith, or Dr. Chunn watching us through the one-way mirror, but the heat of their focused eyes was scorching.

"It's so easy for you; nothing has changed," Dominic whispered.

I gaped. "Nothing has changed for me?" I spread my arms out, my lethal, silver talons elongating elegantly. "Nothing?"

He grinned. "Your physical changes are undeniable, but your moral stance as a revealer of truth, as a beacon to shine light on the darkness, as a guiding hand and protector of this city—those facets of yourself are irrefutably constant. I, on the other hand, despite the constancy of my physical form, am the one who must truly transform."

"Seriously?" I asked. "You're cranky because I'm still a reporter and you're not Master vampire of New York City for a week?"

"Answer the question, Lysander," Greta said, her voice low, and for all she was a weak, insignificant human, dangerous. "Are you with us or against us?"

Mackenzie's eyes widened.

My useless, non-beating heart contracted painfully in my chest.

Dominic's gaze locked with mine. "I'm with you, Cassidy. Wherever you stand, I stand with you."

The electric thrill of his words speared my heart.

"Meaning?" Greta asked.

I smiled, wide and uncaring of the flash of my fangs. "We're in this together, G. All of us—vampires, humans, Day Reapers, whatever the hell my brother is, and all—we're your team."

"This is touching and all," Mackenzie interrupted, "but your unfailing declaration of loyalty to each other doesn't change the fact that there's a reason why a newspaper hasn't been published in eight days. The city's a ghost town. Everyone is either dead, dying, or hiding, and no one in their right mind would risk life and limb just to print a damn newspaper article."

I could hear the light burst of Meredith's laugh even through the makeshift interrogation room wall, and damn it, despite our situation and the complete destruction of New York City, I couldn't help but laugh too. "Let me worry about finding someone crazy enough to care about printing a post-apocalyptic newspaper article."

Chapter 17

"I can't print that article, DiRocco. Have you lost your mind along with your humanity?" Carter bellowed. His words and the underlying bass drumbeat of his anger pounded a double-jackhammer rhythm into my already aching head.

Carter Bellissimo, editor in chief of the *Sun Accord* and my prickly boss, scowled at the pages I'd tossed on his desk, his thick eyebrows nearly merging into one, disapproving bush over his eyes as he read the headline: *Vampires Bite in the Big Apple*. I supposed, considering the *Sun Accord* no longer had a staff and the paper hadn't gone to print in eight days, that Carter wasn't my boss at the moment, but standing in his office defending my work, like old times, I could imagine a full bullpen behind us. Any other day at this bright morning hour, Meredith would be at her cube, craning over the dividers to gauge Carter's reaction to our latest stunt. Other reporters and photographers would be making mad dashes from their computers and out the door to follow leads, talking on their phones to contacts and witnesses, and doing whatever needed doing to make deadline.

Today, however, the building was a ghost town. The bullpen was deserted and Meredith was at the lab, helping Dr. Chunn with her research instead of helping me convince Carter to go to print. Meredith was still on our team, I reminded myself, even if she wasn't my partner anymore. I tried to feel buoyed that I hadn't lost her entirely—she was alive and healthy at least—but we hadn't talked since my transformation, not really. She hadn't said that she was happy to see *me* alive and healthy. She hadn't embraced me, like I longed to embrace her, and I hadn't felt anything besides caution, hesitation, and fear when she'd declined my request to come with me to confront Carter.

Maybe her silence was more telling than anything she could say. Maybe my transformation had changed more than just my person and had irrevocably altered my relationship with Meredith.

Maybe Meredith wasn't my best friend anymore.

Carter looked up, transferring his frown from my article to me. No matter my transformation or his empty bullpen, Carter obviously still considered himself my boss.

I jabbed my finger at the article, moving it subtly closer to him. "Questions of humanity aside, I'm still me, and this article is dynamite."

"Yeah, dynamite in my closed fist. No thank you, DiRocco." Carter leaned back in his chair, creating more physical distance between him and the article, and if I was honest, between him and me.

I raised my hand to indicate the empty cubes through the floor-to-ceiling windows behind us, ignoring his wince at my too-fast movements. "Why? Because you have so many other, more compelling stories to choose from this week?" I snapped.

"Don't," Carter said, his voice brooking no argument. "You don't get to be flippant about the destruction of New York City. Your friends killed my reporters. They killed my photographers, my contacts, and my printers. They killed my livelihood, and you"—he said, his finger trembling as he pointed at me—"they killed you, too, I think."

My heart bottomed out even as my anger skyrocketed. "*They* are not my friends. Did you even read my article?" I snapped. "The monsters who destroyed New York City are the Damned, not the vampires. One vampire is responsible for transforming the night bloods into the Damned. One. And we need to take her down."

Carter nodded. "Yeah, Jillian Allister. So you've said."

I blinked, stunned. Carter had accused me of many things throughout the years, most of it true, but never in all my eight years writing for him—first as an intern and then as a crime reporter—had he ever accused me of lying, sans that one animal-attack article. But that accusation could hardly count, considering he'd been entranced.

"Excuse me?" I asked.

"Where's Meredith? Does she have your back on this?" Carter asked.

I suppressed a wince at the mention of Meredith. "Of course," I said. "She wants to take down Jillian as badly as I do. I've got Greta's loving consent and the full support of the ME's office backing me. This article is going to print."

"Not in the *Sun Accord*, it isn't," Carter said stubbornly.

"What do you need from me to prove it to you?" I asked, dumbfounded. "You want to see the scientific proof for yourself? I'll bring you to Dr. Chunn's lab. You want to see someone transform from a man into the Damned? I'll introduce you to my brother. You want to see Greta in person, so she can vouch for me that I'm not the murdering psycho responsible for the collapse of Brooklyn?"

Carter shook his head sadly. "I know you're not responsible for all this, DiRocco. You don't need anyone to vouch for your character, not to me anyway. You know that."

"No, I don't know that," I said, my voice high and desperate and somehow still growling. I couldn't prevent the growl any more than I could prevent my throat from constricting and my eyes from burning with unshed tears. I took a second to regain control of my emotions, but everything was so new and overwhelming and uncertain, something had to give. The tears crested, and when I blinked, they poured down my cheeks. "If Meredith came to you instead of me, would you consent to printing the article?"

"It's not about that," Carter grumbled.

I shook my head. "If it's public opinion you're worried about, I think that ship has sailed. The citizens of New York City were completely clueless that vampires even existed before being attacked by seven-foot-tall, ravenous, heart-eating monsters. People want answers—they want the truth—and damn it, no matter how fantastic, this article gives them that."

"I know," Carter said, his voice still low and grumbling.

I made a rude noise in the back of my throat, punctuated by the clicking rattle of my growl. "If it's not me and not public opinion that's holding you back, than what the hell's your problem?"

"I was one of the people who were completely clueless!" he shouted.

The underlying bass drumbeat I'd mistaken for anger suddenly detonated. Carter's fury, like a landmine, blasted my senses: the smell of char seared my nostrils, the booming crash of thunder ruptured my eardrums, and the bitter taste of tar coated the back of my tongue. I stood and blinked stupidly at him in the face of his rage, unable to react rationally while my senses were being battered. Although his rage was real, I reminded myself that the char and thunder and nauseating taste of tar were not, but that didn't stop me from gagging.

"Through the glass windows of this office building, I watched as a stampede of those animals flooded the streets. I witnessed them tear people limb from limb, puncturing their chests and eating their hearts, and I knew on sight that those monsters were your story." He shook his head at me, looking betrayed. "And you hadn't warned me."

I swallowed. "I didn't—"

"You knew," Carter spat, his voice so angry and ugly, I flinched in the face of it. "Don't you dare fucking deny that you knew."

"What was I supposed to say?" I shouted. "You flew off the handle when I wrote about animal attacks in Brooklyn. You wouldn't have supported an article about vampires and night bloods and the Damned."

"I didn't expect you to write about it. I expected you to tell me about it!" Carter slapped his desk with the flat of his hand, swiping the pages of my article onto the floor. "I told you to come to me if you were in over your head. I'd have done everything in my power to help you," he said.

"You couldn't have helped me. You—"

"But you didn't come to me. Again and again, you landed in the hospital, hurt on the job, under my watch, but you always managed to survive. You always managed to find and expose the truth, so I looked the other way." Carter shook his head, his expression anguished. "Why didn't you come to me for help?"

"There was nothing you could have done. I—"

"Just look at you, DiRocco!"

I pursed my lips and looked away, unable to meet his gaze. I wasn't ashamed of myself, of what I'd become to survive, but I couldn't hold his gaze while he looked at me like I was one of the monsters.

"You knew the truth about those murders and the existence of those creatures, and you didn't tell me. You let me sit up here in my glass-and-chrome office and watch as the city streets washed red."

"I'm sorry," I whispered, picking up the tossed sheets of my article. "I was scared. I didn't think anyone would believe me without corroboration, so I was building the case and gathering evidence and writing my story, *this* story"—I said, shaking the pages at him—"to prove to you that creatures beyond our imagining exist right here in Brooklyn. But then everything spun out of control so quickly, and I—" My hands fell at my sides, beyond words. "I'm so sorry."

Carter pursed his lips, the vertical lines bracketing his mouth cutting as deep as his disapproval as he eyed the papers in my hand. "That's *the* story? The one you nearly killed yourself to write?"

"Yes," I said. "It's the biggest story of my entire life."

"That's what you never understood, DiRocco," Carter said sadly. "No matter how big the story, it was never worth your life."

I stared at him, shocked. "Of everyone I know, I thought you of all people would understand. Of course it's worth my life. It's worth both our lives, because it's one step closer to saving all their lives," I gestured at the cityscape behind me, which was vaguely anticlimactic because the city looked just as deserted as the bullpen, but I knew otherwise. "People are out there, hiding from the Damned, waiting for someone to rise up and do something about it."

"Waiting to die," Carter grumbled.

"No," I said, slapping the paper back on his desk. "You are going to find your contacts at the printer and convince them to risk coming out of hiding to print this article and distribute it. I want everyone to know exactly what's going on in this city. They're going to know how they can help and where they can get help. I'm rising up, damn it, and so are you, and everyone who survived is going to do something about it, because in the big picture, taking down Jillian is worth all our lives."

Carter let my words ring in the silence, eyeing the article between us. I waited him out, feeling the shifting current of his emotions.

Finally, he picked up the article, caressing its corner between his fingers. "You should have told me the truth." He held up a hand. "I know you didn't think I'd believe you. I understand that you were scared and wanted the evidence in place to back your claim. I get it, DiRocco." He met my eyes squarely. "But you should have found a way to tell me before the shit hit the fan."

I nodded. "I know. And I'm sorry."

"All right then," he said, standing brusquely. "I'm not making any promises, but I'll see what I can do."

Carter's "I'll see what I can do" was as good as a done deal from anyone else. I smiled, exuberant for a fraction of a second before I felt more than saw him recoil. *I have fangs now*, I thought, making a conscious effort to close my mouth and still look overjoyed. It was a difficult expression.

"Thank you," I said, holding out my hand. I made sure my movements were slow and smooth, so he wouldn't startle. At five foot two and under 130 pounds, I'd never been physically intimidating in my entire life, not even before my battle with arthritis and subsequent broken leg had confined me to a scooter. My no-nonsense personality, on-point instincts, and fierce loyalty had earned the respect of my colleagues at the bureau, but I'd had to work to keep that respect every day.

Now, I could cut down grown men with a smile. The power that came with physical intimidation was humbling and suddenly unwanted.

Carter hesitated, but only for a fraction of a second, before taking my hand. I might not have even noticed his reluctance without my heightened senses. His resolve tasted like beef and potato stew—something hearty and warm, something that had taken a very long time and experience to get just right.

His hand engulfed mine. "How are you even out at this hour, in sunlight?" he asked, unable to prevent himself and his reporter's instinct from asking questions, just like me.

I shook his hand carefully, mindful of my superstrength. "As it turns out, I wasn't just any old night blood who had the potential to transform into a vampire. I transformed into a Day Reaper. I'm extra-special," I said, my voice dripping with sarcasm.

Carter released my hand. He shook his palm, a little bruised despite my restraint, but his grin was genuine and his eyes were warm with pride when he met my gaze.

"You didn't need to transform into a Day Reaper to know that."

Chapter 18

Dominic had sent me out this morning with a list of errands to complete during his day rest. Had the errands on said list been grocery shopping, picking up the dry cleaning, and grabbing some Chinese take-out, I would have felt downright domestic. Instead, he'd given me what looked like a hit list: convince Carter to print the article, discover where Sevris's loyalties lay, determine the extent of Jillian's power, and estimate the number of Damned vampires in Jillian's army—as if I could just walk into the coven and take a head count.

I could scratch Carter off the list, but before I moved onto the next item, I had my own errand to run, one that was long overdue. Dominic had thought of nearly everything when he'd designed his underground bunker—essentials like emergency supplies and human food as well as bagged blood, and comfort items like couches, mattresses, and running water—but he hadn't had the time or inclination to grab the overnight bag I'd packed in anticipation of bunkering down for the Leveling. I suppose he'd been a little distracted since then—saving my life and transforming me and all—but after seven days being transformed and another two attempting to convince everyone, including myself, that Day Reaper Cassidy was essentially the same woman as night blood Cassidy, it might help my cause if I changed into a fresh shirt, flat-ironed my bangs, and wore some eyeliner.

I landed on the roof of my apartment building a little after seven o'clock. The sun had fully risen and tingled on my skin, not burning like it would if I were a vampire, but not pleasant like it felt on the skin of a human, either. In addition to the strange new sensation of sunshine, I could feel the effect of my efforts to vampire-proof my apartment: the stale blood around the doors and windows was off-putting, and the silver hardware and silver nitrate spray I'd doused throughout the apartment chafed my skin. I'd deliberately reinforced this apartment with blood and silver to protect myself from vampires when I was a night blood, but now that I was a Day Reaper, it felt like I was breaking and entering into my own apartment. Entering through the rooftop access instead of the front door probably didn't help, but until I looked more like myself, I'd prefer to avoid contact with any of my former neighbors.

Reassuring everyone that I was still me when I didn't even feel like myself anymore was difficult enough with friends and family. Convincing acquaintances that the creature I'd become was friendly would be impossible, especially when the blood pumping through their veins really did smell like a meal.

I tapped the hammock as I passed it on my way to the rooftop-access hatch. Metal squeaked against metal as the fabric swung in its frame, and had I not been distracted by the feel of the hammock's abrasive squeak like an IV under my skin, I might have heard the hum of anticipation vibrating from inside what should have been my empty apartment. I might have hesitated before entering, or at the very least, prepared myself for the unexpected. But I was overwhelmed by the many unfamiliar sounds and smells surrounding me, and if I was honest, distracted by the swamping melancholy of my new existence, so when I opened the rooftop-access hatch and approached the staircase that led to my apartment, the spray of silver bullets that greeted me took me by complete and utter surprise.

Sudden, searing pain pummeled my face and upper chest. I dodged blindly away from the blast, but my foot found nothing but air. I fell, dinged my forehead against the wall, wrenched my back reaching for the banister, and cracked my kneecap as I tumbled head over ass down the stairs to the landing in my apartment hallway.

I sprawled on the floor, dazed. After a moment, my vision cleared and someone swam into focus, blocking the view of my apartment's outdated popcorn ceiling. Ian Walker and his velvet-brown eyes gazed down at me, a cruel grin twisting his lips.

"It's daylight, DiRocco. Not as invincible when it's just you and me now, are you?"

He was wrapping something around my wrists as he spoke, and regardless of the confidence in his words, I could smell the strong odor of his uncertainty billowing from his pores like bonfire smoke. The bindings must be laced with silver—Walker wouldn't use anything less to secure a vampire—but since I was a Day Reaper, I wasn't allergic to silver like other vampires. I had silver talons growing out of my nail beds, for heaven's sake. He secured my ankles with the same material, nevertheless, and to my astonishment and horror, the bindings held strong no matter how hard I struggled.

With me trussed to his liking, Walker disappeared from my line of sight.

I remembered how Dominic had risen as if from the dead after having been ambushed by Walker's bullet blast. He'd ejected the bullets from his skin, a horror movie brought to life. Granted, Dominic was nearly five hundred years older than me, more experienced, and a Master vampire, but I was a Day Reaper. That had to count for something, damn it, so I tried to feel each bullet as an individual injury through the immobilizing wash of pain. I envisioned each one ejecting itself, one by one, from my skin. I imagined hearing them hit and roll on my hardwood floor, but no matter my memories of how Dominic had healed his injuries, the bullets remained lodged in my skin and muscle. I felt weak from the wounds and trapped by the bounds around my wrists and ankles, and no matter my will, my body didn't heal.

Walker returned with a sharpened wooden stake in his hand. He straddled my waist and kneeling in the expanding puddle of my blood, pressed the wooden stake against my chest, directly over my heart.

"I don't care if you're a vampire, a Day Reaper, or fucking the Master vampire of all vampires himself; the sun is shining, and finally, it's just you and me and this stake. No one's coming to save you—not Dominic, not your brother, and certainly not me this time, darlin'—so listen up."

I tried to open my mouth, more to spit in his face than to say anything intelligent—I was so angry that words, for once, were beyond me—but something was wrong with my mouth. Maybe my jaw was broken or maybe the nerves and tendons that worked my jaw were destroyed—too many bullets to the face. The only thing I could do, which perhaps was more menacing than spitting anyway, was let loose a low, feral growl.

The stake against my chest trembled. "You are going to turn Ronnie back into a night blood."

And just like that, with one sentence, my anger wilted.

"I would if I could," I said. My words were barely decipherable between my locked jaw, but despite their garbled enunciation, Walker seemed to understand me just fine.

The stake against my chest pressed painfully into my skin. "You can and you will. You figured out how to turn your brother back from being Damned. You nearly died doing the impossible, but you did it. And you'll do it again. You'll figure out how to turn Ronnie back into a night blood."

"Nathan is still Damned," I wheezed. "He has his mind again, but he's not completely back to normal. He still eats human hearts." Even with a stake at my chest, I told Walker the same thing I'd told Ronnie: the truth. "Sometimes, people can't completely recover from the creature they become. Sometimes, there's no going back. Only forward."

Walker's expression, already grim, hardened with resolve. He cocked his arm back and impaled the right side of my chest with the stake, deliberately missing my heart. The wound was searing.

I gasped, choking on pain and revived rage. My body suddenly felt on fire—like it was being metaphysically incinerated from head to toe—and I thought, *What the hell kind of stake sets Day Reapers on fire,* before I heard Dominic's roar. The stake wasn't the source of the licking flames charring my insides; it was Dominic.

He could feel my pain. He knew I was injured, and screw the sun, he was coming for me.

I closed my eyes, ignoring Walker, the man impaling me with a stake mere inches from my heart, to concentrate on banking Dominic's inferno. I soothed the physical burns and tried to project thoughts of calm and safety to him. *I'm fine*, I lied. *I can hold my own without you.*

Walker pulled the stake out of my chest, and it hurt nearly as much being yanked out as it had going in.

I groaned weakly, my connection with Dominic slipping.

"You figure out how to transform Ronnie back, or next time I won't miss," Walker snarled.

Dominic's roar vibrated inside my skull. I had to ground myself and remember that I was the one who controlled our connection now. I could hide my pain from him, heal his injuries, and know his mind better than he did. Which was why I knew that Walker would be dead when Dominic arrived.

"I get it, Walker," I whispered, panting in pain through my locked jaw. "Your anger, your drive for revenge, even your drive to kill—no matter the blowback or bystanders—I get it. I hate it, but I get it. I even understand you attacking me. Your loyalty to Ronnie is commendable, especially considering she's one of the very creatures you hate so much. I wish you'd had that same loyalty to me."

Walker winced, but he didn't drop his gaze. "She hasn't killed anyone. Even as a vampire, she'd rather starve than attack a human."

"Who have I killed?"

Walker scowled. "Excuse me?"

"You've remained loyal to Ronnie even though she's a vampire because she hasn't killed anyone? You think she's still worth saving."

"She *is* still worth saving."

I raised an eyebrow. "I haven't killed anyone. Why am I not worth saving?"

He pressed the stake hard against my chest, directly over my heart again. "You don't look starved to me."

I laughed, the sound more growl than anything, and blood sprayed from one of the bullet wounds in my neck. "I've drunk blood, if that's what you're implying, but I haven't killed anyone to get it. More than I can say about you."

"Ronnie didn't choose this life. She was attacked and—"

"So was I!"

Walker leaned close, his face spotted with my blood. "You should have been there for her."

"And who the hell was there for me?" I asked. "When Jillian attacked me and tore out my throat, did you have my back?"

Walker just stared at me, the stake trembling between us.

"I was dying, and when the time came to choose between life as a vampire or death, I chose life." I leaned forward, inches from Walker's face, embedding the stake deeper into my skin. "I won't apologize for surviving."

"You're twisting the truth to fit your agenda, but that's not reality," Walker snapped. "The reality is that you're a monster now, like all the rest, and need to be put down."

"The reality is that you can't accept the truth. Would Julia-Marie have been a monster had her transformation been successful?"

"Don't drag her into this," he spat. "Don't even fucking breathe her name!"

"The answer to that is, no. Julia wouldn't have been a monster, and neither is Ronnie and neither am I. There are men and women who are monsters, and there are vampires who are nothing but men and women allergic to sunlight. We are more than our physical being. We are who we choose to be. When you shove that stake through my heart and kill me or I succumb to mindless bloodlust and kill the nearest person with a pulse, it doesn't matter who's vampire and who's human. In that moment, we're the same person: a murderer.

Walker was shaking so badly, the stake inadvertently lodged even deeper into my skin, nicking bone. I could feel its scrape vibrate my collarbone and gritted my teeth.

"I don't believe your lies," he hissed.

"I haven't killed anyone, Walker. I'm not a monster. But if you kill me now, in this moment, you will be."

Walker's expression hardened. The stake suddenly stilled. "I'll do whatever is necessary, even become a monster, to save Ronnie."

I nodded, resigned. I understood and even respected his devotion to Ronnie. I'd done the same for Meredith, Nathan, and Dominic; nothing—not morals, laws, or the risk of death—would stop me from attempting to save a loved one. I'd expect nothing less from Walker.

"I don't know why I waste my breath," I murmured resentfully, slumping back against the floor.

"Excuse me?"

I shook my head. "This isn't the first time you've ambushed someone in their apartment. First Dominic, then Meredith, and now—"

"I've never attacked a woman in my life, let alone Meredith," Walker snapped. "Why the hell would I ambush Meredith?"

"Never attacked a woman in your life," I mocked bitterly. "You just attacked me!"

Walker scoffed. "You're a vampire."

"And you shot out Bex's eye," I reminded him.

He gave me a look. "Also a vampire."

"You held me at gunpoint. You abandoned me when I was dying. You killed Jolene, an innocent woman caught in the crossfire!"

"I held you at gunpoint to convince the vampires to release Ronnie after they'd attacked and kidnapped her. I left you in the woods because saving you would have saved Dominic—once again, a vampire. I killed Jolene to save *you* from Kaden, another vampire," Walker said, exasperated. "You see a pattern here?"

"Cut the bullshit, Walker," I said warily. There was no talking sense into someone as stubborn and fanatical as Walker, but Dominic was nearly here, and I wanted answers before he skewered Walker on his talons. "Meredith saw you. She was half dead, but she remembers your golden hair and brown eyes." I shook my head sadly. "I know you hate vampires. I know you hate me. Attack *me* if you must, but I never thought you'd attack Meredith to get to me."

"I wouldn't. I *didn't*," Walker insisted. "When did this happen?"

"Last week, right before the Leveling."

Walker pursed his lips. "You know she is susceptible to being entranced."

"You think a vampire would deliberately leave the memory of you attacking her?" I asked skeptically.

He shrugged. "It's the only explanation, if that's what she remembers."

I shook my head. "It'd be easier to simply fog her memory and make her forget that she saw her attacker at all than create new ones."

"Easier, sure, but maybe the person who attacked Meredith didn't need easy. Maybe they needed you to doubt me," he said pointedly.

I met Walker's gaze sadly. "By the time Meredith was attacked, you'd already created enough doubt all on your own."

Walker and I glared at each other, both of us so alike in our anger and stubbornness, it was nearly like looking into a mirror.

"Well," I said on a sigh, breaking the silence. "Go ahead, then. Let's finish this."

Walker blinked. "Come again?"

I sat up slightly, and the stake embedded even deeper, scraping past bone and farther into flesh and organ. Walker eased the pressure on his end, careful not to pierce my heart even as I pressed unheedingly forward. "I can't do anything about Ronnie. She is the creature she is now, and whether she chooses to starve or survive or become a monster is her choice and hers alone. So either finish this now or let me go. That's *your* choice."

Walker stared at me, debating his options as if I hadn't just laid them out for him. Seconds ticked by, our eyes locked in silent battle, and I willed with every atom of my being for him to see past my fangs, talons, and other monstrous physical attributes to the friend he'd known and trusted; to the person beneath I'd been all along.

I smelled more than saw the moment when Walker decided not to murder me. The clean, fresh mint I'd come to recognize as uniquely him overrode the fear and anger driving him. The scent reminded me of a time when we'd had much more in common and the excitement of learning all there was to know about this man overrode common sense. A time before I'd known he was living with Ronnie and building a veritable army of night bloods, before he'd held me hostage against Dominic, when right and wrong was still black-and-white. Before I could see Dominic in all his kaleidoscope colors, and when the potential in Walker's kiss had felt like a benediction.

Maybe Walker could still remember that time, too. Maybe humans and the creatures who fed on them could be allies against the monsters who wanted to kill us all.

Walker pulled the stake from my chest and dropped his arm to the side.

I winced. A river of blood flowed toward my stomach and then to the floor, joining the pool from the right side of my chest. "You don't have much time. Dominic will be here any moment."

"Dominic can't venture into daylight," he scoffed

I quirked an eyebrow. "You'd be shocked at what Dominic shouldn't do and will anyway."

Walker narrowed his eyes. "Why are you warning me? You could have let him catch me off guard. We could have ended this"—he gestured between us—"whatever twisted triangle this is, once and for all."

"Whatever *this* is, it isn't a triangle, I assure you," I said, glancing at the stake. "Despite what you think, Walker, I'm not your enemy."

Walker tightened his grip on the stake, his jaw muscles flexing. I froze, wondering if that had been exactly the wrong thing to say.

"When I look at you, I see everything I've spent a lifetime fighting against," he said, his voice low and rumbling. Had he been a vampire, his chest would have rattled. "I've killed people, innocent people, in the name of killing vampires, because I knew beyond a doubt that they were unequivocally evil. They would have killed more than the few I killed to get to them, so I was actually saving lives."

"I know," I whispered. "I don't agree with you, but I understand you better than you think."

"Words don't mean much; they can be just as deceiving as looks—God knows Bex blinded me for years."

I tried to bite my tongue. Until he actually dropped the stake entirely, I needed to mind my words, but I'd never been one to sugar-coat the truth. "Bex saved you and Ronnie from burning in the fire that killed your parents. That has to count for something."

I braced myself for a stake through the heart, but Walker just calmly nodded. "Bex saved us over twenty years ago, and since that time, she killed Julia-Marie and attacked and transformed Ronnie. She's shown her true colors."

I actually bit my tongue and managed not to respond this time.

"But *you*," Walker said, filling my silence with a heavy, frustrated sigh. "You risk your life for everyone around you: vampires, humans, and night bloods alike. And even though I've spent a lifetime fighting against the very creature you've become, your actions match your words. It makes me question where I've marked my lines, who the monsters are, and whether, after all these years, I'm already a murderer."

I gaped, struck dumb by his honesty and sudden, self-clarity.

"That doesn't mean I trust you," Walker said. He stepped back, careful not to give me his back as he retreated. "It just means I don't trust myself."

"Everything I understood about life and humanity and New York City has been shoved through a shredder and fed to a tornado. Given a human lifetime, no one could pick up the pieces, let alone reconstruct the picture. But the one thing nothing can tear apart is true friendship."

—Meredith Drake

Chapter 19

Part of me worried that Walker's insightful self-revelation had been a grand performance to lull me into a false sense of safety, so he could finish what he started all those weeks ago, use me as bait a second time, and kill Dominic once and for all. I struggled to break the binds around my wrists and ankles, but either the material of the binds was stronger than me (unlikely) or the material of the bullets still lodged in my skin had somehow significantly weakened my body. I should have been able to expel regular and silver bullets from my skin, so whatever special ammunition Walker had used must be specifically designed to take out Day Reapers.

He was holding out on Greta and Dr. Chunn big-time. Either that, or Greta and Dr. Chunn were holding out on me.

The living-room wall exploded.

The glass in my floor-to-ceiling bay window shattered. Shards, brick, and drywall blasted across the room like hot shrapnel, embedding themselves in my furniture, scraping across my hardwood, and raining over my body. I winced, instinctively wanting to shield my face and eyes from the debris, even as my body healed near-instantly from those superficial nicks and slices. The rest of my apartment, however, didn't survive the fallout as well.

My coffee table flattened, its legs snapped outward and its frame fractured in spider webbed splinters. My purple, gauzy living-room curtain fluttered in the air, hovering over the wreckage like a frayed, torn shroud, and over everything—the couch, recliner, love seat, television, area rug, and ruined coffee table—a fine layer of powered brick and drywall dust settled in the resounding silence.

My heart plummeted. I tried to rationalize that even if Walker blasted Dominic with the same ammunition as he had me, I could heal him. I was in control of our metaphysical connection now, and I could take the wounds into myself. But irrational or not, I strained to face the living room wall, desperate to catch a glimpse of them—had Walker doubled backed somehow? Was he binding Dominic? Had Dominic been caught as unaware as me and knocked unconscious by the blast? But my living room was empty.

A floorboard creaked behind me; I sensed the displacement of air, the flare of Dominic's fury, and the clean scent of Christmas pine.

Dominic stepped out from behind the wall, his expression thunderous. His eyes moved over my bullet-sprayed face, neck, arms, and chest; flashed between my bound wrists and ankles; and narrowed on the lake of blood expanding around me on the living room floor.

"I liked that wall," I commented, nodding my head at the shattered bay windows.

Dominic knelt next to me, heedless of the blood, reaching for my bound wrists. "I'll kill him."

"Careful, they're—"

Dominic hissed, jerking back as the binds around my wrists burned his hands.

"—something more than silver," I finished lamely. "I can't break them or expel the bullets from my skin. Does Greta know he's developed these weapons, or are they hers?"

He fingered one of the bullet wounds in my arm. "I don't know," he said, his voice grim.

"Obviously *you* didn't know he'd developed this kind of ammunition," I murmured, more thinking than questioning.

"Obviously," Dominic said drily, "Ian Walker needs to be put down."

"We came to a truce."

Dominic's eyes blazed. "This is no truce. This is the gauntlet being thrown down."

"A stalemate then. I—"

The sun peeked out from behind a cloud and washed over us. My words were ripped away by the sudden, overwhelming heat that engulfed my body from head to toe. I refocused on healing Dominic, which only served to worsen my own injuries, since I was healing him instead of myself.

"Cassidy?" Dominic cupped my cheek in his palm. "You're trembling."

"L-l-leave me," I ground out from behind clenched teeth.

"Shut up," he snapped. "Let me think."

"It's mid-d-d-day and I won't have the strength to p-p-protect you from the sun for much longer." I struggled to speak.

"You need blood. Fresh, human blood."

"No," I said.

"This is not the time to remain steadfast to your diet. Stale blood will not be enough to undo this damage." He cupped both my cheeks in his hands and forced my gaze to meet his. "You're ready, Cassidy. You can do this."

I opened my mouth to argue, but then I met the blazing certainty in his icy-blue eyes. I shut up. He believed in me, and maybe, just maybe, it was time for me to believe in myself.

I nodded.

"That's my girl." Dominic leaned down and kissed my forehead. "I'll be back," he murmured, his lips and breath warm on my skin.

"I'll b-b-be waiting," I said, but he was already gone.

Time was indeterminate, marked by waves of pain: my own stinging wounds were swept under the feeling of Dominic's burns only to resurface with a vengeance until I was as battered by the pain as I was the actual injuries. My vision began to tunnel and darken. I fought it; with everything inside of me I fought it, but when a drowning woman fights to breathe, all she finds inside her lungs is water.

"Cassidy?"

I wrenched my eyes open at the sound of Meredith's voice, unsure when I'd closed them or why focusing on her face was so difficult. Or why she had three faces, and they were all spinning in dizzying circles above me.

The spinning made me nauseated, so I closed my eyes again. Someone moaned, and the noise sounded like it had come from a dying animal.

"Cassidy!"

I opened my mouth instead of my eyes this time, but another moan escaped. *Huh,* I thought, somewhat detached from the urgency of the moment, considering how desperate Meredith sounded. *I'm the dying animal.*

Something warm and thick and sweet and spiced and absolutely, irresistibly, unfathomably delicious coated my tongue and poured down my esophagus. My throat swallowed convulsively. Warmth spread outward from my stomach, and a sudden, searing heat, not unlike the sting of the healing enzyme in Dominic's saliva, speared through my entire body.

I screamed.

"Hold still, Cassidy." Meredith's voice was soft but firm. I felt her lock my head in a choke hold, minus the choking, and pour more of that heavenly, hellfire liquid into my mouth.

I swallowed and choked and was forced to swallow more until, eventually, the burning wasn't a full-body blaze but contained to my wrists, ankles, face, upper chest, forehead, and kneecap. My injuries were healing.

And I was drinking Meredith's blood.

I pulled back, turning my face away.

"You're doing well," Meredith encouraged. "Don't stop now. You need your full strength."

"You are so strong, Cassidy. Stronger than me. Stronger than I could have ever imagined," Dominic said, his voice hoarse. He coughed several times before saying, "You can do this."

I struggled against Meredith's grip and turned my face toward Dominic's voice. Opening my eyes this time and keeping them open didn't take force of will, but accepting what was in front of me did. I blinked, but the image of Meredith hovering over me, her forearm sliced to the bone, didn't go away, and neither did the horror of Dominic next to her, peeling and oozing from head to toe with third-degree burns.

Of course Dominic had burst into flames; I'd lost consciousness. And of course, becoming a human-shaped torch hadn't stopped him; he'd managed to find Meredith and convinced her to bleed for me.

"Drink," Meredith encouraged.

I shook my head. Given the ravenous, burning urge to drink and the sight of Dominic's suffering, resisting Meredith's blood was nearly the most difficult thing I'd ever done in my entire life.

Suddenly, Dominic's ravaged, red, blistered face took up my entire field of vision. "You think the blood I keep in our emergency stash doesn't come from humans?" he asked, his voice harsh.

I glared at him.

"A hamburger is delicious, but it's less appetizing after watching the cow being slaughtered and ground and cooked into patties, hmm?" He pushed.

"I. Will not kill. Meredith," I said, my voice stilted and gasping.

His glare softened slightly. "You won't," he said. "And if you try to, I won't let you. I promise."

"Practice makes perfect," Meredith added, wiggling her arm in front of my face temptingly. Blood spattered on my cheeks; I could feel its hot sprinkles like a brand on my soul. "And there's no time like the present. Plus, Dominic looks like shit. You might want to do something about that."

I laughed, barely a match for Meredith and Dominic separately; their combined encouragement was irresistible. When Meredith pressed her sliced forearm against my mouth, I sealed my lips over the wound and drank.

"Sense past the taste of her blood and the heat of its healing," Dominic said. "Focus on the wound and hear the pressure of her pulse. Feel its strength and life with every swallow. Envision that life strengthening you. Can you feel it?"

I nodded, still swallowing, still latched like a freaking leech onto Meredith's arm, but I couldn't feel shame in that—or rather, I probably could if I wasn't so full of so many other feelings. The taste of her blood was exquisite, and its healing was hot and uncomfortable, the way a man inside me was hot and uncomfortable. I wanted more, even if it didn't feel entirely good. Beyond the confusing pleasure-pain of drinking Meredith's blood, I could hear and feel Meredith, too, her pulse and her life, just as Dominic had said.

I refocused on her wound and realized her pulse wasn't quite as strong. Her heart was slowing as mine was glowing, and I wanted more.

I should stop. I was healed. I took Dominic's wounds into myself and healed them, too. We were healthy and whole, and all that was left was the taste of Meredith's blood, now that I could hardly hear her pulse and barely feel her life.

And still, I wanted more.

In the end, it was actually my own want that stopped me. I remembered that feeling, that all-consuming need to have more even if that meant risking my personal health, well-being, happiness, and risking the health, happiness, and well-being of everyone around me. That was addiction, and there was nothing on this earth, absolutely nothing, that could force me down that rabbit hole back into hell, especially not my own selfish want.

I detached myself from Meredith's arm and dared to meet her gaze. She was smiling. The corners of her mouth were pinched and her complexion was perhaps a bit paler than her usual peaches-and-cream, but she was alert, upright, and gazing back at me. She was very much alive.

I sagged against her, my bones suddenly made of noodles, and I realized by the overwhelming extent of my relief that I'd expected to open my eyes and see her vacantly staring at the ceiling. I'd seen her like that once before, and to see her like that again, knowing that I'd been the monster to kill her this time, would have been more than I could have borne.

"Cassidy, are you okay?" she asked, her voice tinged with alarm.

I snorted and then laughed, a sad, wailing noise that would easily turn into a sob if I wasn't careful. I pulled back from her and met her eyes. "That's my line," I said.

"Oh, thank God," she gasped, and she flung her arms around me, pressing me tight against her chest. "You scared the shit out of me."

I wrapped my arms around her, minding my strength, claws, and hunger as the proximity to her carotid did strange things to my salivary glands. Hearing the blood pulsing through her neck was sweet torture, but I buried my face in her shoulder and savored the sound of her pulse and the feel of her life inside her, just for her.

"I scared me too," I murmured.

"You're a natural."

I glanced sideways at Dominic at the sound of his voice. He was healed. I knew I'd healed him, but seeing the evidence of my power—his smooth, healthy skin where there'd been weeping blisters covering him from head to toe only moments ago—was still startling.

I opened my mouth.

He spread his arms out as if for my inspection. "I, too, am fine. I believe we all are," he said, smiling. And then a naughty gleam entered his eyes. "As soon as you close Meredith's wound, that is."

"Oh!" I pulled from her embrace, and sure enough, her wounded forearm was still pouring blood.

I glared at Meredith, as if any of this was her fault, and took her arm in both of my hands.

And hesitated.

"What do I—" I began.

"You know what to do," Dominic said. "You've watched me heal dozens of times."

I eyed Meredith's wound skeptically. Blood trickled down her arm to her elbow, and I imagined licking it clean the way I once anticipated licking clean the cookie dough from a whisk. Her blood would, of course, taste delicious, but licking the drippings instead of the cut itself wouldn't actually heal her.

I shifted my gaze from her elbow to the wound itself. If her dripping blood was the cookie dough, the source of her bleed was without a doubt the freshly baked, double-chocolate-chip cookies hot from the oven. I'd have my regrets the moment I finished half the cookie sheet, but my God, they'd taste divine. From the moment the first cookie passed my lips and hit my tongue, the other half-dozen cookies on the sheet were just sitting ducks.

I was still hungry. Ravenous, really. I suspected that I could never really get enough—I had a never-ending hunger that would result in never-ending regrets.

My grip on her wrist must have tightened uncomfortably. Meredith made a pained noise in the back of her throat.

"Don't hold back, Meredith," Dominic said, his voice both encouraging and deadly serious. "Be honest. Cassidy won't know what she's doing if you don't tell her."

Meredith cleared her throat, obviously uncomfortable with honesty, but just as obviously in pain. "You're hurting me."

Dominic looked at me, waiting on me to loosen my grip.

"I can't do this," I murmured.

"Yes. You. Can," Dominic growled. "Look at her."

"I am," I said, staring at her bleeding arm.

Dominic's growl turned exasperated. "Look at her face."

I forced my eyes up to meet her gaze.

"This is Meredith. Your best friend. Your sister—how do you always…"

I pursed my lips. "My sister-in-love if not in law or by blood."

"Yes, and you prefer her alive, do you not?"

I turned to Dominic, my turn to be exasperated. "Of course I—"

"No, not of course! Look at her." Dominic reached out and with an iron grip on my chin, physically forced me to look back at Meredith. "Look at her! She is in pain. She is wounded. And you are no longer in need of more blood. In fact, to take more from her now when she is clearly injured would be an attack on her person. Would you attack her? Would you further injure her?"

I inhaled sharply. "I would never hurt Meredith."

"Then stick your tongue in her wound and heal her without feeding from her, because to do anything else wouldn't just hurt her, it would kill her," Dominic said, his voice stern.

I didn't even realize I was crying until tears rolled twin, scalding paths down my cheeks. I didn't think. I didn't taste or feel. I held my breath so I couldn't smell the delicious scent of her, licked Meredith's wound closed, and lapped at the cut until it sealed, then scarred and smoothed. When I was done, I pulled back, and the exhaustion that bore down on me from my restraint was like nothing I'd ever experienced. Maybe if I'd been an athlete in my human years, I'd have something to compare to this full-body, trembling, aching lethargy. But I'd never been athletic, and if this was any indication of its aftereffects, I didn't know why anyone would want to be.

Meredith cupped my face in both of hers. "You did it," she whispered.

I blinked, and suddenly, I could see Meredith, really see her now that the wound was closed and I wasn't gripped by the insane, insistent need to kill her. And I was horrified. Her skin was pale and clammy, her expression pinched and slightly dazed.

"I'm so sorry," I said. "We need to get you to a hospital. You need—"

She gave me a look. "What hospital? The one that's deserted and Greta turned into her investigative headquarters?"

I opened my mouth, closed it, and then cursed.

Meredith giggled. She giggled! "I'm fine."

"No, you're not. You—"

"I've been better," she admitted, "but I've been worse too. I'll be fine."

I narrowed my eyes on her, not satisfied in the least. "You're going to the hospital and seeing Dr. Chunn. She—"

Meredith laughed, a fully-blown belly laugh. "Seriously? Dr. Susanna Chunn, forensic pathologist? She's a doctor for dead people." She gave me a look, and I knew whatever was about to come out of her mouth would be outlandish. "She can be your primary-care doctor."

I sighed, but it sounded frighteningly like a growl. I obviously wasn't getting anywhere with Meredith. Nothing could penetrate the loyalty of our friendship, apparently not even my razor-sharp fangs buried in her forearm, so I turned on Dominic.

"How could you bring her here?" I asked, but the words were more accusation than question.

"How could I not?" he shot back, and I had the distinct feeling that he'd somehow anticipated this reaction, my turning on him, and had prepared for it. "You were gravely injured. You needed to feed."

"I understand that," I ground out. "But of all people, you had to bring my best friend?"

"Yes," he said unequivocally. "It had to be Meredith. It had to be someone you cared about to make you strong enough to do the right thing."

"I wanted to be here," Meredith interjected. I turned back to her and realized to my surprise that she was angry. "Of all people, I'm your best friend, and I *should* be here."

"Meredith—"

She pointed at me with her finger. "No, you listen to me. You were there for me when I needed you most. When you had the law and the odds of my survival against you, you damned the consequences, did what needed doing, and saved my life. You risked your career and your life just for me. Do you regret that decision?"

I blinked. "Of course not. I'd do anything for you."

"Exactly. And I'd do the same for you. How dare you try to take that from me, as if you love me so much more than I love you, as if you have more right to give and sacrifice for our friendship than me."

I shook my head, unsure when the conversation had spun so off its axis. "No, I wouldn't. I—"

"I know you're different now, but everything is different now. The world, this city, my life—" She shook her head, nearly at a loss for words. "Everything has changed more than I could have ever imagined it changing just a couple weeks ago. I won't lie to you; when I saw you that first time after your transformation, I was terrified."

"Meredith—"

She held up her hand. "No, this needs to be said. I was terrified. *You* were terrifying. Your claws and fangs and pointed ears, your strength, your eyes, I-I—" Meredith stuttered for a moment, but she took a deep breath and regained her composure. "I needed time to come to grips with reality, because what's real is so far off the spectrum of what I'd ever imagined possible. I look at you, sometimes, like just now when you were drinking my blood, and I know there will be some things that I just won't understand about you. You hear things I can't hear, and feel and see and smell the world in ways I don't even want to know. Your thoughts are simply beyond my comprehension because your brain doesn't fire quite the same as mine anymore."

Tears burned in my eyes. They were brimming the edge of my lashes when Meredith grasped my shoulders.

"But then I realized: when the hell had our brains ever really fired quite the same?"

I laughed, and the tears spilled down my cheeks.

"Some things will never change, no matter who we become or what becomes of this world. You and I are best friends, Cassidy DiRocco. I love you. You are the sister of my heart, and nothing on this earth—not even your transformation into something not human—will ever change that."

"Oh." The sound was more noise than an intelligible word, but it was all I could manage through my constricted throat.

She embraced me, her arms fierce and warm and strong around me.

I wrapped my arms around her a beat later, careful not to crush her in overwhelmed, soaring joy.

Chapter 20

I woke to the smell of banana-nut pancakes and the sound of Keagan's bleating bird, and no matter the pleasant, aromatic scent permeating our room, groaned warily. A sense of déjà vu blindsided me; Dominic and I had never slept together two nights in a row, and now here we were, rising from bed in his underground bunker to greet a second night. Ronnie was once again wasting her time and our meager food supplies, and everyone was holding their collective breath in anticipation of a meltdown. Again. After the insanity of the last few weeks and the freeing serenity of my moment with Meredith yesterday, I did crave the solid surety of routine, but not this routine.

Dominic stirred at my groan. "Something amiss?"

"Don't you smell that?" I asked.

"Breakfast?" Dominic asked, his voice still muffled. He hadn't moved his face from the pillow.

"That's not the smell of breakfast."

"Really? Because if I'm not mistaken, not only do I smell pancakes, I also smell potatoes, onions, and bacon. Definitely bacon."

I shook my head. "That's the smell of disaster."

"Ah, my mistake," Dominic said, but his voice didn't sound as grave as it should. In fact, his voice didn't sound grave at all. If I wasn't mistaken, and I knew I wasn't, his voice was shaking with repressed laughter. "They smell so similar lately."

"Nothing about the dysfunction of our motley little family is funny," I grumbled, covering my ears. "God, the sound of Keagan's annoyance is annoying."

"I'll find time to work with him, as well."

I shook my head. "Better yet, let's get our own place. Either that or the children need to move out."

Dominic turned to face me at that. "I'd check the paper for available listings, but the paperboy hasn't been reliable lately."

I snorted. "You'll have to give him a talking-to. Until then, I guess we're stuck with them until they grow up and build their own underground bunker. Damn it."

Dominic smiled at that, a true smile; his lower lip stretched down slightly from the pull of his scar. "This is what leading a coven means: living with other people's problems as your own and finding ways to solve them. And hopefully, if you're lucky, they don't kill you for it."

I sobered suddenly. His words, though teasing, were irrevocably true. As Dominic's lover and the right hand of the Master vampire of New York City, I couldn't have my own apartment separate from the coven. I would wake every morning from now until eternity surrounded by the sounds and smells and tastes of everyone else's problems.

More than the prospect of drinking blood or being unable to control the disruption of my senses for years to come, that thought was terrifying.

Dominic chuckled. "You look like you've seen a ghost."

"A ghost is nothing; I discovered the existence of vampires."

"I hardly think you stumbling upon me in an alley can be considered a discovery of my entire race," Dominic argued. "People have known of our existence before you; you're just the only one who couldn't keep it quiet."

I blinked, and the horror in my expression must not have subsided, because Dominic sobered on a long-suffering sigh.

"Just nine nights ago you were a night blood, and before that, you had only just barely come to terms with the existence of vampires and your potential to become one. Now, you're not only a vampire, you're a Day Reaper and my Second and the entirety of our coven's troubles is suddenly on your shoulders. It will take time for you to adjust to those responsibilities and everything they entail, but your shoulders are not the only pair to bear that weight. I am in this with you every step of the way."

I'd never wanted any of this. I'd only ever wanted to survive, but now that I'd climbed onto the pedestal beside Dominic, there was no way down. And worse, if being on said pedestal helped us fight Jillian and the Damned, restore Dominic's power, and right the wrongs on New York City, I was exactly where I needed to be, whether I liked it or not.

I squared my shoulders, left the bed, and got dressed, still feeling terrified by my prospective future. "Well, one thing at a time, I suppose."

Dominic nodded. "Exactly. Baby steps. We'll overthrow Jillian and her army first and *then* worry about freeing the other Day Reapers, facing Lord High Henry's judgment, and leading the coven in the aftermath of vampire-kind being exposed to the world."

I'd just finished pulling a crisp, fresh shirt from my overnight duffel—that prize had been hard-won—and I stared at him as I stabbed my hands through my sleeves. "Seriously? That's baby steps?" I shook my head, reaching back into the duffel for my silver rings, pen-stakes, and nitrate spray. "How about we just try to prevent Ronnie from making any more pancakes before someone strangles Keagan in our kitchen?" I frowned into my bag. "Where are my weapons?"

"You're wearing them."

"I am not. They're not—"

Dominic grabbed my wrist and held my hand up to my face. He pinched my pointer finger between his thumb and forefinger and waved my four-inch talon at me. "Yes, you are."

I pursed my lips and tugged my wrist from his grasp. "You didn't bring the pens or spray or jewelry, or *anything*?"

"I brought everything you needed," he said, his eyes darting to my mother's jewelry box sitting atop the bureau, the only surviving link I had to my parents.

I hadn't been able to bring myself to open the jewelry box in the five years since their deaths, and I honestly never thought I would. The debilitating wound of their loss wasn't something I'd ever thought to heal in my lifetime, so I'd stuffed away my memories and mementoes in the locked box of horrors hidden deep in the shadows inside my heart, never to see the light of day. I'd never considered the possibly, however, that I might live several human lifetimes.

I turned away from the jewelry box and nodded, not bothering to hide the raw, septic stink of my grief. Dominic had grabbed the jewelry box along with the duffel of my clothes. He already knew how much it meant to me, and he was the one person I didn't mind knowing. My parents might never escape from the box I'd locked them in, but maybe that didn't matter as much as making sure that my feelings for Dominic—the person still living and capable of sharing this life—never joined them.

Five minutes later, after Dominic had finally dressed—*finally* and *dressed* being two words I'd never imagined thinking consecutively in reference to him—we were standing outside our bedroom door, staring at the scene in our kitchen. Everyone was occupying the same space as they had the night before—Bex stood on the far side of the living room glaring at

Ronnie; Logan and Theresa twittered their disapproval in hushed undertones from the corner; Keagan and Jeremy sprawled on the couch, watching the drama unfold; and Rafe and Neil stood as we entered the room. The only things different were Walker, whose presence was conspicuously absent, and Ronnie. She wasn't making banana-nut pancakes; she was eating them.

And she looked absolutely radiant.

Her hair was thick and wavy down to her shoulders. Her skin, which had been stretched thin from the sharp angles and bony protrusions of her eye sockets, cheekbones, and chin, was now plump and flushed. She was the picture-perfect definition of vitality and health, looking more alive now than she had while still human. She'd been too thin then, her knuckles chapped and split, her features fragile, like fine china. When she was a human, I'd seen her cook uncountable batches of banana-nut pancakes and chocolate-chip cookies, but only once had I ever seen her eat and only then because I'd forced her. Now, even as she looked up at me, staring agog at her, she didn't stop eating. She smiled briefly before dipping a forkful of pancake into syrup and shoveling it into her mouth.

"Where's Ian?" Ronnie asked around her half-chewed food. "No one seems to know, and I was hoping you—"

"He is no longer welcome here," Dominic said, his voice kind but firm.

She stopped chewing. "Why? What happened?"

"Nothing he hasn't done before." Dominic waved his hand in a dismissive gesture. "Please, don't let his absence quell your appetite."

Her appetite for food, I thought numbly. God help me, but like a gruesome car accident on the side of the road, no matter that I was holding up traffic, I couldn't help but slow and stare.

"What?" she asked self-consciously, wiping her mouth with a napkin even as she resumed chewing. "Do I have syrup on my face?"

I opened my mouth and struggled to find the words.

"No, nothing is on your face, my dear," Dominic said, his voice kind and delicate. "Your face is perfect."

Ronnie blushed. "Then what's wrong?"

"Your face is perfect," I said, finally finding my voice. "From eating pancakes instead of drinking blood."

"After Ian left yesterday without even taking one bite, I couldn't very well just let them all go to waste, could I?" Ronnie asked, sounding defensive.

"I guess, but—"

"They were all just sitting there in neat little stacks, all twelve of them golden and fluffy and perfect, absolutely perfect. I couldn't help but think that in a world that had gone completely mad, I still made the best banana-nut pancakes known to man; that little part of my world hadn't changed, and no matter how little, it was still something to hold on to. And then Ian just walked out." She slammed her fork down on the table. "And the pancakes just sat in their neat little stacks, beautiful and perfect and abandoned. No one would know how delicious they were, and if a pancake is delicious and no one eats it, does it even have a flavor?"

"Well, I… er—" I began. Thin ice was spider web-cracking beneath my feet, and no matter how I distributed my weight, I was going to fall through and drown.

"When everyone left to hunt for breakfast, I stayed behind to clean up and do the dishes. And I was alone with the pancakes."

Rafe frowned. "And your first thought was to eat them?"

"Well, my first thought was that Ian was being a jerk, and then yes. My stomach growled. They were just sitting there, and no one else wanted them. So I ate them."

Bex snorted, breaking her stony, silent stare.

"But why?" Neil asked, wrinkling his nose as if she'd confessed to cannibalism. "We left you here because you said you weren't hungry. I thought—"

"You thought I really wasn't hungry?" Ronnie asked, incredulous. "Are you insane? Do you not have eyes? I was starving!" She shrugged. "Just apparently not for blood."

Dominic turned to Rafe and raised his eyebrows.

"Don't look at me! I took her out on hunts. I had her drink blood, and she just threw it up afterward. I tried different blood types, different genders, different ethnicities, as if that would make a difference. But I tried!" Rafe shook his head. "I just never tried solid food."

"If you were so starving, why didn't you just eat?" Bex asked, her voice harsh.

"I didn't know I was hungry for solid food," Ronnie admitted, and I could tell the words cost her by the low rattle of a dying breath—the sound of her anxiety. "I feel a scratchy burn in the back of my throat, just like Rafe said the blood craving should feel like—but every time I tried to drink, I couldn't keep the blood down." She shrugged. "Guess I was hungry, not thirsty, after all."

"What does that mean?" Neil asked, looking more confused than I'd ever seen him—which, for Neil, was a lot of confusion. "Is Ronnie a vampire or still human?"

"Dr. Chunn said that—"

"It means that Ronnie Carmichael is the weakest, saddest excuse for a vampire I've ever seen in my very long existence," Bex growled.

I stared at her, stunned speechless by her words. Apparently, so was everyone else. No one moved. No one spoke. No one so much as blinked.

I opened my mouth—defending Ronnie emotionally and physically was a freaking full-time job—but Ronnie, for once, actually recovered faster than me. "At least I'm figuring my shit out and getting stronger for it," she muttered around a mouthful of onion-and-bacon–sautéed hash browns. "You're a bitter, resentful bitch, and after living such a *very long existence*, I doubt any amount of pancakes or power will ever change that."

I wanted to warn Ronnie to take it slow, that maybe less food would be best for her starving stomach, but the silence in the room after her comeback was cutting. I didn't dare waste my breath trying to save her from vomiting when I might have to save her from being impaled on Bex's claws.

As if completely unaware of Bex's murderous intent, Ronnie swallowed and scooped up another heaping forkful of hash browns. "After hundreds upon hundreds of years of getting over grief and heartache and lost loves and rejection, you should be better at coping with it. Practice makes perfect after all, and during all those long years, you had lots of practice."

Another awkward, electrically charged silence stretched between us before Bex replied, "Losing a loved one, even for a seasoned mourner such as myself, is tantamount to losing a limb. That pain isn't something one becomes used to or can easily live with, not even with practice or the passage of time," she growled, the last two words a mocking bite of Ronnie's voice.

Ronnie shrugged. "I disagree. The first loss cuts the deepest. If I freaked out and slaughtered a houseful of night bloods every time Ian rejected me or someone I loved died, night bloods would be extinct."

"I did not 'freak out.' I took revenge," Bex snarled.

"Then you should be happy. You got your revenge. You had the last laugh. And yet, you're still a bitter, resentful bitch."

Silence.

"Ian will never get over Julia-Marie's death. Ever. It's been ten years, and in another ten years, he'll still hate you and not spare a glance at me. Deal with it." Ronnie inhaled her forkful of hash browns. "I have."

"And now that he hates you?" Bex asked, her voice cruel. "How are you dealing with that?"

Ronnie swallowed and put down her fork. "I always thought that losing Ian was the worst thing that could ever happen to me, second only to losing my parents. But I was wrong. Becoming a vampire was much worse, because not only did I lose Ian, I lost myself too."

That terrible silence consumed the room again. Ronnie picked up her fork and resumed eating, the crunch of golden hash browns, the scrape of her fork against the plate, and the munch of her teeth as she chewed the only sounds in the room.

Finally—and warily, it seemed—Bex's expression broke into a reluctant smile, her fangs gleaming. "Rene was the first of my vampires to ever question me. He was fiercely loyal and his wit was nearly as cutting as his talons, but one of the things I miss most about him was his honesty. He had no tact, and he didn't let fear or rank or power prevent him from seeing and speaking the truth. Very much like our dear Cassidy DiRocco here," Bex said, nodding to me. "And for the first time, very much like you."

Ronnie raised her eyebrows, still chewing.

"Luckily for you, I no longer kill vampires simply for being honest, assuming I agree with them." She grinned suddenly, her smile wide and genuine. "I was a bitter bitch long before meeting Ian Walker, and I'll be one long after he dies. Deal with it."

Ronnie considered that a moment, swallowed her hash browns, and finally nodded.

Dominic sat next to Ronnie at the breakfast bar. "You spoke to Dr. Chunn about this?"

Ronnie nodded. "I thought she'd want to know that I figured out my eating problem on my own, you know, after she'd taken my blood and all. I didn't want her wasting time on me when she has other problems to solve."

"Helping you is not a waste of time," Dominic said softly, and his gentle calmness—the way he spoke to Ronnie like he genuinely cared—made my chest ache.

"Compared to saving New York City? Maybe not a *waste* of time, but certainly a distraction." Ronnie shrugged. "But Dr. Chunn was very excited for me. She wants more blood tests."

Dominic's eyes narrowed. "More tests?"

She nodded and bit into a muffin. "Something about Nathan's eating habits being similar to mine. She needs more samples to run more tests, get more data. I don't know, but if it will help, I don't mind."

I blinked. "Nathan eats human hearts. What does Ronnie eating human food have anything to do with that?"

Dominic grimaced. "They are both creatures whose eating habits do not coincide with their physical form. Ronnie is a vampire who still needs solid food to survive. Nathan is a human, most of the time, who needs aortic blood to survive. They are anomalies."

"The paper came today, by the way," Ronnie mumbled around a mouthful of muffin.

I frowned at her and her bulging cheeks. *Where the hell had that muffin even come from?* I thought, and then her words finally penetrated. "The paper? What paper?"

"Your paper," Ronnie said. She picked up a folded newspaper from where it was buried underneath the griddle, spatula, electric mixer, and baking sheet.

"The *Sun Accord*?" I asked, leaping forward and snatching it from her hands in one swift movement. "And you're just telling me this now?"

Ronnie took another bite, completely decapitating her muffin. "While I was being accused of being the weakest, saddest excuse for a vampire ever, there wasn't an opportunity to sneak in a 'good morning,' let alone share news from the morning paper."

I ignored Ronnie, her words fading into the background as the words on the page in front of me consumed my complete attention. We'd done it. Carter had come through on his word and published and distributed a post-apocalyptic newspaper, featuring *Vampires Bite in the Big Apple* front and center.

"Damn," I murmured, staring at my words in print on the page. Something warm and glowing swelled through my chest and constricted my throat. The feeling was so physical, I'd have thought I was experiencing a heart attack if my heart still functioned that way.

"Cassidy?" Dominic asked, sounding worried. "Did it not print as you had intended?"

I glanced across the bold headline, the hook, the personal experiences I'd sprinkled throughout the piece. It was so tidy and compelling—the complete opposite of how I'd experienced it at the time. I scanned down to the closing, to my call to all others who'd experienced everything I'd experienced, who felt as I'd felt and feared as I'd feared, to come forward, share their story, help us build a case, and fight by my side as I fought to reclaim our city. My eyes took in each paragraph, every word on each narrow line, and I felt my smile burst across my face even as tears bathed my cheeks.

"It printed exactly as I'd intended," I breathed.

My eyes caught on the closing, on my call to everyone to rise up and share their story, too. "Exactly as I'd intended," I repeated, a slow dawning realization breaking through my glow. *Oh, shit.*

I snatched my phone from my pocket and speed-dialed Greta.

"Cassidy," Dominic asked, his voice sharp with concern.

I waved my hand at him and waited, listening to Greta's phone as it rang.

"I'm sorry; I should have found a way to get the paper to you sooner," Ronnie said.

"Ya think?" Keagan muttered.

"Not often, obviously," Jeremy muttered back.

Logan shot the boys a quelling look.

"Is something amiss, Cassidy?" Bex asked, hissing a long, taunting 's' on *amiss*.

Seven rings later, and Greta's phone continued ringing.

Logan crossed his arms. "Well, what the hell's wrong?"

I jabbed the *end* button with my thumb and turned to Dominic. "Meet me at the morgue."

Dominic nodded.

"What's going on at the morgue?" Keagan asked.

"If no one is answering their phones, the Damned may have fought through its defenses," Logan said ominously.

"Ian fortified the morgue himself," Ronnie reminded him.

Theresa scoffed. "Because we all know how well his fortifications hold up when put to the test."

"Excuse me?"

"You heard her," Bex drawled. "If I broke past his defenses, who's to say the Damned couldn't?"

"Fuck you," Jeremy spat.

"She's right. We need to—"

"The hell she is. We should—"

"We don't even know who Cassidy called. If she... Cassidy?"

I could still hear their conversation through the cold evening sky as it whistled past my ears, but I couldn't answer. I'd already left the bunker, my absence unnoticed as they'd argued, and launched into the air, soaring like a targeted missile aimed at Kings County Hospital Center.

Chapter 21

Vampires Bite in the Big Apple was damn effective: as I'd suspected, Greta was slammed by witnesses.

Her makeshift waiting area and interrogation rooms were packed full of dozens upon dozens of people, some still holding the newspaper in hand, folded open to my article. Others were holding children. Some held backpacks stuffed with supplies and weapons. A few just had their arms crossed, holding themselves as their wide eyes shifted uneasily over the crowd.

I couldn't help but look over the crowd with wide eyes myself. These people had abandoned the safety of their bunkers and fallout shelters—God knew no one had homes anymore—to come here in the hope that they could do something more than hide and die in the aftermath of the Damned's attack. They'd found the courage to rise from the rubble, and most astonishing of all, their courage had been inspired by my article.

Everyone's story was curiously familiar: night bloods whose siblings had been transformed; night bloods whose parents had been killed; night bloods who had vampire lovers; humans who had vampire lovers; night bloods who had been attacked by vampires; night bloods who hated vampires; night bloods who wanted to be vampires; humans who had been attacked and couldn't remember by whom. The variations of the same theme were endless, and I couldn't help but think of Dominic and me, Walker and me, Walker and Dominic, Bex and Walker. With the right push or wrong decision, similar circumstances could result in so many different endings.

Story after story, unique and yet exactly the same. I listened to people recount the last moments they'd had with their loved ones, jotted detailed notes, and tried not to feel too deeply, but it was impossible not to feel when

I knew exactly how they felt—the fear that they'd experienced their final moment with their loved one, the anger that such tragedy could happen to their family, the denial that this could be their fate. I watched it play out for them like it had for me when I'd lost my parents and when I'd nearly lost Nathan. Their grief brought all my own padlocked emotions to the surface.

I still had a dozen people to interview before the night was out, but I needed a recharge. I locked eyes with Dominic. He was walking out of the lab with Ronnie in tow after having discussed the acceptable parameters of more tests with Dr. Chunn. I jerked my head to the side before he could sit. He looked around the room at the dozens of people still waiting for me, who had been waiting all day and would continue waiting all night—because who were we kidding, what else did anyone have to do but be here in this moment? It wasn't like anyone had jobs or hobbies or television anymore—murmured a quick word to Ronnie, and walked with me into the privacy of an empty interrogation viewing room.

I waited for him to shut the door behind us before speaking. "How's Ronnie?"

"Fine," Dominic snorted. "Better than fine, obviously. Dr. Chunn is fascinated."

"I'm sure. So are we all," I said.

Dominic sighed deeply and looked out at the crowd through the window between rooms. "What a fucking disaster."

I blinked. His was not quite the reaction I'd had while looking out over the crowd. "Come again?"

"We can blame Jillian all day and all night for the destruction of New York City. We can hate her for betraying me and cast her as the villain in the coming battle to make us feel better when we attack her—my brother's love and my former Second—kill her and attempt to reclaim my throne, but the truth is that everything, from her betrayal to the destruction of the city, is entirely my fault," Dominic said, his voice grave. He waved his hand at the waiting room. "And this is our proof."

I frowned at "our proof" through the window. He obviously wasn't seeing the same room I was seeing. When I looked over the dozens upon dozens of people who had read my article and come here, I felt a sort of bond, an affirmation that I wasn't alone. My entire world had been flipped upside down since stumbling upon Dominic in that alley, and for the majority of that time, even while visiting Walker and meeting other night bloods, I'd felt very much on my own.

The other night bloods—Logan, Theresa, Keagan, Jeremy, and Ronnie—had endured egregious losses, just like me. They'd learned to survive in a dangerous underground world that human laws and law enforcement couldn't touch, and they'd been willing to share that world with me. But they'd also viewed Bex and Dominic and all the vampires universally as monsters. I had at first, too—hard not to do when your first encounter with one is being shoved up against a wall in a deserted alley, clawed mercilessly, and then entranced to shut up about it—but by the time I'd met the other night bloods, I'd begun to question exactly who were the monsters and who were the men.

As I'd come to know Dominic, I'd realized that he wasn't just a ravenous beast intent on slaughtering humans for the thrill of the hunt. He was a man with ambition and responsibilities and deep, carving emotions. As I'd come to know Bex, Rene, Sevris, Neil, and Rafe as people, too, I'd realized the truth: vampires were as unique as humans, created with genes and shaped by experience. They weren't all emotionless murderers. They experienced an array of emotions beyond blood-lust, from hope and joy to despair and rage. They could hate and kill.

And they could love.

I opened my mouth and closed it again, still frowning, unsure how to express myself and everything this room of people meant to me.

"I don't see what you're seeing," I said.

Dominic raised an eyebrow.

"This room isn't proof of your faults. At the risk of sounding cocky, it's proof of my success," I said bluntly. "And proof that we're not alone in this fight. All this time I thought night bloods were *so* rare, that our relationship was *so* taboo—a night blood falling for a vampire, betraying her kind, and being tempted into hell by the devil himself." I gave a mock shiver.

Dominic's other brow rose to match the height of the first. "Am I the devil in this analogy?"

"I'm not saying that what we have isn't special. And in a city of millions, a few dozen night bloods are pretty rare," I said, backtracking slightly. "But look at them. They're us, and they're willing to help us fight for our city, people we didn't even know existed just yesterday. I searched for weeks for a credible witness to corroborate my article. *Weeks*. And now, here they are."

"But that's the crux of the problem, isn't it, Cassidy? You didn't know they existed. I should have."

I blinked at the bitterness and self-condemnation in his tone. "How could you? Humans are… how did you once put it? 'Food you want to fuck, but food nonetheless,' isn't that right? Did you ever think you and I would really bridge the gap between predator and prey and—"

"From the moment I saw you, I knew you would be mine."

"Let me finish!" I said, stomping my foot. The movement would have been childish except for the fact that I accidentally cracked the tile under my heel. "Did you ever think you and I would bridge that gap *before* turning me into a vampire?"

He hesitated, his mouth still open.

"Had Jillian not attacked me, torn open my throat, and forced your hand, I might still be a night blood, and we would be lovers as human and vampire. Considering that I wasn't ready to willingly become a vampire, we might have continued in that relationship for some time."

Dominic only shrugged. He finally saw where I was going with this, but judging by his expression, he still wasn't convinced.

"Given our volatile relationship when we first met, could you have ever foreseen such a relationship between us?"

He cut his head once to the side in a negative.

"Okay then," I said with finality, but I could see by Dominic's mutinous expression that this debate wasn't over. "If you couldn't even foresee such a relationship between us, then how could you have possibly foreseen it developing between others? This," I waved my hand at the crowd before us, "was completely unpredictable and unprecedented. You couldn't have known it would happen any more than I could have known vampires existed before seeing it with my own eyes."

"Jillian knew."

His words were so soft that I might not have even known he'd spoken had I not seen his lips move. "What?"

Dominic's face was still hard and inscrutable as his gaze swept the crowd. "Jillian knew that many of the vampires in our coven wanted to come out of hiding, and this was why. Vampires in love with humans, and those humans fighting and lying and dying to keep our secret. How many times did it nearly kill you, both physically and emotionally, to know the truth about the creatures in this city, to be at the same crime scene as Greta and know exactly what was causing those crimes, and know that you couldn't say a word? That even if you did, not only would she not believe you, she'd be entranced to forget by the next day?"

I pursed my lips. "You know how much it killed me. You finally broke down and let me write my animal-attack article, knowing how much it killed me."

Dominic nodded. "And imagine all these dozens upon dozens of lovers, friends, and family doing the same, keeping our secret, alienating themselves from their day-lives because they were forced to keep their night-lives secret. I'd always thought that the few who wanted to expose our existence to the public were just power hungry, and Jillian was using that weakness to her advantage to take control of the coven." He shook his head sadly. "But there was a real need in my coven, one I knew nothing about, and this is the proof of my failure."

"*Failure* is a strong word," I objected. "You had the best interests of the coven at heart when you fought against Jillian. You knew that if vampires in your coven went public, the Day Reapers would come. And you knew if the Day Reapers came, they would take control of the coven, execute its leader"—I gave him a pointed look—"and mind-wipe the public into forgetting your existence."

"The Day Reapers did come, and look how that worked out," Dominic said drily. "But you're right: without the Council's support, going public would have immediately alerted them to our coven. They would have deemed our actions treasonous, and they would have executed swift punishment."

I nodded cautiously, waiting for the "but."

"Had I known about these people and how my coven was struggling under the burden of secrecy, I might have softened my stance. I still would have fought against Jillian's betrayal, but I might have petitioned the Council. I could have made strategic moves to eventually sway their laws."

And there it was. "You think that would have worked?" I envisioned High Lord Henry's unyielding expression as he stared down at me like a spider does a fly caught in its web, and I couldn't imagine that man allowing his stance to sway on anything.

"I don't know. Probably not," he admitted, "but at least I could have tried. As Master, it is my duty to lead the coven, protect it, know my coven's heart, and represent it. And on every front, right before the Leveling when Jillian had the opportunity to seize my rule, I failed them." He shook his head in disgust. "I didn't deserve to continue as their Master."

"As your Second, had she truly been loyal, she would have told you what was going on in the coven and helped you lead them, helped you approach the Council, if that's what it took. But she didn't. She—"

"She did! For years she told me that the coven wanted to reveal their existence to humans. She—"

"I heard her speech," I interrupted him right back, refusing to give ground. "In all her raving and justifications for betraying you, never once did she say anything about this," I said, indicating the roomful of morose night bloods and frightened humans, all worried about a missing loved one. "She talked a lot about being tired of hiding in darkness and feeling imprisoned by your secret existence, but never once did she mention that vampires were falling in love with night bloods and had families with humans. She told you what she wanted, but she didn't tell you the truth. You might not have known this was happening in your coven, which was remiss of you—"

Dominic snorted under his breath.

"But she knew, and instead of representing the coven as she was meant to, she used that knowledge to rebel against you and usurp your power, and in doing so, she tore the coven apart. Look at these people, Dominic. She might have revealed your existence to the world, but these people aren't finally with their loved ones like they'd hoped; their loved ones are missing."

"I should have seen her deception and protected the coven against her."

I rolled my eyes. "Fine! You failed them! You should have known Jillian was going to stab you in the back and betray you. You should have known that members of your coven were deceiving you, breaking your one sacred law, and allowing humans—loved ones, but humans all the same—to remember their existence." I threw my hands up in the air, completely exasperated. "With everyone going behind your back instead of having your back, it's no wonder you failed them. They set you up to fail them. But they still need you."

Dominic met my eyes, his expression unfathomable.

"More than ever, now, since they've been betrayed by the woman they'd hoped would free them, they need you to save them from her rule."

"Us," he whispered.

I blinked. "What?"

"I can't save them by myself. As you already said, I need something I've never had: I need someone at my back." His eyes blazed with a deep, volatile emotion I recognized all too well. I no longer shook in fear of that emotion, but I could still feel my body tremble. "I need you."

I cleared my throat. I couldn't act on that look. We were at the morgue, in the makeshift interrogation viewing rooms. The thought of Greta or Rowens—or my brother, for God's sake—walking in should have tempered the heat between us. But knowing that I shouldn't tear the shirt from his body, rip off his pants, and impale myself on him made the desire to do so that much more poignant. I had to clear my throat a second time before I could speak. "That's why we're here. That's why I've brought everyone together and why we have dozens of witnesses to interview. I've got your back, they've got my back, and together, we're taking that bitch down."

The heat in his eyes sizzled, and he closed the distance between us, taking the step toward me that I'd refused to take toward him. "Never in my very long existence would I ever have considered allying with the human police force and Day Reapers to regain my lost position as Master." He smirked, and his lips tipped lopsidedly. A real smile. "But I've seen firsthand the things you're capable of when you have a team behind you. I've seen firsthand the things you were capable of all by yourself when you were a night blood, confined to a wheelchair—"

"Scooter," I corrected stubbornly.

"—and put your mind to do something, to saving someone. In the very short time that I've known you, you've saved my life and Bex's life. You saved Nathan from a fate worse than death. You saved Meredith's life, and you saved the many people Nathan would have continued to prey upon had you not transformed him. You saved the countless civilians Kaden would have continued murdering had you not been willing to play bait to help me stop him."

I let loose an unprofessional snort. "That's one sacrifice I wouldn't willingly repeat," I muttered.

"And yet you did. Over and over again you sacrificed your safety and sanity for the chance to protect this city and its citizens. You acted as bait to allow us to draw out Nathan when he was Damned. You stood up to the Day Reapers while I was being interrogated by them when you couldn't even physically stand. You—"

"I get the point. I'm the sap who risks everything to save the day. What's your point?"

Dominic blinked. "The sap?"

"Everything I've sacrificed—over and over again, as you so eloquently stated—and look at us. Look at the state of our city! It's in ruins, and we're all that's left," I said, shaking my head. The sight of so many people coming forward in reaction to my article had bolstered my spirits with a bolt of optimism, but the longer I spoke to Dominic, the more reality set in.

Dominic cupped my cheeks in his hands, forcing me to face him. "I wouldn't trust anyone else to take what we have left and form it into the weapon we need against Jillian and her army."

I eyed him warily.

"Don't let my melancholy ruin this for you," Dominic said, and I started, wondering if he'd skimmed the thoughts from my mind. "This room debatably encompasses my failure, but I was wrong to share that with you now, on the cusp of your success. You are quite right, and I am going about this all wrong. You—"

"I'm right and *you're* wrong?" I raised my eyebrows. "Are you feeling all right?"

"Let me finish!" he thundered.

I snapped my mouth shut and waited.

"You are more than all this, and I, no matter my seeming omniscience, could never have predicted what you would mean to my coven and this city, and most all, what you would mean to me."

"What are you saying?" I asked.

Dominic stared into my eyes for a long, lingering moment before growling—the sound low and rattling deep in his chest. His grip tightened on my face, and that was my only warning. Suddenly, his lips sealed over mine. His tongue swept into my mouth. His body molded to my body, and my body melted. The smell of chai and hearth embers—the scent of our desire—ignited from our collision, but I could sense something more from us, too. Everything he couldn't find the words to express was in his kiss—in his hands, which burrowed under my shirt until they reached skin; in the goose bumps that flared over my body in heat instead of chills; in the urgency of his hitched breath—the hard evidence of his feelings for me surrounded me and illuminated me from the inside out, without the words.

Someone cleared her throat behind us.

I tore my tongue from Dominic's mouth and snapped my head around to face Greta and Rowens, who were standing behind us. The fact that I hadn't heard them approach spoke volumes about my level of distraction.

I would have detached myself from Dominic's unprofessional embrace—I'd never been caught necking on the job before, ever (probably because I'd never necked on the job before)—except that Dominic didn't loosen his hold. Forcing him to loosen it would involve kicking his ass and possibly a broken table, thrown chair, or shattered plaster. I didn't want to cause a worse scene than the one we'd already been caught in.

Instead, I gritted my teeth and simply raised an eyebrow. "Yes?" I asked, as if being caught necking in an interrogation viewing room during a mass-murder investigation was a common occurrence.

"We've got a problem," Greta said, but I could see the very minute twitch of her lips. If I didn't know better, I'd say she was amused.

"It's a lead, not a problem," Rowens interjected. He eyed us and added, "However, *this* is a problem."

Dominic snorted. "It's an inevitability, not a problem."

"So much of this case is already breaking procedure, we can't afford another liability," Rowens said, dead serious. "Besides the obvious, everything else needs to be by the book."

"Procedure?" Dominic laughed. "Where in your book is there a procedure on a hostile vampire takeover?"

"I said, 'besides the obvious.' That includes the existence of vampires, Damned, Day Reapers, and night bloods. Otherwise, we can pretty much follow procedure for a terrorist attack." Rowens eyed us critically. "And nowhere in that procedure does it outline the need to fuck in an interrogation room."

I jerked back from Dominic, and this time he let me go. "Can we focus on the case, please?"

Greta shrugged. "Keep it professional at work, and we won't make it personal."

"My bad," I said, grimacing. "It's been an intense few days. It won't happen again."

I felt the vibration of Dominic's growl on my back.

"We have a lead?" I asked, attempting to get the conversation back on track.

Greta rolled her eyes heavenward. "We've got something, all right. The woman in interrogation room three claims her son is a vampire and leading the 'vampire revolution.'"

Dominic made a choked noise behind me. "Well, we can rule her testimony out as false. Jillian is leading the uprising, and in case you haven't noticed, she's a woman."

"Still, I figured you'd want to talk to her, see what inside information you might be able to squeeze out," Rowens said.

"It's bullshit," Greta snapped. "She just wants attention. She's scared and lonely and wants to be a part of our efforts here."

Rowens shook his head, unconvinced. "That's not the read I'm getting from her. She doesn't want to be here. She's never trusted the police, and it took a 'vampire revolution' to get her here. Maybe she's misinformed or confused, but she isn't doing this just for attention."

"I don't like encouraging false testimony," Greta said tightly.

"A few more questions can't hurt."

I frowned. "Who is she claiming as her son?"

"Someone named Kaden Alexander," Greta said.

I turned my head to look at Dominic, the denial on the edge of my lips—Dominic had sentenced Kaden to his final death for his crimes against the coven, for his crimes against me, and that sentence had been carried out weeks ago—but his expression had smoothed to unyielding, unfeeling stone.

Chapter 22

The woman sitting at the interrogation-room table had had a hard life. Granted, the past week had been rough on everyone, but for Luanne Alexander, life had been rough long before this past week. The deep frown lines scoring her face and between her brows, the nicotine-stained fingernails, the pockmarks on her cheeks, her gaunt frame, and, most telling of all, the cut of her sharp green eyes as she stared me down told a story of struggle and abuse that had started years before vampires had ever darkened her doorstep.

But I'm sure the vampires hadn't helped.

Rowens and Greta had already teamed up, playing good cop-bad cop, and when that hadn't worked, bad cop-bad cop. When *that* hadn't worked, Greta had let Rowens try to peel the truth from her by himself. His FBI-trained interview skills were honed and dangerous—I knew firsthand how he could crawl under a person's skin without flexing a muscle—but even he couldn't quite crack Luanne's hardened exterior.

I don't know what they thought was missing from the puzzle, but I knew exactly what was missing from mine. Kaden Alexander was supposed to be dead—he'd been sentenced to death, and his sentence had been carried out by Dominic Lysander, the Master vampire of New York City, himself—but according to this woman, by her account Kaden's mother, he was alive and well enough to lead a vampire revolution.

Jesus wept.

I walked into the interrogation room and held out my hand. Luanne eyed the proffered appendage like I might a cockroach. "Mrs. Alexander, it's a pleasure to—"

"Like I told that one-armed officer, it's Ms. Pyle now. Husband's dead, good riddance, and I'm taking back my maiden name," Luanne said, her voice nothing but gravel from decades of chain-smoking.

I resisted the urge to glare through the one-way glass. So much for building a rapport. "Ms. Pyle, my apologies. I'm Cassidy DiRocco, a reporter with the *Sun Accord*, and I—"

"I know who you are," she rasped. "You're the idiot who tried to pass off vampire attacks as animal attacks. When Lysander caught wind of that, he shut you down right quick." She made a terrible sound, almost like clearing a throat filled with tar, over and over again until I realized she was chuckling.

Fuck it. "Good. Then let me be frank. From all accounts, your son is dead."

Luanne shook her head. "Still an idiot, I see."

I narrowed my eyes. That hadn't been quite the reaction I'd anticipated. "Lysander sentenced him to death after finding him guilty of treason and attempted murder."

"Killing a human ain't murder for them. It's good eatin'," Luanne snorted. "Fool girl."

I struggled to keep my face composed. This woman was unreal. Even if her son was a vampire, she was human, for Christ's sake. "Your son attempted to kill Lysander, Master vampire of New York City, and me, his night blood at the time. He was found guilty and his death sentence was carried out."

Luanne narrowed her eyes at me, considering. "And when did all this nonsense take place?"

"A little over a month ago."

"Thought so," Luanne said. She leaned back in her chair, unconcerned.

I raised my eyebrows. "Don't you care about your son's well-being?" I asked.

"Not when I saw him alive and well just yesterday."

I let a mocking smile tip my lips, so Luanne would think I didn't believe her. "Sure," I said, and every vertical wrinkle around her mouth crinkled.

Luanne struck me as a woman who, despite her sharp eyes and keen sense, hadn't been listened to very much over the years. Put on the defensive, she might trip over her own good sense to prove her version of the truth.

Sure enough, Luanne tilted her head and pulled aside the collar of her shirt, baring a neck ravaged by mounds of keloid scar tissue. "What do you make of this, then, hmm?"

I stared at her scars and forced my expression to remain bland. "Whoever you let munch on your neck did a slipshod job of healing you afterward. Doesn't look like the work of a loving son to me."

"Never said he was loving," Luanne said, releasing the collar of her shirt.

I remembered the untamed savagery of Kaden's bite all too well. Unlike Dominic, whose bite was pin-needle precise, Kaden feasted on flesh like a dog with a bone; Ms. Pyle's neck could certainly be the result of Kaden's enthusiasm, but it could just as likely be the result of any number of savagely enthusiastic vampires.

"That doesn't prove shit, lady," I said. My words were deliberately harsh. People didn't hear you unless you spoke to them in a language they understood, and for Luanne, direct and abrasive seemed to be her fluent language.

"You want proof?" she sneered.

I crossed my arms. "It doesn't matter what I want. You came to us. Most of the people here today want to file missing-persons reports. Their loved ones are missing, and they came here looking for answers. But here you are, telling us that we're wrong, that you saw your son just yesterday. If you don't have a missing loved one and you already have all the answers, than why the hell are you here?"

It was a risky move. If I pushed her too hard, she might lose her temper and just leave, but if I pushed her just right, maybe she'd lose her temper and spill her guts.

"I've got fucking proof," she snarled, reaching in her jeans back pocket.

The door slammed open, gouging its handle into the wall, and Greta and Rowens burst into the interrogation room, guns aimed at Luanne's head.

"Freeze!" Greta and Rowens said, their movements and command simultaneous, nearly choreographed.

Luanne froze.

I thought about telling Greta and Rowens to back down; even if Luanne was pulling something nefarious from her back pocket, like a gun—which was unlikely, considering everyone had received a thorough pat-down before entering the waiting room—at this distance, I could probably disarm her before she even pulled the trigger, and if I wasn't close enough for that, I could dodge the bullets. With the exception of Walker's weapons, guns weren't a threat to me anymore.

I could do many things now that Greta couldn't, but I remained silent and let Greta do her thing. No matter how much I had transformed from my former self, I was still just the crime reporter she'd invited into this investigation, and the moment I allowed my newfound vampire strength and abilities to interfere with Greta doing her job, that would make me something else entirely. And I very much liked being a crime reporter, even if I had to report to work with fangs. I'd never been particularly conventional anyway.

Besides, if push came to shove, I could lunge forward to shield her and Rowens from the bullets.

"Raise both hands, slowly, into the air where we can see them," Greta said, her voice low and steady. "Now."

Luanne did, slowly, just like Greta said, and her hands were empty.

Rowens jerked his head, his aim as steady as Greta's.

Greta put up her gun and approached Luanne. She patted her down again, and when she reached her back pocket, found what the woman had been reaching for: her cell phone.

Greta held up the phone and glanced meaningfully at Rowens.

Rowens put up his gun.

"That's what I thought," Ms. Pyle said, her glare as sharp as ever, but she couldn't hide anything from me. I could hear the most minute, nearly undetectable quaver in her voice. She was shaken.

Greta slapped the phone onto the table with the flat of her hand and leaned down to hiss into Luanne's ear. "One wrong move, and your brain is nothing but bullet spatter. Got it?"

Luanne glared back, but nodded.

"Good. Got anything else in your pockets you want to whip out now before we go back behind that glass?"

Luanne shook her head mutely.

"Last chance. You move to pull anything else from your behind, and we shoot first, ask questions later. Hear me?"

"Loud and clear," Luanne ground out from behind clenched teeth.

Greta nodded curtly, and she and Rowens left the room.

Luanne didn't watch them leave, however. Her eyes were all for me.

I lifted my eyebrows. "Problem?"

"Renfield much?" she sneered.

I stared at her for a long moment and tried to compose myself, I really did, but in the end I couldn't help it, not even after years of conducting interviews and being at the receiving end of a few from Greta and Rowens myself. I laughed. "Hypocrite much?"

Luanne shook her head, the disgust she felt etched into every wrinkle across her weathered face. "It was bad enough when the vampires were psychopaths stalking the night, but at least I knew the rules. If Kaden murdered someone and I kept my trap sealed shut, no one remembered come morning. Kaden was stronger and more powerful as a vampire, which was hell on our neighbors—the few who survived—but at least I didn't have to worry about covering his tracks like I did when he was human."

I blinked. I'd always suspected Kaden of having serial killer tendencies, but having his mother outright admit it still took me aback.

"Now here you are in daylight, exposed as the monster you are, with human friends and part of an investigation to hunt and kill my son." She shook her head. "And here I am jumping from one cage to the next, trapped first by the secrets and lies of knowing the truth about your existence, and trapped now by the truth. I prefer the first, thank you very much. At least then I had my son. At least then I knew my place."

I shrugged, feigning nonchalance, and forced myself not to grind my teeth. "So leave," I said.

Luanne stared at me for a hard moment, and I tensed, doubting whether I was playing this right.

Luanne came to us, I reminded myself. *No matter how tough she acts, she has something to say or else she wouldn't be here.*

"Fuck you," she spat. But she didn't leave.

I hid the self-satisfied grin that spread like fresh blood through my limbs.

I blinked. *Warm coffee*, I corrected my thoughts. The self-satisfaction I was feeling spread like warm coffee.

Luanne leaned forward, unaware of my internal struggle. "Mark my words, my Kaden will take you out," she said, her voice more growl than words through her smoke-damaged throat.

"Is that a threat?" I asked, my own voice low and menacing, and unfortunately becoming familiar.

She shook her head. "It's a fact. He's had a vendetta against Lysander for years, and since you helped imprison him, he's got one against you now, too. Nothing, and I mean *nothing* will stand in the way of that monster. He'll rule this city. He won't be satisfied until he's king of everything he's destroyed, and even then, he'll be on the lookout for whatever peon might have survived, so he can bathe in its blood, too."

I let out a huff of a breath. "'That monster' is your son." *Supposedly*, I added to myself.

"Only by blood and not anymore." She picked up and unlocked her phone, and for the first time during our interview, Luanne's fingers visibly trembled. "He ripped out my heart."

I raised my eyebrows, staring at the smooth, unblemished skin of her intact chest.

"Figuratively speaking," she clarified.

"You can't be too literal these days," I commented.

Luanne cackled that terrible, rattling laugh of hers and turned her phone toward me to show me a photo. My mouth watered. My throat closed in a burning ring of thirst and convulsed hungrily. And my face transformed. I couldn't help it; I could feel my fangs elongating, my ears pointing, my forehead thickening, and my nails lengthening to talons from a mere photo, and I couldn't stop my reaction any more than I could have stopped my stomach from rumbling as a human; it was an automatic, physical response to being hungry.

But Luanne wasn't showing me a photo of a hamburger.

Although the synapses in my brain could fire faster than a human's, all my eyes could see at first was the blood. The volume of blood that had sprayed from her wounds and saturated the carpeting, walls, and curtains around her was astounding.

Eventually, I saw past the blood and recognized the human toddler at its center, and I pried my eyes from the image. I was still hungry, my fangs hadn't retracted, my talons hadn't receded, and my face hadn't returned to its human-like curves, but my voice when I finally spoke was calm. For that small accomplishment—that and not attacking Luanne on the spot to satisfy the swift, overwhelming hunger—I gave myself a few brownie points. But only a few, considering my rumbling stomach.

"Your heart, I presume?" I asked.

Luanne nodded. "Lucy was my granddaughter, the only good that bastard ever produced in this world. She was my second chance at doing it right, at raising something that didn't take joy from tearing someone's throat out."

"Goal of the year, right there: don't raise a serial killer," I muttered.

"I made a go of it all alone," Luanne said, her voice as hard as her face, and I suspected, as hard as life had been to her. "I didn't beat him any more than I'd been beat. I protected him from the rapes and scars and sights I'd seen and survived growing up, but somehow, he became one of the fucking monsters I'd always protected him from."

Her eyes filled with tears as her gaze swept over the photo. She relocked the phone and let it lie on the table, its screen black.

"What happened?" I asked softly.

"We holed up in my apartment when the Damned stormed the city. Kaden would visit to feed from me, but I'd fortified the back hallway bathroom against vampires. Lucy and I spent the majority of our time in that bathroom, except when Kaden visited, but even then, I locked her inside until he left."

I frowned, wanting to know why she'd chosen the bathroom of all places to hide a child, but that detail wasn't important enough to interrupt her story, so I let it go and just nodded.

"A week in, we ran out of food," Luanne continued. "I left the apartment to see what I could find and locked Lucy in the bathroom. I didn't know how long I'd be gone—God only knew what was left of the city in the wake of those fuckers—but I told Lucy I'd be back soon."

I bit my lip, knowing exactly where this story was headed, and tasted blood. Damn fangs. "You were away longer than you expected."

Luanne nodded. "And Kaden visited to feed while I was gone."

"I'm so sorry."

She met my eyes squarely. "Have you tasted young blood yet?"

I shook my head.

"It's sweeter, supposedly, and doesn't have that cinnamon heat that you creatures find so irresistible. Not ripe enough, I guess," Luanne said, shaking her head. "But my Kaden was always fond of children; even as a human, he took pleasure in carving flesh and spilling blood. I think killing was just an unfortunate by-product. The body doesn't bleed as well once the heart stops, you know. He told me that once as a boy, staring at the neighbor's butchered dog, and I knew then that he wasn't right. Never would be." Luanne sniffed coldly. "He was a monster long before becoming a vampire."

I stared at her, encouraging her with my attention more than with words. Anything I said would be inadequate.

Luanne took a shuddering breath, the vibrating tremor of her inhale the only sound in the hollow room. Eventually, she spoke. "When I came home with the groceries, Lucy was already stiff and cold on the kitchen floor, like… well, like you just saw her."

I pursed my lips, willing my tongue to swallow the question, but this time, I couldn't help myself. Even with the craving burning my throat, my mind could still discern right from wrong, even if my body couldn't. "And when you found her, your first thought was to take a picture of her?"

Luanne's eyes snapped up to meet mine. "Fuck you, you sick shit sack," she spat. "Kaden took the picture. I found it later, after I'd already cleaned and buried her."

I frowned. "Why would he—"

"I'd left the phone with her, so she'd have it in an emergency. As if 911 would even work. As if there was anyone to call for help besides me," Luanne said, her voice nothing but gravel-ground glass. "Kaden messaged the photo to his own phone. A souvenir."

"He could have used his own phone," I murmured.

"And spare me the pain of stumbling across the photo and reliving that horror?" She shook her head. "Right."

I pursed my lips. "When did all this happen?"

"Didn't you see the date above the photo? Or were you too focused on all the damn blood?" Luanne sneered. "Two days ago. Lucy was attacked and killed by Kaden, my son, her own damn father, two days ago. I buried my baby yesterday." She met my gaze. "And then I read your article. If Kaden was sentenced to death last month, and if that sentence was carried out, how the fuck did he do this to my Lucy two days ago?" she said, flashing the photo at me again, her hand and the phone visibly shaking.

She was telling the truth. I could tell by the steady contractions of her heart, the cinnamon spice of her constant fear, and the weight in her unyielding eyes. She was frightened by me because I was a vampire, but she wasn't nervous and she didn't falter. Even the best, most sadistic, sociopathic liar alive couldn't lie to me unnoticed anymore; she couldn't control the flavor of the words as they spilled into the air any more than I could effectively describe their taste, but the taste of her words convinced me like nothing else could of a much harder truth to swallow.

Humans couldn't lie to me anymore, but vampires could.

Five weeks ago, while I'd recovered in the hospital from our confrontation with Jillian and Kaden, Dominic had assured me that both Jillian and Kaden had been brought before the coven on charges of treason and attempted murder, found guilty, and sentenced to death. He had told me that their sentence had been carried out. Their final death.

Jillian was alive and well, having usurped his coven, but I could understand Dominic's reluctance to kill Jillian. She had been his Second, and the most trusted and beloved vampire in his coven, right up until the moment when she'd betrayed him. Love was annoying that way; it didn't matter that she had stabbed him in the back—literally and with her own talons—the love was still there, bitter and biting, but there all the same. So instead of carrying out the full weight of her sentence, he'd condemned her to an eternity in the Underneath, which honestly was a worse sentence than death, but that's what love does to a person: it confuses right and wrong, hope and the hard truth.

What I couldn't understand, and in fact resented, was him allowing me to believe that Kaden's sentence had been carried out. There had been no love lost between those two.

"I don't know how Kaden could have killed Lucy if he was already dead," I said, in answer to Luanne's hanging question. "But I intend to find out."

Chapter 23

"You said Kaden was dead. You said the coven had found him guilty of treason, and for his crimes against the coven, for his crimes against *me*, you said he was sentenced to death and that sentence had been carried out." My words were clipped and hard and echoed hollowly in the interview viewing room I'd dragged Dominic into, the very same room we'd been caught kissing in less than an hour ago, back when I'd thought we'd known everything important about one another. I wasn't fool enough to think I'd ever know everything about this man—it was impossible to know everything about anyone who'd lived a normal human lifespan, let alone someone who had already been alive for over four hundred years before my birth—but I'd have staked my life on the fact that we no longer withheld secrets from one another.

Dominic had the nerve to meet my eyes. He didn't even flinch when he spoke. "I know what I said."

I stared at him, shaking my head slowly from side to side. I couldn't seem to stop the movement, as if I could deny it all as a nightmare. But this was one truth I couldn't wake up from. "You let me think you'd killed Jillian, and I spent weeks suffering from her lingering hold on my mind—I suffered through her cravings and pain and constant taunting—"

"Had I known, I could have helped you. You should have told me that you could feel her. I could have—"

"You should have told me that she was still alive! I thought I was going crazy, hearing and feeling the thoughts of a dead woman!"

"We've already had this argument. I thought we'd come to terms with all this. We've *moved on*," Dominic growled, slashing his hand through the air as if he could will away the argument as easily as he forced his will on everything and everyone else.

But not on me. Not anymore. "I thought we had to, but now here we are, weeks later, after I've trusted you to transform me, trusted you in my life, inside my body, convinced Greta and Rowens to trust you on this investigation, and you *still* don't trust me with the truth."

"I didn't mean for you to find out this way. I—"

I could hear the bleat of his backtracking like a lamb being dragged to slaughter, and I realized another truth he'd hidden. "You knew Kaden had been released from his confinement when we rescued Bex from the Underneath," I said. It wasn't even a question. It was fact: I could hear it in the desperation of his eyes, in the taste of his words. I knew the truth of it in my bones the way I used to know bread was burning from the living room long before turning to see the flames from the toaster, because I could smell the stink of it.

"Yes," he admitted.

"You left me vulnerable all over again." My head was still shaking, still in denial. "Did you learn nothing from what happened with Jillian? Do *I* mean nothing?"

"You mean everything," Dominic growled.

I laughed. The sound was bitter and scraped painfully against my own eardrums. Dominic winced.

"Why?" I asked. "After everything we've been through and survived together, after all the times I've saved you and you've saved me, why continue to lie?"

Dominic's eyes blazed. "You know exactly why. Jillian was my Second, and Kaden a member of my coven, the survival of which I've spent the majority of my four hundred years ensuring. As Master, it's my duty to carry out their death sentences, but I couldn't, Cassidy. No matter their crimes against the coven, no matter even their crimes against you, no matter their betrayal of me—" Dominic's voice broke. He shook his head warily, taking a second to regain his composure. "God knows, Kaden is a sick, murdering evil piece of shit," Dominic said, his tone proper and clipped despite the vulgarity. "But I'm not. I couldn't give them their final death."

I nodded, waiting.

"But the coven expected me to uphold the duty of their Master, so I condemned Jillian and Kaden to the Underneath—an arguably worse sentence than final death—and told the coven that their sentence had been carried out." Dominic stared at me, his eyes pleading. "With the Leveling approaching, I was steadily losing my strength and power over the coven;

had the coven discovered my weakness, they would have used that to strip me of what little power I still maintained. Don't you see, Cassidy? I had no choice."

I stopped shaking my head. "You're right. The coven might have turned your compassion and empathy against you had they discovered your secret. But I'm not concerned about why you'd lie to the coven. Dominic"—I let loose a long, sad sigh—"why did you continue to lie *to me*?"

Dominic opened his mouth, closed it, and opened it again, at a loss.

"I don't care that you didn't carry out their execution. I understand exactly why you didn't, and in fact, I respect you for it. What I can't understand, or abide, is you not telling me the truth," I said softly. "Is there anything else I should know? Anything else you've been keeping from me that may or may not bite me in the ass tomorrow?"

He shook his head vehemently. "No, there's nothing else. There are no secrets between us."

"That's what I thought, too, until I got into that interrogation room half-hour ago, and she shattered that illusion 'right quick,'" I said bitterly. "You always saw the potential in me and our relationship. From the first, you wanted me as your night blood, demanded my loyalty, and coerced my aid in your diabolical schemes to save your coven. You had such high expectations for us long before I saw you as anything but a monster. But you"—I shook my head and my finger at him—"you shattered every expectation I had for you. From the first, I thought you were a monster, a murderer, and evil, just like all the others of your kind." I placed my hand gently on his cheek, and he closed his eyes at the feel of my touch. "I was wrong about nearly everything about you and your kind, but being wrong this time was the first time it broke my heart."

His eyes flew open. "Cassidy, please, I—"

I gripped his face tighter in my hand. "Promise me, by the final certainty of the sun, that there are no more secrets between us."

"Jesus Christ, have we really come to this?"

I hadn't realized how cold my face was until tears overflowed from my eyes and scalded my cheeks. I could only imagine how gaunt and monstrous I looked. "Swear it!"

"I swear by the sun, Cassidy, that there are no secrets between us." Dominic gripped my shoulders and shook me, gently but firmly. "I swear, Cassidy."

Part of me expected all the hard-won bonds connecting his soul to mine to snap and fall limp between us with that final lie, the lie that would break us apart permanently, irrevocably. But they didn't. His promise held true, the bonds between us remained unbreakable, and his promise tied us closer. We were more permanently bound than we had been a moment before, even if I still felt fragile enough to shatter.

"Good," I murmured, releasing him. "That's good."

His hold on my shoulders tightened. "Cassidy—"

"We should go. Everyone's waiting on us."

I turned away, but Dominic pulled me back roughly. "They can continue to fucking wait."

He sealed his lips over mine, stealing my breath along with my sanity. The hearth between us, separate from my hurt and reservations, ignited as bright and scalding as ever. It seemed a simple fundamental action-reaction inside me with this man: he kissed me and I burned. But I wasn't alone in the reaction. I could smell the electric sting on his skin, the brand my kiss had on his soul as surely as he scorched mine. As unlikely and unequal a paring as we had begun, the force driving us forward and together was equal between us, and in that equality, I couldn't find purchase to fight back.

I should have raked my talons across his face and told him exactly where to stuff his kisses and excuses, but when the person in your arms has already claimed the very deepest, darkest depths of yourself, where do you dig down to find the strength to pull away?

"I'm sorry," he murmured against my lips between kisses, so I couldn't discern where his kiss started and apology ended.

"I know," I whispered, biting his lip and soothing the bite with a quick lick.

He growled, his grip on my upper arms tightening. "Condemning Kaden to the Underneath was my burden to bear, and by the time it should have been yours as well, we'd become so tangled in the war with Jillian and saving Nathan and transforming you and just *surviving* that I never found the right moment to share the secret. I didn't deliberately keep it from you, but I should have found a way to tell you before now." He leaned back from the kiss and met my eyes. "It won't happen again."

I could taste the truth in his words like the final, decadent smears of cream from a cake—no kaleidoscope-confusion of hidden and mixed emotions from him anymore—but my cold heart still felt bruised. Funny, how it could go both ways, the head and the heart refusing to listen to each other. Reason, no matter how reasonable, never could convince emotion.

"Prove it," I murmured, softening my words with another fierce kiss before finally, agonizingly, pulling away.

Chapter 24

"As far as last-ditch efforts go, I suppose it's not the worst plan I've ever heard," Rowens conceded.

Even without my newfound, heightened senses, I would have felt the uncertainty and tension filling the room. With my new senses, I actually smelled it like the acrid warning of smoke. If we inhaled too much, we'd succumb before the real battle even began.

"This is *not* a last-ditch effort," I defended. "This is our best shot at taking down Jillian and reducing the risk of casualties to both us and the night bloods she's transformed."

"You mean the mindless, monstrous, heart-eating army of Damned guarding her front door," Greta clarified.

"They can be saved," Nathan insisted. He raised his hand. "I was once a mindless, heart-eating monster, and look at me now."

Greta snorted. "Now, you're a lucid heart-eating monster. Such an improvement."

"It is," Rowens said, calmly, as usual.

I sighed. This meeting of the minds was going as well as could be expected, I supposed, except for my creeping suspicion that perhaps "as well as could be expected" wasn't going to be enough to win this war. Not nearly enough. Jillian had an army of almost one hundred Damned vampires and the entire New York City coven at her back. I looked around at the players who had my back: Greta and Rowens were sitting as far as possible from Bex and her murderous eye, which was currently trained on Ronnie, who determinedly ignored her regard. Rafe, Neil, Keagan, and Jeremy sat around Ronnie, but Theresa and Logan sat slightly apart from their group, next to Keagan. They were cold and rarely participated.

Nathan and Dominic sandwiched me. Next to Nathan sat Meredith and Dr. Chunn, and in the far corner away from everyone was an empty seat where Walker should have been.

"As well as could be expected" was going to fail.

"But it doesn't matter how good—or 'not the worst'—the plan is. It won't work unless everyone is on board," I said.

Rowens raised his eyebrows and glanced at the empty chair in the corner. "Everyone?"

"He'll be here," Ronnie insisted, but even she looked a little sheepish as she added, "I hope."

"He won't," Dominic growled. "He knows better than to show his face with me here."

Greta cocked her head at Dominic and then settled her eyes on me. "I thought we were all on the same team."

"We are." I squeezed Dominic's knee under the table. No one wanted to know if Greta and Dr. Chunn had supplied Walker with his Day Reaper ammunition more than me, but now was not the time or the place. If Bex knew what Walker was capable of, she would kill him—or at least try to—and we needed everyone to put aside their personal battles in favor of fighting the war against Jillian. Granted, leaving her unaware and vulnerable to Walker's potential attack didn't sit well with me, either, so the faster everyone was on board, playing nice, and focused on the common enemy instead of each other, the better.

"Except for Walker," Meredith said.

"What else is new?" Bex scoffed.

I groaned to myself. I could do many things now as a vampire, and Day Reaper to boot, but reaching under the table like Stretch Armstrong to unobtrusively squeeze Meredith's knee on the other side of the table was not one of my many talents.

I kicked her shin under the table instead.

Nathan grunted and glared at me. Wrong shin.

"Whether or not Walker is on board is his choice," I said, soldiering forward. "We all have choices to make, the most important of which, in my opinion, is uniting as one force against Jillian. Everyone here at this table needs to commit to that, or we're just planning a mass funeral."

Rowens pursed his lips. "Run through it again."

Jeremy made an imperceptible noise in the back of his throat. I could hear it because I could very nearly feel the rubber-band snap of his brain synapses firing, but even Jeremy knew better than to groan loud enough for Rowens to hear.

I leaned forward, more than willing to comply. "The coven has a hidden underground entrance, but thanks to our little mishap while smuggling out Bex, Jillian is likely now aware of that entrance. We'll need leverage to have a hope of actually infiltrating the coven and making it to the honeycombs."

Neil frowned in confusion, and Rafe opened his mouth.

"The great hall," Dominic clarified.

Rafe grunted. Neil still looked confused.

"Kaden is our leverage," I said, refocusing the conversation. "He visits his mother to feed from her every night. We plan a stakeout, ambush him, and before Jillian gets wind of it, we infiltrate the coven. When she makes her move against us, we'll use Kaden to force her down. At the very least, she'll hesitate long enough for us to make our move."

"And what exactly is our move?" Ronnie asked hesitantly.

Jeremy snorted. "I'd forget it, too, if I could. Our move sucks."

Logan growled something admonishing under his breath.

"Well, it kind of does," Keagan admitted, "considering our move is to save people who are more likely to kill us than the Damned."

"When we release the Day Reapers, they aren't going to kill anyone, not the Damned and not us. They're going to help us save the Damned."

"In the interest of full disclosure, the Day Reapers may very well kill me," Dominic added.

Bex raised her hand. "And me."

I forced a grin and hoped it looked more pleasant than just a baring of fangs. "That's why it's in your best interest to convince them otherwise."

Rafe crossed his arms over his chest. "We should just leave them to rot in the Underneath, where they belong."

Bex growled low under her breath.

Dominic sighed. "Rafe—"

"They're tyrants, and you well know it!" Rafe said. "No offense," he added as an afterthought to Bex and me. "But if Jillian hadn't locked them up when she did, they would have hunted down Lysander for transforming you and killed him for it, even though he *saved* you. Screw them!"

"We need them," I said calmly. "Jillian has transformed dozens of night bloods into the Damned, and there's only three of us here who can fight them. Bex, Nathan, and I need all the help we can get. We can't do this on our own."

"You entranced every Damned vampire in her coven. Dozens upon dozens of them paused at your command," Bex said, her tone half wonder and half disgust. "Y'all don't need jack shit."

I sighed. "I will, of course, attempt to entrance them again, but Jillian won't make the same mistake twice. She'll deflect the command next time, I'm sure. In which case, I need to be careful with my commands, and we need backup," I insisted. "Hence the Day Reapers."

"We may still take Jillian by surprise. There's still a chance—miniscule but possible—that she believes we are dead," Dominic said.

A slow grin spread across Bex's face. "Considering she adopted only some of your Master's power, we have much more than a miniscule chance. She's never been a Master and has no idea the all-encompassing power she should have obtained. She may think whatever fraction of power she obtained is the full power and therefore an indication that you indeed died at the Leveling."

"Nevertheless, we should stay the course," Dominic insisted. "If we release the Day Reapers ourselves, *rescuing* them from the Underneath and Jillian's reign, the Lord High Chancellor might be grateful."

"So grateful as to absolve you of your crimes and not execute you?" Neil asked, his voice nearly childlike with hope.

Rafe grunted, unconvinced.

"The Day Reapers might help us; they might not. We can't predict their mood, so let's move on to something we *can* predict," Nathan said. "How we are going to leverage Kaden after we ambush him?"

"We restrain him, bring him with us into the coven, and when the timing's right, we threaten his life, forcing Jillian to back down." I raised my eyebrows. "I thought that part of the plan was pretty straightforward."

Nathan shrugged. "Do we really want Kaden in close proximity to Jillian, giving her the opportunity to save him?"

I cocked my head to the side. "What did you have in mind?"

"Something simple and effective, like video chat. We keep Kaden at the apartment and threaten Jillian with his death from across the city."

Greta nodded. "Sounds simple and effective to me."

"That would be brilliant," Dominic agreed, "except that we don't have service everywhere in the coven. It's spotty at best in the great hall and nonexistent in the Underneath."

"We don't need service for video chat. Just Wi-Fi," Nathan said.

Dominic grinned. "Wi-Fi we have."

I blinked. "Since when does the coven have Wi-Fi?"

"Since you showed me the necessity of carrying a cell phone. Do you know how much data one hundred and fifty-three vampires accumulate?" Dominic sighed, shaking his head.

"Wi-Fi was a necessary evil," Rafe agreed ruefully.

"Finally," Neil muttered.

I shook my head; the generational differences in Dominic's coven were mind-boggling, only rivaled by the logistics of attaining Wi-Fi in an underground lair. "But it would be near impossible for the signal to penetrate the coven's stone walls. I have enough trouble getting a decent connection in my apartment! You would need a wired connection to a Wi-Fi—"

"To a Wi-Fi access point in each room," Neil finished for me. "I know. I did most of the drilling. Do you know how much fishing wire it takes just to—"

Rafe clapped him on the shoulder. "She doesn't. And she doesn't want to know."

I did, actually, but not today. "Jillian may have changed the password," I pointed out.

Neil shook his head. "She didn't."

I frowned. "How do you know? She could have—"

"The password can be changed?" Dominic asked.

Neil held out his hand, his expression near comical. *You see what I live with?* his face said.

"Just because Dominic's Kryptonite—besides the sun—is technology, doesn't mean that it's Jillian's, too."

Rafe nodded. "Neil drilled everything into place, and Sevris waved his techy wand over everything until it worked. No one cares how. When was the last time you changed your home Wi-Fi password?"

"Okay," I said, regrouping. "We have Kaden. Miraculously, we have Wi-Fi, and—"

"I'm sorry, but I don't think we have Kaden," Theresa interrupted. "No mother would willingly give up her own son. Something's up there."

"He murdered her baby granddaughter," I said. "She's good for it."

"She's unreliable, but I agree, she's good for it," Greta said. "What I'm not sure I agree with is why we're wasting our time and risking our lives breaking into the coven. Why not use Kaden as leverage to coax Jillian out?"

I narrowed my eyes on Greta. Her face was neutral and sincere. Too sincere. If she wasn't human, I'd suspect her of deliberately kaleidoscope-confusing her emotions, like Dominic had taught me, so I couldn't get a read on her. Then again, considering Greta and her many talents, I wouldn't be surprised if that was exactly what she was doing.

"There's nowhere else we can keep everyone contained," I said, "and we'd be showing our hand too early if we sent—what, a ransom note?" I shook my head. "We'd lose the element of surprise, and we need every advantage we can get. You want another Prospect Park massacre on our hands?"

"Of course not," Greta said.

"Because that's exactly what we'd get. The moment we held Kaden hostage and made our demands, Jillian would hone in on Kaden's location and descend on us with all the rage of her Damned army," I said. "This time, we're bringing the battle to Jillian, and any casualties will be people who signed up for this craziness. No innocent bystanders."

Greta nodded.

I looked around the table—Nathan, Meredith, Rowens, Keagan, and Jeremy were all grimly nodding their agreement, too. Theresa and Logan shared a look, but they didn't voice an argument. For the first time during this entire meeting, everyone was actually in agreement.

The telltale wind chime of Greta's pleasure lit the air between us as she took in everyone's nodding heads, and I suppressed a grin. Greta was good.

"So…we ambush Kaden, infiltrate the coven while the majority of the Damned are out hunting, and confront Jillian after they return. Then—"

"It'll be easier to subdue Jillian without having to simultaneously battle the Damned," Nathan interrupted. "If we can confront her before the Damned return for the day, we have a better chance of surviving."

"Yes," I conceded, "but we don't know how much control she has over the Damned. What if she has a mind connection with them like she had with me? She'd be able to warn them that we're there."

"Let them be warned," Nathan said. "Whether they come with the knowledge that their master is in distress makes no difference. They're too consumed with bloodlust to care about anything else."

"If Jillian has the ability to communicate with the Damned, what's to stop her from communicating with Kaden?" Rowens asked.

"Jillian transformed the Damned with her bite and blood," Dominic explained. "She created that connection with them, but she doesn't have that connection with Kaden, because I transformed Kaden."

I raised my eyebrows at Dominic.

"Not one of my better judgment calls, I'll admit," he said, his tone grim. "I'm lucky Jillian was a stronger vampire, or he might have inherited the position of Second."

"Yeah, you're so lucky that Jillian—your betrayer and the force behind the destruction of New York City—became your Second instead of a serial killer," I said, my voice saturated with sarcasm. "After we confront and overthrow Jillian, Bex will release the other Day Reapers from the Underneath and convince them to help us subdue and drain the Damned.

The humans will feed the Damned their blood to transform them and…" I paused to steel my nerves. This was the part of the plan that no one really liked—as if there were a part that everyone actually liked. "And then Dominic will kill Jillian to seal the transformations."

For the second time in as many times as I'd outlined the plan, the room erupted, everyone arguing and no one listening.

"We can't force the public to help. They're the innocent bystanders we were just talking about protecting."

"Technically, 'sealing the transformation' isn't real. You know that, right? There's nothing to support that Nathan hasn't fully transformed back from being Damned because Jillian is still alive. Not that Jillian shouldn't face the consequences of her crimes, but—"

"Dominic just wants the full Master's power to transfer back to him."

"As former Master, that power is mine by right."

"With Jillian's death, it's likely the Master's power will transfer to her Second, not the former Master."

"It's possible it could transfer to the person who actually kills her, former Master or not. We've never had a new Master claim the hearts of the coven following a Leveling in which the current Master lived. It's unprecedented among our kind, and we can't predict how the power will transfer. If it transfers cleanly at all."

"All that is irrelevant. The Day Reapers will just slaughter us and call it a day."

The various bullhorns, bird squawks, thunderclaps, and sirens—the sounds of everyone's anger and annoyance and frustration—drowned out the sounds of their words as they argued over one another. I covered my ears, feeling trampled by their emotions, and when that didn't work, I lifted the table and threw it over everyone's head and across the room.

The table pounded a hole in the drywall and cracked in half when it hit the floor. People in the waiting room on the other side of the wall shrieked; the sounds and smells of their fear lit the air. Rowens and Greta cleared their guns from their holsters, but I'd already sat back down, my hands neatly folded in my lap, still and waiting. Everyone was tense and uncertain, but the move, although perhaps a bit dramatic, had had the desired effect.

The room fell quiet, and I could actually hear my own thoughts and feel my own emotions instead of being swamped by everyone else's. The silence was a reprieve after such sensory overload, so I breathed in that feeling, the peace of quiet, if not of serenity, and steeled myself to face everyone's concerns, one by one.

I turned to Greta first. "The public will help because their loved ones need saving. They're not innocent, because they know exactly what they're signing up for, and they're not bystanders, because they want to help. They left the false security of their underground bunkers and safehouses to report their family and friends missing. They're primed for this plan."

Greta lowered her gun. "What if no one is willing?"

"Then their loved ones die. Either way, after tonight, there won't be any more Damned in New York City."

Greta nodded.

I flicked my eyes to Dr. Chunn next. "I don't care if sealing the transformation is necessary or not. Jillian does not come out of this alive. After everything she's done, after everyone she's killed and tried to kill, she can*not* rule the New York City coven, and the only way to strip her of the little power she's stolen is to kill her."

Dr. Chunn nodded. "That, I support."

Then I met Bex's gaze. "Do you have a problem with Dominic reclaiming his position as Master vampire of New York City?"

Bex shook her head. "No problem here. Just an observation: he lost that power once. Doesn't seem wise to allow him to have it again."

Dominic narrowed his eyes. "Looking to expand your kingdom, *Beatrix*?"

"Just an observation," Bex said again, and she let it go at that.

I glanced at Rafe last. "You're right. We can't predict how the Master's power will transfer. We just need to stick to the plan and roll with the punches, but"—I glared at Ronnie, who'd shrunk in on herself—"no matter what happens, we will not panic. None of this is irrelevant. We will adapt as needed and survive. Jillian and Kaden will not. Agreed?"

Everyone, even Theresa and Logan, nodded this time.

Rowens tapped a finger on the table, thinking. "The earlier in the night we infiltrate the coven, the better. Our plan is established and well planned, but it has a lot of moving parts that may take time, especially when hiccups arise."

Greta nodded. "What are your thoughts on countering that?"

"Currently, we can't control when we infiltrate the coven because we need to ambush Kaden first. He may decide to stalk the city all night before visiting his mother, in which case, we'd get a late start infiltrating the coven. We need to split into two teams, so our timing isn't based on his. Team one ambushes Kaden while team two infiltrates the coven. By the time team two confronts Jillian, team one will need to have Kaden subdued and detained."

"We won't be bound by Kaden's schedule," Greta said, nodding. "I like it."

"I don't," Dominic growled. "The only people in this room capable of confronting Kaden are Nathan, Cassidy, Bex, and me. We need Bex with us to release the Day Reapers from the Underneath, and I refuse to be separated from Cassidy for such an extended time. So…" Dominic lifted his hands, waiting for more suggestions.

"That leaves me," Nathan said. "I can do it."

I shook my head. "I need you in the coven with me to confront Jillian and subdue the Damned."

"You'll have Dominic at your side for Jillian, and the Day Reapers can handle the Damned without me," Nathan reasoned. "There's no one else here who can ambush and subdue Kaden."

I opened my mouth, determined to find a solid reason for him to remain on team two, my team, besides pure selfishness—when the meeting-room door opened.

I didn't need to watch Greta and Rowens clear their guns only to relax; I didn't need to witness Ronnie's face bloom and blush only to shutter closed again. Nor did I need to turn around to know that Walker had just entered the room. He was standing behind me. I could smell the peppermint effervescence of his scent. Honestly, I should have smelled it earlier, but considering the many overwhelming sounds and tastes and smells battering my senses, I wasn't surprised I'd missed it.

"I beg to differ," Walker said, his drawl low and smug. "I can damn well ambush and subdue anything I want. Isn't that right, DiRocco?"

I closed my eyes, keeping the hurt and rage and stabbing betrayal locked inside the padlocked safe hidden deep inside myself, but I was the only one. The last thing I heard before the soft whoosh of air being punched from Walker's gut was Dominic's unmistakable, rattling growl.

Chapter 25

Greta and Rowens had their guns out and aimed—a second time in as many seconds—at Dominic, but had Dominic intended to inflict permanent damage to Walker's person, he could have done so before anyone even processed his movement, let alone retaliated with bullets. Instead, he'd only punched Walker in the gut with his closed fist. He hadn't sliced open Walker's throat with his fangs or eviscerated him on his talons. And he'd pulled the punch. He was restraining his strength and power to human proportion, and in acknowledgment of that, Greta and Rowens kept their aim but held their fire.

"Lysander," Greta said, her voice low but sharp in warning. "Don't force my hand."

"I apologize for interrupting the meeting with violence," Dominic responded, his voice nearly unintelligible though his rattling growls, "but he forced *my* hand."

I stood and turned to face the brawl behind me, putting eyes to the scene I'd already envisioned from its sounds. Heedless of the guns and the futility of fighting Dominic, Walker punched back, clipping Dominic on the chin with a strong left cross, and Dominic—eager for any excuse to pummel Walker—snatched Walker by the neck and slammed him into the wall. But even that movement, as theatrical as it was, had been measured. The drywall behind Walker didn't even crack, and Dominic was careful to prevent Walker's head from whiplashing.

Their noses nearly touching, Dominic snarled in Walker's face, "You are not welcome here!"

Walker grinned and then spoke, proving that Dominic's hold on his neck was pretty much for show. "I was invited."

Ronnie wrung her hands nervously. As usual, her instincts for survival were nil. "I'm sorry," she whispered.

Dominic didn't even bat an eyelash in Ronnie's direction. "You know well enough that Ronnie does not speak for us. I speak for us, and I say *you are not welcome*."

"It's not a matter of welcome. It's a matter of necessity." Walker's grin widened. "You need me."

Dominic's growl swelled the silence.

Rowens sighed. "He's got a point."

"The hell he does," Dominic said, his words scraping from his throat like the grindings from a wood chipper.

"His skills would be a tremendous help to our mission."

"No matter if we need him, do we really want him?" Neil asked, uncertainly. His eyes darted between Dominic, Walker, and me nervously and then settled, surprisingly, on Greta. "We're all supposed to be allies, working together as a team against our common enemy, and despite our differences, we *have* been working together. Except for Walker. If we give him a task as important as capturing our leverage, the very thing ensuring Cassidy and Lysander's relative safety when infiltrating the coven, I don't trust him not to deliberately sabotage everything in favor of the personal pleasure of thwarting Lysander and seeking revenge on Cassidy."

Greta pursed her lips and turned to me. "Give it to me straight, Cassidy. What the hell happened between you two?" She held up her hand. "The short version, please."

I considered my options with Bex still present, but hell, Dominic was already half choking Walker. Bex would have to get in line. I'd been waiting for the right time and place to confront Greta about Walker's ammunition, but maybe I'd been procrastinating more than waiting. The time had come, and worse than facing the business end of Greta's handgun, facing her now on the teetering cusp on our friendship made something hot and trembling close like a vise around my own throat.

I pinned Greta's gaze with mine squarely. "Walker ambushed me in my own apartment," I said. "He had weapons I didn't know existed and used them against me with the intent to cause real and permanent harm. He attacked me."

Bex growled. "He had *what*?"

Dr. Chunn leaned forward. "He had weapons specifically engineered for Day Reapers?"

Greta had faced criminals ranging from petty thieves to serial killers in her line of work, and she could face both with whatever mask she chose—good cop, bad cop, flirt, hard ass—whatever got the job done and done right. But Greta's mask couldn't hide her true feelings from me, not anymore. No matter her decade-developed dead-eyed stare or bored-washed expression, I could smell and hear and taste her nonverbal reaction just as vividly as, if not better than, Dr. Chunn's inquisitive excitement.

And no matter that Greta tried to act as if she was in complete control of her team, that Walker's possession of weapons capable of killing a Day Reaper wasn't a complete and utter shock, a whirring siren blasted from her body, perfuming the air with burned rubber and exposing the truth.

Greta and Dr. Chunn hadn't provided Walker with ammunition to kill me. They'd been left to founder in the dark as much as me and everyone else.

Relief swept through me, so sudden and swift it nearly hurt. I cleared my throat, but when I spoke, my voice trembled. "Don't sound too excited, Doc."

"Sorry. It's nothing personal. I've developed some ammunition that might pierce the Damned's hide and not be expelled, but we're down to the wire. If we have another resource to tap for effective weapons, we need to seize it."

Bex rolled her eye. The sequins stitched on the patch over the other winked under the overhead lights. "Maybe if you focused less on pointless theories about oxygen deficiency, we wouldn't have to borrow weapons from a man who continues to field-test his ammunition on our faces."

Rowens's patient, impassive expression never faltered, but a tsunami of bees swarmed stinger-first into my face from the blast of his anger, and his anger wasn't even directed at me. "Dial it back, Bex," Rowens warned softly.

Dr. Chunn placed a quieting hand on Rowens's shoulder—his residual limb, really—and he relaxed back in his chair.

"My 'pointless theories' regarding the diet of re-transformed night bloods such as Nathan have been *delayed* due to lack of resources, limited time, and order of priority," Dr. Chunn clarified pointedly, "but my top priority, developing ammunition against the Damned using a synthetic replica of your blood, has been successful. And you're welcome for not field-testing them on your face," she added.

"Field-testing Damned ammunition on me would be pointless; I'm a Day Reaper." Bex did grin then, baring fangs. "A pointless test to prove your pointless theories," Bex teased.

Dr. Chunn grinned back, and even without the fangs, through her glasses, and past her flawlessly groomed person, her grin was savage. "Not completely pointless."

"We digress," Greta interrupted. "Dr. Chunn is apparently not the only one of us who has successfully developed new ammunition, but she is the only one sharing her developments with the team."

She turned back to face me, and I sucked in my breath sharply at the feral protectiveness in her gaze. Greta wasn't fooled. She could see through my mask with her human eyes nearly as well as I could sense the world in vampire Technicolor. She'd known me too long and too well, and she was too good at her job to see otherwise. For once, her perceptiveness worked in my favor because she could see plain as day, no matter my fangs and pointed ears and five-inch talons, that I was telling the truth.

Which meant that Walker had been holding out on all of us.

"Do you think Walker would jeopardize our entire mission just to get back at you?" she asked me point-blank.

"I can't speak for him," I said, trying to be fair, "but if you're asking me if I trust him at my back with a weapon that can potentially kill me—a weapon he's already used against me—the answer is no."

"His actions speak for him," Bex said, her voice once again nonchalant as she gazed at her painted, pointed talons. "During our last mission to save and transform Nathan, he betrayed us, killed Rene, shot Dominic, and left us all for dead." She shrugged. "He'll betray us again if given the chance, I have no doubt."

"He has attacked many of us several times," Rafe agreed. "He can't be trusted."

"Maybe he attacked the lot of you with good reason," Rowens said, still in his calm, considering voice.

"He could have proven himself a team player by sharing his knowledge of Day Reaper ammunition, but he didn't," Dr. Chunn said softly.

"Of course not," Dominic growled. "Not when he could keep the ammunition to himself to use against Cassidy."

Rowens nodded, but when he spoke, he said, "It could have been self-defense. Let the man speak for himself."

"I don't hear him defending himself now," Neil muttered.

All eyes, like choreographed theater lighting, focused on Walker.

Walker gurgled an unintelligible response around Dominic's grip. I bit my lip, wondering how long his chokehold hadn't been for show.

Rowens leveled his eyes on Dominic in reproach. "Lysander, if you please?"

The rattling hum of Dominic's reluctance growled through the room. He loosened his grip, but only enough to allow Walker the ability to speak again.

Walker cleared his throat. "It's always self-defense against a vampire."

His words, though roughened by Dominic's bruising grip, were unmistakably wary, and I had the sudden, strange impression from the dual sound of his words and the creaking floorboard whine of his emotions, that he was saying the words by rote. He didn't actually believe them anymore, but for appearance's sake and pride, he would still say them.

For appearance's sake and pride, would he still stake me in the back if given the chance?

Dominic's rattling hum escalated to an engine's roar.

Rowens pursed his lips. "Maybe we should just stick to the facts."

"I told you the facts," I said. "I walked into my apartment, and Walker ambushed me. The ammunition he used, like all of Walker's weapons, was very effective," I said ruefully. "I have no doubt his weapons would come in handy on this mission if used for us instead of against us."

Bex snorted. "I don't doubt the weapon. I doubt the man."

Rowens settled his eyes back on Walker, colder than before. "Is this true?"

Walker's jaw tightened. "You've only known about vampires and night bloods for what, three weeks now, if even? I was raised in this world. I know better than anyone that if you wait to defend yourself, it's too late. They're faster, stronger, and more lethal than any creature alive, and the only way for people like you and me to stay alive is to build weapons that are faster, stronger, and more lethal than they are. And that means using those weapons when necessary, not hesitating so the vampire can entrance you, take your weapon, and kill you with it. I've seen it happen." Walker's eyes flicked to meet Dominic's. "I've *lived* it, and I learn from my mistakes."

"But you didn't kill me," I said, not sure why I was defending him except that I could still hear that floorboard creaking between his every word, and for the life of me, I couldn't let it go, not until I'd unearthed the truth. "You attacked me, and when I was vulnerable and at your mercy, you could have killed me. But you didn't."

Walker was silent for a long moment. When he finally met my eyes, I lost my breath at the uncertainty and pain in his expression. "That wouldn't have been self-defense, and I'm not a murderer," he said, and then more quietly, he whispered, "For once, I chose not to be a murderer."

But no one else heard his second sentence, no matter their superhuman hearing, because everyone was too busy verbally eviscerating him for his first.

"Was it self-defense when you hid in the woods and killed Rene?" Bex interjected.

"Was it self-defense when you shot me and left Cassidy for dead?" Dominic asked. "We were fighting to save her brother, for God's sake, and because of you, Jillian escaped."

"Was it self-defense when you broke into my apartment and attacked me in my living room?" Meredith asked.

Her words choked off everyone else's grievances. Silence filled the room as rolling thunder, buzzing bees, squawking birds, and the crack and pop of an inferno blasted my mind. I could barely hear myself think through the chaos of everyone else's thoughts, and for once, that wasn't hyperbole. I'd never been so drowned in noise during complete silence in my life.

He's got the nerve to show his face here and make demands from...

...killed our loved ones, now he thinks we'll welcome him like...

...never thought it would come to this when we came to him for help.

They'll never believe me.

I groaned as that last thought broke through the others. Walker was right; after everything he'd done and everyone he'd deliberately hurt—physically and emotionally—they would never believe him.

But they would believe me.

"That may not be true, Meredith," I managed to shout between my clenched teeth. My voice was shockingly loud, and I remembered belatedly that the room had been struck silent. I released my head—unsure exactly when I'd clamped my hands over my ears—and slowly and deliberately folded my fingers neatly on my lap. No one would take me seriously with my hands clamped over my ears like a crazy person, and it's not as if my hands could block metaphysical sound waves anyway.

"What do you mean?" Meredith asked. "I know what I saw, and I saw him attack me that day. He—"

"You saw a man with golden, curly hair and brown eyes," I countered. "You may have seen exactly who your attacker wanted you to see."

"What are you saying?"

The emotional racket battering my mind abated slightly as everyone stilled in anticipation of my next words. Except for Meredith's emotions; her spitting, sizzling inferno continued to burn.

"We argued about it when he ambushed me. I accused Walker of attacking me like he attacked you," I said

I could feel the soft contraction of Meredith's throat as she swallowed. "And what did he say?"

Walker's eyes flashed.

"He denied it," I admitted.

Meredith licked her lips. "Do you believe him?"

Everyone's eyes volleyed back to me.

No matter what I said, they would believe me. Meredith, because of our lifetime of friendship; Greta, because of years of professional and personal trust; Rowens and Dr. Chunn because of my reputation and their experience with me as a straight shooter; Nathan because he'd have my back anytime, anywhere, against anyone; Ronnie, Keagan, Jeremy, Theresa, and Logan, because Walker had abandoned them, and they knew what he was capable of; and Rafe and Neil out of loyalty to the coven. Dominic was the only one that would have the ability and wit to detect the truth from a lie from my lips.

I met Dominic's eyes and inhaled sharply at the poise I saw there. He was just waiting on my word, unconditionally.

Dominic had once said that I was in the business of finding and spreading truth, and even though I'd denied it at the time to spite him, he was right.

"Cassidy?" Meredith prompted.

I sighed reluctantly. "Unfortunately, Mere, I don't know who attacked you. I wish to God I did, but I don't."

The ice of Meredith's instant denial shivered down my spine, and I fought to keep my face relaxed, as if the banshee of her aching, raging bitterness wasn't making my ears bleed. Crimes go unsolved every year. The evidence runs dry over time, witnesses' memories become uncertain, leads go cold, and no matter the savvy inquiries of a dedicated detective, new crimes are committed—kidnappings, rapes, attempted murders—with witnesses who actually saw what happened, and the mystery that seemed so immediate last month takes a back seat to a higher-priority case. It doesn't mean the victims of that mystery deserve justice any less than the new crime's victims, but sometimes justice just slips away, along with the murderer and the truth.

Unsolved crimes are the hardest for victims to overcome because the first step in healing is acknowledging that they will never see justice.

Meredith cleared her throat. "But you said that you thought it was Walker," she said, her voice hoarse. "You accused him."

"When you described your attacker, yes, I suspected Walker, but I believed him when he denied it. He didn't even know you'd been attacked." I turned to Walker and met his wide, shocked gaze. "You have committed many sins against me and mine, but I don't think attacking Meredith is one of them."

He stared at me, and then, as if we'd come to some unspoken accord, he nodded.

Dominic growled. "It doesn't matter who he *didn't* attack. It matters who he did attack. Three members of this team have been betrayed and injured by his hand when he should have had our back. How many more people does he have to hurt before he's off this case?" Dominic glared at everyone around our circle of chairs. "Or doesn't it matter how many? Just who."

"Of course it matters," Greta said, "but without proof—"

Bex laughed. "How much proof do you need when he confessed?"

"Self-defense isn't always as cut-and-dry as we would—"

"We've already established that Walker's version of self-defense is bullshit."

"We need as many people on our side as we can get, and Walker's particular skill set is an undeniable advantage," Rowens interjected.

"I won't deny that this case would benefit from his expertise," I agreed. "Assuming he doesn't keep attacking me."

"Then where does that leave us?" Ronnie asked, her voice wavering.

Rowens placed his hand on Ronnie's shoulder and squeezed. I watched the casual offering of comfort from Rowens, a night blood, to Ronnie, a vampire, and glowed.

"We've heard Dominic's, Bex's, and Cassidy's reservations regarding Walker's role in this investigation. Would anyone like to speak on his behalf?" Rowens asked.

Keagan raised his hand hesitantly.

Bex raised her eyebrows.

"Put that hand down," Logan hissed.

"We're all in this together," Rowens encouraged, unflappable as always. "Please, I want to hear what you have to say."

"We're in this together?" Logan asked, but it was more accusation than question. "Were you attacked and transformed into the creature you spent a lifetime fighting against? Were you then abandoned by that monster and forced to seek help from the sister of the murderer who killed your son?"

Nathan visibly shriveled into himself. My heart ached for them both.

"Are you stuck between loyalty to a man who took you and your family into his home, fed you, and protected you and your family, who are now in danger from that same man?" Logan continued. "I don't think you can rightfully say we're in this together. I know better than anyone that when the going gets tough, the people who supposedly have your back will turn around and shoot you between the shoulder blades if it means saving themselves."

"We *are* in this together," Ronnie whispered, her voice as insistent as it was thready. "I can't pretend to know the grief of losing your son, Logan, but in every other way, I know *exactly* how you feel. I was attacked and transformed against my will. I lost my home and my life and, God help me, I think I lost my sanity for a bit. I lost Ian." She reached out even as Logan recoiled from her and held his big, beefy hand in her tiny one, refusing to let go. "I'd been starving and scared and lost long before being transformed into a vampire, and now that I'm the very creature I spent a lifetime hiding from, I might finally have the chance to live. Assuming we survive the next few days. And for the first time in a very long time, I'm willing to fight for that life." She squeezed his hands. "Are you, Logan? Because I can't fight on my own. I can't do much of anything on my own, but damn it, with all of us together we actually have a chance."

Her words were encouraging all on their own, but all that courage and strength and hope coming from Ronnie made my heart swell with a protective urge to rise above our pettiness and fight on her behalf. Every word she said was true. She couldn't fight on her own as so many of us could, but if we could find the strength to fight together, we could all survive.

I wasn't the only one moved by Ronnie's words and sentiment. Bex looked a little shamefaced, Greta was grinning, Jeremy looked less churlish than usual, and Logan was actually returning Ronnie's hold, sandwiching her little hands in his.

"Ronnie is exactly right," Rowens said. "We need to come to some sort of an agreement, so we can work together. Only a united force can stand against Jillian and the might of the Damned. Are we all agreed on that statement?"

I nodded along with most everyone else. Walker didn't nod, but that may have had more to do with the threat of Dominic's lethal talons beneath his chin than disagreement.

"And despite Walker's previous offenses to several people on this team, his skill set would benefit this case. Agreed?" Rowens asked again.

Bex snorted. "Yeah, and despite my leadership skills and beauty, no one's appointing me queen of England, no matter who would benefit. Some dreams just don't come true, darlin'," she drawled.

"And sometimes," Greta snapped back, "even convicted criminals make a deal in exchange for information that leads to the arrest of many, more criminals." She met Dominic's eyes. "Walker's crimes against you matter just as much as his crimes against everyone on this team, but that's not the question on the table. What we need to decide today is if holding him accountable for his crimes now is more important than using his skills to take down Jillian and the Damned."

Dominic curled his lip. "We can't trust him to use his skills against Jillian and the Damned. He'd as soon as kill us as kill her."

"You need someone to stay behind to ambush Kaden as leverage," Walker said. "Let me play my part, and I'll be a team player. I promise."

Dominic grinned in Walker's face, all of his fangs gleaming. "Playing on this team means having my back, knowing I have yours."

"It means protecting people you've spent years trying to kill," Bex said.

"And sticking to the plan, even if an opportunity to kill us presents itself," I added.

The silence stretched as Walker ruminated on that.

Greta raised her eyebrows. "Well? Are you a part of this team or not?"

"Yes," Walker insisted, but his words were a little too certain and came too fast for my taste. "I'm a part of this team."

I let my nails grow into talons and held out my hand in offering. "I want your word that you've got our back against Jillian. And then—only then—I'll promise that we've got yours."

Walker hesitated. His eyes slid past Greta and met ours one by one: the former night bloods he'd given shelter and protection to; his childhood friend and lifelong companion; his childhood idol turned nemesis; and me, his former flame; plus my brother, a former Damned; and Dominic, the former and contending Master vampire of New York City—all of us the dictionary definition of his worst nightmare standing before him and asking to be allies. I didn't think he'd be able to swallow a lifetime of grief and hate and anger long enough to even contemplate shaking my hand, let alone agreeing to work with us, but I was wrong. After a long moment of staring at my talons as if they were a contagious disease, he reached out and took my hand in his.

"So, what's the plan?" he asked.

Everyone groaned this time, but Jeremy loudest of all.

Chapter 26

"Jillian must have changed the Wi-Fi password," Dominic said. And then his face brightened. "Try it again with a capital *N*. It may be case-sensitive."

I ground my teeth against the first response that came to mind and dutifully entered in the coven's Wi-Fi password into my phone for the eighth time, suspecting that Dominic simply couldn't remember the correct password.

We had infiltrated the coven half an hour after sunset, ensuring the Damned had left for their nightly hunt, and our teams had gone their separate ways: Bex and Nathan along with five willing human donors were on their way to free the Day Reapers from the Underneath; Dominic and I had gone ahead to scout Jillian's location; Rafe and Neil were scouting the honeycombs for Sevris and other potential allies; and Meredith, Rowens, Greta,Ronnie, Keagan, Jeremy, Logan, and Theresa were babysitting the remaining two-dozen human volunteers at the coven's entrance, armed with a combination of Dr. Chunn's and Walker's ammunition to combat a possible Damned and/or Day Reaper attack. Trusting Bex's theory that Jillian hadn't adopted the full Master's power and therefore wouldn't sense our infiltration—assuming we refrained from using walkie-talkies this time—was a small leap of faith, but half an hour in, and the plan was unfolding with only one hitch: we didn't know whether Walker had successfully ambushed Kaden, and until we connected to the Wi-Fi, we had no way to find out.

The password—even with a capital *N*, with and without a special character, with and without the numbers 1723 and every combination thereof—did not work.

"Nope, that's not it either," I said.

Dominic cursed. "Did you try it with an exclamation point?"

"I tried it every which way." I looked up from my phone and met his eyes. "We need to consider an alternative option to video-chatting Kaden's kidnapping." I sighed, and the reluctance I felt at considering my next words made my sigh end on a low, rattling growl. "I know we had decided against it, but if we can't get online to leverage Kaden virtually, Walker needs to bring Kaden here so we can leverage him in person."

"Nathan's arguments against that were valid," Dominic reminded me. "Keeping Kaden away from Jillian and using him as leverage from afar was brilliant, not to mention the double benefit of keeping Walker away from us."

"You think I don't know that?" I snapped. "But if we wait much longer, we won't have time to double back to get service, and then where will we be? No Wi-Fi, no service, and no Kaden means no leverage. You tell me: what other choice do we have?"

"We don't," Dominic growled. "Let's double back and make the call."

Twenty minutes later, we were standing just outside the coven's entrance, and Walker picked up on the second ring.

"Do you have Kaden?" I asked.

"No, 'hello?' No, 'how are you'?" he asked. "What happened to keeping it civil, DiRocco?"

Dominic cleared his throat suspiciously.

I glared daggers at him; I could feel the tremor of his amusement through his nonchalant facade. "You know me: straight and to the point."

"Actually, I don't know you very well at all."

I rolled my eyes. "Do you have Kaden or not?"

Walker sighed. "Not. He hasn't shown up yet."

"Well, when he does, we have a change of plan," I said and updated him on our Wi-Fi failure.

"We'll make it work. I'll let you know when I have Kaden," Walker said.

"Great, I—"

But I heard the *click* from his end. I was talking to myself. "Bastard," I muttered.

"No one employs proper phone etiquette these days," Dominic commented.

I wrinkled my nose at him.

Two hours later, we still hadn't heard from Walker, but we'd reconnected with Rafe and Neil and located Jillian. She must have already left the coven, hunted, and returned in the first few hours of sunset because she was positively aglow with good health. From our ten-story vantage atop the highest honeycomb in the coven's great hall—the central location where New York City vampires slept during the day and either hosted dinner parties or slashed throats during the night depending on the guest of honor's appetite—I could just tell her apart her from the vampire she was speaking with. The other vampire was also a lethal-looking woman wearing leather, but there was no mistaking the glow of Jillian's ice-and-blue eyes, so eerily similar to Dominic's eyes, and her blond, pixie-short hair. When we'd first met, her hair had been a riot of curls down to her waist, but after losing her long locks during her imprisonment in the Underneath, she'd chosen to keep the short style.

The other vampire left, and another replaced her. When that conversation finished, Jillian spoke to a third and a fourth and a fifth vampire, and my heart bottomed out into my stomach. I jerked my head back to Dominic, and we retreated from the overlook. Rafe and Neil were waiting for us at the back tunnel of the top level, guarding the entrance to the honeycombs. I put my finger to my lips for silence and waited until we were far away, buried back beneath the main coven by layers of earth and stone passageways so that we couldn't be overheard, not by anyone, before speaking.

"Bex was wrong," I whispered. "Having fully-adopted the Master's power or not, Jillian knows we're here."

Dominic shook his head. "Jillian knows *someone* infiltrated the coven, but without the full Master's power, she has no way of knowing with certainty that it's us."

I gave him a flat look. "Who else would infiltrate her coven but us?"

"For all she knows, we may be dead. She doesn't know the extent of our plan, and she won't anticipate Day Reaper or human involvement. How could she? Not even I could have foreseen such a united stand again her," Dominic argued. "We have the advantage."

"What's wrong?" Rafe asked. "What did you see?"

"She's consulting with people," I said. "She's being very discreet, but one by one, she's giving orders, making plans," I glanced at Dominic. "Planning a big move."

"Our move is bigger," Dominic argued. "Once we have our leverage and the Day Reapers are released, we'll have the advantage."

I sighed and turned to Rafe. "Did you find Sevris?"

He shook his head.

"Keep looking," Dominic said, but we both knew the only thing more disheartening than Jillian planning a counterattack was imagining that Sevris was planning it with her.

Another three hours later, I'd gnawed all ten nails down to the quick and grew them back, but Walker finally called with good news: he'd ambushed and successfully subdued Kaden. At least one thing was going according to plan, even if it was the one thing Walker was in charge of. Dominic and I met him at the coven's subterranean entrance. Kaden was draped over Walker's shoulder, his arms and legs bound with the same debilitating material that Walker had used on me, but Kaden looked significantly worse than I imagined myself looking after being ambushed.

The majority of the skin on his face, neck, and upper body had been shredded, either by some sort of blast or excessive bullet spray. His long, auburn hair was matted with unidentifiable, mangled pieces of muscle or maybe skin and clots of blood, or all three, and his scalp, separated from most of his head, flapped in time with Walker's stride, rhythmically revealing and concealing the skull beneath. The majority of Kaden's extremities were visibly broken, evident from their unnatural angles, and in some instances, visibly exposed. His left ear and nostril were dangling by threads.

The contrast between Kaden's beefy, muscle-bound body and its complete destruction was startling. There'd never been any love lost between Kaden and me—hard to feel anything but resentment toward a person who continually and unapologetically attacked and attempted to murder you—but even I couldn't see Kaden's injuries and not cringe. He was so unrecognizable that if it wasn't for the fact that his remaining violet-hued eye was clearly glaring spears of hatred and vengeance at me instead of staring vacantly, I would have thought him dead, or perhaps, not Kaden at all.

"Could he have possibly shot more bullets into his face?" I hissed.

"Yes," Dominic said coolly. "The right eye and part of his nostril remain intact."

I pursed my lips and shot Dominic a look under my brows.

Walker dropped Kaden on the ground at our feet and stepped back. "Problem?"

Kaden coughed, and bloody foam spewed from the hole in his lower face that was once his mouth. The movement caused his ear to detach from his head.

I raised my eyebrows.

"He's alive, which means he's leverage, and his wounds are debilitating, which means he's not a danger to us. I did my job." Walker crossed his arms. "Let's see you do yours."

I could have said a lot of things; my gut reaction to Walker lately was more emotional than rational. I would have loved to feel the muscles in his jaw clench and smell the blush of his anger, like hot sauce, knowing that I could get under his skin and singe him in places he'd wounded me. But that kind of thinking was nothing but shackles to the past, and by God, I was moving forward, even if that meant gnawing off the shackled limb.

I nodded. "Thank you," I said, my voice bland but sincere. I couldn't work up a smile, but smiling with fangs was counterproductive anyway.

Walker swayed back slightly, relaxing where I hadn't even noticed he'd already been tense. "You're welcome."

Dominic stepped forward and lifted Kaden into his arms, slinging him over his shoulder like a sack of potatoes. Kaden made a noise, something between a growl, a gasp, and a sob, but otherwise, remained deadweight. I shouldn't have felt anything but satisfaction at a plan well executed—Kaden was a sociopathic serial killer, he'd attacked me multiple times, murdered dozens upon dozens of people, and was just as responsible for the deaths and destruction in New York City as Jillian—but that noise, even from a man like him, still chafed.

I picked up his ear and shoved it in my back pocket. If everything went according to plan, he wouldn't need it, but bleeding hearts make you do things that go beyond logic.

I nodded to Walker and turned to leave.

"I could help."

I glanced over my shoulder doubtfully, but by the earnest clarity in his expression and grim determination tightening his pinched lips, the offer was sincere.

"You've already been an extraordinary help," I said carefully, nodding at Kaden curled over Dominic's shoulder. "We couldn't have done this without you."

Walker glanced askance at the wall, looking extremely uncomfortable with my praise and suddenly fascinated with the slick, uneven cavern. "Yes, you could have. Not as easily, maybe, but you'd have figured it out. You always do."

"True," I conceded, "but like you said, not as easily, and we certainly don't need anything more difficult than it already is. So thank you."

He nodded. "Everyone's a part of this fight—Greta and Rowens, Logan, Keagan, Theresa, and even Jeremy, for Christ's sake—but somehow along the way, I became one of the people to fight against instead of one of the people to fight alongside. I'm not saying we're friends, but tonight, we're allies," Walker said, standing his ground. "I promised, remember?" he said ruefully. "Let me see this through to the end. This is my fight, too, as much as everyone else's."

Walker would be a distraction, no matter his sincerity. I couldn't focus on Jillian if I had to watch over my shoulder for Walker. Handshake promises and good intentions aside, that's exactly where I'd be looking—back instead of forward. People get hurt easily enough when they trust the people covering their six; people die when they don't.

But I hesitated, unsure how to reject his offer without also rejecting our tentative truce.

Dominic squeezed my shoulder. "Everyone is a part of this fight, including you," he said, calm and sure and sincere, a voice that had led hundreds of people for hundreds of years and had had to speak even when he couldn't find the words. "You've already done your part." He shrugged, indicating Kaden over his shoulder. "We couldn't ask for more."

"I'm offering," Walker insisted.

"Let me rephrase," Dominic said, still sure. Still sincere. "We won't ask for more."

Walker's expression didn't change. "If it's a matter of trust, I gave you my word. I'm good for it, right, Cassidy?" He turned to me. "If you know me at all, you know that."

I pressed my lips together to stifle a knee-jerk, sarcastic reply. The truce between us was a lie; I could feel it every time his eyes settled on me and his fist tightened in reaction. I could hear his bitterness and loosely leashed rage like the rattle and howl of a gale-force wind—but a lie that kept everyone alive was better than a truth that killed one or both of us.

So I looked him dead-straight in the eyes and spoke a half-truth I could live with.

"It's not a matter of trust," I said softly. "It's a matter of planning. We have a mission laid out, which is already unraveling, and I want to stick to our original plan as closely as possible. We have enough foreseen obstacles to face; I don't want to add unforeseen factors into the equation, no matter the good intentions behind them."

I lifted my hand to touch his shoulder in comfort and to convince him of my sincerity. The movement was natural to me and unthinking, and when Walker jerked back violently and lifted his arm, I didn't understand at first. I didn't even react, but Dominic did. He was suddenly between us, twisting Walker's wrist until the gun in his hand clattered to the floor.

I let my hand drop back down to my side.

Walker realized his mistake when I didn't continue my advance, and he actually looked a little chagrined. He blushed and wouldn't meet my eyes even after Dominic stepped back.

"Maybe it *is* a matter of trust," I amended.

Walker sighed. "You can't just transform into a vampire, into a Day Reaper for fuck's sake, and expect everyone to just blindly jump on board the support train. I don't agree with your decision and what you've become, and knowing my stance on vampires, which I've never been shy about sharing, it's not fair of you to expect my blessing."

I nodded slowly, careful to let my anger simmer and expel before speaking. Walker wasn't the enemy I needed to fight right now. He was the enemy I could fight tomorrow, assuming we survived today.

"Thank you for carrying out your part of the plan," I said, wringing every last drop of graciousness from my body. "You really pulled through, and I appreciate your efforts."

"You're welcome," he said, nodding. "I guess this is goodbye, then."

I nodded back, and we stood there for an awkward minute, just nodding at each other. Dominic watched us with his arms folded over his chest, like a nightclub bouncer. I didn't need protection—I could take down an army of Damned vampires, for heaven's sake—but my defenses never seemed adequate where Walker was concerned.

"Good luck," he said. He didn't offer his hand, even knowing we were entering into a battle from which we might not return. Without another word, he picked up his gun, his movements slow and deliberate with Dominic looming over him, and turned his back on me without a second glance. I watched him leave, every inch of him armed—his shoulders draped with silver ammunition, wooden stakes in holsters tucked into his boots, coil-spring projectile watches at his wrists, silver-nitrate sprays clipped to his hip, and a bulletproof vest wrapping the entire package—and somehow, I worried that he was leaving alone. We had been friends once—very good friends that had saved each other's lives—even if I was the only one of the two of us who remembered that friendship fondly.

But fond memories of friendship or not, I wasn't here to mend the past. I turned my back on Walker and stood beside Dominic with more to lose now than I'd ever risked while waging and losing the battle behind me. As surely as Walker was my past, the only thing certain about my future was that I'd have to fight for it.

Chapter 27

Five hours later, I'd bitten all ten of my nails down to the quick, again, had regrown them, and was working on round three while watching Jillian from the vantage of the highest tier of honeycombs. She had finally ceased one-on-one meetings with her vampires and was alone in the great hall. The sun was due to rise in four minutes, thirty-two seconds and counting. I was starving—literally, I could feel my skin shriveling like shrink-wrap around my muscles as I slowly but surely devolved into my day form—and not one Damned had returned to the coven.

Not one.

"Her big move is bigger than ours," I grumbled.

Dominic shook his head. "It's not a move at all," he said, his words precise and perfectly enunciated around his elongated fangs.

He hadn't completely transformed into his gargoyle-like day form yet, but without a ready food source—the humans were for the Damned and Day Reapers, not us, no matter that I could hear all thirty-seven of their hearts beating inside their chests like a siren song—he might as well just give up on the pretense of civility and embrace the change sooner rather than later. I had.

"We can't fight her and her army if her army isn't here to fight," I pointed out.

Dominic grinned. "Good thing, then, that we have the leverage to make her order them back."

Kaden growled, its deep rattle sounding more broken than menacing.

I repressed a wince and met Dominic's eyes. "Stay here and follow my lead. You'll know when to join me."

"I remember the plan." Dominic grinned ruefully. "You rehashed it a dozen times. I couldn't forget it even if I wanted to." He reached for me with his four-inch talons, wrapped his long fingers around the back of my neck, and pulled me close. "Good luck," he whispered against my mouth before pressing his lips to mine.

Kissing is not part of the plan, I thought, and would have said as much except my lips were otherwise occupied. We'd been waiting over nine hours for the ripe moment to confront Jillian, and after all that time together, now he decided to linger in sentimentality. But I wanted to want this kiss, to embrace what little time we still had and not let nerves or grudges or anything ruin this memory, so I pushed aside my anxiety and frustration and let my eyes flutter closed. I let go of where we were and why to savor this moment and this man, because the last nine hours together, spent in worry, might have been our last.

I opened my mouth, and the sound of his satisfaction, like thunder, vibrated down my spine. He tasted like honey and smelled like Christmas pine, and the chill of his powerful arms around me was like aloe on sun-chapped skin. The shock of his touch nearly hurt, but only at first. My body, starved for him no matter what my mind thought, thrilled at his touch, drowned in his smell, and became drunk on his taste.

I wrapped my arms around his back and pulled him to me just for the feel of his body pressed against mine, but when we collided, the rough edges of Walker's borrowed bulletproof vest blocked our embrace. The reminder of the danger Dominic would soon face simultaneously stoked my urgency for him and forced my hands, now fully transformed to claws, to release him. We had a mission to carry out, and that mission started now and ended in either our victory or our deaths. But no matter the ending, I could take courage in the knowledge that we'd face it together.

"Good luck to you, too," I whispered hoarsely.

He nodded and stepped back, but the rigidity in his movements betrayed him. The last thing either of us wanted was to let go.

I stole a final look into his icy-blue eyes—now achingly dear—and braced myself on the top story of the honeycomb's ledge. Against everything sane and normal, I jumped.

The feeling of helpless, breathless freefall was one I'd become intimately acquainted with several times in the past few weeks. When we were visiting Walker in upstate New York, I'd been pushed down a mining shaft—the entrance to Bex's coven—as a joke. I'd fallen from the top branches of a very high tree, twice, while being chased by my Damned brother, and just last week, I'd been thrown from the top of a fifty floor apartment building by a Damned vampire after witnessing it eat my friend. All four times, I'd been caught and saved by a nearby friendly vampire before smashing into the ground below. This time, I was in control. I was the vampire. And unfortunately for Jillian, I wasn't friendly.

I had assumed Jillian was aware of our moves even before we'd made them. But when I landed behind her with a loud thud, she didn't twirl around and lunge at me with her claws. Hidden Damned didn't descend from the rafters to protect her. None of the various scenarios I'd prepared and braced for happened.

Instead, she screamed.

The high note of her shriek echoed through the cavernous honeycombs even after I caught her neck in my hand and choked it off. Unused to my own strength, I felt the bones of her spinal column buckle and crack under my hand, but I didn't ease my grip. The whites of her wide eyes and the desperation of her trembling hands clawing at my wrist spoke volumes without words. She was frightened. I could smell the rich cinnamon of her shock and fear, and God help me, the creature I'd become felt empowered by it.

"Miss me?" I asked.

Jillian blinked rapidly, obviously taken aback by my presence. "You're alive," she recovered enough to choke out. "How?"

"You seriously underestimated my drive to survive. I'm not a 'little night blood' anymore," I snarled. "I'm the big, bad wolf."

"Come to blow down my house?" she wheezed, somehow managing to infuse the barely audible words with droll sarcasm.

"Close." I grinned. "Come to blow you out of it." I held up my free hand and wiggled my four-inch talons in her face. "Do you recognize the color of my nails? They're all natural."

Jillian's face blanched. She nodded.

"I'm told that if I were to slice your throat, like you sliced mine, you might not regenerate. It's a perk of being a Day Reaper, one I've only put to the test on the Damned." I scraped my thumb talon lightly across her cheek. "Should we test it on a vampire now?"

Jillian shook her head minutely, careful of the claws at her throat, but I could almost smell the electric connections of her synapses firing as she calculated her options, their risks, and her advantages, just like I would in her position.

I needed to play a card before she drew an ace.

"I'm going to release your throat, and you're not going to scream," I said. "If you do, I'll remove your throat, just like you did to Rafe all those months ago," I growled. "Just like you did to me. Do you understand?"

She nodded.

I eased my grip on her neck. She coughed and cleared her throat several times, excessively, in my opinion, for someone who didn't need to breathe to live, but maybe I'd damaged her esophagus. I gave her a moment to collect herself.

"Where are the Damned?" I asked.

She smiled, beaming as bright as the first rays of dawn from behind a mountainous horizon. "They're out at the moment. Did you want to leave a message for one of them?"

I'd known she wouldn't make this easy, not on either of us. I forced myself to smile back. "Cheeky." I leaned close, nose-to-nose. "I don't like cheeky."

I sliced my thumb talon across her cheek, splitting it to the bone. A waterfall of blood erupted from the wound and bathed the side of her face.

She shrieked, more reaction than a call for help, but I choked it off, just like I promised I would.

"No screaming," I reminded her. "Last warning."

She glared at me, a fine mix of hate and fear and bold, righteous desperation in her eyes. I recognized that look. I knew it like the taste of bile in the back of my throat. I'd lived and breathed that look since I'd discovered the existence of vampires, from the night Dominic had attacked me on the street to the day Jillian had torn out my throat. When a person is backed into a corner by her worst fears and certain death, she'll either wilt and die, fight and die, or kill to survive.

I had no intentions of dying. Not today.

Judging by the determination in Jillian's eyes, neither did she.

"I'm going to ask again, and you're going to give me a real answer this time," I said calmly. I eased the pressure from her throat so she could speak, but kept my talons poised over her neck, caressing her carotid, so she wouldn't move. "Where are the Damned?"

"I don't track their every movement, and they don't necessarily all stay together," Jillian snapped, her indignant tone at odds with her stiff, upturned jaw, attempting to create more than a mere hairbreadth between her throat and my talons. "Who could say, really, where creatures like that go during the day?"

I leaned closer. "The creatures are mindless, but you created them. You know exactly where they go. Wherever they are, you're going to command them back to the coven."

"No, I'm not."

I stabbed a talon into her other cheek and carved a chunk of muscle and flesh from her face. The sinew and fat was sticky yet slick under my talon. I flicked it off, and a glob of her cheek fell with a wet splat at our feet.

I forced myself to snarl, to meet her eye to eye even as I wanted to wash my hands and vomit. Jillian had done worse to me, I reminded myself. She'd betrayed Dominic, attempted to murder me multiple times, broken human and vampire law, and created an army of mindless, ravenous creatures that destroyed New York City. All in all, she'd earned every cut and scar I inflicted, but all the reasons in the world didn't curb my gag reflex.

Before Jillian could sense my crisis of conscience, I refocused my thoughts on other memories and emotions. I thought of the worst moments of my life—my parents' deaths, Nathan being Damned, nearly losing Meredith, dying from Dominic's wounds—and alternately, the best moments of my life—retransforming Nathan, saving Meredith, making love with Dominic—just like Dominic had taught me, so Jillian would sense only the kaleidoscope of my emotions and not the truth.

To her credit, Jillian didn't scream this time. She gasped, composed herself, and met my eyes, fury roiling in hers. "You can slice and dice me from head to toe, but you will never have my Damned, and you will never regain power of this coven under his name. We are released from Dominic's rule and the chains that bound us to darkness. We are free!"

"I was hoping it wouldn't come to this, Jillian, but I had a feeling that slicing and dicing you wouldn't be enough incentive." I smiled, making sure my fangs gleamed. "So I'll slice and dice someone else."

Kaden's body fell from the highest honeycomb and slammed into the floor at my well-phrased words. He landed like a ragdoll, his limp limbs unbound and flopping. His left leg bent beneath his back at an unnatural angle, the bone exposed.

I focused on Jillian and continued to think my kaleidoscope thoughts.

Jillian raised her eyebrows, but otherwise, she remained calm and unmoved. Not the reaction I'd anticipated her having upon seeing Kaden.

"Stealing back the coven by torturing its members won't endear you to them," she said. "Seems counterproductive to me."

"We won't need to torture everyone. Just that one."

Her eyes flicked to Kaden, but when her gaze met mine again, it was still indifferent. In fact, she smiled. "Oh? And what is so special about 'that one'?"

I could feel the glass shards of Kaden's breath as he struggled to speak through his shredded vocal cords, and it occurred to me that Jillian couldn't look at Kaden, her Second, in this state and not be moved. She simply couldn't. Jillian wasn't evil, and only the devil herself could see a person she cared about in such pain and not be pained. But there wasn't any strong emotion wafting from Jillian—not even the kaleidoscope confusion of an attempt to mask her emotions and hide the truth.

Which was when the truth hit me: she didn't recognize him.

I cocked my head, and for the first time, even as I prepared the killing blow, I felt every inch the monster I'd become. "I don't know. I never saw the potential that drew you to him. You tell me: what makes Kaden so special?"

Jillian's gaze snapped back to Kaden and narrowed on him for a long moment. She took a deep breath, confirming to me that she hadn't recognized him by sight; she needed smell to determine his identity. She probably hadn't even cared about his identity until now, until the realization that the lump of raw meat and broken bones that had just fallen ten stories and slammed to the floor like overripe fruit might actually be the one person in the coven she cared most about.

The damage to his face and body and the odors that came with those injuries were pungent, but I could still smell Kaden's subtle, earthy scent beneath the carnage, like grass after a shower.

And so could Jillian.

Her knees buckled, and I had to adjust my hold on her neck so my talons, poised at her carotid, didn't accidentally decapitate her.

"No," she gasped. Her mask of calm indifference shattered, and she shrieked. "No!"

"I tried to reason with you. I came to you last week in a last-ditch effort to convince you to pull back your Damned, but you ripped out my throat instead," I said. "Maybe now you'll listen."

She shook her head slowly back and forth. Her eyes were all for Kaden, but her words were all for me. "You fucking bitch. How could you—"

"Call back the Damned, now, or I finish him off."

"You can't simultaneously hold me and kill him, and the moment you move, my vampires will tear you to shreds. You might be stronger and faster than any one of us but not all of us."

I felt a slight, uncertain movement in my periphery—the shifting of weight from one foot to another, the creeping lean of someone thinking about stepping forward, the hardening of a muscle in anticipation of an attack—just the anticipation of attack, but there all the same.

Luckily, my backup wasn't slight or uncertain.

I bared my fangs in a hard grin. "I'd love to put my strength and speed to the test, but that's not necessary. Is it, Lysander?"

I didn't need to turn my head to know that the light touchdown beside me was Dominic landing at Kaden's side. Jillian's expression was telling enough.

"Not necessary at all," Dominic murmured.

Jillian stared and blinked and shook her head side to side in stunned silence.

"Tell me you missed *me* at least," he said drily.

Jillian's words emerged in a croak. "But I have the Master's power."

Dominic chuckled darkly. "You think the little strength you stole from me was the comprehensive scope of my powers?" he tsked.

"I killed you through your connection with Cassidy. I killed both of you!" Jillian sputtered.

"Surprise," Dominic said with relish. "We survived the Leveling. We survived the Damned's attack, and we will survive you. This coven is rightfully mine."

"Bullshit," Jillian spat.

Dominic bent over Kaden, yanked back his head, and poised his claws over Kaden's throat. "Command back the Damned, or I tear out his esophagus. It's your call."

An eerie sense of déjà vu slammed into me. The last time the four of us were together in this coven and Dominic had threatened Kaden's life, Jillian had impaled me on her talons. This time, Jillian was the one being impaled, albeit metaphorically, but our switched roles suddenly filled me with trepidation.

"Don't," Kaden said. His voice rattled wetly in his chest.

"Yes, Jillian, don't," Dominic taunted. He flexed a claw, and a pearl of blood bloomed on a tiny patch of hitherto undamaged flesh on Kaden's neck. "I dare you."

"To think, all the decades I stood by your side, and we've come to this," Jillian said, her voice despondent.

Dominic laughed in the face of her despair, and Jillian jerked back, stung.

"My words exactly when I discovered that you had betrayed me and planned my murder. After I saved you from my brother and trusted you with my coven, trusted you with my very life for decades as my Second, you repaid me by betraying me. You were my closest, most trusted companion. So please, look at what we've become, and let it cut deep, as deeply as you've cut me. You created this," Dominic said, words ending in a snarl. "Don't attempt to pull my heartstrings now, my dear. I have none concerning you, which should come as no surprise since you're the one who severed them."

"I didn't want this. I *never* wanted your place as Master," Jillian said, her voice a sob. "Until recently, I couldn't imagine this coven without you, but it doesn't matter how much I love you. You left me no choice."

"Which is exactly what you have left me," Dominic said coldly. "Make your choice before my hand slips. I have a twitchy trigger finger. This one right here." He pressed his talon deeper, hooking it beneath Kaden's chin.

Kaden twitched in pain. Considering his injuries, I was surprised he could manage even that much movement.

"Stop, please," Jillian pleaded. Kaden's agony reflected in her eyes."Dominic Lysander, I command you to stop!"

Dominic gave her a bored look and pressed his talon knuckle-deep into Kaden's neck.

Jillian turned to me. "Cassidy DiRocco, I command you to release me!"

To my surprise, mirrors weren't even necessary anymore. Her command was like a single gnat, annoying but harmless. I tightened my grip on her neck. "Nice try."

Jillian screamed her frustration. She was losing this battle and she knew it. Her guttural sobs were heart-wrenching; no matter how Dominic claimed otherwise, I knew this was killing him. It had to be. I barely cared for Jillian, and the raw, desperate noises coming from her stirred compassion even in me.

"I'll call them back. Stop, and I'll call back the Damned!" she shouted.

"No!" Kaden roared. He didn't have much of a mouth or throat to speak with, but that single word and the rage behind it were unmistakable.

Dominic slit his throat. Blood poured from the wound, thick and viscous, like lava.

"Stop hurting him! Didn't you hear me? I said I'd call them back!" Jillian slashed her talons across my face.

I ducked, dodging her attack easily, and slashed back in one smooth motion. "You call them back, and he'll stop," I growled.

"Dominic, please. I beg you," Jillian pleaded. "Have mercy, brother."

I retightened my grip on her neck even as my heart bled for her.

"You are no longer family," Dominic said, his voice cold and certain. "You ripped whatever mercy I once had out along with my heart when you betrayed me. Command the Damned to return, Jillian. Now."

Jillian laughed, high and hysterical. "Fine. Let them come. Let them massacre us all."

Chapter 28

For a moment, nothing happened. The grating cackle of Jillian's maniacal laugher echoed off the high ceiling of the honeycombs, and I hesitated, wondering who was more crazy: Jillian backed into a corner, or Dominic and me, uncertain whether we'd won this round or were being played. Dominic's arm tensed to finish off Kaden, and although I didn't quite agree with such a premature, drastic measure—he was our only leverage over Jillian, after all—I wasn't certain enough to stop him.

Until I felt the tremor beneath my feet.

The vibration was rhythmic at first and became increasingly constant as their pounding stampede drew closer.

The Damned were approaching.

Dominic dropped Kaden's limp body and stepped over him to stand at my side. "They're coming."

"No shit, Sherlock," I quipped. "What was your first clue?"

"The vibration of their approach beneath our feet," Dominic answered, straight-faced.

I rolled my eyes.

"Ah, sarcasm," Dominic said ruefully. "You're more difficult to read now that I can't sense your every shift in emotion and thought."

"Good," I said flatly.

I released Jillian to Dominic's tender care and stepped back from the wall to concentrate. I closed my eyes and opened my awareness to the coven's tunnels and secret passages. Its labyrinth snaked outward from the honeycombs, some passages winding and twisting and splitting off into passages that also winded and twisted, some leading to dead ends, some leading to hidden entrances, and others descending to the Underneath. I could feel the different energies and emotions of everyone within those passages, and of the hundreds upon hundreds of vampires within the coven, the few people I recognized made the fine hairs on my skin stand alert.

Rafe and Neil were making their way toward the great hall, Bex was flying around the Underneath instead of guarding her position with the Day Reapers, and Nathan had left her and was running through the tunnels toward us. The dozen or so vampires surrounding the great hall were edging closer, spurred by the impending wave of approaching Damned, and leading them was a vampire whose widow's peak was as undeniable as my warring relief and apprehension at recognizing him: Sevris.

There were others at the outskirts of my periphery: Greta, Rowens, and Meredith with the humans; someone shifting in the rafters of the honeycombs; and hundreds of coven watching and waiting, knowing another power shift was erupting beneath them and wondering if they'd survive the fallout this time. I pushed the uncertainty and distraction of everyone from my mind and honed my concentration on the approaching bloodthirsty, stampede of death barreling toward us.

The connection between me and the Damned—between me and everyone, if I was honest with myself—wasn't the same taut bowstring I remembered from last time. Even as I concentrated on the world around me and the people in it, I felt more like a passive observer than a force to influence their actions. I couldn't feel their intent in my bones like my own. I couldn't even sense a dull impression of their thoughts, and I realized that, unlike every other time I'd entranced someone, even as a night blood, I didn't have a metaphysical string connecting me to their minds.

I tried to form a connection with the Damned, but I couldn't create something from nothing. When I was a night blood, I'd connected with others through the consumption of blood. As a Day Reaper, however, the connection had been as present and unmistakable as my claws and fangs; it had seemed to simply occur as a result of my transformation.

Except now, when I needed it most, of course, the connection wasn't there.

I came back into myself and met the intensity of Dominic's glacier gaze.

"I still feel the acceleration of their approach," Dominic said. As dramatic as his words were, his voice was calm and collected.

"That's because they're still approaching and accelerating," I said.

"You've entranced them before," he reminded me.

"I know, but it's not working now."

"What you've done once, you can do again," he encouraged me, still so fucking calm and collected, I wanted to shake the reality into him that now might be the time to panic.

"In theory," I ground out between my clenched teeth, "but in reality, I'm telling you that we have a big problem. I need to form a connection somehow. Maybe they need to drink my blood."

"Is that what you did last time when you entranced the Damned? You formed a blood connection?"

"No, but I don't know how I formed the connection last time. It was just there. Now, it's just not," I said.

"What's different this time compared to last time?" Dominic pondered as if he were posing the question over tea and crumpets.

I suppressed the urge to scream. "I don't know, but I don't think we have time to—"

As if to prove how little time we really had, a single Damned burst from one of the honeycombs and soared through the air with an incredible, soul-shaking roar. I held my breath, spellbound in horror by its power and menace, until it turned its head and the sparkling stud of its nose ring winked in the light from the candelabra.

He landed a few feet from me, shaking the entire coven with the force of his landing. Dominic tossed Jillian on the ground next to Kaden and tensed to fight.

I squeezed Dominic's arm to hold him off, but Nathan's words—barely discernable in the rumbling rattle of his growl—spoke volumes. "We have a problem."

Dominic eased back. No other Damned had the ability to talk but my brother.

I sighed. "Tell me about it."

He took me literally. "I can't, not in front of our present company." He flicked his eyes at Jillian.

"I don't think subtlety and surprise will win the day anymore," Dominic said drily. "With the Damned coming, we're past that now."

"Our 'big move' won't work," Nathan said. "We can't find them."

I cursed. "What do you mean, you can't find them?"

"They're not where Bex had anticipated. She's still searching for them, but the Underneath is massive. It's very possible that the Damned will be here before she finds them, assuming she finds them at all."

"Jillian must have moved them after we broke out Bex," Dominic hissed.

Nathan glanced at Kaden and Jillian on the floor beside us. "At least our leverage worked as planned."

"About the only thing that's gone as planned," I grumbled.

He shrugged. "We have you. It'll take longer to drain all the Damned without the other Day Reapers, but once you entrance them, who cares how long it takes?"

I sighed. "About that. I can't entrance them."

Nathan blinked at me. Confusion on his scaly, monstrous face was nearly a comical expression. I suppressed the insane urge to burst out laughing.

"You've done it before," Nathan said. "What's stopping you from doing it again?"

Dominic lifted his palms and gestured them at Nathan. "Thank you."

"I haven't figured it out yet, and until I do, we'd better prepare for plan B."

"I don't remember planning a plan B," Nathan said doubtfully.

"We're planning it now. Any ideas?" I asked.

Nathan shook his head. "I know you need me here, but Bex needs help finding the Day Reapers. There's a lot of ground to cover and not a lot of time."

I turned to Dominic, about to suggest he join Bex instead.

"No," he said before I could even open my mouth.

"You don't know what I was going to say. You can't read me anymore, remember?"

He gave me a flat look. "Splitting up is a mistake."

"You can't fight the Damned, and Nathan can. We'll hold them off until you and Bex find the Day Reapers," I reasoned.

Dominic shook his head. "You can't simultaneously fight the Damned and babysit Kaden and Jillian."

"So take them with you."

"That wasn't part of the plan," he argued. "You need them here. She created the Damned, and you need her to retransform them."

"You think I don't know that?" I snapped. "None of this was part of the plan, but the plan is fucked and so are we if we don't adapt to survive."

Jillian's cackling laughter interrupted the conversation. "Too late," she murmured.

It took a moment for me to realize why she was gloating, a testament to how emotion could cloud even the most enhanced senses. We were surrounded, not by Damned—the impact tremors of their impending arrival still vibrated the ground beneath our feet—but by the silent approach of the coven's rebel vampires.

They were still hiding in the far corners of the great hall, but close enough now that the double glow of their eyes glinted from the darkness. Hundreds of eyes, probably the majority of the coven, surrounded us. They stepped out from the shadows in one smooth, nearly choreographed movement, and at their lead, one step ahead of all the rest, was Sevris. Behind him on either side were two vampires holding Rafe and Neil in front of their bodies as hostages, their talons poised over their throats.

Dominic's expression didn't so much as twitch. "Sevris," he inclined his head. "It's a relief to see you alive and well."

"I'm sure it is," Sevris said coolly. "You as well."

The two of them might be able to hone their anger into formal frigidity, but I'd never been known for my restraint. My anger ran red, boiling and loud. "You motherfucking bastard," I spat. "How dare you?"

I could take them out. Maybe not all of them, but without a doubt I could take out Sevris and steal back Neil and Rafe before anyone landed a killing blow.

Some of my intentions must have leaked because Dominic placed a staying hand on my shoulder and squeezed, hard. "It's all right, Cassidy. Sevris made his loyalties to the coven known from the very beginning. I knew he'd support the strongest Master despite personal preference. One must adapt to survive—isn't that what you just said, Cassidy?"

"Yes, but—"

"Then how can we begrudge Sevris his survival?" Dominic asked, his posed question more philosophical than practical.

I blinked at him. *Was he kidding?* "But what about Rafe and Neil and—"

"Don't worry about us," Rafe growled. "Just take the bastard down."

Neil's hearty agreement wasn't forthcoming. His eyes darted between Sevris, Rafe, and us, just watching and waiting and hoping for a loophole out of an impending slit throat.

The Damned's approach was getting louder. A few of the framed canvases on the walls had tilted and figurines were jumping from their mantels and smashing on the stone floor. Sevris's boots crunched over the shattered remains of a porcelain vase as he stepped forward. The swarm of vampires closed in around us, following Sevris's lead until he reached Jillian and knelt down in front of her.

She smiled, and the symmetrical slashes across both her cheeks widened grotesquely to reveal her molars.

"Sevris," she breathed in relief. "I always knew I could rely on you."

For the briefest, barest of moments, I swore I saw something akin to regret surface as he looked at Jillian. "For years, you were the only hope this coven had at convincing Dominic to release us from a prison of darkness," he said.

He offered his hand to help her stand.

I shrugged Dominic's grip off my shoulder. With the coven against us, the Damned approaching, all our leverage played out, and the Day Reapers MIA, Jillian was all we had left. If Sevris took her now, we could kiss transforming the Damned goodbye.

I tensed to attack.

"You understood that to build a better future, we couldn't allow the mistakes of our history to repeat themselves," Sevris said to Jillian, but his words echoed a conversation we'd had weeks ago regarding the care of vampires and the protection of the coven.

Jillian placed her hand in his. "Thank you."

I inhaled sharply and let his words stay my hand.

"It's up to us to break the cycle," Dominic murmured.

Sevris nodded. Whether he was responding to Jillian's thanks or Dominic's words was an imperceptible distinction. Every muscle in my body hummed in uncertain anticipation.

Sevris helped Jillian to her feet, and when she stood in front of him, he wrapped an arm around her shoulders and poised his talons across her throat.

"Sevris?" Jillian asked, shocked.

"For years, you were right about the wants of this coven," Sevris said, "but for the past week, you've been dead wrong."

He cut his head to the side, and the vampires behind him released Neil and Rafe.

The relief that flooded through my body nearly took me out at the knees.

"I did what Dominic was too afraid to do," Jillian growled. "I defied the Day Reapers and their tyranny and gave us our freedom!"

"You went too far, Jillian, and you know it," Sevris said.

Jillian looked around at the vampires that had been surrounding us, now surrounding her on all sides. "Jacqueline? Daria? Are you going to let him betray us like this?" No one moved, and Jillian's eyes became frantic, looking for one friendly face in the crowd. I tried to harden my heart against her, but even after everything she'd done to me and mine, I couldn't help but ache for her as she realized that they were all betraying her.

"Nikko? Lorna? K-K-Kip?" Tears streamed from her eyes and dripped into her sliced cheeks. I could feel the press of her desperation like the struggle against suffocation.

One of the vampires stepped forward, obviously torn with guilt, but she folded her arms, resolute. "You transformed our friends, potential night bloods, and future family into abominations that wiped out our food source. The humans, what little are left, are scarce and in hiding. I haven't eaten in days!"

Another vampire stepped forward in support of the first and squeezed her shoulder. "We liked being at the top of the food chain," he said, his voice less frantic and more resigned than the woman sobbing angrily next to him. "Now the Damned are ravaging everything, murdering the humans and ruining our homes. We wanted to live in New York City, not destroy it!"

All the vampires surrounding us were nodding their agreement, and I stared in awe at them. This was the same coven that only a few, short months ago had challenged Dominic as their Master as I lay broken and bleeding beneath him. Dominic had had to force their obedience, but here they were now, willing and ready to stand with us against Jillian. If we stood with them and offered to champion the very goals they'd wanted all along, maybe we had a real shot at taking back the coven, not only in name but in heart, too.

I opened my mouth—unsure what to say but knowing I needed to find the words to turn their rage and despair toward Jillian to our advantage—when an unholy cacophony of roars shook the coven.

Chapter 29

Eight-dozen Damned against two vampires. The odds weren't great to begin with, but factor in the liability of three hundred vampires to protect, and our odds were shit. Unless I packed some serious punch into this plan before the Damned arrived in the next minute, people were going to die—the very people we'd just unexpectedly gained on our side—and that was unacceptable.

We needed more Day Reapers, and if Bex needed help finding them, by God, she'd get that help.

"Nathan and I will hold off the Damned. Dominic will guard Jillian and Kaden," I commanded. "Sevris, I need you to lead everyone to the Underneath, and help Bex find the Day Reapers."

Everyone had turned to Dominic after realizing the Damned were descending on us, but when I spoke, they jerked their heads to face me and in nearly choreographed befuddlement, gave me a slow blink.

"It's hot down there," the female vampire spoke up between the hiccups of her tears.

The man beside her nodded. "Scalding."

"Suck it up." I stomped on the ground in frustration, cracking the stone floor. "Now!" I shouted.

They jumped to do my bidding without a second glance at Sevris or Dominic. Sevris neatly tossed Jillian back to the ground next to Kaden and led the masses fleeing the great hall to the Underneath.

With the exception of Rafe and Neil. Rafe glanced at the tidal wave of approaching Damned and back at me. He knew his fate should he stay. "We're in this together," he said.

I shook my head. "Take Neil and go with Sevris."

"You need us," he insisted.

"I can't simultaneously protect you and hold off the Damned, and you better believe my priority will be holding off the Damned."

"But—"

"Go!" I roared, and my voice was a physical force that actually pushed Rafe back and to his knees. He recovered quickly and escaped with Neil exactly as I'd ordered.

I stared at his retreat, taken aback by myself. I'd only ever seen one vampire's roar detonate in physical compulsion.

I turned to Dominic.

He stared back at me, wonder and worry warring in his gaze.

But neither of us had time to voice our thoughts. The Damned poured from the honeycombs—not one, not two or three, but dozens of them—each blindly following the one before it, to rain over us. I gaped as the first few Damned leading the charge soared through the air and landed in the great hall. They shook the coven on impact like an avalanche. The cacophony of their stampede was only rivaled by their slavering, rage-filled roars, and from one moment to the next, nothing else filled my mind but the grace and speed needed to survive.

Nathan and I fought in an orbit around Dominic, Kaden, and Jillian to create what probably looked, to the human eye, like a veritable tornado of slashing claws, fists, and fangs. The Damned were relentless, but their onslaught was unplanned and disjointed. They fought each other as readily as they fought us, clawing and biting their way to the front of the horde, and the Damned who did fight us only had one, predictable move; they jabbed at my chest for my heart every time.

As a human, I had thought their speed and strength unimaginable and undefeatable, but now, Nathan and I easily blocked their strikes, dodged their claws, and landed jabs of our own. The one chink in our armor, as the Damned attempted to disembowel and dismember us, was that we wanted to take them down alive. Our moves were faster but theirs were more lethal. We were stronger, but they were more brutal. Even pitted against our superior skill, their savagery was unstoppable. Their drive was endless, and superior skill or not, we couldn't fight forever. And I had a sinking suspicion that by sheer numbers and the insanity of their rage, they could.

We were in the middle of a paranormal battle in which my brother was a vampire-Damned hybrid and I was a gargoyle-like creature in my day form, yet I was suddenly struck by the absurd notion that our parents would be proud. Obviously not in the traditional sense, but our combined strength and power, and most of all, our indelible bond was undeniable.

The iron of our loyalty and fierce love, even challenged by fire—many fires over the course of this past year—had strengthened into something even more unbreakable than it already was.

As the Damned pounded relentlessly forward, undaunted by their wounds and fallen brethren before them, I channeled the pride and love for my family into every slash, every block, and jab. We were two against dozens, but our two had the heart of hundreds.

Beneath the grunts and screams of battle, I heard Dominic arguing with Jillian, demanding she control the Damned and stop their attack, but he wasn't making much headway, no matter how he threatened or reasoned with her.

"You're their creator," he insisted. "You brought them here, so you can damn well halt their assault. Call them off."

"I can no more control them than you can control Cassidy," Jillian said. "Sometimes the birth of our creation takes a life of its own far beyond what you thought possible. I doubt you intended for Cassidy to be more powerful than you, but here she is, a force of nature more devastating than you'll ever be again."

A Damned jabbed at my chest as another swiped at my head; I dodged the first, ducked the second, and sliced the tendons in both their wrists with a double downward swipe of my talons. Blood erupted like a geyser into the air, but even hemorrhaging and slack-wristed, they pressed their attack, snapping at me with their jaws.

Jillian was panting; between shaking breaths, she let loose a desperate, maniacal laugh. Dominic must have followed through on one of his threats; I could smell the cinnamon effervescence of her fresh blood.

"Command them to stop," Dominic growled.

That laughter grated on my nerves. I sliced harder than I'd intended and severed an arm.

"Careful," Nathan said.

I growled, low and rattling, under my breath. Even knowing he was right, curbing my strength and skills was difficult when they had no such qualms. Given the opportunity, they would not only sever my arm, they'd sever every limb from my body before ripping a hole in my chest and eating my heart. And once I was out of the way, they'd do the same to Dominic.

But *I* needed to be careful.

Jillian's laughter cut short on a sudden gasp. Dominic must have choked her. Hopefully, he'd only choked her; we needed her timely death to seal the transformation.

I glanced over my shoulder and hesitated. Dominic hadn't choked her. He hadn't slit her throat or ripped out her esophagus or torn out her heart. She was just staring at him, touching his cheek; tears rolling silently down her face.

"Don't you think I would command them if I could? This entire army of ferocity under my trigger finger would be the ultimate weapon, but look around you, Dominic. They can't be contained."

Dominic frowned. "You commanded them here."

She shook her head. "I called to them, like a ringmaster tugging on her lion's leash, but a leash only keeps the lion tethered; it does nothing to protect her or anyone else from the lion's attack."

Dominic blinked at her. "You created an army of ravenous, murdering monsters that you can't command," he said flatly.

"You think I wanted New York City in ruin?" she asked, desperate for him to understand. "I wanted us free. But this," she said, looking around her, "this is just another prison."

"Why did you keep creating them?" Dominic said, disgusted. "If you knew from the first, with Nathan, that they couldn't be controlled, why did you make another hundred?"

"I didn't know that, not for certain," she said, insistent now. "Nathan was more cognizant than anything Desirius had created in his first attempts at transformation. I couldn't control him, but I improved with practice. Now when I call for them, they all come."

"They come and *attack*," Dominic hissed. "What is the point of having a lion on a leash if all it wants is to eat you? And no, you didn't just leash one lion, you had to leash a hundred lions!"

"With more practice and time, I could—"

Dominic slapped her across the face.

And a claw slashed across mine. For a moment I thought I was vicariously feeling the pain of Dominic's hand on Jillian's cheek, but then the force of the Damned's blow rocketed me through the air and across the great hall. I crashed in a tumbling heap. My leg snapped and my head slammed back hard into the stone floor, and although I could already feel those injuries along with the ragged edges of my torn cheek healing, the damage was done. I'd been distracted, and now I was across the room, leaving Nathan to protect Dominic, Jillian, and Kaden on his own.

The Damned swarmed me, which at least relieved some of the pressure on Nathan, but their massive bodies blocked my view of everything except their slathering, ravenous rage. I fought back—slash for slash, dodging their claws and swiping with my own—but protecting myself was all I could do. I couldn't make any forward progress back to Nathan, and for all I could see of him, he might have already succumbed to the Damned's overwhelming numbers without me. For all I knew, Nathan and Dominic were already dead.

I tore my talons across the Damned in front of me in a helicopter spin to create some space to maneuver; if I couldn't fight through them, I'd jump over them.

I envisioned the spring in my legs as my strength launched me high over their heads. I felt the curl of my stomach as I tucked my body into a somersault, and I remembered to lock my eyes on the ground where I wanted my feet to land, not my ass. But the Damned had sardined themselves shoulder to shoulder surrounding Nathan, so there wasn't a spare square of floor space.

I landed with my right foot on a Damned's stomach and my left on a thigh; I turned my ankle, tripped, and the ground rushed up to meet my face.

Nathan caught me by the shoulders before I could eat stone and hauled me up next to him. I turned, braced to fight the Damned, and froze. There were no more Damned, not attacking us, anyway. The Damned who were in front of me—that I'd gracelessly landed on—were all writhing on the ground, roaring in pain. They were hobbled—their legs visibly broken in some cases and reduced to nearly bloody stumps in others. I opened my mouth, about to ask what had happened to being careful, when an approaching Damned's legs were shot out from under him. He dropped on top of his already-wounded brethren and rolled to the ground to writhe next to them.

A metal casing caught my eye. I picked it up—one of many, now that I was seeing it—and I remembered the person I'd sensed shifting in the rafters of the honeycombs. Considering the stampede of Damned descending on us at the time, I hadn't bothered to pay much attention to the man, but now, with my senses focused in that direction, I smelled him. And his minty scent was indisputable. It was Walker. He was picking off the Damned one by one, sniper-style, protecting Nathan and Dominic while I'd been preoccupied.

Unfortunately, I wasn't the only one to deduce the cause or location of his assault. The Damned indiscriminately tracked and killed anyone in their way. Three Damned vaulted into the air, soaring toward the far-right corner of the rafters.

My instinct was to give chase, but I hesitated, glancing back at Nathan. He couldn't hold the Damned off on his own.

Before I could decide, the Damned were shot in midair, and all three crashed to the ground like bowling balls, knocking down five others below. The inconvenienced Damned tossed the bodies of the fallen aside, then looked up at the rafters, searching for the source of the disruption. Their eyes swept the ceiling left to right as they sniffed the air, growling. Hunting.

Five Damned leaped into the air this time, soaring toward the rafters, and once again, they flew about halfway before five shots rang through the coven and all five Damned crashed back to the ground. Eight enraged Damned leaped to attack the source of the gunfire, and when they fell, twelve more gave chase. The cycle continued and escalated as more and more Damned discarded their fight with Nathan and me to pursue Walker. The uncomplicated stink of their anger was like the musk of a skunk. Anger, not grief. They were affronted that they'd been knocked down by their dead bodies and determined to kill the source of that affront.

I might have laughed at their logic if the sight of their determination wasn't paralyzing.

Faster than I would have imagined, the waves of Damned leaping toward the rafters became a constant stream, and that stream grew into a tidal force. Walker's shots were well aimed, but relentless now. Sooner or later, there would be more Damned than he could shoot. It would only take was one Damned to dodge his bullets, and distracted by all the others in the swarm, he wouldn't be able to protect himself.

"What the fuck are they doing?" Nathan asked, looking bemused.

I held the shell casing up for Nathan's inspection. "They're taking out the person shooting them."

"Who the hell is shooting them?" Nathan asked, sniffing the air.

I threw the casing down, frustrated. "Who the hell do you think?"

"Walker wasn't included in this part of the plan."

"Was any of this?" I asked, nearly laughing at the ridiculousness of that statement, but one look at Nathan's face and I swallowed the reaction.

"Is he killing them?" he asked grimly.

"You're seeing what I'm seeing," I said, swiping my hand at the pile of dispatched Damned in front of us, some unconscious, some dismembered, some roaring their anger, some dying and dead, but all too wounded to seek revenge.

"We promised to take them out alive. He's gunning them down like dogs."

I sighed. "Can you blame him? Look at them, Nathan. They're not swarming him to make his acquaintance."

He cursed. "What now?"

"Maybe this is just the distraction we need. If Walker can keep them more focused on him than us, maybe we can—"

The gun stopped firing.

"Maybe he's reloading," Nathan offered.

The silence, filled now by the crescendo of the Damned's collective roar, stretched.

"Maybe his gun jammed," Nathan said. "He must have more than one gun."

Dominic snorted. "Maybe he ran out of ammunition."

I waited, and as the seconds ticked by and the Damned drew closer, the absence of return fire was deafening.

"Maybe he ran," Jillian hissed, "and left you to deal with me and my army of murderers all on your own."

I cursed under my breath, the ultimate truth undeniable. It didn't matter whether or not Walker had run, if he was reloading, his gun had jammed, or he'd run out of ammunition. He was being swarmed by our enemy because he'd provided us with cover. My transformation into a vampire, and subsequently a Day Reaper, had undeniably changed me in many ways—physically, emotionally, mentally—but I was essentially the same person at heart. No matter the personal risk, I wouldn't let someone else fight my battles.

And I'd certainly never let someone who had my back face a battle alone.

"The woman I knew five years ago who took a bullet for Harroway is the same woman who used herself as bait to solve a case last month, and she's the same damn fool today that she was back then. People don't change. I don't care if the heart inside her chest still beats or not. It's still the biggest heart I've ever had the privilege to know."

—Greta Wahl

Chapter 30

I vaulted into the air, past the Damned, and landed in the rafters moments before the first Damned reached the landing. Walker was tensed with his pen-stake raised, his watch dart aimed, his sunbeam flashlight lit, and several empty guns at his feet. For a moment, I wondered if he would see me as an enemy or ally.

But the Damned were only a heartbeat behind; I didn't have another moment to second-guess myself. I turned my back on Walker and his weapons—no matter how woefully inadequate, they were raised against me—to face the swarm.

I slashed my talons at the front line, spilling blood and organs in my haste. *Be careful,* I reminded myself, but even with Nathan's words ringing in my mind, when the second line of Damned attacked, as fierce and relentless as the first, my instinct was to fight back, matching deadly ferocity with deadly ferocity.

I didn't have the space to maneuver on the rafters like I'd had on the ground, but we weren't open to 360 degrees of attack either. We were in the corner of the ceiling, and even though that trapped us on three sides, the Damned only had one side on which to attack. Walker's bullets had been a decent deterrent, but now, they had to get through me.

Walker stepped up beside me, aiming over my shoulder with what was left of his weapons. His older weapons didn't penetrate the thick, scaly hides of the Damned as effectively as his newer, modified firepower, but an attempt to help was better than an attempt to harm.

"Well, you were right. I should have just left while I had the chance," Walker said, trying and failing to be funny. Still, trying.

I cursed, blocking another Damned and saving Walker from losing his head by inches. "I didn't want to be right. I wanted to win."

He pursed his lips. "Now would be a good time to make our big move."

I twirled, slashing a Damned with my left talon and blocking the strike of another with my right. "Yeah, about that—"

"I know, I know, no Wi-Fi. Here." Walker slapped a walkie-talkie into my hand. "Have at it."

I blinked, so caught off guard by Walker slapping anything into my hand—besides maybe a grenade—that I almost missed a Damned as it lunged for his chest. Walker pegged it square in the face with the sunbeam of his flashlight. It reared back, blinded, and I roundhouse kicked it off the rafter. It fell to the ground with a thundering shudder ten stories below.

"Where did you get this?" I asked.

"I brought it with me when you said there was no Wi-Fi. I figured there might be a need," Walker said.

"Does Bex have one?"

Walker gave me a look. "As if I had time to take a stroll into the Underneath."

"You had nearly nine hours to—"

"You're lucky I had time to give one to Greta."

"Then what good does—"

"It puts your voice on a different frequency, remember? She'll hear you."

"And so will Jillian," I snapped, frustrated with our failed plan almost as much as I was frustrated with all of Walker's interruptions.

"We're not going for stealth and surprise anymore," Walker insisted, his words a mirror of Dominic's words not twenty minutes earlier. "We need backup, and we need it now. Tell Bex to make her move."

I wanted to continue arguing—really, I could stretch an argument with Walker all day without even trying—but when both Walker and Dominic were in agreement over something, it was time to listen. I squeezed the walkie-talkie and shouted into it, hoping Bex would hear me over the shrieks and roaring growls around us. "Reaper to Reaper, I hope you copy. Release the other Reapers if you have them. I repeat, release the Day Reapers. Over."

"*If* she has them?" he asked.

I tossed the walkie-talkie back at Walker to free both my hands against the Damned. "She had a little trouble finding the Day Reapers in the Underneath. They weren't where we had left them."

"So entrance the Damned, and we'll deal with the Day Reapers later," Walker said.

"About that—" I began.

Walker aimed his watch and shot three Damned in a row with deadly accuracy, piercing their eyes with his little watch spears. Their roars shook the honeycombs, and when I roundhouse-kicked their chests, eviscerating three others with my talons with one power swipe, all six tumbled backwards off the rafters.

"We had a little trouble entrancing the Damned too," I admitted.

"What didn't you have trouble with?" Walker snapped.

I slashed two more Damned and tossed them from the rafters. "We found the Damned, no problem."

He snorted. "Not funny."

"You used to like my humor," I said.

"I used to like *you,*" he countered.

I blocked a Damned from eviscerating Walker with a smart kick to its elbow and used the momentum to impale my claws in another's chest. I glanced at Walker over my shoulder. "You're welcome."

He grimaced. "We can't defend against this assault forever."

"Speak for yourself," I growled, kicking the wounded aside to deal with the next in line. "Besides, we don't have to fight forever—only until Bex comes with reinforcements."

"And then what?" Walker said, reloading his watch and taking out three more eyeballs. "Unless you can entrance the Damned, so we can drain and transform them, the Day Reapers won't have any choice but to kill them."

I didn't justify Walker's comments with a reply. He was right. He knew he was right and admitting as much wouldn't help solve our problem. Neither would hiding behind a Pollyanna facade and denial, but I let his comment fester in the air between us and took out my frustration on another round of Damned.

The last round of Damned.

I stared at the empty air in front of me, at a loss. We hadn't fought them all. There were too many of them for us to have possibly fought and beat them all. I leaped to the edge of the rafter and peered down at the scene ten stories below. The Damned had another battle to wage against a new adversary: the Day Reapers.

"Stay here," I said.

"Where are you—"

I jumped from the rafters.

I'd known Walker would be right, but knowing it and living it were two different things entirely. The Day Reapers weren't just defending themselves against the Damned. They were slaughtering them.

Lord High Chancellor Henry Lynell Horrace DeWhitt looked fantastic, considering he'd just been resurrected from the Underneath. Feeding from our willing human donors had obviously helped; the Chancellor's skin was plump and blushed with the bloom of health. His dark, chestnut-and-white–striped hair was thick and wild around his blood-spattered, chiseled jaw, and his eyes—those piercing, unyielding, unforgiving humanlike eyes—were trained on me, even as he decapitated three Damned with one powerful swipe of his silver talons.

The myriad of emotions—recognition, shock, awe, respect, anger, and eventually cold resignation—in that man's gaze would have been laughable if not for the fact that it was also everything Dominic had predicted and feared. He broke our gaze, faced Dominic, and with one swipe of those silver talons, ripped out Dominic's throat.

The stabbing heat of his claws across my throat was staggering, a physical pain from my metaphysical bond with Dominic. Flashbacks of Jillian raking her claws across my throat distracted me for a moment, but I shook off the vulnerable, horrible feelings that memory evoked in favor of the present horror. The wound was devastating; Dominic wouldn't have been able to heal it, might not even have survived it, without our metaphysical bonds—without me—and that made me furious. I took the injury into myself, healed it, and refocused all that fury toward the nightmare confrontation come to life before my eyes. Someone had to, because the Chancellor—high on his all-knowing, all-powerful, all-ruling pedestal—either couldn't see or didn't care that while he was engaging in an unnecessary, personal battle with Dominic, his Day Reapers were losing against the Damned. Again.

The other Day Reapers weren't as recovered from the injuries they'd sustained within the Underneath. Their movements weren't as quick or as effective. They were weak and malnourished, and without the Chancellor giving them focus and strength, I could see why they'd lost against the Damned at 432 Park Avenue. Besides the fact that they would have been distracted by entrancing Greta's SWAT team, they didn't fight like a team; they fought like they could single-handedly take on the Damned on their own. Which they couldn't.

When one Day Reaper took a hit to his forearm to block the Damned's claws from raking his chest, the Day Reaper next to him didn't cover his back while he healed. She ignored his injury, decapitated the Damned she was fighting, and moved on to the next, letting her partner struggle to both recover and block another strike. He nearly didn't, but while the Damned's claws embedded in his other forearm, he couldn't help the Day

Reaper on his other side, who hadn't healed her injuries in time to block the next strike to her chest. The Damned impaled her sternum with its talons and tore out her heart.

She hit the ground, not quite dead yet, but that was only just a matter of time. The Day Reapers stepped into the gap her absence left in their defense, closing the circle and protecting the Chancellor. But they weren't protecting each other.

By the time I dropped into the center of their circle, four more Day Reapers had fallen, and no one even spared me a second glance. I wasn't a Damned, and honestly, I don't think any of them—having remembered me as the night blood who could barely walk—really anticipated facing a version of me that was not only strong, fast, and powerful, but stronger, faster, and more powerful than them.

The Chancellor raised his bloody claw for a second strike against Dominic. Dominic's chest was soaked in a waterfall of blood, and although his wound was already healed, a second wound so soon after the first might just be a killing blow despite our metaphysical bonds. I leaped between them, shielding Dominic's body with my own, my hand raised to catch the Chancellor's wrist. His sharp, silver talons halted inches from my face.

I'd thought long and hard about how to react upon seeing him, knowing he would be duty bound to kill Dominic for transforming me. I could grovel, beseeching his empathy; I could rationalize Dominic's actions, appealing to his logical mind; I could feign innocence and ignorance of his crimes. But all of those options implied that we were somehow wrong in our actions and needed the Chancellor's forgiveness. A very good friend of mine once told me to never apologize for surviving, and although lying was worth my pride if it saved Dominic, it wasn't worth our lives; the Chancellor was the one creature who would undoubtedly be capable of detecting a lie, and he would punish it with death.

Instead, I'd wield the only weapon I had against the most powerful vampire on earth: the truth.

"Hi, Henry," I said, smiling bright and wide, showcasing every one of my many pointy fangs. "Aren't you happy to see me?" I asked.

The Chancellor cringed. "I am Lord High Chancellor Henry Lynell Horrace DeWhitt, Master vampire of London and—"

"And Lord of all vampires," I finished. "I know. We met in this very room little more than a week ago. Guess I didn't make a big impression. I'm Cassidy Di—"

"Cassidy DiRocco, Dominic Lysander's *former* night blood. Yes, I quite remember," the Chancellor finished. "But as I am your Lord, you may refer to me as such."

"Listen, *Henry*, I know you follow this infallible adherence to propriety and titles, but considering you just attacked my master, I'm beyond adhering to anything remotely resembling propriety right now." My voice was calm and reasonable-sounding in tone if not in words. "You can call me DiRocco. Everybody does."

The Chancellor's other hand darted for my throat, and I blocked that strike, too.

His eyes widened.

I imagined that it wasn't every day, if ever, that someone stood up to him. He was too fast to allow me to counterstrike, but I was strong enough to defend myself and protect Dominic, and really, that's all we both needed to know.

"According to Council law, I know that you're the only vampire permitted to transform a night blood into a Day Reaper, and I know that, by saving me, Dominic broke that law," I said, my voice still steady. Still calm. "I also know that breaking Council law is punishable by death. But *you* should know that I'm prepared to break *every* law if it means keeping Dominic alive."

The Chancellor didn't react. He didn't so much as blink.

"I could have left you to rot in the Underneath," I said, driving home my point, "but I saved you, hoping we could be allies against a greater evil."

The Chancellor lifted his left eyebrow—a very Dominic expression of doubt—and I wondered if that's who Dominic had adopted the expression from. "Hoping I could save you from a greater evil, you mean," he said.

I shook my head. "I could take on the Damned myself, but I thought that having you and the other Day Reapers on our side would give us a better chance at winning. You failed against them last time because you were working against Greta and the other humans, like you're working against me now," I said. "Look around you," I added, spreading my hand out to the steadily shrinking circle of Day Reapers around us. "You're losing again. You might be willing to make that same mistake again, but I'm not. Either we work as a team, or this plan doesn't work at all."

Rage blazed like fire in the Chancellor's eyes. "The humans are here? You revealed the existence of vampires and the location of their coven?" he thundered.

I snorted. Probably not the most intelligent response to his rage, but I couldn't help it. "The Damned ravaged New York City, and with you, Bex, and the other Day Reapers imprisoned within the Underneath, Dominic caring for me, and me undergoing a week-long transformation, who was there to entrance the humans?" I asked, deliberately including Dominic and myself in the same breath as the Day Reapers. Subliminal messaging at its finest. "The humans have been fully aware of the existence of vampires for over a week. Jillian's been running the show, and she certainly didn't restore order to the city." I shot a look at Bex. "Why is he not up to speed?"

Bex rolled her eye. "Considering his impeccable sense of hearing, he is a surprisingly poor listener."

The Chancellor pinned his fiery gaze on Bex.

She inclined her head. "My Lord."

That seemed to appease him slightly, or at least mollify him enough not to physically strike Bex. I could only protect so many people at once, and unfortunately, I had my priorities.

He took a step back, slowly and deliberately, and I released my hold on his wrists, hoping for the best but tensed for the worst.

"Assuming all of what you say is true," the Chancellor said, his voice heavily laced with skepticism, "why has no one yet killed our betrayers?"

Jillian shrank back, petrified.

Kaden's body vibrated with a gurgling growl.

"They will receive their due comeuppance," Dominic said, his voice grave through his shredded vocal cords.

"But right now, we still need them to complete our plan," I finished.

The Chancellor's right eyebrow rose to match the height of the left. "And what might that plan be?"

"To save the several dozen night bloods who fell victim to Jillian and her evil, unlawful rise to power," I said, hoping to mask the fact that I was referring to the Damned.

The Chancellor blinked, and his eyebrows climbed higher, nearly merging with his hairline. "Your plan is to the save the Damned?" he asked, blatantly incredulous. "To *save* them?" He gestured at the ravenous, snarling, mindless riot of creatures raging around us, being held in check—barely—by his dwindling circle of Day Reapers.

"She saved me," Nathan said. The focused calm of his steady gaze was unnerving coming from him—as was the voice of a man coming from the lips of a monster—and I couldn't have paid to have a more convincing advocate for my argument.

The Chancellor was silent for a long moment before he finally spoke. "What do you need from me?"

Relief rushed through my body, making me nearly weak-kneed. "We need to drain the Damned enough to incapacitate them, but not kill them, and then feed them human blood."

"Ah." The Chancellor grinned unpleasantly. "The only beings capable of piercing the Damned's flesh is their maker"—he eyed Jillian cowering and defeated on the floor—"a former Damned, and Day Reapers. Without us, it's only you and your brother against hundreds."

"And me," Bex said, raising her hand.

"Against several dozen," I said, eyeing the horde. "Eighty at most," I corrected wearily.

"That's being overly generous, but for the sake of argument, three against eighty may as well be two against hundreds."

"Yes, I need your help," I hissed. "We don't have time for petty arguments. Are you in or are you out?"

His eyebrows finally disappeared behind his hair. "And where are we obtaining that many humans on such short notice?"

"We have them waiting on my signal to join us here and donate their blood," I said.

"And why would they do that?" he snapped. "Why would humans, nothing more than our food, bleed to save hundreds of Damned? The same Damned who—how did you put it? *Ravaged* New York City?"

"Because those Damned vampires are their brothers and sisters, fathers and mothers, husbands and wives, and dear friends that they've loved for a lifetime, and just like I was determined to save Nathan, they are willing to risk their lives for a chance to save that love," I said fiercely.

The Chancellor stared at me. Slowly, his brows settled to a normal position above his eyes. "It's certainly easier to kill them than subdue and drain them in battle."

"It doesn't have to be in battle," Bex said. "Cassidy can entrance them."

"No one can entrance them," the Chancellor scoffed.

"She can. I was there," Bex insisted.

"No, I can't," I said, and the confession was as physically painful as if I'd jammed my talons into my chest and ripped out my own heart.

"I was there," she insisted. "I saw you. You can—"

"I know I've done it before!" I screamed. Bex's tone wasn't condemning in the least, but after hearing that same statement from Dominic, Nathan, and Walker—and knowing damn well that I'd entranced them before—hearing those words yet again made me snap. "That was then and this is now, and for whatever godforsaken reason, I can't now!"

A Damned broke through the wall of Day Reapers around us, and on instinct, reflex, and blind hot anger, I swiped at it savagely. The blow severed its throat straight through to the spine; its head tipped back, the wound gaping like a spitting mouth, and fell off its twitching body.

I glanced sheepishly at Nathan. He was shaking his head in aggravation.

"Sorry," I muttered.

A second Damned broke through, and Bex blocked that one, humming thoughtfully as she fought. "What did you do then that you're not doing now? We were surrounded, Dominic was injured, the situation was hopeless—"

"So the situation was actually identical to now," Nathan interjected.

"We were in the Underneath, not the great hall. The sun had just risen. She was newly transformed and had not yet drunk fresh human blood," Dominic rasped.

"Those differences are inconsequential," the Chancellor said, dismissing Dominic with his best High Lord sneer. "A skill of that magnitude accomplished once should easily manifest itself in a different location, and having fully transformed and consumed human blood would only strengthen that skill."

"Besides those inconsequential differences, Nathan is correct. Our situations are identical," Dominic said grimly.

"I was fully transformed when I entranced the Damned," I argued. "The sun had just hit me and…" My voice faded along with my thought as the realization of what I'd just said slammed home. "The sun! That's the difference! I was bathed in sunlight the last time I entranced the Damned!"

Everyone stared at me and then in unison at our surroundings in the honeycombs, the deepest, most subterranean section of the coven where the vampires safely took their day rest hidden from sunlight.

"Fuck," Nathan said, generally speaking for everyone.

"Well, I hate to state the obvious," Bex said drolly, "but we're in the one room in this entire coven specifically fortified *against* letting in sunlight."

The Chancellor growled, "Whose bloody brilliant plan was this?"

Everyone looked at me.

I bit my tongue. "If the sun can't get to me, there's got to be a way to get me to the sun."

"I can help with that," Walker said smugly.

I jerked around at his voice behind me. "How did you—" and then I noticed the rappelling harness still hooked around his hips. Sure enough, one glance over his shoulder revealed the telltale cable hanging from the rafters. "I told you to stay put."

"I don't even like you," Walker said genially. "Why would I listen to you?"

I threw my hands up, gesturing to the many Damned attacking around us. “Why, indeed.”

Without any more warning than a sly little grin, which really, I suppose should have been warning enough, Walker unstrapped his sunbeam flashlight from his hip and bathed me in artificial sunlight.

Chapter 31

Sunlight flooded over and through my body, its effect as potent as the actual sun. Warmth, light, and calm settled over me, like the comfort and weight of a down blanket on a chilly morning. I could hear the hisses and screams to "watch your aim" and the putrid stench of someone—hopefully Kaden, but likely Dominic, damn it—catching fire, but the people around me and their movements and panic were suddenly a world away. In this moment, a second that stretched to infinity, I wasn't Cassidy DiRocco, former night blood now Second to Dominic Lysander, former Master vampire of New York City; I was reduced to light and blood and the electric snap of synapses—the essential elements of my entire being.

The sunlight felt different than last time and not because of the light source. This time, the light wasn't a catalyst to my transformation; it was a rejuvenation of everything I already possessed: strength, power, light, and insight. Everything I already was and had learned over a lifetime combined with everything I'd become, beaming down on me like a mirror, reflecting a reminder of true self.

A person who had diligently trained for a marathon and had successfully run one before wouldn't be able to run one again without drinking water and eating properly for the days leading up to the big event. No matter the person's skill and determination and commitment, failure was inevitable if the person wasn't properly fueled.

I basked in the light, shutting out the fighting and screaming and flames around me, and within that illuminating luminescence, I rediscovered the strings connecting us—hundreds upon thousands of strings linking me to each individual Damned and to Dominic, and interwoven between me and everyone. I could feel the frayed bonds between Dominic and his vampires. I could feel Jillian and the broken bonds between her and her followers, her leash on the Damned, Bex's tenuous bond on her own coven, and the Chancellor and his iron-clad bonds with everyone. And in its infancy, I could feel the fragile, inadvertent bonds I'd created with Dominic's coven. Now, my coven, too.

I reached out with the metaphysical fingers of my mind and severed the leash between Jillian and the Damned. With the swift, practiced precision of a cellist, I plucked all nine-dozen strings connecting each individual Damned to me.

"Stop," I thought, and the timbre of the command vibrated down each string and through each of the Damned, halting their movements and minds.

"Fuck, she really did it."

"Bloody hell."

"I told you she'd done it before."

"She saved me when I was one. She can do anything."

"There's a difference between being told that someone has the ability to perform miracles and actually witnessing it for oneself."

"Cassidy."

I felt a hand on my shoulder, warm and rough and trembling.

I touched the hand but kept my eyes closed. Dominic was struggling to remain conscious. His burns were severe, head to toe, and to the bone. I didn't need his touch to know he was suffering. Although he was attempting to hide his pain, he couldn't successfully hide anything from me anymore. Never mind the trumpeting fanfare of Walker's joy as indication of Dominic's egregious injuries. I could feel them as my own. I took Dominic's wounds into myself, made them physically mine, and healed them.

His hand relaxed on my shoulder for a moment—in relief, I suspected—but then his grip became steel.

"Cassidy!"

I opened my eyes.

I'd been so consumed by the sun, literally, and the echoing cords of the strings I'd plucked that I hadn't realized that utter and complete silence had blanketed the great hall. Walker had flicked off his flashlight some time ago, but I hadn't registered that either because the warmth and light were still radiating under my skin. The Damned were no longer snarling, the Day Reapers were no longer battling, and Dominic was no longer screaming. He was staring at me, his body healed and his eyes proud. I sank into that gaze like a warm bath at the end of a long, hard day, and it cleansed me, body and soul.

Someone growled.

I glanced past Dominic and started. Everyone was staring at me with varying degrees of awe and nervous apprehension.

"What are you waiting for?" I snapped. "We don't have all day, and there's nearly a hundred Damned. Start draining them!"

My exclamation was more than words; they packed a physical punch equal to my raw emotions. Every Day Reaper, including Bex, but excluding High Lord Henry, jumped to my command. They flew out into the crowd, latched onto the nearest Damned, and one by one, severed their carotids. The Damned remained complacent throughout the onslaught, theirs eyes glazed and for all intents and purposes, seemingly unaware as the Day Reapers bled them dry.

The underlying growl grew louder. I could feel its vibration under my feet. The source was nearby and likely against the floor for the vibrations to be so tactile.

"Call them back to action. Command them to attack," Kaden hissed.

I peered behind Dominic where Kaden and Jillian lay, and sure enough, found the source of the growling. Kaden and Jillian were charred around the edges, having been shadowed from the majority of Walker's light by Dominic's body, but the burns may have actually cauterized some of their wounds. Neither Kaden nor Jillian's injuries were actually bleeding anymore. They didn't even look fresh. And although Kaden's wounds were still devastating and debilitating, he was now healed enough to enunciate words and string them into full sentences.

And those sentences were clearly not happy.

"Call them back to you," Kaden insisted. He squeezed Jillian's shoulder, much like Dominic was still squeezing mine. "Now, before it's too late!"

Jillian shook her head, her morose resignation a stark contrast to Kaden's urgency. "I can't," she muttered, her voice deadpan.

"What do you mean, you can't? You created the creatures! You've called to them before," Kaden growled.

"They're no longer mine to call," she said, staring at me. Her expression never shifted, but tears gushed down her cheeks. "I can't feel my connection to them anymore."

"After everything we sacrificed, everything we worked so hard to achieve, after how far we've climbed, scraping and killing and fighting our way to the top—just when we've finally won, you're going to let it all just slip away," Kaden said, his voice a grating growl. "Fight for it, damn it! Fight for us!"

"No one wants the future we created. I don't even want it," Jillian said. "There's nothing left to fight for. It's done. We're done."

Kaden shook his head, an expression of disgust and rage like I'd never seen before wrinkling his handsome face. "I'm not done."

Considering my newly heightened senses, I should have been able to anticipate his next move, but I hadn't really thought Kaden capable of movement. Kaden's wounds, although cauterized, weren't the least bit healed. Both his left leg and arm were visibly broken. The bones had torn through his flesh and protruded from his skin, a startling white in contrast to all the blood. Only his right arm, although bruised and sliced to ribbons by shrapnel spray, didn't appear broken, and apparently that, and rage, was all Kaden needed.

Fangs fully extended, Kaden tore open Jillian's throat to her glistening spinal column. She pitched forward, hands clutching her neck, and impaled herself on Kaden's waiting talons.

I watched him catch the waterfall of blood from her neck in his mouth. I watched him rip his fist from her chest, hold her heart in his hand in front of her face, and smile. His movements weren't even really that fast, but for the life of me—or I suppose, really, for the life of Jillian—I could only stare in shock as Kaden tipped back his head and squeezed the blood from her upended heart into his mouth.

Chapter 32

Some moments are so devastating and cataclysmically life-altering that a person becomes paralyzed—physically and mentally—as if the brain and body create a shield against the pain, and all that's left is a vague feeling of numb denial. I'd felt that way seven, nearly eight years ago now, when Nathan had called to tell me that our parents' New York apartment had been engulfed by flames, and that no one on their floor—not even Bonnie Boo, the neighbor's temperamental calico—had survived.

His words, "engulfed by flames," had echoed around me, separate somehow from the phone in my hand, Adam stroking my leg, and my own cat, Whiskers, flicking her tail agitatedly under my chin. My phone, Adam, and Whiskers lived in another reality, one in which those words, "engulfed by flames," didn't exist. And for a long while after I'd ended that call, neither had I.

One would think that seeing Jillian's exposed heart in Kaden's hand would be one of those moments that paralyzed reality, but it wasn't. It was the moment before.

Jillian looked down at her chest, Kaden's arm nearly elbow-deep inside it, and her gaze traveled up from his elbow to his face. Her eyes were wide and her mouth gaped, and despite my heightened vampire senses that could hear the squawk of Keagan's annoyance, smell the sriracha bite of Walker's rage, and taste the nutty crunch of Ronnie's longing, I couldn't sense anything from Jillian in that moment. She'd been utterly stunned stupid by Kaden's betrayal. One moment, she'd been lying beside a trusted loved one, battling for the right to rule the city—a battle she'd been arguably winning, until recently—and in the very next second, she faced her own death at the hands of that loved one.

And then Kaden held her heart, was actually drinking from it. Dominic recovered faster than I did. He launched himself at Kaden; the two of them streaked across the room in a black-and-blue blur, and Jillian collapsed face-first into the hard stone of the coven floor.

I knelt down, keeping my eye on Dominic even as I reached to roll Jillian onto her back. Dominic had fought against Kaden and overpowered him once before, and I had no doubt that he could overpower him now, especially considering the uncountable broken bones and blood loss Kaden had suffered at Walker's hands. Dominic should have easily pinned him to the ground and twisted off his head or slashed his throat or ripped out his heart tit for tat, or whatever Dominic deemed a fit punishment—banishment to the Underneath, more than likely, if history was anything to go by—but what Dominic should have easily done and what he was actually accomplishing were two different things. I watched, confused at first and then with growing unease, as I realized that somehow, whether he'd been faking his weakness before (unlikely) or had somehow been imbued with sudden and overwhelming strength, Kaden was fighting back. And he wasn't losing.

I tensed to join Dominic in battle against Kaden, but Jillian made a strange noise as she rolled onto her back, a sort of wet *splat* like the pop and gush of a water balloon. The hole in her chest where her heart used to be was gushing blood, and yet she weakly, but persistently, attempted to reach for her heart. Kaden had dropped it a few feet away after having been tackled by Dominic. It lay on the stone floor, bruised and a little torn, just out of arm's reach.

Jesus, not again, I thought, remembering how I'd shoved Bex's heart back into her chest after Nathan, Damned at the time, had ripped it out. From that experience, I knew that Jillian's injury wasn't fatal, assuming the heart was placed back where it belonged.

Moving on instinct more than logic—because, had I thought through my actions, I might not have acted at all—I snatched Jillian's heart in my bare hand and shoved it and my entire fist into the gaping wound of her chest. The wound was much wider than my arm, perhaps because Kaden's claws were much bigger than mine, so I held the heart in place, unsure if the heart would remain in the right position without me holding it—assuming I was even replacing it in the proper position. I'd been equally uncertain concerning the placement of Bex's heart, and hers had healed just fine. Granted, I'd had the power of Dominic's blood in a handy pendant around my neck to help heal her wound. All I had now was grit and a prayer.

With my hand inside Jillian's chest, heart in place if not necessarily in position, my eyes drifted back to Dominic.

Kaden was indisputably winning. He lashed out with his claws, and Dominic dodged to the side but not out of range. Blood bloomed across his stomach as he lifted his arm to counterstrike. Dominic's claws slashed at nothing but air, and the momentum of his missed swing unbalanced him. Kaden seized the advantage and lunged at him, taking the fight to the ground. Dominic tried to kick him back, trap him between his thighs, and pin him to the ground, but although Dominic was strong—nearly the strongest creature I knew besides my Damned brother—Kaden was somehow stronger. He pinned Dominic back, and the stone floor fractured under the force of Kaden's grip. If the floor buckled under his strength, no doubt so would Dominic's bones.

Dominic was faster and stronger than this. He might not have the full Master's power anymore, but Kaden had been teetering on the brink of unconsciousness, if not death, for the last several hours. How was he suddenly stronger than the former Master vampire of New York City?

"Because he's my Second," Jillian rasped.

I tore my gaze away from Dominic and glanced down at Jillian, stunned. My hand was still buried inside her chest, her wound still hemorrhaging around my arm, and she was looking up at me, not looking the least bit stunned. In fact, given the dull certainty in her eyes and the deflated ache I could feel in her chest—a separate pain from the gaping physical wound, but just as fatal—she was resigned.

"What?" I asked.

"Kaden. He—" Jillian coughed, and I could feel her muscles contract around my fist. A fresh spurt of blood and thicker things seeped from her organs and spilled out around my arm.

"Hush," I said. "You'll be fine. It's just a flesh wound for someone like you. You've healed much worse."

"He's my Second," Jillian persisted between gurgles. "His blow," she coughed, "is a death blow."

"It's not the Leveling," I argued. "This isn't the end for you."

"He's becoming Master vampire of New York City."

"No," I denied.

Jillian breathed to gain enough air to speak, and her lungs trembled against my hand as they inhaled more blood than air. She coughed, and I turned my face away from the spray. "Lysander should have regained all his powers after surviving the Leveling and didn't. What little I retained is transferring to Kaden as we speak."

I glanced up and watched as Kaden dodged another of Dominic's powerful punches and punched him back with more speed and force and precision than Dominic could hope to evade. Dominic took the strike square in the face and ate stone.

"Kill me."

I tore my gaze from Dominic and stared. Every time Jillian spoke, I became more dumbstruck. "What?"

"Kaden would not be a good Master for this city," Jillian said, and the certainty in that statement seemed to predate the last few moments of his sudden betrayal.

I blinked, equally certain. "No, he would not."

"Dominic was a wonderful Master, but he never listened to his coven and their needs. I told him over and over again throughout the decades that we yearned to break free from the confines of living in secrecy, but he wouldn't listen to me. He thought he knew what was best, even if it killed him. Even if it killed us." Jillian lifted her hand and gripped my arm in her chest. "But he listens to you."

I shook my head. "I don't think—"

"In all my hundreds of years serving as Second by his side, he never once, ever, opposed the Council, not even at the risk of losing his own coven." Her grip on my arm tightened. "But when faced with the risk of losing you, he didn't just oppose the Council; he flat-out betrayed them." She tried to inhale again, but her lungs seized. Her next words came out with more blood than sound. "Together, you can accomplish what I never could."

I was still shaking my head. "We can't—"

"Finish killing me. Prevent Kaden from adopting the Master's power, and take it for yourself. Save the city."

"Damn it," I cursed, still shaking my head as if denying everything would rewind time to the version of reality that made sense. In that reality, we were good, she was evil, and killing her would right the injustices in the world. Everything she was saying was everything I wanted—hell, it fit perfectly in place with our original plan to take back the coven—except for one thing. "But if I kill you, *I* will adopt the Master's power."

"Only what little I had of it," Jillian said, but we both knew she contained more than just a little. She contained enough to rule the damn coven.

"I don't want to be Master," I growled.

She lifted an eyebrow. *Either you or Kaden,* she mouthed, her words no longer audible.

I glanced up at Dominic, torn. He could kill Jillian and take back the Master's power himself, but he was a little preoccupied. Dominic was now battling Kaden from the impossible position of being pinned on his back with Kaden astride his waist. Jillian would die in the next few moments, giving Kaden the last bit of power he needed to kill Dominic once and for all.

Luckily for me, Kaden was preoccupied, too.

I leaned over Jillian, my lips so close they brushed her ear as I spoke. "You once said that in another life, we would have been allies. Friends, even."

Jillian exhaled on a sob.

"But in this life, we're so much more than friends or allies. In this moment, for this city and for our coven, we are sisters, and I am so very sorry for what I'm about to do to you."

I know, Jillian mouthed, blood now pouring from her mouth nearly as steadily as it poured from her chest, *it's how I felt when I killed you.*

"Be at peace," I said, stealing the words she had once whispered to me. I let the bitterness of this inevitability pour from me—in sight, sound, smell, and stabbing pain—so she could sense the truth and depth of my regret. "No more pain."

No more pain.

I squeezed the hand still inside her chest into a fist and punctured her heart with my silver talons.

Black fissures, like poisoned veins, erupted over her chest and spread outward over her neck and shoulders, snaked down her arms, and swept across her face. I remembered those fissures. They had looked exactly the same when Rene had died.

Something suddenly occupied the air behind me. Her eyes shifted from my face to over my shoulder, and that one small movement was enough to break her body apart into a million microscopic pieces. Skin flaked from muscle and muscle from bone; nothing remained but dust.

I stared into the empty air where Jillian had lain just a moment before. Her ashes alight on the air. My fist was in front of me, now empty, but still gloved in blood. I watched my fingers move as I opened my palm, and I had the sudden, strange sensation that it wasn't just my hand that I opened. Even though I could see that my palm was empty, it felt as if I were somehow still holding her heart. But that wasn't quite right, either. Jillian was gone, consigned to ash by my own hand, but in her passing, she'd gifted me with something far greater than the weight of one heart. She'd gifted me with many hearts. Hundreds of hearts.

The heart of the entire coven.

I could feel them like I couldn't feel anything before, not even as a Day Reaper. I was tied to them, each of them, and their dreams were suddenly my dreams. Their secrets were my secrets. Their unuttered hopes, unrealized desires, darkest fears, deepest scars—everything a person keeps locked in a padlocked box inside themselves because to reveal it to the scrutiny of light would be worse than death—were suddenly my hopes and desires and fears and scars. Like I was bound to Dominic and Dominic was bound to me, the coven was suddenly bound to me and I to it.

I opened my eyes, struggling not to buckle under the staggering sensation of being splintered into hundreds of beings at once, and then blinked at the sight in front of me.

Walker was there, his crossbow raised, cocked and aimed directly at my heart.

Chapter 33

Less than a second passed between the moment that I met Walker's eyes and the moment he squeezed the trigger of his crossbow, but it felt like years. Time enough for me to notice both the rage and the pleasure flushing his cheeks but, distracted as I was by my new connection to the coven, not enough time for me to physically react and dodge his aim. I recognized the expression on his face, the fanatical relish in his eyes tempered by the tight, grim set of his mouth. It was the very same expression he'd worn while aiming at Nathan to save Bex back when my brother had been Damned. He had aimed, but he hadn't fired, hadn't been able to bring himself to pull the trigger to save her—not even as the mindless, ravenous monster that was my brother thrust his claws into Bex's chest and ripped out her heart—because after all the years of resentment between them, Walker had realized that my brother was his best chance to be rid of her.

Now Walker gazed upon me, and I doubt he saw a former girlfriend and night blood. He didn't see a crime reporter who could squeeze the truth from any witness or a sister who had saved her brother from being Damned. And he certainly didn't see a friend who would willingly die to protect this city, including the stubborn, insufferable man aiming at her heart.

He saw a target and an opportunity.

Walker squeezed the trigger.

And the broadhead grazed my shoulder and soared behind me. I blinked, shocked that Walker's aim had been anything less than true, and then heard the swift *whoosh-thud* of the arrow hitting flesh, someone losing their breath, and a body's hard impact with stone.

Walker grinned, lowering his crossbow. He hadn't been aiming at me after all.

I whirled around and caught sight of the arrow protruding from Kaden's chest. Black fissures spread outward from the wound, over his neck, and up his face, just before his body crumbled to dust.

Dominic staggered back and fell to the ground.

I rushed to his side, my hands fluttering over the gaping wound above his right eye, his split lip, the ribbons of torn flesh across his abdomen, and the hole in his sternum where Kaden had attempted to reach his heart.

Attempted and failed, because I'd stolen his power, and Walker had delivered the deathblow that had saved Dominic.

I chuckled to myself at the irony.

Dominic glanced down at the hole in his chest, looking almost puzzled. He fingered the edge of the wound. "He was becoming a Master. I couldn't match his strength and speed because, as Jillian's Second, he was adopting her power."

I sobered. "I know."

"An arrow—even tipped by a silver broadhead—shouldn't have killed him. As a Master, he'd have been injured, but it shouldn't have been a mortal wound."

I opened my mouth, but the words jammed in my throat. How could I bring myself to admit that I'd killed his sister-in-law—albeit our enemy—and invariably stolen the Master power from Jillian before Kaden could receive it? He'd never forgive me, and knowing how much the coven meant to him—as much as New York City meant to me—I didn't expect him to.

Instead, I took Dominic's wounds into myself and healed him. I didn't have the words, nor the courage to speak them, so I let him feel the truth within me. Through our metaphysical connection, the dozens of promises sworn by the certainty of death, I shared my power and strength. I mended the hole over his exposed heart, rejuvenating the torn muscle and knitting the split flesh. I felt the bone-deep fire of his wounds across my chest and stomach, the ache over my brow where his eye had swelled, and the throbbing of internal bruises and fractures I couldn't see. They were mine and then they were gone, and without the distraction of pain between us, Dominic could feel me through our connection as easily as I could feel him.

I could feel his emotions as he saw life through my eyes. The sensation was disturbing, but only slightly—I'd experienced stranger things, like Jillian's blood cravings. At least, this time, I was feeling emotions I could understand. I felt his awe at my power and control. I felt his pride in my strength and how grateful he was that I'd found him that night nearly six weeks ago, a lifetime ago, and unwittingly saved him from the sun. That even after I understood who and what he was, I'd chosen to stand by his side.

And then he felt something more inside me, something he hadn't anticipated. I sensed his tentative query and then instant denial as he saw the hundreds of threads connecting me to the vampires in our coven.

When I opened my eyes and met Dominic's gaze again, I knew that he knew. He didn't ask after Jillian's body, and I didn't present him with my bloody talons still dripping with her aortic blood as proof. We were beyond words.

And I knew that our relationship, so newly blossomed, was beyond repair. I'd betrayed him as surely as Jillian had, and look how their relationship had ended: in nothing but soiled memories and ash.

"The Damned are drained and ready for transformation," the Chancellor said, his haughty voice impatient. "Who is transforming them?"

"The humans, I believe," Bex said drolly.

"Humans transforming vampires. Who would have thought?" the Chancellor murmured. "Where are they?"

There was an extended pause. I knew that was my cue, but I was beyond speech. It took all my concentration to keep my mouth shut, because I knew once I opened it I'd vomit my emotions all over Dominic, humiliate myself, and make everything worse between us.

As if there was anything worse than this.

"I'll radio them," Walker offered.

"Tell them to run," Nathan said. "The Damned are bleeding out as we speak."

The crackle of the walkie-talkie blended with a low growl.

"What, pray tell, is he doing here?" The Chancellor's voice was low, but even so, I could taste the electric anger of his words biting the air.

"Walker to Wahl, do you copy? Over."

"How should I know?" Bex asked blithely.

"Wahl here. Over."

The walkie-talkie crackled again. "The Damned are down and ready for transformation. Over."

"On our way. Over and out."

"All of this was your plan, was it not?" the Chancellor's voice rumbled like the warning of a coming storm.

"Cassidy DiRocco was the mastermind behind tonight, including your release from the Underneath," Bex said. I could have kissed her until she added, "*His* part in her plan ended ages ago."

Dominic broke our gaze, his eyes shifting on the scene unfolding behind me. "The Chancellor is about to murder Walker."

"We're on the same team now," Walker said. "Tell him, Bex."

"You want me to defend you? To come to your aid at just the right moment and prevent your demise?" Bex's voice was the ugliest I'd ever heard a voice sound. It tasted like hot tar. I nearly gagged at the sound of it. "But this may be my only chance to be rid of you."

Bex's callousness—Walker's own words coming back to haunt him—filled the air with silence.

"I just saved Dominic's life," Walker said. "That must be worth something."

"I will appreciate being able to kill Lysander myself, but I hardly think that one commendation worthy of expunging your own sins," the Chancellor said, his voice flat and dooming.

I took a tiny, terrible satisfaction in the note of near-panic wafting from Walker. He was a good man who had done a few very horrible things in the effort to survive; if I could understand one thing in this mess of a life, it was the drive to survive. I couldn't completely forgive him, not yet—some of those very horrible things, he'd recently done to me—but I could understand.

But I wouldn't, under any circumstances, stand for the Chancellor threatening Dominic. Becoming Master of New York City might kill everything between us, but the extra power, combined with my already incredible Day Reaper strength, had some benefits, one of which was the certainty that I could defend us against anyone who meant us harm, even the Chancellor.

I turned to face the Day Reapers closing in around Walker and hesitated, stunned into immobility. The scene unfolding before me was unbelievable. Dozens upon dozens of Damned, the entire horde of Jillian's army, were bleeding and unconscious across every inch of the great hall, even piled atop each other in some places. The humans were running to save them, and the sight would have been nearly comical—humans running to, instead of away from, the Damned—if it hadn't constricted my throat.

The humans, by everything right and ordered in the universe, should have either run screaming from the Damned or rejoiced in their deaths. They were directly responsible for destroying and terrorizing New York City, but they were also parents and siblings, friends and loved ones, and they were not themselves and not completely in control of their actions any more than Nathan had been completely responsible for the people he had murdered. I knew how it had felt when I'd realized that Nathan and the monster we were hunting were one and the same. I'd recognized the man within the monster, and I'd wanted to die, knowing that he'd killed all those people, knowing that to protect more people from dying, I'd have to kill him.

And I remembered the agonizing fear that accompanied the realization that maybe, just maybe, I didn't have to kill him to stop him. Maybe I could save him.

Daring to hope for a happy ending had been nearly more painful than accepting the necessity of his death, but when we'd lain in adjacent hospital beds and I'd gazed upon the smooth lines of his human face, I remembered the aching bliss of realizing that I'd attained that happy ending. Maybe not completely happy—not for Nathan as he struggled under the weight of his sins—but Nathan was alive, and after everything we'd suffered through, that was enough.

Surviving was more than enough. It was everything.

As I watched the humans running toward the Damned, I understood their hope-filled fears, their tangled emotions of recognition and horror and relief. They'd found their brothers, their wives or dear friends, and they embraced them. They bled for them. They came together against fear and anger and doubt, against overwhelming, seemingly insurmountable odds, and saved them.

The Chancellor advanced on Walker. I blocked his strike with one smooth sidestep between them.

We stared at each other; he measured the likelihood of being able to juke my stand as I dared him to try. No one had ever survived an attempt to defy the Chancellor. He still thought he could win against me—he had the confidence of someone who had never lost—but I had scraped my way back from the dregs of hell, both emotionally and physically, so I knew exactly what I was capable of. And if he forced my hand, I was more than willing to prove it.

He narrowed his eyes at me, like I was a bug that could be crushed beneath his boot, but he wasn't sure whether the effort was worth staining the leather sole with my insides. "You developed this plan to overtake Jillian and save the Damned."

I nodded.

"And part of your plan was to save me and the other Day Reapers," he said. His tone didn't rise on a question, but his words hung between us all the same.

Again, I nodded.

"I'm not your maker. You knew that, when you released me, I would kill Lysander, your Master, and in doing so, kill you as well," he said.

"I knew you would try."

The Chancellor blinked, unaccustomed to such confidence when facing… well, anyone. "Knowing I would *try* to kill Lysander, and inadvertently you, you released me anyway."

I nodded, still not hearing a question in any of this.

He growled, and the sound reverberated throughout the honeycombs. "Do you have so little care concerning Lysander's life? So little care for your own?"

I smiled. "On the contrary, I knew that Dominic and I could hardly survive without you. Now that the world knows about vampires, we're going to need a strong, fearless leader more than ever. We need you," I said, making sure my smile was firmly affixed in place as I added the cherry on top of the whipped cream, "my Lord."

The Chancellor's incredulous blink turned nearly twitchy. "The *world*?"

I nodded. "The government nearly bombed New York City to kill the Damned, but we managed to communicate with them just in time. Once I'm done writing *this* story—" I waved my hand at the scene behind him. "—the world will know that, with the help of the humans and night bloods, the Day Reapers saved New York City."

"You've always wanted to expose the existence of vampires," the Chancellor murmured, his voice all the more dangerous for its softness. "You're getting exactly what you wanted, and you're enjoying every moment."

"And aren't you?" I countered. "Don't you want what's best for the continued survival of vampire-kind?"

"This is *not* what's best," the Chancellor scoffed, "but for the time being, it is what's necessary, thanks to you."

"Thanks to me, you're here and alive to point fingers," I reminded him.

"I could fight you," he said after a long pause, his voice dropping an octave when it had already been impossibly deep. "I could kill you, and then Lysander and Walker after you, all your supporters and sympathizers, your brother, all the humans who know of our existence, force that bomb you mentioned, and cover up the entire incident as a terrorist attack. With mass casualties and heavy entrancement, I could still preserve the anonymity of vampire-kind."

"You could," I said sadly. "But knowing everything you would lose, do you really want to?"

He laughed. With the balance of my world in his hands, he laughed in my face. "You're the one with everything on the line. What, pray tell, do *I* possibly have to lose?"

"Me," Bex said. She had been watching our conversation with nearly a bored expression, but she stepped up now to stand in front of Walker and face the Chancellor by my side.

The Chancellor stopped laughing. "Bex?" he asked, blinking rapidly as if he could blink away the confusion of Bex standing with me against him.

"I abandoned my coven to finally take my rightful place at your side when I transformed into a Day Reaper," Bex said, her voice gentle but firm, "but I cannot abandon the side of the person who saved me and you and all our fellow Day Reapers. That is wrong, and even you can recognize that."

"You would stand against me?" the Chancellor asked, incredulous. "I waited for you for decades, patiently indulging your wish to rule your own coven before ruling the world by my side, and this is how you repay me. In favor of them, in defense of *him,*" the Chancellor said, glaring at Walker, "you would stand against *me*?" He looked stricken, and for the first time, I wondered at the Chancellor's feelings toward Bex. How long could a man really wait for someone who fell in love with and pined and nearly died for another man? How could his pride survive, knowing she would defend the man who had, literally, broken her heart?

"Never," Bex denied. "I'm asking you to stand with me." She stepped forward and touched the hard, unyielding plane of his cheek. The muscle there jumped and twitched as he clenched his jaw against her touch.

"I can't do that," he said, his voice hoarse. He cleared his throat and stiffened his posture against whatever debilitating emotion was weighing it down. "But you know, after a decade apart, that neither can I stand against you."

Bex let her hand drop to her side. "Where does that leave us, then?"

The Chancellor shook his head and gazed upon the miracles surrounding him—at the humans saving the Damned, the Damned successfully transforming back into night bloods, and me, the Day Reaper who had entranced them all—as if in search of the elusive answer to that question. Suddenly, Lord High Chancellor Henry Lynell Horrace DeWhitt, Master vampire of London and Lord of all vampires, threw back his head and laughed. From the very deepest depths of his stomach to the highest rafter of the honeycombs, the peals of his laughter echoed.

When his amusement subsided, Henry reached out to Bex and stroked a thumb across her cheek, mimicking her touch from a moment before.

"Really, Beatrix," he murmured, sweeping his hand to me and then to the great hall behind him. "Where does this leave any of us?"

The Damned were being transformed. Some were still hemorrhaging, others still thrashing and seizing, resisting the change—because most change, even good, is embraced at some level unwillingly—but a few were already returned to their night blood form. Gone were their impenetrable scales, flared nostrils, pointed ears, massive bodies, and thickened foreheads. In their place were brothers, wives, cousins, daughters, and best friends. Their bleeding loved ones clutched them, each and every one of them crying over their unconscious forms and smiling through their tears.

"Sevris!"

Mackenzie was running across the great hall, her arms outstretched and her face radiant despite the blood pouring liberally from a ragged wound at her neck.

"Mackenzie?" Sevris's eyes nearly dropped from his head. I could hear the little pops of his strained capillaries as he refused to blink. "Fucking Christ, your neck."

Mackenzie jumped over the body of a re-transformed night blood and collided with Sevris midair. The soul-deep ache of his love constricted my throat as I watched him pull her into his embrace, and the bittersweetness of hers, like chocolate, wrapped around him along with her arms, needing to hold him as much as she wanted to strangle him. The fact that I knew such intimate details from a simple glance made me look away.

But countless precious, private moments surrounded us, and I couldn't look anywhere that wouldn't intrude. Rowens was dipping Dr. Chunn into a searing kiss. Keagan and Jeremy were fist-pumping and grunting like apes. Ronnie was squeezing Logan's and Theresa's hands, and Logan—my God, Logan was smiling.

I could feel my lips trembling as I smiled along with him, my throat constricting tighter, nearly completely closing, clogged with everyone else's overwhelming emotions as much as my own.

Meredith and Greta were standing across the great hall, taking in this moment, as was I. Our gazes locked with the fruits of our sweat and blood and sacrifice between us, and I felt the hot slide of my own tears flood down my cheeks. A fierce, triumphant lion's roar burst from my body, unheard by Meredith and Greta, but I knew they shared my emotion because I could feel their pride and relief and surging, incredible joy roaring from them as loudly and boisterously as mine.

For the first time in weeks, the future was beaming down on us with warmth and hope. High Lord Henry, Walker, Bex, and a few others who hadn't had an anchor grounding them in the storm might feel adrift now that the gale-force winds had died and the clouds had parted, but I knew exactly where the storm had left me: a place I'd never known existed, that I'd fought to find and that I'd fight to keep for the rest of my—hopefully—very long, extended existence.

Excerpt from ***Vampires Bite Back, Save the Big Apple***
Cassidy DiRocco, Reporter

Vampires are intimidating creatures, their fangs lethal, their talons deadly. Their strength, power, and ability to heal after injury makes them nearly indestructible. They are creatures that human society has little knowledge of, and, more often than not, should fear. However, as the proverb goes, you shouldn't judge people until you've walked a mile in their shoes; I am living proof that vampires are not everything they appear.

I was once a night blood, a human with the potential to transform into a vampire, and tenacious woman that I am, I couldn't allow potential to go untapped. A few drops of blood, and suddenly I had fangs and talons, strength, power, and abilities I could never have imagined having. But despite the many physical differences between my current and former self, I am still very much me. My friends can attest to the fact that I'm the same loyal, sarcastic, short-tempered, tenacious woman I was before I transformed into a vampire. My diet is altered and my senses are enhanced, but otherwise, I still want to expose the truth, help serve justice, and see good triumph over evil. And good certainly did triumph this time, finally, but only because all the many people who were good—humans, night bloods, vampires, and Day Reapers alike—came together for one united purpose: to win back our city.

The coming together was, admittedly, almost as dangerous and nearly just as difficult as fighting to win back the city, and it's easy to see why. Trust is a fragile thing, rarely given and easily broken, and to give it to people who have broken it before is nearly impossible. Imbecilic, even. A person can't distinguish between good and evil by sight alone; we never could, not even when the only monsters out there were other humans. The only thing a person can use to truly judge the intent of another person are their actions.

The past actions of the many vampires in my acquaintance were suspect: they fed on human blood without consent and then entranced their victims to forget. And they survived, like clever ticks living off our blood, for eons. Until today. After centuries of tyranny, the vampires broke free from the laws of their Council, the Day Reapers, which forced them to exist in secret, and their first action upon having attained that freedom was to join forces with the humans and night bloods to free us from the Damned. They could have left New York City. They could have fed. They could have rejoiced in their newfound freedom and bathed in our blood. If they had been so inclined, they could have inflicted more physical and mental harm on us than we could possibly imagine. But the majority of them are not so inclined. Although people who do terrible things are just as terrible after the transformation, loyal, courageous, wonderful people who are transformed into vampires remain just as loyal, courageous, and wonderful as vampires, too.

I don't need to believe in the paranormal to believe in monsters; they existed long before I ever discovered the existence of vampires—men strangling wives, women stabbing lovers, children shooting children. Violence and death seemed to surround me my entire life: my parents' early and unexpected deaths, the crimes I covered as a journalist, my transformation into a vampire. So imagine my surprise in discovering the good in something so inherently bad: a being that survived on drinking our blood. The truth of their innate humanity wasn't something I could easily accept or readily trust.

Until I saw it in myself.

I can look into a mirror (yes, that's a myth) at the features that once inspired such fear and hate—fangs and claws and unimaginable strength—and instead, see the people we protected, the friends and family and loved ones we saved, and the city we helped restore.

Claws and fangs alone don't make a monster, and neither do a few drops of blood.

Chapter 34

I stood on the rooftop of my old apartment, overlooking the city and watching the sunrise over the skyline. I wasn't the only one. People were emerging from their safehouses, peeking out from basements, unlocking themselves and their children from their guest-bedroom closets, and venturing from their back-alley hiding places. Tonight was the first night in over a week in which the Damned hadn't descended over the city and hunted. Carter had printed and distributed my article just before sunset, a paper version for the citizens of New York City and a digital version submitted to the World Press, but for once the public had exercised caution over elation; they'd waited out the night.

And now that they were emerging, it wasn't in celebration. They tipped their faces up to the warmth of the sun, their eyes closed and tears streaming down their cheeks. I remembered emerging from Dominic's coven after he had kidnapped me that first time; I'd spent the night, just one, caged underground before Walker had helped me escape. And that first breath of fresh air and those first warm rays of sun lighting my cheeks had brought an exquisite ache of relief and bitter joy.

After a night of peace, my article had proven true in at least one regard, really the most important one: the Damned had been defeated. Being witness to their awe, disbelief, and bitter joy of realizing, if not quite believing, that they'd survived—emotions that I understood all too well—was almost too precious to bear.

I had freed New York City from her cage. I'd reunited families. I'd watched monsters transform back into sisters and husbands and loved ones. Time would only tell how the coven would heal from being torn asunder under Jillian's rule, how New York City would rise in the coming weeks, and how we would all carry on in light of this new dawn, but the beauty of today was that we had time: time enough to write more articles and host press conferences to convince the public of our (relatively) peaceful coexistence; time for Dominic to regain the favor of his coven; time for Dr. Chunn to continue her research to help Nathan and all the other recently re-transformed night bloods who would now crave human hearts to curb their appetites, no matter how much Dominic insisted that her research was a wasted effort. Jillian had been killed before their transformation and therefore, according to his logic—folklore, Dr. Chunn insisted—the re-transformed night bloods were doomed to make do with their new diet. Certainly, we had time enough to debate folklore versus fact, and better yet, discover the truth together.

Even with the memories of yesterday's victory so vivid in my mind and the hope for all our futures so bright, I couldn't quite enjoy the solitude of my rooftop like I used to. The quiet peace I usually experienced was replaced by loneliness, and I was afraid I knew exactly why. While everyone else was emerging from their cage, I was slinking back to hide inside mine.

After everyone we'd saved and everything we'd accomplished, I'd failed the one person I feared meant the most to me: I'd stolen Dominic's power from Jillian, and unless he killed me—which I wasn't sure he was physically capable of at this point—I'd forever stripped him of his rightful place as the one and only Master of New York City.

I couldn't bear to face him. I'd slipped from the great hall and the coven while everyone else celebrated. I'd submitted my article to Carter, skipped dinner, and fled here, to the one place I'd taken great pains to make safe: my apartment.

But I wasn't safe, not even here, from my memories. My hammock, which had always been a comfort, reminded me of Dominic entrancing me beside him, of him kissing me senseless and me, unable to resist kissing him back. The city lights and skyline, previously a reminder of my roots and everything I stood for and believed in, was now the view I remembered from Dominic's embrace. Memories of Dominic were everywhere inside, too—the couch, the rug, the kitchen counter, the bed, the recliner—oh God, that recliner. Hell, even the shattered window and glass scattered over the living room floor reminded me of Dominic coming to my rescue. I couldn't escape him or my feelings for him any more than I could escape myself.

"I thought I'd find you here," he said.

I whirled around, startled but hardly surprised by his presence. Considering our indelible metaphysical connection, he could probably hear the sound of me dying inside.

He stepped out from the shade of the trap door.

"Dominic, no! Stop!" I shouted, holding my hand up even as he stepped forward into sunlight. "Don't risk it."

"I'd risk everything for you," he said, grinning like the idiot he was. "I'd walk through fire for you."

I snorted. "You'd *become* fire for me, you mean."

"An even more apt analogy for my devotion," he conceded.

I rolled my eyes, but when I felt my own skin begin to smolder, I lunged forward and shoved him out of the sun. I joined him in the shade, so he wouldn't be tempted to join me where he'd burst into flames.

He raised his eyebrows. "Why all the fuss? You've protected me from sunlight before."

"And I had entranced the Damned before. We saw how well that turned out," I grumbled.

"Yes, we did," he said slowly, patiently, as if speaking to the mentally deranged. "We won."

"But it took us forever to figure it out. I'm still learning my new body, and I'm not accustomed to all its new powers and strength," I insisted. "There's no reason to…well, play with fire," I finished, grinning in spite of myself.

He grinned back, his scar pulling his bottom lip lopsided. His fangs were so straight, his icy eyes so blue, and his expression so dear that I couldn't help myself. All the fear and guilt and overwhelming love erupted at once inside me.

"I'm sorry!" I blurted, my words a wail followed by a geyser of tears.

Dominic jerked back, my misery like a physical slap. "Cassidy, what—"

"I never wanted this. I never would have—" *stolen the coven from you*, I finished in my mind, but my mouth couldn't form the words. Just the thought made me die inside.

He shook his head, looking perplexed. "Never would have what?" he asked.

And he *was* perplexed, I realized. I could smell the cinnamon of his proximity to me, his desire and need and desperate want that was never far from the surface. I could hear the sound of his confusion, like a dull, droning hum, and I could feel his helpless panic at the sight of my tears.

I'd been aching with guilt and bone-chilling fear, had actually considered whether he might attempt to kill me to steal back the power, but with him in front of me now and his confusion obvious, maybe—just maybe—I'd been wrong. And hoping to be wrong had never felt so sweet.

His utter confusion gave me the courage to say it out loud as his reassurances never could have. "I killed Jillian, and I stole your Master's power from her."

"To save me."

"I'm sorry," I whispered.

"I'm not," Dominic said, his voice firm and certain. "I love you, and I can't imagine sharing this coven with anyone else." He took my hands in his, but my brain had stopped and stuttered on the words "I love you." It took me a moment to realize that he was still speaking. "—learned from my experience with Jillian is that I can't do this alone anymore. I must listen to my co-Master and consider her advice, or the coven will fall into ruin. Again," he added warily. "The coven accepted your power over them before you had even accepted the Master's power. There's no stopping you." He grinned. "There's no stopping us."

"You love me?" I whispered.

He raised a haughty eyebrow. "Who else would I allow to share the coven with me? What is mine is yours: my coven, my power, my life. Everything, Cassidy. Don't you know that by now?"

I shook my head, not necessarily in answer to his question, but just in general. "I love you, too," I murmured.

Dominic smiled. "I know."

I scoffed, a rough, rude noise from the back of my throat. "But I don't know anything about being a vampire, let alone leading a coven of vampires. I don't know anything about being a Master," I said, my words tumbling from my lips. "I can't do this."

"I have some experience, don't worry," Dominic said flatly, "but I no longer have their trust. You, my dear, sweet Cassidy DiRocco, have earned their trust." He let go of my hands and wrapped his arms around me, pulling me close. "As you have earned mine."

His head dipped down and then his lips sealed over my lips, fervent and fevered, and I kissed him back with equal passion. Trust wasn't something that came easily to either of us, but ironically, it was the one thing Dominic had earned from me while he'd lost it from his coven. After nearly six years in the news industry, interviewing witnesses, reporting the grizzliest of crimes, and helping Greta clean the underbelly of Brooklyn, I'd come face-to-face with people who were more monster than man. Hearing more-often-than-not remorseless confessions had hardened me in ways I hadn't even realized until I'd come face-to-face with a real monster.

Dominic had been my worst nightmare when we'd first met, but time and again, he'd defied my initial judgment of his character. He'd saved my life, mended my broken heart, and returned something precious to me that I hadn't even realized I'd lost: hope. My future was suddenly bright—startlingly exquisite, if overwhelming—simply because he was in it. In that clarity, I saw more than just my future; I saw past Dominic's frightening exterior to the man beneath the monster.

I'd witnessed the worst humanity had to offer—I reported murders, rapes, assaults, and robberies every day—but after discovering Dominic in that back alley six long weeks ago and finally seeing the world, myself, and Dominic with clear eyes, I saw redemption now, too.

I didn't need to believe in fairy tales to believe in happily-ever-afters.

I was living one.

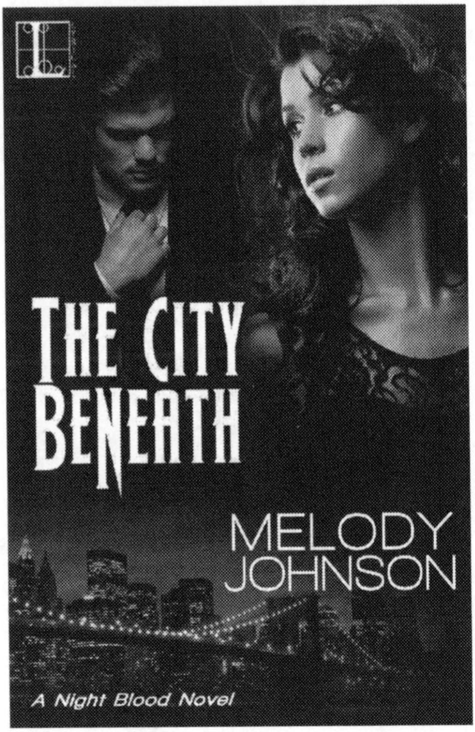

THIS TURF WAR NEVER SLEEPS…

As a journalist, Cassidy DiRocco thought she had seen every depraved thing New York City's underbelly had to offer. But while covering what appears to be a vicious animal attack, she finds herself drawn into a world she never knew existed. Her exposé makes her the target of the handsome yet brutal Dominic Lysander, the Master Vampire of New York City, who has no problem silencing her to keep his coven's secrets safe…

But Dominic offers Cassidy another option: ally. He reveals she is a night blood, a being with powers of her own, including the ability to become a vampire. As the body count escalates, Cassidy is caught in the middle of a vampire rebellion. Dominic insists she can help him stop the coming war, but wary of his intentions, Cassidy enlists the help of the charming Ian Walker, a fellow night blood. As the battle between vampires takes over the city, Cassidy will have to tap into her newfound powers and decide where to place her trust…

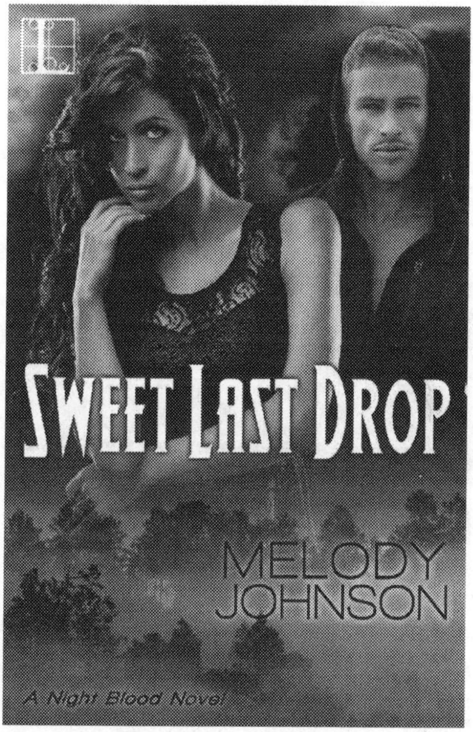

TRUST NO ONE

Cassidy DiRocco knows the dark side intimately—as a crime reporter in New York City, she sees it every day. But since she discovered that she's a night blood, her power and potential has led the dark right to her doorway. With her brother missing and no one remembering he exists, she makes a deal with Dominic Lysander, the fascinating Master vampire of New York, to find him.

Dominic needs the help of Bex, another master vampire, to keep peace in the city, so he sends Cassidy to a remote, woodsy town upstate to convince her—assuming she survives long enough. A series of vicious "animal attacks" after dark tells Cassidy there's more to Bex and her coven than anyone's saying. That goes double for fellow night blood Ian Walker, the tall, blond animal tracker who's supposed to be her ally. Walker may be hot-blooded and hard-bodied, but he's hiding something too. If Cassidy wants the truth, she'll have to squeeze it out herself…every last drop.

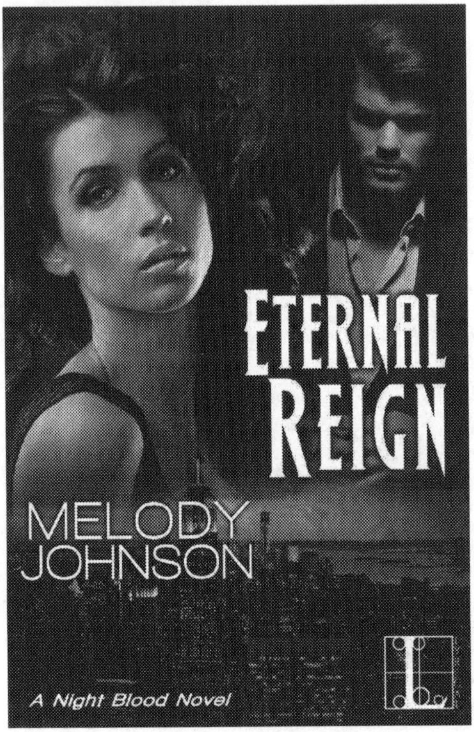

THE LEVELING

Last week, Cassidy DiRocco had some influence over the vampires that stalk the streets of New York City. She was never completely safe, but with her newfound abilities as a night blood and her honed instincts as a crime reporter, at least she had the necessary skills to survive.

Now, thanks to the injuries she sustained while saving her brother from a fate worse than death, she's lost her night blood status just as another crime spree hits Brooklyn. Dozens of people are being slaughtered, and each victim bears the Damned's signature mark: a missing heart.

Cassidy will need the help of all her allies to survive the coming war, including the mysterious and charismatic Dominic Lysander, Master Vampire of New York City. But as his rival's army threatens his coven and his own powers weaken with the approaching Leveling, even Dominic's defenses might not be enough protection.

With nothing left to lose, Cassidy must find the power inside herself to save Dominic, his coven, their city, and survive.

About the Author

Melody Johnson is the author of the gritty, paranormal romance Night Blood series set in New York City. The first installment, *The City Beneath*, was a finalist in several Romance Writers of America contests, including the "Cleveland Rocks" and "Fool for Love" contests. Melody graduated magna cum laude from Lycoming College with her B.A. in creative writing and psychology, and after moving from her northeast Pennsylvania hometown for some much needed Southern sunshine, she now works as a digital media coordinator for Southeast Georgia Health System's marketing department.

When she isn't working or writing, Melody can be found swimming at the beach, reading at the pool, and exploring her new home in southeast Georgia. You can learn more about Melody and her work at www.authormelodyjohnson.com and connect with her on Facebook, @ authormelodyjohnson.

Printed in the United States
by Baker & Taylor Publisher Services